HE KISSED HER, THERE IN
THE MOONLIGHT

Kissed her, and it wasn't enough. He wanted to inhale her, to drink her essence, to absorb her very soul into his own. She was sweet, so sweet. Heat sizzled between them, hotter than the sun he would never see again. Why had he waited so long?

"Oh, Edward . . ."

Kelly looked up at him, breathless. She was soft and warm and willing. He covered her face with kisses, whispered praises to her beauty as he adored her with his hands and his lips. He closed his eyes, and desire rose up within him, hot and swift, and with it the overpowering urge to feed. He fought against it. He had fed well before coming here, yet the Hunger rose up within him, gnawing at his vitals, urging him to take what he wanted.

"This is crazy," she murmured breathlessly. "We hardly know each other."

"Crazy," he agreed. Her scent surrounded him. The rapid beat of her heart called to the beast within him. He deepened the kiss.

AFTER
SUNDOWN

Amanda Ashley

ZEBRA BOOKS
KENSINGTON PUBLISHING CORP.
http://www.kensingtonbooks.com

ZEBRA BOOKS are published by

Kensington Publishing Corp.
850 Third Avenue
New York, NY 10022

All Kensington titles, imprints and distributed lines are available at special quantity discounts for bulk purchases for sales promotion, premiums, fund-raising, educational or institutional use.

Special book excerpts or customized printings can also be created to fit specific needs. For details, write or phone the office of the Kensington Special Sales Manager: Kensington Publishing Corp., 850 Third Avenue, New York, NY 10022. Attn. Special Sales Department. Phone: 1-800-221-2647.

Zebra and the Z logo Reg. U.S. Pat. & TM Off.

First Printing: February 2003
10 9 8 7 6 5 4 3 2

Printed in the United States of America

TIME

deep inside the core of humanity
is the anguish of death
its cries like thunder
thrusting into the virgin air
moving with the power of hate

suck inside that last gasp of air
oh, God, hold it
longer than you're able
to live

why do we
move with time
as a lover
moves with his mate

let me walk away from
this path that pulls me
down
my soul scraping the
harsh reality of lost life

I savor your breath
as I inhale my pain
looking up
I see the lifting of souls

where is my blanket

my warmth
where is my comfort
my safety
fear rapes me
as my eyes seek
the end

I open my soul
hoping for one touch
I open my heart
thirsting
for one kiss . . .

as I leave this time
will I know tomorrow
as I walk with death
will I hurt

please
let the darkness cover me
and hide what I am
please never forget
time as it curses
us all

—M. Dearmond

Chapter 1

It was late Friday night. Steeped in black despair at the thought of what he had become, Edward Ramsey walked slowly down Hollywood Boulevard, unmindful of the moviegoers, the drunks, the panhandlers, the tourists, the endless parade of transvestites and whores.

Occasionally, he glanced at the faces of the strangers he passed by: young people talking about the scary movie they had just seen, homeless men and women clad in ragged clothes looking for a place to spend the night, well-dressed couples emerging from the Pantages Theater discussing the play they had just seen. Hah! They had no idea what scary really was, but he could show them. What would they think? he wondered. What would they do if they knew what he was? Would they recoil in horror and disgust, or stare at him in stunned disbelief?

Last night, the fourth since his life had turned upside down, he had considered awaiting the dawn and stepping out into the bright California sunshine to put an end to his cursed existence. As a new vampire, he would have little resistance to the pure light of day. The touch of the sun on newly made preternatural flesh, a quick burst of flame, and his life would be over, extinguished like the flame of a candle in the wind.

Vampire. How could he be a vampire? He had spent most of his life stalking the undead, destroying them. The Ramsey family had hunted the undead for centuries. Vampires were evil, abhorrent creatures, forever doomed. Forever damned.

But he didn't feel evil, didn't feel damned. Only unnatural, as if he were living inside someone else's skin. His senses were heightened: touch, smell, sight, hearing—all were more sensitive, more acute, than ever before. It was amazing how differently he perceived the world through his newborn vampire senses.

His vision was nothing short of miraculous. He could see great distances, detect minute details that ordinary mortals never saw. Each stitch in the fabric of his coat was visible to his eye. Colors were sharper, richer, almost as if they had texture and depth. Bright light hurt his eyes.

The noise of the city now seemed endless and sometimes deafening! And sometimes so overwhelming, he thought he might go insane. How had Grigori Chiavari stood it for so many years? There had to be a way to shut out the constant barrage of speech and music and traffic sounds that bombarded him from every side, but if there was, Ramsey hadn't discovered it yet.

He felt physically stronger than ever before. Indeed, that sense of physical power was so intoxicating that he might have wished he had been a vampire years ago save for the awful craving for blood. The smell of it was all around him on the boulevard, a pulsing flowing river of crimson. It called to him, excited him until he thought he would go crazy. He needed to feed but didn't know how. The hunger, the pain, had been with him every minute of the past five days, clawing at his vitals in bitter, relentless agony. He had made one clumsy attempt on a streetwalker but had fled the scene before his goal was accomplished.

He passed a man and a woman, heard the woman gasp, her eyes widening when she saw his face. He knew in that moment that he must look like death itself. He had seen that expression of horror before, when he had looked into the depths of Grigori Chiavari's hell-black eyes and seen his own death lurking there.

Chiavari. Of course! He would go to Chiavari. The vampire had cursed him with the Dark Gift. The vampire could damn well tell him what to do with it.

There were lights burning in the big house that Grigori Chiavari had bought shortly before marrying Marisa. Hard to believe only a few days had passed since he had seen Alexi Kristov destroyed in this very house. It seemed centuries had passed.

Marisa opened the door at his knock, a warm smile of welcome curving her pale pink lips. "Edward!" she said, extending her hand. "Come in."

"Where is he?" Ramsey demanded.

Ignoring Marisa's outstretched hand, he swept past her into the hallway, his angry stride carrying him into the living room.

"Where is he?" he demanded again. "Is he here?"

"What do you want, Ramsey?"

Ramsey pivoted at the sound of the vampire's voice.

Grigori Chiavari glided soundlessly into the room. He exuded an air of self-confidence and invulnerability that Ramsey envied in spite of himself, and never more so than now.

For a moment, the two men looked at each other.

They had never been friends. At best, they had been uneasy enemies allied against a common evil. But Alexi Kristov was dead now, his body burned to ashes. But for Grigori's timely but uninvited interference, Ramsey would have been dead, too. Hard to believe he had actually thanked the man for turning him into a monster. He remembered Marisa asking him, shortly after his transformation, if he would rather be dead. He had replied instantly: *Of course I would.* But afterward, he had found himself drowning in a wave of indecision. Confused, dazed by all that had happened that night, he had stumbled out of the house, needing to be alone.

The horror of that night was still fresh in his mind. He and Chiavari had spent months hunting Alexi Kristov, months that had culminated in this very house. He recalled it all so clearly, being caught in the vicious web of Kristov's power, helpless to resist the ancient vampire. Captive to Kristov's will, Ramsey had drugged Chiavari, drained him of enough blood to weaken him, and bound him with heavy silver chains. And then he had waited. Waited for Marisa. She had been surprised to see him. . . .

"Edward!" she had exclaimed as he stepped in front of her. "You scared me out of a year's growth. What are you doing here? Edward?"

He had stepped behind her and closed the door. "Go sit down, Marisa."

"What's wrong?"

"Nothing, and everything."

"You're not making sense."

"You'll understand everything soon enough." He had given her a little push and she had stumbled forward.

She had seen Grigori then. Chiavari lay still as death on

the bed, bound by a heavy silver chain. The same chain that had once bound Alexi.

"What have you done to him?" she asked.

Edward had pulled a syringe out of his coat pocket. "I put him to sleep, and then I bled him." He had nodded at the basin on the table beside her chair. It was a large bowl, filled with blood. Grigori's blood. Enough to weaken him.

"He's not . . . not dead?" Marisa had asked.

"Not yet."

"Edward, please . . ."

He had pushed her toward the chair in the corner. "Sit down, Marisa. Alexi will be here soon."

"Alexi!" She had looked at him in alarm. "He's coming here?"

Edward nodded sadly. "I'm sorry, Marisa."

She sat down heavily. "Why are you doing this?"

"I have no choice."

"What do you mean? Of course you do. . . ." The words had died in her throat. "He's done something to you, hasn't he? Oh, Lord, you're like Antoinette."

"No. She had no mind of her own. Alexi has left me my mind, Marisa, but he has robbed me of my will. This is worse. I know what I'm doing, and even though I don't want to, I can't refuse."

"Fight him, Edward! You've got to fight him."

"I can't." He remembered pacing the floor. "He's too strong. He took my blood, made me take his. I can hear his thoughts in my mind. I can't shut them out! I can't shut him out!"

"He's going to kill us, isn't he?"

"He's going to kill Grigori. I'm afraid he has worse things in mind for you." He had dropped to his knees in front of her and pulled a short piece of rope from his pocket. "I'm sorry. So sorry."

Marisa had jerked her knee up in a hard, swift motion. It had caught him under the jaw. His head had snapped backward and she had kicked him in the chest with all her might.

Jumping to her feet, she ran for the door, but he had caught her by the ankle.

"Let me go!" she shrieked. "Let me go!"

She had struggled against him, but he was too strong for her. Twisting her arm behind her back, he quickly tied her wrists together, then guided her back to the chair and pushed her into it.

"Marisa, I'm sorry."

She was shaking now, frightened beyond words.

There had been a ripple in the air, a stirring, as Grigori began to emerge from his drugged sleep. Edward had pulled a stake from inside his coat.

"Edward, don't!"

"I won't," he said. "Alexi wants that pleasure for himself."

"Edward, please, please don't do this. Please. I'd rather be dead than become Alexi's creature."

"Marisa." *He had struggled against Alexi's hold on his mind, but to no avail.*

"Please, Edward. He'll make me like Antoinette." *A soulless zombie, a creature without a mind of her own.*

"I can't fight him," *he had said, panting heavily.* "He's too strong. I can't help you." *He had doubled over then, racked by pain.* "Stop," *he begged.* "Please stop." *He had writhed in pain, all else forgotten, as Alexi's power washed over him.*

And then Alexi was there. Darkness seemed to trail in his wake.

"So," *Alexi said.* "We are all together at last. Edward, it's time I made the woman mine. You will leave the room. Wait for me in the hallway."

The vampire had sniffed the air, his nose wrinkling as the smell of cold blood reached his nostrils. He jerked his chin toward the bowl. "Get rid of that." *Cold blood. It was an abomination.*

"Yes, master," *Edward had replied. Moving like a robot, he had picked up the bowl and moved toward the door.*

"Edward," *Marisa cried.* "Don't leave me! Please, help me!"

But he had been helpless. He had tried to turn to face her, his whole being longing to help her, to strike Alexi down, but the vampire's power was too strong to resist. He had told himself to stop, to turn, but his body refused to obey. One step after another, he had moved toward the door.

"Edward!"

He had heard the fear and anguish in her voice, but there was nothing he could do. Nothing. And then he had heard Chiavari's voice inside his head. "Ramsey, I've taken your blood, made you a part of me. Listen to my voice. Draw on my strength. You can fight him. Think! Combine your will with mine. Together we can defeat him."

"I can't." He had stared into the bowl, at the blood that was so dark it was almost black.

"You can!" Grigori's voice echoed in his mind. "Marisa needs help, help I can't give her. Damn you! Fight!"

Cradling the bowl in one hand, he had opened the door and stepped into the hallway. He heard Marisa's shriek of terror as he closed the door behind him. Standing outside the room, he heard Alexi laugh as Marisa struggled against him. He had looked at the blood again and then lifted the bowl to his lips.

Grigori's blood had filled him with power, lessened Alexi's hold on his mind. Bursting into the room, he had hurled himself at Alexi, the stake in his hand driving toward the vampire's heart. But the vampire was strong and fast, and the stake had missed his heart. Alexi had flung him against the wall and buried his fangs in his throat, not to drink, but to kill. . . .

And he would have died, had it not been for Chiavari. Grigori had slain Alexi and then, at Marisa's urging, forced the Dark Gift upon Edward. He had a vague memory of Grigori holding his bleeding wrist to his lips, urging him to drink. The vampire's voice had been soft yet compelling, soothing as a mother's lullaby. "Drink, Edward," he had urged. "Drink your fill."

And he had suckled the vampire's wrist like a babe at its mother's breast. . . .

He looked into Chiavari's eyes and knew the other man was also remembering.

"What brings you here, Ramsey?" Chiavari asked brusquely.

Ramsey clenched his hands into tight fists. It galled him to ask Chiavari for help, not only because he thoroughly disliked the man, but because Chiavari had won Marisa's heart.

Grigori lifted one dark brow. "Ramsey?"

"I'm hungry, damn you."

"Ah," Grigori murmured, and there was a wealth of understanding in that single word.

Ramsey glanced at Marisa, beautiful Marisa with her dark-brown hair and deep green eyes and warm, sweet smile. Marisa. He had asked her to marry him, but she had refused him in favor of Chiavari. Marisa. His gaze was drawn to her throat, to the pulse beating there. Her blood beckoned him. Hot and sweet, it called to him. She had willingly given her blood to Chiavari when he needed it. Ramsey licked his lips. Would she share it now, with him?

Ramsey took a step forward, oblivious to the other vampire, oblivious to everything but the woman's warmth, the rich red blood thrumming through her veins. Just a sip, he thought; just one sip to ease the horrible agony burning through him. And if she would not give it, then he would take it. . . .

Marisa stared at Edward. He was as tall as Grigori, with the same trim build. She had never thought of Edward as a handsome man, but now, enhanced with the glamour of the Dark Gift, he looked far younger than his forty-two years. There was a dark sensuality about him that had been lacking before. His pale blond hair had turned a deeper, richer color that gleamed like burnished gold, his ice blue eyes were darker, more intense, aglow now with a fierce need. The faint scar on his cheek only added to his mysterious allure.

His lips parted, and she saw his fangs. She moved quickly to Grigori's side, her heart pounding. She knew vampire blood lust when she saw it.

It is all right, cara. *Have no fear.*

Grigori's voice whispered in her mind. It was a bond they shared, the ability to read each other's minds.

I'm not afraid, she replied, *as long as you're with me.*

Ramsey took another step forward, seemingly oblivious to everything but her.

"Ramsey, no." Grigori's voice cut across the room, as sharp and deadly as a blade.

Ramsey came to an abrupt halt. With a shake of his head, he looked around the room, his expression slightly dazed, like a sleepwalker abruptly roused from sleep. "Marisa, I'm sorry."

"It's all right," she replied gently. "I understand."

Grigori brushed a kiss across Marisa's lips. "I'll be back later, *cara.* Ramsey, come with me."

Wordlessly, Ramsey turned and followed the vampire out of the house and down the narrow flagstone walkway that led to the garage.

"Have you fed since I brought you across?" Chiavari asked.

"No."

"Nothing in five days?"

Ramsey shook his head. He had made two attempts. The second had been on a kitten he had found in an alley. He had held the terrified creature in his hands, but in the end, he had let the animal go. "I don't think I have what it takes to be a vampire," he said ruefully.

"Nonsense. Any man who can track a vampyre to its

lair and cut off its head shouldn't have any trouble finding something to drink."

"Are you mocking me?"

"Merely stating a fact." Chiavari slid behind the wheel of a sleek black Corvette, reached over, and opened the passenger door. "Get in."

"Where are we going?"

"Hunting."

With a sigh, Ramsey got in the car and closed the door. Once, he had hunted vampires. Now he was hunting humans. "I don't want to kill anyone."

"That's up to you."

"But you told me you killed, in the beginning."

Chiavari switched on the ignition and backed the Corvette out of the garage to the street. "I shall teach you to hunt without killing."

"I don't think I can drink . . . blood."

"Of course you can. You have done it before."

Ramsey stared into the darkness. Blood. The elixir of life. He had said he didn't think he could drink it, but he knew it was a lie, a taboo that no longer had any meaning. He remembered the warm, rich coppery taste of Chiavari's blood on his tongue. Once it had sickened him; now he craved to taste its like again. "Where are we going?"

"My first rule," Chiavari said. "Never hunt where you live."

Chiavari drove down to the beach. It was one of his favorite haunts. He parked on a dimly lit side street near a run-down bar, switched off the engine, turned off the lights.

"You are Vampyre now," Grigori said. "You have powers of which you are not yet aware. Few mortals have the strength to resist you. You have the power to mesmerize them, to compel them to do your bidding, to wipe your memory from their minds. You can drink your fill from one and take his memories and his life as well, or you can drink only enough to sustain your own existence. The choice is yours."

"How have you stood it for so many years, Chiavari?"

"What do you mean?"

"The noise, the light, the constant hunger. Sometimes I think I'm going out of my mind."

"In time, you will learn to block the noise, to shut out the siren call of the heartbeats around you." He pulled the key from the ignition and slid out of the car.

Ramsey followed Chiavari into the dimly lit bar. It was a little after eleven, and there were only a handful of people in the place.

Ramsey grimaced at the stench of old smoke and old sweat that flooded his nostrils.

Chiavari took a seat at a back booth, and Ramsey slid in across from him.

"Look around you," Chiavari said. "What do you see?"

Ramsey shrugged. "Men and women talking too loud and drinking too much."

"No. You see prey. Food. You are a young vampire. You will need to feed often, at least for a while. Forget what you were before. *Who* you were before. You are Vampyre now, and you can never go back to what you were. That life is gone. That man is gone. You have been reborn. Accept it. If you want to live, you will embrace your new life. If not, then go out and meet the sun and end it. There is no worse hell than being caught between worlds."

Ramsey clenched his hands as he listened to the vampire speak. They were hard words—hard to believe, harder to accept. He looked at the other patrons. Once, he had protected them from the undead; now they needed protecting from him. In his mind, he saw the chasm between himself and the rest of humanity grow deeper, wider—saw it fill with an endless river of warm, rich crimson.

Vampire. I am a vampire. I must drink blood to survive.

Chiavari regarded him through narrowed eyes. "Are you strong enough to be Vampyre, Ramsey, or should I have let you die?"

Ramsey thought of the night Chiavari had brought him across, how tenaciously he had clung to the vampire's arm, to the pulsing promise of life. "I want to live."

Chiavari nodded. "Then you must accept what you are. You do not have to be like Kristov. You can be a man with a peculiar lifestyle, or you can be a monster. You must make the choice, as does every man, mortal or otherwise."

Ramsey stared at the cross tattooed on his right palm. "Damned," he murmured. "Forever damned."

Grigori lifted one brow in amusement. "You did not think yourself damned when you killed my kind." He grinned faintly. *"Our* kind. Why are you damned now?"

"Because of what I am!"

"Murder is murder, Ramsey, whether you are killing vampires or killing humans for their blood. It is all the same; only the reasons are different. You can be as good, or as bad, as you wish."

Ramsey snorted. "You don't understand."

"No, it is you who do not understand. But you will. If you live long enough. Now, look around and decide who will be your prey."

"How do I decide?"

Grigori shrugged. "Probe their minds. Find the one who is most susceptible to your power. Plant the suggestion in their mind that they are ready to go home."

"I can't do that."

"You can. Try."

Ramsey glanced around the room. A middle-aged

man sat alone at the far end of the bar. There was an elderly couple in a front booth, a couple of young punks playing pool in the back. His gaze settled on a woman standing beside a cigarette machine. She was about twenty-five, dressed in a pair of jeans and a bulky red sweater. Her hair was brown, her eyes blue. He stared at her, wondering how to go about probing her mind, when, as if a door had suddenly opened, he was aware of her thoughts. She was recently divorced, lonely, searching for something to ease the pain.

He swore under his breath, exhilarated and frightened by this strange new power. How often in the past had he wished he could read another's mind? But to actually have that ability . . . could he actually impose his will on this strange woman?

Look at me. Ramsey sent the thought to her, felt a thrill of satisfaction when she turned in his direction. She regarded him a moment, then smiled uncertainly.

Come to me.

Slowly she began to walk toward him, her expression slightly puzzled.

"Good evening," Ramsey said.

"Hello." She had a sexy, breathy voice. "Have we met before?"

"No."

Ramsey gazed deep into her eyes. He had never had time for women, or for love. He had spent his whole life hunting vampires, moving from town to town, country to country. Like most hunters, he had never married. Families all too easily became victims, hostages, pawns in an endless war.

A curious sensation swept through him as he felt his mind connect with hers, felt her will bend to his. Felt her desire reach out to him. It was something he had never felt before, never known before. Women had respected him, trusted him, confided in him. They had never desired him. And even now, it wasn't *him* she wanted, but the creature he had become. An immortal creature clothed with the vampire's mystic allure.

"Come," he said. "I'll walk you to your car."

She nodded, and he took her arm. Ramsey glanced over his shoulder to make sure Grigori was with them.

Outside, some of Ramsey's confidence waned. The woman stood beside him, her expression blank.

He looked at Grigori. "What do I do now?"

"Follow me."

Grigori led them into the alley that ran between the bar and a vacant lot that was overgrown with weeds and littered with empty beer cans and bottles. He gestured at the woman, who stood unmoving, like a robot waiting for instruction. "She is in your power now. You can do whatever you wish."

"But how do I . . . you know."

"Think only of her blood. Listen. Can you not hear it flowing like sweet honey through her veins?"

Grigori took the woman in his arms, ran his fingertips ever so lightly over her cheek, down the length of her neck.

"Smell the blood," Grigori said, and he felt his own fangs lengthen as he bent over the woman. Her head fell back, exposing the tender skin of her throat. "You must always be gentle," he said, his voice changing, growing deeper, rougher as the hunger within him stirred to life. "Human flesh is so very fragile."

The woman made a small sound of pleasure as Grigori's mouth closed over her throat, his fangs piercing the skin. He took only a sip, and then he thrust the woman into Ramsey's arms. "She is yours. Take her."

Ramsey stared at the woman, at the single drop of crimson sparkling on her throat. "What about . . . how do you know her blood is . . . don't you worry about disease?"

"You would know if her blood was unclean."

Ramsey nodded. Feeling as awkward and self-conscious as a boy on his first date, he gathered the woman into his embrace. She didn't resist. Pliant as a rag doll, she allowed him to hold her. She smelled of soap and perfume and cheap brandy. And blood. It called to him like a Siren's song: loud, insistent. Irresistible. He felt an ache in his gums as his fangs lengthened.

With a low growl, he sank his fangs into the warm tender skin of her throat, felt the thick richness of her blood fill his mouth.

"Gently," Grigori admonished. "It can be a pleasant experience for her, as well, if you choose to make it so."

Ramsey drank, disgusted by what he was doing, yet compelled to take more and more, overcome with the warmth of it, the way it eased the pain that had clawed at him. He drank her memories, her strength, her dreams. The sound of her heartbeat echoed in his ears. How had he ever thought such an act repulsive? Her life filled him until he felt drunk with it. And still he wanted more. Wanted it all.

"Enough, Ramsey. Enough!"

Dazed, drugged with blood and a sense of unlimited power, Ramsey lifted his head, his lips drawn back in a silent snarl. The woman was his. He would not share her.

"Enough," Grigori said again.

Ramsey looked down at the woman in his arms. Her heartbeat was faint, her face pale. She stared up at him through vacant eyes.

"What have I done?" he moaned. "What have I done?"

"Only what you had to do."

"Is she . . . will she die?"

"No."

Horror-stricken, Ramsey shoved the woman into Chiavari's arms and backed away. He dragged a hand over his mouth, grimaced when he saw the blood there. The thrill he had felt earlier was gone, replaced by a sense of horror and self-disgust. "I can't do this."

"You can, and you will. Abstaining will only make the pain worse. Waiting, trying to fight it, will only make it harder for you to control the Hunger. And when you are out of control, people will die."

"How have you stood it for so long?" Ramsey asked bitterly. "How have you stood the separateness, the aloneness?"

Grigori took a deep breath and loosed it in a long, slow sigh. "Being Vampyre is not for the weak. There are drawbacks, but they grow fewer as the years pass. And the advantages far outweigh them."

"Advantages!" Ramsey scoffed. "What advantages?"

"Think, Ramsey. Think of all the things I have seen, the changes in the world, the inventions. I have powers you cannot imagine. As for the other, the loneliness, the separateness . . ." He shrugged. "One can get used to anything."

"Easy for you to say."

"Ramsey, I could have killed you years ago. But I did not because I have always admired your tenacity, your will to live. Do not disappoint me now."

Ramsey gestured at the woman in Chiavari's arms. "Will she be all right?"

"She will be fine."

"I . . ." Ramsey looked away, embarrassed by the need that had driven him to Chiavari. "Thanks for your help."

Grigori nodded. "Give yourself time, Ramsey. Call me if you need me."

Ramsey grunted softly. Going to Chiavari for help had been one of the most difficult things he had ever done, not only because it had pricked his pride to ask the man for help, but because it had meant seeing Marisa again, having her see what he had become.

Marisa. Once, he had hoped she would he his. "I would have thought you'd have brought her across by now," he remarked.

"No. She wants to wait a while, to spend time with her family while she can." Grigori shrugged. "There is no hurry."

Ramsey nodded, jealous because Marisa had chosen Chiavari over him, because Chiavari would have her love for a dozen lifetimes to come.

"Is she happy?"

Grigori nodded.

Ramsey glanced at the woman in the vampire's arms. "Thanks again for your ... your help."

"Give it time, Ramsey," Grigori said again.

"Yes, time." Ramsey smiled ruefully as he turned and walked away. He had plenty of time.

Chapter 2

Marisa stood at the window, staring out into the dark, waiting. It made her nervous, thinking of Edward and Grigori together. They had never liked each other, though they were indebted to each other. A life for a life. She tapped her fingers on the windowpane. What were they doing out there?

She did not like to think of the answer that quickly came to mind.

They were hunting. Hunting for human prey.

She could picture it so clearly: the old vampire teaching the young one how to find and stalk his prey, how to drink the warm living blood that was necessary to ensure his immortality. The ancient and horrifying rituals of the Dark Gift. Would the gravity of this transfer of knowledge—of power—overcome the antipathy Grigori and Edward held for each other? Or would the uneasy truce between the two them continue?

She pressed her forehead against the window as a new thought pushed its way into her mind. She had promised Grigori she would accept the Dark Gift so that they could be together forever. Grigori was in no hurry to bring her across, willing to let her have as much time as she needed to bid farewell to life as she knew it, but one day Grigori would bring her across. Then it would be her turn as pupil, stalking the unwary.

She shuddered at the thought. Did she truly want to be a vampire? And yet, wanting to be with Grigori forever, what other choice did she have? For a vampire, "forever" was not a hollow promise made in the throes of infatuation. She knew he would never force her, would not try to sway her decision. But if she didn't accept the Dark Gift, she would have to watch herself grow old while he stayed forever young. Would he stay by her side while she aged? Or would he find another, still-young woman in one of his midnight prowls? Some woman who would not hesitate to accept the Gift? She couldn't imagine—didn't want to imagine—such a betrayal.

She sighed as yet another thought crossed her mind. Sooner or later they would have to leave this place, this house. If things stayed as they were between them, they would have to move before people noticed that she aged while Grigori did not. And if she accepted the Dark Gift, they would still have to move on within a few years, but at least no one would look at her and think she was his mother, or worse, his grandmother!

What was it really like to be a vampire? Never to see the sun? To live only at night? To drink warm blood from the veins of a helpless victim? Did she love Grigori enough to embrace the Dark Gift?

She thrust the thought aside. She was still young. She had plenty of time to decide before anyone began mistaking her for Grigori's mother.

She went to the door and opened it when she heard

his car pull into the drive. And then he was striding toward her, tall and dark, graceful as a cat.

"How did Edward seem to you?" she asked. "Is he going to be all right?"

Grigori shook his head. "I don't know."

He followed her into the living room. Marisa had done wonders with the old house. What had once been little more than a drafty old mansion had become a home, filled with soft colors and antique oak and a warmth that came from the woman herself.

Marisa sat down on the sofa. She expected Grigori to join her, but he began to pace in front of the fireplace, and she knew something was bothering him. She never tired of looking at him, of watching him. His thick black hair fell to his shoulders; his brows were straight above ebony eyes. His skin was pale, though not sickly looking. He was tall, with the firm, trim build of an athlete.

Tall, dark, and handsome, she thought. It described her husband perfectly. *Husband*. How she loved the word and all that it meant. He was the most wonderful man she had ever met. The thought made her smile. He would have said he wasn't a man at all.

She had first met him at a carnival on Halloween night. She had gone to the Roskovitch Carnival because they claimed to have the body of *"Count Alexi Kristov, the oldest vampire in existence."* She had not believed in such things, of course, had never believed in ghosts and goblins or the like. Even now, she wasn't sure what had drawn her to the carnival that night. Surely she had never dreamed that she would see not one but two vampires that evening.

She had met Edward because of Grigori. Both men had been hunting Alexi Kristov—Grigori during the night, Edward during the day. Looking back, it all seemed like a nightmare come true.

She had gone to the carnival, curious to see the vampire. It was a sight she would never forget: the casket on a dais in the center of the floor; the "vampire" clad in a shiny black suit, his skin as white as the satin that lined the casket. His hair had been long and limp, the color a dull reddish-brown. He had looked dead. Or rather, not alive. A wax figure of a man laid out in the casket to fool the gullible. So certain had she been that it was a hoax, that when she found herself alone with the figure, she had climbed the dais and touched its hand. It hadn't been made of wax, but flesh. The skin had been cool. Smooth and dry, it had reminded her of old parchment. She had gasped when the skin grew warm beneath her hand, shrieked when the fingers moved. She had stumbled away from the casket, fallen down the stairs, and scraped her leg.

It had been the scent of her blood that had roused Kristov from his long sleep. He had gone on a rampage, killing over a dozen people before Edward and Grigori joined forces and destroyed him. In the hunt for Kristov, they had discovered that Grigori's first wife, Antoinette, whom he'd thought dead for two hundred years, had not been dead at all. Transformed by Kristov, she had existed for two centuries as a revenant, a creature with no mind or will of her own. In the end, it had been Edward who had freed her soul and laid her body to rest. Even now, it was all so hard to accept. So many things she would never have believed had played out before her eyes.

She shook off the grim thoughts of the past as she watched Grigori pace the floor. "Something's troubling you," she remarked. "What is it? What's wrong?"

He turned to face her. "He's very powerful. More powerful than I would have expected."

"Edward is? Really?"

Grigori grunted softly. "He has Kristov's blood in his veins. And mine. And Khira's," he added, thinking of the beautiful vampyre who had brought him across over two hundred years ago.

"How can he be so powerful so soon?"

"He has good blood," Grigori said with a wry grin. "When a very old vampyre brings a mortal across, he bequeaths a part of his strength." And Kristov had been a very old vampyre—indeed, the oldest vampyre Grigori had ever met. Kristov's blood, combined with Khira's and his own, made for a very powerful combination.

"Is that a problem?" Marisa asked. "His being powerful?"

"It could be. He is powerful, but he is a young vampyre who does not yet fully understand what has happened to him, what powers he possesses. He lacks wisdom and experience. It could be a dangerous combination."

"I'm not sure I understand."

"The Dark Gift affects people differently. Some get drunk with the power. Some go insane. Some look for ways to help mankind. And some turn into monsters, like Kristov."

"A monster? Edward?" She smiled. In spite of what Edward had done for a living, she couldn't imagine him as a monster. There had been an old-world courtliness about him, a gentleness. An innate goodness.

"It cannot be easy for him to accept that he has become what he once destroyed."

"No, I guess not. I wonder what he'll do now. For a living, I mean." She looked at Grigori and laughed. A living. That was funny. "You know what I mean."

"He is an intelligent man. I am sure he can find a suitable career." A faint smile tugged at Grigori's lips. "He will have plenty of time to find one." He sat down beside her on the sofa and drew her into his arms. "Enough talk about Ramsey."

Marisa snuggled against him, loving the feel of his

arms around her. She felt safe in his embrace, loved, cherished. All her doubts and fears faded away. In time, she would accept the Dark Gift from him, and they would truly be one. Soon, but not yet.

"*Cara* . . ."

She gazed up at him, felt her skin tingle as his preternatural power moved over her skin like a dark warm wind. They had been married only a short time, and the fire that had ever smoldered between them quickly sparked to life. It was exhilarating to be in his arms. He was a creature such as she had never known before—a man who had lived for centuries, who had incredible strength, who possessed powers she did not fully understand. He could mesmerize her with a look, destroy her with a touch, charm her with a smile. He had the strength of ten men, yet he was ever gentle with her.

Her eyelids fluttered down as he dropped kisses as light as rain upon her brow, her cheeks, her eyelids. His tongue was like a flame against her throat, a silent entreaty. She moaned softly, tilting her head to one side, inviting him to take what he needed.

"*Cara* . . ."

There was no pain, just an oddly sensual feeling of euphoria as his fangs grazed her throat. And she surrendered to him completely, lost in the wonder and the magic that was Grigori.

Chapter 3

Ramsey felt stronger, more confident, when he woke the next night. He showered, then dressed in a brown pullover sweater and beige slacks. He grimaced when he looked in the mirror. It was time to change his image. No more beige and brown for him. He had been dull and boring long enough.

Shoving his billfold into his back pocket, he left his room, deciding, on a whim, to head for the mall. He was surprised to find himself there, among the bright lights and the throng of late shoppers, almost as soon as the thought crossed his mind. For a moment, he was overcome by a wave of dizziness, intoxicated by the scent of so much blood, the dull roar of so many heartbeats. The lights hurt his eyes; the noise pounded at his eardrums. He closed his eyes, focusing his will, and found that he could mute the noise, control the dizziness, and concentrate on his purpose here. Once again, Chiavari had been right.

He went into an exclusive men's shop and indulged

himself beyond anything he would have imagined before he had received the Dark Gift. He purchased a complete new wardrobe. Shirts, slacks, sweaters, socks, underwear. Nothing brown or tan. Nothing beige. He was heartily sick of brown, sick of tweeds, sick of dressing like some stuffy sixty-year-old college professor. He bought several pairs of shoes and, on a whim, a pair of snakeskin cowboy boots.

One night next week he would start looking for a new place to live. Perhaps he would buy a new car, something sleek and sporty. He had never owned a house, never owned a new car. He had spent his whole adult life in hotels and motels. Well, all that was about to change. He had a rather tidy sum saved up. Vampire hunting had been a lucrative career. Ramseys had been hunting vampires for hundreds of years. The first Ramsey had turned vampire hunter to avenge the death of his wife. His knowledge and wisdom had been handed down from father to son for generations, as had the instinct to hunt, which, over time, had become second nature. In the old days, hunters had been paid in corn and wheat more often than gold or silver. But not anymore. The Ramsey family had money behind them now, thanks to a vengeful millionaire who had lost his only daughter to one of the undead.

Brian Francis Throckmorten had been so grateful when Harold Ramsey had staked the vampire who killed his daughter, that he had set up a fund to ensure that the Ramsey family and its heirs would always have the means to hunt and destroy the undead. Only there would be no heirs now, Ramsey thought bitterly. He was the last of his line. In fifteen or twenty years, should he survive that long, he would have to pretend to be his own son in order to continue drawing on the trust. He grunted softly. Perhaps he could donate funds to some obscure university with the stipulation that they use the money to research diseases of the blood in hopes of finding a way to reverse the effects of the Dark Gift. Or maybe he could open a training school for vampire hunters. . . .

Returning to his room, he rummaged through his purchases, deciding on a pair of black jeans and a bulky white sweater. He paused in front of the mirror, a faint smile playing over his face. He had never been a handsome man. Had anyone asked, he would have described himself as ordinary. Now, transformed by the blood of the three vampires that burned in his veins, he looked younger, more virile. Not handsome, he mused—even the blood of a vampire couldn't work miracles.

But . . . powerful. Dangerous.

A vampire.

Vampire . . . He shook his head ruefully. "I am a vampire."

Even as he said it, he didn't quite believe it, not deep down. But his blood sang in his veins at the declaration, stirring him to action.

He ran a hand over his hair, worn short ever since he had been a boy learning the lore of his vampire-hunting ancestors, absorbing the seriousness of his family calling. But that was over now. Past history. He had become what he had hunted.

Perhaps he would let his hair grow long.

Sitting on the edge of the bed, he pulled on his new cowboy boots and left the hotel.

Some of his newfound confidence waned as he entered a small neighborhood bar. Country music blared from a loudspeaker. Half a dozen couples were line dancing.

He went to the bar and ordered a drink, which he held but didn't taste. He was studying the crowd when a slender young woman with wavy brown hair and large green eyes sidled up to him.

Hands on hips, she looked him up and down. "You don't look like a cowboy," she remarked with a come-hither smile.

She was a pretty thing. She wore a tight-fitting cowboy shirt, fringed blue-jean shorts, and a pair of white boots.

"Perhaps because I am not," he replied with a faint smile.

"I don't remember seeing you here before."

"I have never been in here before." He swore under his breath. She was coming on to him, something no woman had ever done before, and he had no idea how to respond. While other boys had been dating, he had been out with his grandfather, learning how to track and slay vampires. Not exactly suitable training for the dating game.

She placed her hand on his chest, her fingers making slow circular motions. "Would you like to dance?"

"I fear I must refuse."

"That's too bad. It would be a good way for us to get to know each other better."

"I'm afraid I never learned how."

She slid her arm through his, tilted her head to one side, ran the tip of her tongue over her lower lip. "That's okay, honey. I know a quiet place down the street where I can teach you."

He felt a surge of excitement as he placed his untouched drink on the bar and took her hand in his.

She chatted about some country singer he'd never heard of as they walked down the street. When they reached an alley, Ramsey pulled her inside and pushed her up against the wall.

She looked startled, then laughed nervously. "What are you doing?"

He didn't know what to say, felt all his doubts rise up to mock him. *You are a vampire. Play the part.* He gazed deep into her eyes. Summoning his power, he bent her will to his, felt her body relax at his suggestion. Her eyelids fluttered down, her head lolled to one side, exposing the smooth expanse of her neck.

He took a deep breath. *"Any man who can track a vampyre to its lair and cut off its head shouldn't have any trouble finding something to drink."* Chiavari's words echoed in the back of his mind as he bent over the woman's neck.

Revulsion warred with his hunger. The hunger won, rising up within him, hot and hungry and overpowering. He drank quickly, sickened by what he was doing, filled with bitter self-loathing because even though the act disgusted him, he found pleasure in it. Power flowed through him, thrummed through his veins, expanded his mind.

Not too much! He was proud of himself as he drew back. He had taken only a little.

I can do this. He repeated the words aloud. "I can do this." He didn't have to kill. He didn't have to be a monster like Alexi Kristov. The woman caught in his dark embrace would never miss the small amount of blood he had taken.

Pleased with his self-restraint, he put his arm around her shoulders and led her out of the alley. Releasing his hold on her mind, he took her by the hand and started walking.

She blinked at him several times, like someone who had just been roused from a deep sleep.

"Is this the place you were talking about?" Ramsey asked.

"What?" She looked up at the blinking neon light that identified the place as *The Sea Nymph Motel.* "Yes. Yes, it is."

"Is something wrong?"

"No. No, I guess not." Her flirtatious manner was gone. She looked suddenly shy, nervous in his presence, unsure of herself. She glanced up at the neon sign again, her face wan in the artificial light. Her brow furrowed. "Do you mind if we do this another night? I feel sort of . . . strange."

"I'm sorry to hear that. Can I see you home?"

"What? Oh, no, I'll be fine. Good night." She stared at him a moment, then turned and hurried back down the street.

Whistling softly, he headed for home.

"Move over, Dracula," he muttered wryly. "Look out, Lestat. Ramsey is here."

Chapter 4

She stood on the far edge of the pier, staring down into the still, black water below. It looked cold, cold enough to numb her pain. *Jump,* she thought. All she had to do was jump and it would be all over. What did she have to live for, anyway? She had no family, no lover or any prospect of one, no friends to speak of. No job, no money. No reason to go on.

How long would it take to drown? Not long, she thought, since she couldn't swim. Would it hurt? At this time of year, the water would be cold—one sudden, gasping shock and she would probably be unconscious. As a child, she had been afraid of the dark, terrified of dying. She had slept with a light on until the summer her grandmother came to stay with them. Grandma Hansen had told her stories of heaven, of the blue-eyed, golden-haired Angel of Death who came to earth to escort the spirits of the dead into the next world.

As she grew older, she had stopped believing in angels. There were no such things as heavenly escorts.

There was no heaven, and surely life was hell enough for anyone. She found it strangely comforting now to believe that there was nothing after this miserable existence, to believe that she could plunge to her death and find peace in the endless black void of eternity. No more pain, no more tears, no more heartaches. She had achieved success once, and blown it big time. She wouldn't fail at this. One last success—and oblivion.

Taking a deep breath, she closed her eyes and let herself go. Just let herself go. And then she was falling, falling, the wind rushing against her ears, her arms involuntarily outstretched. It was, she thought, almost like flying. . . .

Ramsey stood on the pier near the stairs, gazing down into the ocean, his expression thoughtful. The moon was reflected on the face of the dark water, a brilliant yellow that rippled and shimmered. He cast no reflection at all. But that was to be expected. He was one of the undead he had hunted all his adult life. Yet he could still see himself in a mirror. He pondered that for awhile, thinking how odd it was that a looking glass reflected his image but water didn't, and then shrugged. Still, casting no reflection in the moonlit water was unsettling, as if he no longer existed. A fitting irony, he thought, that he should spend eternity as the very creature he had spent his life destroying.

He grinned ruefully. In point of fact, he didn't exist anymore—at least not as anything the world would recognize. Perhaps the natural world—free-flowing water, the glowing moon—mocked his peculiar existence now. It was all like a bad dream, a nightmare from which he would never awake.

But did one feel that throbbing hunger in the middle of a nightmare? he wondered with grim humor, thinking it was just the sort of sardonic musing he had come to expect from Chiavari. He shook his head at the irony. More than just his wardrobe had changed in the past month.

But he wasn't thinking just then of his new Porsche, or of the new house he had acquired, all in this relatively short time. He had thought it would be difficult to convince the real estate people to come to their office at night to close the sale, but he hadn't reckoned with his new powers of persuasion.

His mood lifted, and he grinned into the darkness. His new house, located near the end of a quiet street in an old neighborhood, looked like something out of *Dark Shadows*. It was two stories high, with an attic and a basement. The windows were high and arched. There was even a turret on the southeast corner. It was, he thought, the perfect abode for a vampire.

The sense of power, of invincibility, flowed strongly through him, overcoming his lingering repugnance. With each succeeding night, each feeding, his qualms seemed to grow weaker. And his power to grow. Perhaps one day he would be as powerful as Chiavari.

A sudden movement on the far end of the pier interrupted his reverie.

With his preternatural senses, he had been all too aware of the young woman lingering there, easy prey on a cold dark night.

Now she was climbing over the rail, plunging toward the water, arms outstretched. Caught in a wash of silver moonlight, she looked like a raven-haired angel plummeting to earth.

She hit with a loud splash, disappeared for a moment, then bobbed to the surface like a cork, her hair spreading across the rippling water like silken seaweed. The tide was coming in, and it swept her toward the shore, her clothing dragging her under. He left the pier and went around to the steps that led to the sand. Hurrying now, his gaze swept the dark water. At first, he saw nothing, and then he saw her, her body tumbling in the tide that was carrying her toward the shore.

Wading into the water, he grabbed her by the shoulder. She was unconscious, no doubt from the impact of hitting the frigid water. There were dark smudges under her eyes. Her face was pale, her lips tinged with blue. She was far too thin. Kneeling, he laid her on the sand, took off his coat and wrapped it around her, then gathered her into his arms once again.

He stared down at her. He had not yet fed. The Siren call of her blood whispered to the hunger within him. He suppressed the urge, pleased by his power to do so. She was unconscious, weak, her life force feeble. To feed now, while she was unconscious, was somehow repugnant. More important, it would put her life at risk. Thus far, he had left all his victims with their lives. This frail waif would be no exception. He gazed at the planes of her face, bared and vulnerable in the moonlight, felt the damp swing of her heavy hair against his arm as he gained his feet. Looking at her filled him with a kind of aching tenderness. He would take her home, revive her, strengthen her. And then he would feed, at his leisure.

She woke slowly, reluctantly, surprised to find she was still alive. Where was she? It was too much of an effort to raise her head.

She was lying on a bed not her own.

In a room. Not her own.

Panic slithered down her spine when she realized she was naked beneath the covers. Jackknifing into a sitting position, she glanced around the room. Pale mauve-colored walls. Deep mauve carpeting. There was a large walnut dresser against the far wall, a rocking chair in one corner.

She frowned as she swung her legs over the edge of the bed. She didn't know where she was. She didn't remember how she had gotten there, but she was leaving. Now.

She stood, the covers clutched to her chest, swaying as a wave of dizziness passed over her. What had she done? How had she gotten here?

Pills. She remembered taking a handful of pills, leaving the squalid boardinghouse where she had been staying. Walking for what seemed like hours. Falling . . . Falling? And then she remembered the dark water beckoning to her, the wind in her ears as she tumbled over the end of the pier . . .

With a faint cry, she fell back on the bed, suddenly too weak to stand. The pier. She had jumped from the pier. She had wanted to die. Still wanted to die. Why wasn't she dead?

She gasped as the overhead light went out and the room went dark. Panic swept through her when she realized she was no longer alone. "Who—who is it? Who's there?"

Pulse racing, she peered into the dark, but she saw nothing, heard nothing but the frantic pounding of her own heart. Was it her imagination, or had she felt a breath of cold air against the back of her neck?

"Do you really want to die?"

"Yes. No. I don't know." She jumped as an unseen hand brushed her cheek. "Who are you?"

"I am no one."

"Are you the one who brought me here?"

"Yes."

She was afraid to ask why. Terror rose up within her. She didn't stop to wonder at this; she had been ready to die on the pier, had thought she had died in that last moment of consciousness when she hit the icy water that felt as hard as cement on impact, driving the consciousness from her. But she had not died. Why? So that she could die now? One thing was certain: she was closer to death now than she had been when she plunged off the pier.

"Have you come to take me?" she asked. "Are you the Angel of Death?"

A soft chuckle rippled through the air. "You could call me that."

"Grandma was right," she murmured, her voice tinged with wonder. "Will it hurt?"

"Only a little."

"I'm ready."

He looked down at her. He could see the pulse beating in her throat, hear the blood thrumming through her veins, smell her fear. Yet she lay on the bed, the blankets drawn up to her chin, her arms extended, her eyes closed, like a virgin about to be sacrificed to some heathen god.

She is yours. You have only to take her. . . .

The voice of his hunger whispered in the back of his mind, urging him to feed the demon that now lived within him, to slake his thirst, to ease the coldness of his existence by filling himself with her life force, weak as it still was. His noble sentiment at the pier, of strengthening her so that she would not die, seemed a distant memory in the exquisite agony of this hunger. She wanted to die anyway. What would it be like to take it all?

"Angel?"

"I'm here."

"Please hurry. I'm . . . I'm so afraid."

The fear in her voice, coupled with an almost childlike trust, reached deep down inside him, stirring his best and worst selves. Moving swiftly, he knelt beside the bed and drew her into his arms, blankets and all. His fangs lengthened, pierced the tender skin at her neck. He closed his eyes and drank . . . and knew her.

She had no one. She lived alone. Once, she had aspired to be an actress. Once, she had dreamed of a romantic love everlasting. Then that love had abandoned her for another woman. Devastated, depressed, she had lost her dreams of stardom, drowned them in alcohol, burned them away in drugs. Now she was out of money, and out of hope. . . . Her choice had been prostitution or death. . . .

He drew back. Though the room was dark, he saw her clearly. She was thin. Too thin. There were hollows in her cheeks. He could feel each rib beneath the blankets that covered her.

And she was young, much younger than he had first thought.

"Angel?" she murmured.

"I'm here."

She lifted a trembling hand to her neck. "Am I dead?"

"No." He searched her mind for her name. "No, Kelly. You are not dead."

"I'm cold."

He drew the bedspread over her, lifted her into his arms—bedspread, blankets, sheets, and all—and carried her to the faded overstuffed chair in the corner. Sitting down, he cradled her to his chest though he doubted his body—his cold, *dead* body—could offer her much heat.

Gazing deep into her eyes, he whispered, "Go to sleep, Kelly. There's nothing to be afraid of. You are warm now, warm and safe."

He felt his mind connect to hers in that curious bond common between vampire and prey, felt that curious sense of power sweep through him as he bent her will to his.

Obediently she closed her eyes. "I'm not afraid anymore," she murmured. "Grandma was right. There's nothing to be afraid of."

"No," Ramsey said as he lowered his head to her neck. "There is nothing to be afraid of."

He brushed his lips over her throat, his nostrils filling with the scent of her skin, her blood. The faint musty smell of the river clung to her hair. But her blood was warm and sweet, infinitely sweeter and more satisfying than any he had tasted. The first taste chased away the coldness that gripped him, banished the hunger, filled him with a sense of euphoria. Sweet, so sweet.

He drank slowly, wondering that her blood did not repulse him, even as he cursed Chiavari for transforming him, cursed himself for what he was doing. He drew back a little so he could see the girl's face. She was, if possible, even paler than before. Her lashes lay like dark fans against her cheeks. Her breathing was slow and shallow. He had been so pleased the other night, proud of his self-control, of his ability to subdue the raging demon that now lived within him. Why was he having such trouble tonight? Why did the thought of draining her dry hold such appeal even as it sickened him?

He stared at the droplets of bright-red crimson at her throat. He had done that. He ran his tongue over his fangs. Long. White. Sharp. He had only been kidding himself.

Monster. The word rang out in his mind. He was one of them, a creature of the damned, doomed to prey on the blood of innocents.

And even as the thought crossed his mind, he bent his head and drank again.

Chapter 5

AFTER SUNDOWN

The vampyre stirred while the sun hung low in the sky. Lying amid an array of black silk sheets and feather pillows, she contemplated the events of particular interest to her that had transpired halfway across the world.

Alexi had been destroyed.

Grigori had bequeathed the Dark Gift to another.

Her blood flowed in the veins of a newly made vampyre.

Grigori. She had not seen him in centuries. She let her mind expand then fold in on itself, and she knew, within that part of her being that had created him, that he was well.

Rising, she went to the window and drew back the heavy velvet draperies that shut out the sun during midday, when she was the most vulnerable. She ran her hand over the soft velvet. She was a sensual creature, and she smiled, enjoying the feel of the velvet beneath her palm, the texture that was smooth yet rough, the material still warm from the heat of the late-afternoon sun.

Her timing was second nature now, precise. The sun had descended just beyond the distant hills moments before she parted the curtains. The sky was ablaze with streaks of bloodred crimson and scarlet and lavender as the sun descended behind the distant hills.

Sweetest night, mistress mine, a toast to thee with mortal wine. She smiled as she recalled a poem Grigori had written for her centuries ago, when he had been enamored of her. It had been his first attempt at poetry. Caught up in his new life, he had been hungry for every new experience. Hungry for blood. Hungry for her. How romantic he had been then, she mused as she remembered the rest of the poem.

> *Moonlight, fangs, glitter, shine, harvesting the human vine. Eternal game, Hunter, Prey, mortals always slower, they. Instinct sends them running, madly; always ending the same, badly. Chase them, tease, feed their fear; whisper in their dying ear. Too soon 'tis done; they are gone, horizon lightens, hated Dawn. As morn approaches, I am prey; soon I must secret away. Coffin waiting, satin lined, soon I shall be deaf and blind. Deepest sleep through bitter light, come swiftly beloved, Mother Night.*

Grigori ... She had never met a male, human or vampire, who challenged her as he had, excited her as he had—as he still did, though she had not seen him in decades. He had been a lover without equal, tender and gentle, yet masterful, sure of himself, secure in his masculinity. She had been older, stronger, but he had made her feel young, vulnerable.

"Grigori." She whispered his name, and felt the old sweet stirring in her veins.

In centuries past, she had visited all the countries in

Europe, but she had never been to the United States. Perhaps it was time. It had been years since she left Italy. No matter where she went, she always returned here, to the place where she had met Grigori.

A faint smile curved her lips as she contemplated seeing him again. He had always held a special place in her affections. She recalled the first night she had seen him, grieving over the graves of his children. His grief had burned like a bonfire in the night, drawing her with its warmth. Even in the mire of his desolation, his life force had been powerful, throbbing. He had looked right through her, blind to her beauty then, his whole being infused with pain and hate.

"What are you doing here?" she had asked, and he had told her what had happened—how Alexi had taken his wife and killed his children.

"And do you wish to join your children in death?" she had asked.

"No!" he had declared vehemently. "I want to avenge them! But how can I? How can I?"

"How indeed," she had replied softly. "Shall I show you how?"

"Only show me," he had replied with a bravado she had known was false. "And I will do whatever you ask."

She had smiled then, and he had recoiled from the sight of her fangs. "You're one of them!"

"Will you not join me, my handsome one? It is the only way you will ever be strong enough to find the vengeance you seek."

"You're asking me to become the same kind of monster he is!" Grigori had exclaimed.

"We are not all monsters," she had replied. "Look at me. Do I appear a monster to you?"

"No," he had replied. "Who are you?"

"Khira." She had offered him her hand. "Will you join me?"

He had cocked his head to one side, giving her easy access to the large vein in his neck, and she had taken what he offered. It was always so much sweeter when they were willing, when they didn't fight.

She had bestowed the Dark Gift on only a few, and her blood and her power were strong. She had taught her fledgling how to find his prey, how to survive. He had taught her a depth of passion she had thought long vanished with her mortality. She began to entertain thoughts of an eternal relationship, and taught him all the things she wanted him to know: how to read and write, and the complex etiquette of the upper classes.

She had introduced him to all the finer things: art, opera, literature, architecture. He learned it all with zest, and seemed to have forgotten his vow of vengeance. But she knew better. He could not hide his inmost thoughts from her, but she did not press. There was world enough, and time enough. He was strong yet gentle, full of passion and tenderness, if a bit arrogant. And he was handsome, so very handsome. He had embraced the Dark Gift fully, and the Gift's powers had enhanced his natural good looks; she was sure that all women wanted him. She knew his prey submitted willingly as he eagerly explored his new life. In one sense, she had watched him, as proud as any mortal mother watching a child of her womb mature into his manhood. In another sense, as his powers grew stronger, she began to feel uncertain—she, who had never doubted her own allure. Would he leave her? Would he find some mortal woman more desirable than she?

But it had not been another woman's beauty that took him from her. She closed her eyes tightly, remembering. It had been her own insatiable hunger. In his enthusiasm for his new life, he had pushed all thought of Alexi into the back of his mind until the night he saw her bending over a child and remembered his own children, his own reason for becoming Vampyre. He had taken the child from her, his eyes blazing with contempt, and she had never seen him again. . . .

She sighed as she turned away from the window, wondering if he had yet forgiven her. She had destroyed others who had left her side before she tired of them, but not Grigori. She had loved him at first sight. She recalled the sweet taste of his blood the night she had bestowed the Dark Gift upon him, and all they had shared before her foolish error.

Surely time enough had passed by now. Time enough to heal his anger. Grigori had his revenge at last; Alexi was destroyed. Perhaps he would be in a forgiving mood, and if not, then she would have to persuade him to see things her way. She was not without her own power, her own irresistible charm.

Her mind made up, she threw off her melancholy mood as easily as she changed her gown. She had never been one to brood or lament the past. Grigori would see her whether he wished it or not.

Humming softly, she fastened her cloak, excited and intrigued by the journey ahead. She contemplated the distance, careful to time her departure so she would arrive in the New World after sundown. Young vampires who wished to travel long distances had to make careful plans so that they might travel safely in their coffins on long trips. But she was no longer a young vampire. Mortals grew weaker as old age set in, losing youth and strength and beauty. It was not so among vampires. Increased age brought increased powers and the ability to travel great distances with supernatural speed.

She closed her eyes, and in moments, she was where she wanted to be.

Chapter 6

Ramsey stared at the woman on the bed in horror. Kelly. Her name was Kelly, but he could not bear to call her that. Acknowledging her by name only made what he had done seem more monstrous somehow. Her skin was as white as the sheet upon which she lay. And she was still, so still. What had he done? He had kept her here for three days, trapped between life and death.

He backed away from the bed. He hadn't meant to kill her. Never that! He was not a murderer.

Aren't you? The voice of his conscience whispered down the tortured corridors of his mind. *What of all the lives you have taken in the past?*

"But they were monsters. Vampires who preyed on the innocent . . ."

Sardonic, silent laughter mocked him. And now you have become one of them. You are what you hunted, Edward Ramsey, what you and your family have hated and destroyed for centuries. . . .

"No!" Anguish sliced through him, and he screamed

the word in denial, even though he knew it was true. He was a vampire. He had become what he had hated, what he had spent his lifetime destroying.

Vampire. Vampire. Vampire!

He pressed his hands to his temples in a vain attempt to block the word and the horror it entailed, but it seemed to echo off the walls, the ceiling, even the floor.

Vampire . . . vampire . . . vampire . . .

Killer of innocents.

Drinker of blood.

Unholy.

Unclean.

Monster.

"No, no." He sank to his knees and closed his eyes to shut out the image of the woman on the bed: her body limp, lifeless, the single drop of blood that lay like a scarlet teardrop on the pale skin of her neck—but her image was burned into his brain.

She had wanted to die. . . .

But even that thought offered no absolution. The Ramsey of old would have offered her comfort and solace. His family had provided protection for the innocents of the world. Yet he had feasted on her blood, drawn on her life force, until he had taken too much, taken it all. The self-satisfied restraint he had prided himself on had been nothing but an illusion.

He had only been kidding himself, thinking he could do this, live like this. The thought that he had taken her blood, and found an almost sensual pleasure in it, burned through him like acid.

He had killed her. He was a vampire. There was nothing to do but accept it, just as there was only one way to ensure that such a thing would never happen again. Not for the first time, he thought of walking out into the sunlight and ending his existence. Did he have the nerve to end his own life? After what he had just done, how could he not?

Lost in his own misery, he failed to realize he was no longer alone.

"She is not dead," a low, throaty voice said. "Soon, but not yet."

Ramsey jumped to his feet and spun around, his nostrils filling with the scent of jasmine. His gaze pierced the darkness, focusing on the woman standing in the doorway. Wrapped in a long black cloak, a shadow within shadows, she was tall and slender, with silver-blond hair. And she was a vampire. A very old vampire. Her power slid over his skin, raising the hair on his arms.

"Who the hell are you?" he demanded.

A faint smile tugged at her lips. "You might say I am your grandmother."

Ramsey frowned, surprised that he was no longer afraid. "Grandmother?" He laughed softly. "What big teeth you have."

"The better to eat you with, my dear," she replied, and her laughter joined his. "I am Khira."

"Khira!" The vampire who had brought Grigori across.

"The very same. May I come in?"

He hesitated, then shook his head as the habits of a lifetime of vampire hunting took over. "I'll come out."

She laughed softly and stepped aside so he could join her outside. "What will you do with her?" she asked, gesturing at the woman lying on the bed.

"What do you mean?" He couldn't bring himself to look at the woman lying so cold and still.

"You seemed grieved when you thought she was dead. Will you bring her across?"

"No! I don't make vampires. I destroy them."

"So you did. As did your forebears, as well. A long

line of nuisances, your ancestors." She laughed softly. "Trust Grigori to be the first one to bring a Ramsey across! What delicious irony. Tell me, my handsome new vampire, why do your thoughts reek of self-destruction?"

He looked at her, mute, disconcerted by the ease with which she read his mind.

"You are strong for such a young one. You have restrained yourself with your little mortal—amazing control for one so young. But you must not drink from your prize every night if you wish her to live," Khira went on. "And you must feed her well. Thick soup. Red meat to strengthen her blood."

She drew her cloak more closely about her. It was a gesture with no real meaning. She did not feel the cold. "It will be interesting, I think, to see which of your natures prevails," she mused. "The conscience-stricken mortal, or the strong young vampyre."

And in the blink of an eye, she was gone.

Chapter 7

Grigori leaped to his feet in a fluid motion and stood staring toward the window, his heart pounding.

"What is it?" Marisa asked. They had been sitting on the sofa, watching the late movie. "What's wrong?"

"She's here."

"She?"

"Khira."

"Here?" Marisa glanced around the living room. "She's here? Where?"

"In the city." Rising from the sofa, Grigori went to the window. Sweeping the curtains aside, he gazed out into the darkness.

Darkness shrouded the street below, broken only by the faint yellow glow of a streetlamp. Khira's power rode the wings of the night like the wind before a storm, sending shivers of awareness down his spine.

He unleashed his own power, let it flow through the sleeping city. Ramsey had fed and fed well, and now he paced the dark streets, sated but restless.

And Khira drew ever nearer. She was a mile away. A block away.

"Grigori?"

"It's all right, *cara.*"

He heard the intake of Marisa's breath, the rustle of her silk nightgown whispering against her skin as she clicked off the television, her near-silent footfalls as she moved up behind him.

She slipped her arms around his waist. "What do you think she wants?"

"I don't know. Perhaps I should go down and ask her."

Marisa peered around Grigori and looked out the window. At first she saw nothing but a faint shimmer in the darkness, a sparkle that reminded her of Tinkerbell's pixy dust, and then, to her amazement, the shimmer coalesced, transforming into a tall, slender woman clad in a long white gown and ankle-length black cloak. A wealth of silver-blond hair flowed over her shoulders.

"Stay here," Grigori said. He pulled on his boots, then took Marisa in his arms. "Remember, she cannot come inside unless you invite her."

"Don't go."

"I don't think she means me any harm."

Marisa looked up at her husband. Her handsome, virile husband. Wherever they went, women turned to stare at him, their eyes hot. "That's not what I'm afraid of."

Grigori laughed softly, then brushed a kiss across her lips. "Stay here."

Before she could argue, he was gone.

"I am here, Grigori."

He turned slowly, and she was there, tall and slender,

graceful as a willow, her luxuriant silver-blond hair shimmering like a halo in the lamplight's soft yellow glow.

For a moment, they stared at each other in silent appraisal. She was as beautiful as he remembered. The silk of her gown clung to her figure like a long-lost lover, outlining every delectable curve. Her skin was pale and flawless.

"You are as lovely as ever," Grigori remarked.

"And you . . ." She trailed the tip of her finger down the side of his cheek. "You are still the most handsome of men."

He said nothing, only continued to look at her, wondering what had brought her here.

"Do you still write poetry, my handsome one?"

He frowned. "Poetry?"

"Have you forgotten? 'Sweetest night, mistress mine . . . ' "

He laughed softly. "That was my one and only attempt, clumsy at best."

"But so full of passion," she murmured, her eyes luminous. "Full of your growing power."

"Be that as it may, I am no poet."

"Perhaps it is just as well. You are far too attractive to women already without having poetry in your arsenal." She looked at him, her blue eyes glittering. "Grigori . . ." Her voice was a soft, sultry purr.

"What do you want? Why have you come here?"

"Have you forgiven me yet, *mi amour?*"

Without his willing it, the night they had parted rose up in his mind, as stark and vivid as if it had happened only yesterday. With an effort, he fought down his revulsion. He had been very young then. He had learned much in the centuries that had passed.

"It is not my place to forgive you," he said quietly. "We are what we are."

She looked up at him, her smile as radiant as the sun. She took a half-step toward him, her arms outstretched.

"Why have you come here, Khira?" His words, cold and abrupt, stopped her.

"Why?" she repeated. She lowered her arms, let her shoulders droop as she took on a look of wounded innocence. "Is there some reason why I should not come to see you?"

Grigori shrugged. "It's been over two hundred years," he replied wryly. "Why this sudden urge to see me now?" He took a deep breath, and the answer to her visit filled his nostrils. "How is Ramsey?"

Khira laughed softly. "He is an interesting choice for the Dark Gift. Trust you, *mi amour*, to do something so vastly unconventional, even for one of us!" The sound of her laugher was like fairy bells in the night. "I cannot imagine he was willing. Not the last of the Ramseys!"

"He was not willing, but like all creatures, he wanted to live."

"I find myself liking him."

Grigori lifted one brow but said nothing.

"I think perhaps I shall seduce him." She ran her hand along his shoulder, down his arm, to curve over his biceps. "Young vampyres make such wonderful lovers. Insatiable in their new strength, so eager to explore every facet of their new world. Remember, *mi amour?*"

He remembered all too well. And so did she. He could read it in her eyes. She had been an ardent lover, tireless, inventive . . . He shoved the memory away, aware of her power moving over him, compelling him to remember the long, tempestuous nights he had spent in her arms. With an effort, he pushed her from his mind and closed the door on memories now best left forgotten.

Khira laughed again. It sounded remarkably like a

schoolgirl giggle, something he found quite incongruous coming from a woman who was close to a thousand years old.

"Did you come here to discuss your love life with me?" he asked in a fine attempt at his old bravado with her.

"No." The warmth in her eyes cooled. "I came to meet the woman you married."

Something that might have been fear slithered down Grigori's spine.

"Don't you want to introduce me to her?" Khira purred. She raked her nails over his cheek, exerting just enough pressure to break the skin. The scent of his blood filled the air. Slowly, as though daring him to object, she leaned up against him and ran her tongue over the faint line of blood. "She does know what you are, doesn't she?"

Grigori took a step back, resisting the urge to wipe his cheek. "Of course."

Khira took his arm and smiled up at him. "Well, then, shall we go in?"

There was no way to refuse.

Marisa whirled around as the front door opened and the woman she had seen on the street entered the room, followed by Grigori. This close, the vampire was breathtakingly beautiful. Her skin glowed with a pale opalescence; her eyes were the bluest blue Marisa had ever seen. Her figure was perfect.

"I am Khira," the woman said, extending her hand.

"Marisa."

Khira's hand was soft, her skin warm to the touch. Warm as only a well-fed vampire could be warm.

"She is lovely, Grigori," Khira said. Her gaze ran over Marisa, coolly assessing. "Really lovely."

"I think so." Grigori moved to Marisa's side and draped his arm around her shoulders. It was a warning, a blatant gesture of possession and protection.

Khira smiled in amusement. "I have not come to harm her, Grigori." She glanced around the room, like a queen visiting peasants. "The decor suits her."

"I'd appreciate it if you wouldn't talk about me like I'm not here," Marisa said.

"I am sorry," Khira said. "I did not mean to offend you, Marisa. May I call you Marisa?"

"Of course." Marisa looked at Grigori. "Why don't we sit down?"

Grigori nodded. "Khira, please make yourself at home."

Marisa watched the other woman glide across the room. Like Grigori, Khira moved with fluid grace, almost as if she were floating above the floor. She sat on the love seat beside the fireplace, the hem of her cloak spreading in graceful folds at her feet.

Marisa sat down on the sofa, and Grigori sat beside her.

Silence hung heavy in the room.

"So," Khira said, her gaze moving from Grigori to Marisa and back again, "tell me everything. How you met. How long you have been married."

"Is that why you came here?" Grigori asked.

Khira shrugged. It was an elegant gesture. "I came for many reasons. To see the fledgling you made. To see if you had changed after so many years." She smiled faintly. "To see America. I have heard so much of this country over the years. I am thinking of staying awhile. But now I want to hear all about you. About both of you."

Grigori glanced at Marisa. She was watching him, her eyes filled with love and trust. Did she have any idea of the power of the woman sitting across from them? Now that Kristov had been destroyed, Khira was, as far as he knew, the oldest, most powerful vampire in existence.

Grigori told Khira, succinctly, of Kristov and Ramsey and all that had transpired between them.

Khira sat listening quietly, her body still as only a vampyre can be still, her gaze intent upon Grigori's face.

"And so," Khira mused in a voice that was softly condemning, "you had your revenge on Alexi at last."

Grigori nodded. There was an unwritten law that vampyre did not kill vampyre. He had broken that law when he killed Alexi.

"I would do it again," he said, his gaze meeting Khira's.

She laughed softly. "I do not fault you for what you have done. How could I? Did I not bestow the Dark Gift upon you for that very purpose?" She stood up and walked slowly around the room, her slender hands moving gracefully across the back of a chair, over the satin finish of an antique oak table. "You may have to destroy Ramsey, as well."

Grigori frowned at her. "What do you mean?"

"He is uneasy in his mind about what he is. He cannot control the hunger, yet he despises himself for what he has become. He wishes for death, yet he craves blood, and the life it gives him. Do not underestimate him, *mi amour*. He is powerful. More powerful than he should be, for one so young. Unless he learns to accept what he is, he may become a liability to our small community."

Grigori shook his head. "I don't think so."

"He is a hunter by nature," Khira remarked. "He spent his mortal life hunting those he considered evil. Now he has become what he hunted."

Grigori nodded. "He must work it out for himself."

"I hope so. If he does not . . . well, he is a Ramsey,

after all. You must have known the risks inherent in bringing a hunter across.''

Grigori frowned, troubled by the thinly veiled threat he heard in Khira's voice. "He will find a way to live with what he has become, in time, as we all must do."

Marisa looked up at Grigori. "How did you learn to accept being a vampire?"

"There was nothing to accept." Grigori glanced at Khira, who was standing in front of the fireplace. A wave of her hand, and a blaze sprang to life. He looked back at Marisa. "I wanted it."

"He is one of the lucky ones," Khira remarked. "Many seek the Dark Gift, thinking only of cheating death. They do not realize that death comes to a vampire with each new dawn for as long as he survives."

Marisa shivered at the image Khira's words evoked. There was a time when she had been certain she wanted to share all of Grigori's life, but now she wasn't so sure. Had she really thought it through? Was she prepared for all the drastic changes it would make in her life? It would mean no more vacations with her family, no more lazy summer days at the beach, no long walks except at night. Was she ready to give up the pleasures of food and drink, of dark chocolate mousse and root-beer floats, for a warm liquid diet?

She looked up as she felt Grigori's arm wrap around her shoulders. He knew what she was thinking. She read the knowledge in his eyes.

"What about you?" Marisa said, speaking to Khira. "Did you want to be a vampire?"

"No." Khira sat down on the love seat again. "I fell in love when I was very young. I did not know what he was. Like all young girls who fall in love for the first time, I told him I loved him, could not live without him. And one night he showed me what he was, and then, against my will, he brought me across." Hatred flared in the depths of her eyes. "I killed him for it."

Marisa pressed against Grigori as Khira's hatred flooded the room. It crawled across her skin like a living thing and then slowly receded.

"Later, I was sorry for what I had done," Khira went on. "Being a vampyre was not as horrible a fate as I had imagined. And even though the little death that came with each dawn frightened me for a long while, I grew used to it in time." A faint smile played over her lips. "And now, so many years later, the little death has little power over me. I wish now that I had not killed him."

"If it was your choice, would you accept the Dark Gift again?" Marisa asked.

"Perhaps. I have done much. Seen much. Loved much. And yet . . ." She lifted one pale hand and let it fall. "I have lost much. It is a hard thing, to watch those you love wither and die, and I have seen it many times through the centuries. And children . . . never to have a child."

Khira shook her head, as if to dispel unpleasant memories. "And now I must go and find a place to pass the day."

"You are welcome to stay here," Grigori said. "We have plenty of empty rooms."

"I appreciate your offer, *mi amour,* but I must decline." Khira rose effortlessly to her feet and floated across the floor. She smiled faintly as she took Marisa's hand in hers. "It was a pleasure to meet you, my dear. Perhaps I shall see you again."

Marisa nodded. "Yes, perhaps," she replied. But she was thinking of what Khira had said. *Never to have a child.* She felt a deep, piercing stab of regret. In marrying Grigori, she had forfeited her right to bear children.

Khira smiled at Grigori. "She is a treasure, *mi amour.* Take good care of her."

"I will." He brushed a careless kiss across Khira's cheek, wondering if her warning had been real or imagined.

With a wave of her hand, Khira vanished from sight, but her voice echoed loud and clear in his mind: *Ramsey could be dangerous. Be wary of him. . . .*

Chapter 8

Khira's words echoed in Grigori's mind as he waited for the dawn. *Ramsey could be dangerous. Be wary of him.* Lying in bed, with Marisa's head pillowed on his shoulder, he pondered the vampyre's words. *Ramsey could be dangerous.* To whom? To Marisa? He knew Ramsey had been in love with Marisa. Who wouldn't be? She was a beautiful woman with a generous heart and a beautiful soul. He knew Ramsey had proposed to her, knew the man had been hurt when she refused, but he had never given it any more thought. Marisa was his wife, and that ended it. Perhaps Khira's warning had been for himself. There was little doubt that Ramsey despised him for bringing him across, for making him what he had hated and hunted. Or had Khira merely been warning him that Ramsey was still a danger to their kind? Ramsey the mortal, obsessed with slaying vampyres, had been dangerous enough, with his accumulated knowledge of the hunt. If Ramsey the vampyre retained that obsession, despite his altered state, that would be another level of danger indeed.

Slipping out of bed, Grigori padded noiselessly to the window, drew back the heavy drapes that shut out the rest of the world, and gazed into the darkness. In the past, he had drunk of Ramsey's blood to survive; Ramsey had taken his blood to cheat the grave. They were bound together now, linked by a bond of blood that could not be broken until one of them was dead.

The community of vampyres was small. Because of what they were, because of the kind of lives they led, they tended to be solitary creatures, distrustful of others, even their own kind. He had known, when he invited Khira to stay, that she would refuse. Most vampyres preferred to sleep alone, keeping their resting place a secret from others of their kind. But there was no way for him to hide from Khira. She had made him what he was; she would always be able to find him.

Not long ago, he had thought himself and Kristov the only vampyres in the city. But, once Kristov had been destroyed, he had learned there were four other vampyres living in the general vicinity. One was a rock star who lived in West Hollywood and called himself Prince Dracul. The second, Noah Fox, was a reclusive businessman who made his home in Brentwood. He was wealthy enough that his odd hours were considered eccentric and not abnormal. Kyle LaSalle, author of a dozen successful techno-thrillers, lived in a mansion in Beverly Hills. And then there was Madame Rosa. She was a mystic of some renown whose paranormal ability to read minds had gained her a remarkable reputation, and an equally remarkable fortune. She had appeared on all the late-night talk shows; one of them had offered ten thousand dollars to anyone who could prove she was a fake.

Ramsey upped that number to five. And now there was Khira.

Too many, he thought, for such a small space.

He wondered if the other vampires were aware of Khira's presence, wondered if their lives were in danger. If Khira decided to stay in this area for an extended period of time, she would not allow the others to remain. Indeed, she might insist that Grigori and Ramsey leave the city, as well. She had never shared her hunting grounds with any save for him, but they had been lovers then. Might have been lovers to this day had he not seen her bending over that child, her fangs extended, the lust for blood hot in her eyes.

He shivered with the recollection. Until that moment, he had been lost in the intoxication of his new condition, preoccupied by Khira's attention, as dazzled as a schoolboy by her lovemaking. But that night he had seen her for what she was: a ruthless, soulless hunter, a predator without feeling or remorse. She had been a vampire for so long that she was no longer hindered by any empathy for her victims. And in that frozen moment of time, he had seen what he was well on his way to becoming, what she wanted him to become. In his mind's eye, her victim that night had blended with his lost children and reawakened the furious hatred that had spurred him to accept the Dark Gift. Mesmerized as he had been by her, he had forgotten why he wanted the Dark Gift in the first place.

He had looked deep into her eyes when he wrested the child from her grasp. He had seen no remorse reflected there, no regret, no shame—nor any love for him. He had, however, seen his own destruction in the depths of her hungry eyes.

But, to his surprise, there had also been a trace of fear. Fear of his strength, his power.

Grabbing the boy from her arms, he had fled into

the night. She had not followed him. He had shaken
her to her core with his rebellion. It was a simple matter
to probe the boy's mind and discover where he lived.
He had returned the boy to his home, confident Khira
would not follow, that she would not dare to attack that
particular child again. He knew other innocents would
fall prey to her hunger, but he could not protect them
all. And there had been a far darker evil in the land,
and his name had been Alexi Kristov.

As soon as the boy was safely home, he had gone in
search of Kristov.

It had been a long and frustrating quest, but Kristov
was dead now, destroyed with Ramsey's help. Had it not
been for his search for Kristov, he would never have
met Marisa.

Turning, he let his gaze wander over her face. With
his preternatural senses, he could see her clearly in the
darkness, hear the whisper of her breath. A faint smile
tugged at her lips, and he wondered if she was dreaming
of him. They had made love earlier. As always, her tenderness, her total acceptance, touched a chord deep
within him. It still amazed him that he had won her
heart, that she looked at him with love and desire instead
of fear and revulsion. When she was ready, he would
bring her across, and she would be his forever. It was
a possibility he looked forward to with mixed emotions.
He loved her as she was—vital and alive. He had no
wish to watch her beauty fade, to see her steps slow,
watch the sparkle dim in her eyes; and yet, on a level
he did not quite understand, he was reluctant to bestow
the Dark Gift upon her. She would be the same as she
was now, and yet not the same.

He stood at the window a few moments longer. In
the distance, the sky was growing lighter as dawn lifted
her curtain on a new day. Next door, a dog barked at
an early-morning jogger. His body grew heavy, heavier,

as the sun climbed higher. Once, the deathlike sleep had claimed him at dawn's first light, but no more. With each passing year, he was able to rise a little earlier, seek his rest a little later.

With a sigh, he returned to bed. Sliding under the covers, he drew Marisa into his arms, where she belonged.

Marisa woke slowly. Though it was after three, the room was as dark as night, due to the heavy curtains that covered the windows, shutting out the glare of the sun. She had changed her lifestyle to accommodate Grigori's, staying up until dawn so that they could be together before he surrendered to the Dark Sleep.

Sitting up, she glanced over her shoulder at Grigori. She knew now where the term "sleeping like the dead" came from. It was a little disconcerting, seeing him when he was trapped in the Dark Sleep. She knew he would hear her if she spoke to him—knew that, with a great deal of effort and energy, he could fight off sleep's hold for a short time.

Rising, she went into the bathroom to shower and brush her teeth. She dressed quickly in a pair of well-worn jeans and her favorite *Beauty and the Beast* T-shirt, then went downstairs. Grigori often teased her about the T-shirt, claiming she was indeed the beauty and he was the beast.

Going outside, she strolled down the long driveway and picked up the newspaper. Moving back up the walk, she recalled the first time she had seen the house. Situated on an acre of land, surrounded by a high brick wall, and shaded by tall trees both front and back, it had reminded her of the spooky old houses Dracula always haunted in the movies. Since moving in, they had spent a small fortune fixing up the inside of the old place, but it had been worth it. The rooms had all been restored to their former elegance, but the outside was still in need of work. She stared at the peeling green paint. Next week she would see about hiring someone to paint the exterior, assuming she could decide on a color. She didn't care for green, wasn't fond of white or yellow. Perhaps driftwood or sand. It was hard to believe that this house was hers, that Grigori was hers. Never in her life had she expected to live in such a fabulous place, or to be loved by such a fabulous man.

She stopped to pluck a few weeds from the flower bed alongside the driveway. Once the house was painted, she would hire someone to landscape the yards. Some fruit trees would be nice. And roses, lots of roses. Maybe a fountain or a small waterfall.

Returning to the house, she fixed herself some toast and a cup of hot chocolate, then sat down to read the paper. She stared at the headline.

FOUL PLAY IN WESTWOOD. ROCK STAR PRINCE DRACULA MISSING, BELIEVED KIDNAPPED

Marisa frowned as she read the story. Dracul had been reported missing by his manager. Police reported that bloodstains had been found on the floor mats of the rock star's car. They suspected Dracul might have been kidnapped; however, there had been no demand for ransom.

Grigori had told her that Dracul was a vampire, making her wonder if the blood in the man's car had been his own, or that of some foolish fan who had followed her idol and got more than she bargained for.

She was reaching for her cup when she saw the second headline, smaller than the first.

BODY OF UNIDENTIFIED YOUNG WOMAN
FOUND IN SANTA MONICA

It was with a sense of déjà vu that she read the story. The woman's body had been found behind a restaurant near the waterfront. Her body had been drained of blood.

"No," she murmured. "Please, not again."

She had thought such horror had ended with Alexi's demise. She stared out the window, wondering if the kill was Dracul's. Grigori had told her he was a reasonably young vampire. And if it wasn't Dracul's, then whose? Edward's? Khira's? She shook her head, unable to believe that Edward would murder an innocent girl, and equally unwilling to believe that the beautiful vampire she had met the night before could be capable of such a thing. Yet she knew Khira killed and enjoyed it. Grigori had left her because of it.

She glanced at the clock. It would be hours before Grigori awoke. Needing something to do to occupy her mind, she went out into the backyard and began pulling weeds. In spite of the warmth of the sun on her back, in spite of the blue sky and the gentle hum of insects, she couldn't help feeling that something terrible was lurking just out of sight. Time and again, she glanced over her shoulder, but there was nothing to be seen but the house and the yard and an occasional bird flitting from one tree to another.

She told herself it was just her imagination, that one body drained of blood didn't mean another vampire was running amuck; but she knew in her heart that she was only kidding herself. Any vampire was capable of killing, and though she didn't like to admit it, she knew that included Edward and Khira. And Grigori.

She shivered, suddenly cold in spite of the heat. And

what if she became a vampire? Would she then be capable of killing?

She put the thought from her. She wouldn't think of that now. There was plenty of time to make that decision.

Grigori regarded her through hooded eyes. "What do you want me to say, *cara*?"

"I don't know." Wrapping her arms around her body, she watched the sky turn dark and wondered if she would ever feel warm again.

"It wasn't me."

"I know that," she said quickly. "Do you think it was Edward? Or . . . or Khira?"

"Khira would not leave a body behind. As for Ramsey . . ." He shook his head. "I don't know." Grigori moved to the window and looked outside. Night was making her way across the land, slowly spreading her dark cloak over the earth, stealing the last bit of the day's light from the sky. A woman drained of blood. A missing vampire. Coincidence? He blew out a deep breath. In his experience, there was no such thing.

He sensed Marisa standing behind him, felt her hands slide down his back. "I know it wasn't you." She pressed her face into the hollow between his shoulder blades and kissed him. He could feel her breath through his shirt, feel it warm his skin.

Turning, he drew her into his arms. "It will be all right, *cara*."

She rested her head on his chest and closed her eyes, and hoped he was right.

"Marisa."

"Hmm?"

"Do you want to tell me what it is that is bothering you?"

"Nothing," she said guiltily. "Why?"

"You cannot lie to me, *cara mia*. Something has been troubling you since Khira's visit. What is it? Are you having second thoughts about accepting the Dark Gift?"

"Not exactly." She looked up at him, knowing there was no point in lying. He could easily read her thoughts if he desired. "It's just that, well, I was thinking about what Khira said, about not having children."

"I see."

"Maybe we could adopt a child." She had thought of it earlier. They could adopt a baby and raise it. She looked up at Grigori, wondering what his reaction would be.

"Do you think that would be wise?" he asked gently.

"No, I guess not. I'm sorry I mentioned it."

"If you are having regrets, you have only to tell me."

"I'm not!"

"If you ever do, I will let you go."

"Just like that?"

He nodded. "Just like that."

"You told me once you would never let me go."

"It would not be my choice, but I would not keep you against your will, *cara*. Your happiness means more to me than my life."

Tears glistened in the depths of her eyes as she placed her hand over his. "I'm not going anywhere."

Chapter 9

It was full dark when Ramsey awoke. It was something he hadn't gotten used to yet, the sudden lethargy that engulfed him at the sun's rising, the sense of disorientation when he first woke from the Dark Sleep. How long would it take before he got used to it? Months? Years? He knew that Chiavari was able to move about for short periods after the sun's rising, that he woke before sunset. Something to look forward to, he mused grimly. A benefit of growing older as a vampire.

He showered and dressed, the urge to feed driving him out of the house and into the darkness. . . .

The darkness. He had never realized how much he would miss the sun—the feel of it on his skin, the warmth of it, the brightness. Like most people, he had always equated light with goodness, dark with evil. Was he evil now? Candlelight, electric light, firelight: none of them could compare to the natural heat and beauty of the sun. So many things he had once taken for granted: a brisk morning walk, a cup of strong black coffee, the sound of birds singing. Chiavari had stolen them from him just as he had stolen his life, and in return, the vampire had given him an eternity of darkness, inside and out.

He paused at the corner, perusing the front page of a newspaper in one of the vending machines while he waited for the light to change. The headline hit him like a blow to the gut.

They had found the woman he had preyed upon late last night. The fact that her body had been almost drained of blood was related in lurid detail. It was the kind of story that would have fired his instinct to track down and destroy the monster whose pathetic leavings now resided in the city morgue.

Only this time he was the monster.

He swore softly, his guilt rising up to haunt him. He had not meant for her to die, had not meant to take so much, but she had been so sweet, so sweet. Perhaps, if he had taken her to her home and warmed her, offered her something to drink, she would have lived. But the flashing lights of a passing police car had filled him with a sudden panic and he had fled into the shadows. Left alone in the cold, the woman had died. With grim determination, he read the details of her family and life. A life cut all too short. He had not intended to kill her, but she was dead just the same. No matter how long he survived, he would never forget the look of fear in her eyes, the sudden silence when her heart beat its last. No more. He would not kill again. No matter what the cost, no matter if his accursed hunger went unfed and he endured the pains of hell, he would not kill again. He thought of Kelly. Perhaps he could atone for his sin by seeing that she was returned to vigorous health.

He laughed softly, bitterly, at his rationalization. The hunter had become that which he had once hunted.

He had never hesitated to destroy the creatures of the night when he found them. Why had he not destroyed himself? He was no better than those he had hunted. What made him think he deserved to live? Sadly he admitted that he lacked the courage to take his own life. He was ashamed to ask Chiavari for help. But what about Khira?

He dismissed the idea as soon as it formed. She intrigued him even as she filled him with a growing sense of unease. She was an ancient vampire, her powers without compare. Would he become like Khira in time? Indifferent to mortals, incapable of caring whether they lived or died? Once, he would have viewed Khira as the ultimate trophy for the last of the Ramseys—a difficult quarry to be hunted down, staked, beheaded. He would have been as indifferent to her fears as she was to the hapless mortals she hunted. Was he already changing? Would his rationalizations become fewer with each victim until he saw them as nothing more than a ready source of food? Them. In his mind, he had already separated himself from mankind. He was no longer a part of their world, no longer human.

"Edward."

He swore as Khira materialized beside him. "Damn it," he exclaimed irritably, "don't do that."

"Aren't you happy to see me?" she asked, pouting prettily.

"Yes, of course. What are you doing here?"

She smiled up at him, her eyes glowing like sapphires. She was outrageously beautiful. The moonlight shimmered in her hair like liquid silver. Her hand was warm on his arm, her skin flushed, her cheeks almost rosy. She had fed recently, he mused, and fed well.

"I felt your thoughts," she said, her voice low and sultry.

"Did you?"

"Indeed." She tilted her head to one side, her gaze fixed on his. "You've not yet fed."

An image of the woman lying in his bed at home flashed through his mind. "No."

Her predatory grin revealed perfect white teeth. "Let us go, then." She slipped her arm through his. "I find I still have room for dessert."

Ramsey grunted softly. She had already fed, yet she was eager for more. Chiavari had told him that vampires required less nourishment as they aged. It was not hunger that drove Khira, he thought, but the love of the hunt, the chase. The kill.

Hunt. Chase. Kill. It was easy to get caught up in the excitement of it all. Khira made it seem like fun, hunting the dark streets, chasing her prey. She was the perfect predator. She was not troubled by matters of conscience, didn't worry about right and wrong. Her eyes glowed a clear, bright blue during the chase, glittered a hellish red as she sank her fangs into her prey.

Her eyes blazed like sapphires in the lovemaking that came later, a fierce and tumultuous coupling that burned between them when a different kind of hunger claimed them. . . .

Later, when their passion had cooled, she smiled at him, rather like a well-satisfied cat.

"You were as hungry as I," she said softly. "You must have been a long time without a woman. Though not as long as I have been without a man!"

"I will not discuss that with you," he said flatly as, unheeded, an image of Katherine rose in his mind. Katherine, young and innocent, a victim of the kind of monster he himself had become . . .

"Shh . . ." Khira placed a finger gently against his lips, and he knew she was reading his thoughts. "We have all had losses, *mi amour*. The Dark Gift never comes without its price."

Her gaze turned inward, and something like regret crossed her flawless features. Then she smiled again, and he wondered if he she was capable of feeling anything other than a lust for blood. And flesh.

And then she fixed him with her glowing gaze. "The first thing a vampire must learn is to dispose of the remains. You were careless with that kill. The one reported in the press. Did you learn anything from tonight?"

Ramsey met her harsh gaze with one of his own. "Far more than I ever wanted to," he said grimly.

"Ahh . . ." A long sigh escaped her lips. "Do not spoil this moment for us. Who knows when, if ever, it will come again?" She stared at him, her expression speculative. "While you struggle with your quite active conscience, pay attention to what I say. A careless vampire is a danger to us all, Edward." She ran a long, blood-red nail down the side of his neck, the implied threat very clear. "Do you understand?"

Ramsey nodded. "It won't happen again."

She kissed him lightly on the lips, then rose from the bed, graceful as a cat, to slip into her carelessly discarded clothing. "See that it doesn't," she whispered—and vanished from his sight.

The girl, Kelly, was awake when he got back to his house. Though it had grieved him to do so, he had tied her hands to the bedpost to ensure that she would be there when he returned.

She stared at him through frightened green eyes when he entered the bedroom. "Where am I?" she asked, her voice weak. "Who are you? What are you going to do with me?"

"You have nothing to fear."

She tugged on the rope binding her wrist. "Don't I?"

Moving to the bed, he released her hands, knew a moment of guilt as she massaged her wrists. The skin was red and slightly swollen.

"I'm sorry," he murmured.

"You're not an angel, are you?"

"A dark angel, perhaps," he remarked, his gaze meeting hers. "Are you strong enough to stand? I've brought you something to eat."

"Who are you?"

"Edward."

She looked at him warily when he offered her his hand.

"You have nothing to fear, Kelly," he said, and hoped it was true.

She hesitated a moment more, then placed her hand in his and let him draw her to her feet. He led her down a dark hallway, through a living room furnished with a black leather couch and matching chair. The end tables were also black. There was no light in the room save that provided by the fire burning in the hearth. The kitchen was painted white. The appliances were mirrored black and looked new. A covered tray waited on a small round table.

She sat down, her stomach growling as he uncovered the tray to reveal a bowl of vegetable soup. There was a thick steak, rare, and mashed potatoes, beets, a slice of corn bread dripping with butter and honey. And a large piece of apple pie for dessert.

"I did not know if you preferred coffee or milk," he said, "so I ordered both."

Kelly nodded. "Thank you. Aren't you going to eat?" She felt a chill slide down her spine as his gaze moved to her throat.

"Perhaps later," he said with an ambiguous smile.

She felt uncomfortable eating while he watched. He hovered over her, reminding her of a vulture. The steak was very rare, thick, and juicy. He licked his lips as she cut into it.

She turned her attention to the meal, always aware of the man standing nearby.

Ramsey took a deep breath. Needing a distraction, he went into the living room and turned on the television. Sitting in the easy chair, he flipped through the channels, pausing when he heard the name Dracul. A female reporter stood outside the gates of a mansion, informing the public that Prince Dracul, well-known rock star, had disappeared.

He frowned. Dracul was a young vampire masquerading as a human. Had someone discovered the singer's true identity and destroyed him? Was there another accomplished vampire hunter in the area? Or was it merely some sort of ploy to gain media attention?

Thoughts of Dracul faded, overshadowed by the enticing scent of the girl in the next room. Her heartbeat echoed in his ears, he felt his own heart begin to beat in rhythm with hers, felt his fangs lengthen as the hunger stirred to life within him.

He had just fed; he had no need to do so again. And yet he rose to his feet, unable to resist the siren call of her blood. Khira's facetious remark about having room for dessert crossed his mind.

The girl looked up at him, fear reflected in her eyes. "No! No, don't."

But he was past hearing, past caring about anything but the need roaring through him. The pain . . .

She ran for the door, but he caught her easily. He gathered her into his arms, his mind seeking to calm hers. She fought him, her nails raking his cheek, until he bent her will to his.

When she lay pliant in his embrace, reason asserted

itself above blood hunger. The woman had just eaten; there had been no time for her metabolism to have converted the food to life-giving strength. She was still weak. He had vowed just this night to exercise restraint . . . and failed. Had witnessed the extinction of yet another human life, had shared in its extinction.

Khira had said if he wanted to keep his "little human" alive he needed to treat her well, feed her well, ensure she was strong enough for his purpose. It was time for him to prove he was strong enough to do so. No more killing. It was time to make good on his vow.

Gently he carried her to her bed and tucked her in.

He stalked the dark streets, his mind filled with the memory of the horror in the girl's eyes as he had bent over her. He had seen enough bloodthirsty vampires to know how he must have looked to her, his skin taut, as pale as old parchment, his eyes glowing hellishly red and hungry. She had screamed when she saw his fangs, struggled against him until he took control of her thoughts.

He lifted a hand to his face. She had raked her nails across his cheek hard enough, deep enough, to draw blood, yet the scratches were already healed.

He had no need to hunt, but he prowled the night restlessly. He wasn't surprised when he found himself standing in front of Chiavari's house. Taking a deep breath, he climbed the steps, knocked on the door.

"Edward." Marisa smiled, surprised to see him.

"Is Chiavari home?"

"No, but he'll be back in a few minutes."

"Do you mind if I wait?"

"Of course not." She stepped back. "Come in. I was just fixing myself something to eat."

He followed her into the kitchen. It was a large room,

painted a pale, pale yellow. White curtains covered the windows. There was a small table for two in one corner.

She gestured at a chair. "Sit down."

His vampire senses automatically separated and cataloged the domestic odors of the kitchen: frying chicken, flour and cooking oil, potatoes and corn, soap and cleanser. And, over all, the warm, womanly, mortal scent of Marisa herself.

She slid a pan of biscuits in the oven, then took the chair across from him. "How've you been, Edward?"

He shrugged. Only a few weeks a vampire, yet it seemed like centuries since he had tasted solid food.

"Fried chicken used to be one of my favorites," he said wistfully. "Now just the smell of it makes me sick to my stomach."

She laid a hand on his arm. "I'm sorry."

He gazed down at her hand on his arm, saying nothing.

"Edward? Is something wrong?"

He blew out a deep breath. "Are you happy with him?"

"Is that why you came here?" she exclaimed softly. "To find out if I was happy?"

"I don't know. Are you?"

"Yes, very happy. I love him, Edward."

Her words cut through him like a knife. He wanted to grab her, shake her, make her love him instead. He gazed deep into her eyes, felt the Dark Gift unfold within him, fueled by frustrated love and lust. She loved a vampire, did she? Then why not him? His power flowed through the room, gathering like storm clouds. His vampire senses expanded, filling with the sight of her, the scent of her. Desire welled within him—not a desire for blood, but for the feel of her in his arms. Caught in the web of his power, she was his for the taking. She leaned slowly across the table toward him, her gaze cloudy and unfocused. . . .

"That's enough!"

Ramsey jerked backward as Chiavari's voice cut across the thick stillness.

"What the hell do you think you're doing?" Grigori glared down at Ramsey, his black eyes smoldering with fury.

Marisa blinked up at her husband. "What's wrong? What happened?"

"Nothing. Ramsey was just leaving."

Ramsey pushed away from the table and stood up, never taking his eyes from Chiavari. Chiavari's rage was a frightful thing to see. He felt his own power rise to the challenge. He had been close to death before, he thought, but never as close as he was now. The tension in the room was palpable.

Confused but sensing the danger, Marisa started to rise, but Chiavari put a hand on her shoulder. "Stay here, *cara*. I will see him out."

Without taking his gaze from Chiavari's face, Ramsey made a courtly bow in Marisa's direction. "Forgive me," he murmured, "I must be going."

He stalked out of the room, with Chiavari close on his heels.

"What the hell was going on in there?" Chiavari demanded when they reached the street.

Ramsey shook his head. "Nothing. I . . ." He ran a hand through his hair. "I loved her, damn it. She should have been mine."

Fury emanated from Chiavari like heat from a forest fire. When he spoke, his voice was a low growl. "So you came here to seduce her with the Dark Power?"

"No." Ramsey shook his head. "I came to see you. I don't know what happened in there. I . . ." He began to pace the sidewalk in short, jerky steps. "Sitting there with her, I remembered how much I wanted her, and I knew I could make her love me . . . knew I could make her forget you . . . Damn! What is happening to me?''

Grigori took a deep, calming breath. "One does not adjust to being Vampyre overnight, Ramsey. Give yourself some time. What did you want to see me about?''

"I can't go on like this. I want you to destroy me. Now. Tonight.''

"What has happened?''

"Happened?'' Ramsey repeated. "Happened? You happened! You saw what happened in there! I can't go on like this. Damn it, you did this to me. Now undo it!''

"Calm down, Ramsey, it has been but a few weeks. Give yourself some time.''

"Time.'' Ramsey groaned. "I feel it weighing down on me like the earth that should cover my grave. I can't bear an eternity of this. I can't and I won't!''

"Calm down.''

"I am calm! Damn it, you've killed before. Why not me? You made a mistake. I'm not cut out to be a vampire. Now undo it. Release me from this accursed existence!''

"It can be a good life, if you let it. Think of all you will see, experience, as this new century unfolds! And the next one . . .''

"Damn you!'' Past reason, past hope, Ramsey lunged at Chiavari, determined either to kill the creature who had bequeathed this curse . . . or be killed.

They struggled in silence. The ancient blood that ran through Ramsey's veins gave him a strength almost equal to Chiavari's. For a moment, he almost believed he would win. But Chiavari had more than physical strength on his side; he had experience and a cool head.

Breathless, Ramsey quickly found himself on the sidewalk, flat on his back, Chiavari's fangs only inches from his throat. "Do it,'' he urged. "Do it!''

Chiavari's eyes blazed like hell's own fury. Ramsey

felt strangely peaceful, awaiting the end. Then, as if someone had banked the fires, the rage faded from Chiavari's gaze.

He stared down at Ramsey with preternatural calm. "Are you ready to listen now?"

"Damn you."

"Give it some time," Chiavari said. "Six months. Then, if you still want to die, come and see me."

Ramsey started to speak, but before he could form the words, Chiavari was gone.

Ashamed and humiliated, Ramsey gained his feet. He could not endure this for another six months, not for another six days. He would not!

He was a vampire hunter, a destroyer of the undead. He was now a vampire. And he would do what he had been born and raised to do. Do what he should have done from the beginning.

Destroy the vampire.

Chapter 10

Ramsey stood in the backyard, his face turned toward the east, and waited for the sunrise. Would he burst into flame at the first touch of the sun? Would it be quick?

He thought of Marisa. He thought of Chiavari. But mostly, he thought of Kelly. In another life, he might have loved her. Perhaps she would have loved him.

Before leaving the house, he had untied her hands, covered her with a blanket.

He had written a will, leaving her everything he owned: the house, the car, the money in the Ramsey family bank account. He smiled to think of her bemusement at learning she now was the trustee of quite a considerable fortune—the heritage of generations of successful vampire killers.

His heart and soul aching with grief and regret for the abominable way he had used her, he had stood beside the bed, watching her sleep, one hand lightly stroking her hair.

"Rest now," he had murmured. "You have nothing more to fear. Soon the angel of death will be gone."

Now, standing in the predawn light, he closed his eyes, and the image of her fragile beauty rose up in his mind, her hair like a waterfall of black silk, her dark-brown eyes fringed with long, dark lashes. He remembered how perfectly she had fit in his arms, the sweetness of her blood, the touch of her skin, soft and warm, beneath his hands.

He opened his eyes, his skin crawling with the knowledge that dawn was near.

His last dawn.

Fear uncoiled deep within him as the dark sky gradually grew lighter, the black fading to indigo then exploding with color as the sun peeled the cloak of night from the sky. It was the most beautiful sunrise he had ever seen. Gold and crimson, lavender and fiery red.

For a breathless moment, he basked in the beauty of it, in the warmth of the sun upon his face. But only for a moment. All too soon, the pleasure turned to pain.

He groaned as the light seared his eyes, trembled as the warmth increased, until what would once have been a pleasant warmth became intolerable, scorching heat. The skin on his face, hands, and arms blistered under the touch of the sun.

The sun rose higher, hotter. His body grew heavy, lethargic. Darkness called to him—the darkness of sleep, of death. The preternatural blood in his veins grew hot, burning him from the inside out.

A cry rose in his throat and he choked it back. Pain. Agonizing. Excruciating. Beyond bearing. Pain unlike anything he had ever known or imagined.

Terror engulfed him. A scream clawed at his throat as the torment became unbearable. With a strangled cry, he turned toward the refuge of the house, his only thought to escape the agony that engulfed him.

The house. So close. There was blessed darkness there, relief from the pain. It was so near, so near. His arms and legs felt heavy. His feet were like lead. The sunlight burned through the clothes on his back, seared the skin beneath.

He dropped to his hands and knees, fighting the dark sleep as he dragged himself toward the door, his fingers plowing deep furrows in the earth as he pulled himself, inch by slow inch, across the grass.

He was moaning helplessly when he reached the house. Grasping the door knob, he opened the door and then fell across the threshold. Crawling into the kitchen on his hands and knees, he dragged himself toward the door that led down to the cellar. He pushed it open with the last of his strength, felt himself pitch headlong into darkness as he tumbled head over heels down the stairs . . .

The sound of her own screams woke Kelly from a deep sleep. Breathing heavily, she jackknifed to a sitting position. The nightmare had been so real. She looked at her arms, surprised to see they weren't burned, only then realizing that she was no longer tied to the bed.

The dream faded as she glanced around the room, her gaze searching for the monster who kept her here against her will. She shuddered as she remembered the way his eyes had burned red as he bent over her, her helpless horror as his fangs pierced the skin of her throat, the weakness that had spread through her, the uncanny sense of two hearts beating as one as her blood mingled with his . . .

She shook off the memory. That, too, must have been a nightmare, she thought. It had to be a nightmare. There was no such thing as a vampire, not really. She knew there were people who pretended they were vampires. They dressed in black and drank blood and avoided the sun. No doubt some of them actually believed they were vampires.

Perhaps the man who had brought her here, wherever "here" was, was one of those. No less frightening or dangerous than an actual vampire, when it came right down to it.

She threw off the covers, surprised to find that she was wearing a nightgown, embarrassed because she knew he had to have undressed her.

Rising, she tiptoed from the bedroom. The house looked familiar, but she had no memory of having been here before, no recollection of how she had gotten there.

In the kitchen, she found an envelope with her name scrawled across it.

Curious, she picked it up and withdrew a single sheet of paper. She read it once, and then again:

I, Edward James Ramsey, being of sound mind and body, do hereby give and bequeath all my worldly goods and property, both real and monetary, to Kelly Lynne Anderson. Ms. Anderson is hereby vested by me with trusteeship of the Ramsey Trust Fund, to do all acts and perform all duties as she sees fit.

It was signed and dated.

What did it mean?

She had the irrelevant thought that he had not had a witness sign the document, so it probably wouldn't amount to much if it was contested, and dropped the paper back on the table. Whatever he had been thinking, he had left her unguarded. It was time to make good her escape.

She glanced down, wondering what he had done with

her clothes. She couldn't very well go running down the street wearing nothing but a nightgown.

It was when she turned to go back to the bedroom that she saw the open cellar door. She moved cautiously toward it, her heart pounding as she stared down into the darkness below.

She stood at the top of the steps, recalling every horror movie she had ever seen where the foolish young girl, usually attired in a nightgown, walked down a dark flight of stairs to her death.

"Not me," she said. "No way."

Yet even as she spoke the words, she was compelled to move forward. She saw her left foot moving toward the top step, and it was like watching someone else's foot. Her right hand searched the wall, hoping to find a light switch, but to no avail.

Unable to help herself, she took another step, and another, her heartbeat pounding like thunder in her ears.

When she reached the bottom, she tripped over something. Something large. She put her hand on it to push herself away, shrieked when she realized it was a body. Scrambling to her feet, she backed away, gasped when she smacked into a wall. A light switch jabbed into her arm and she whirled around, her fingers trembling as she flipped the switch.

Light flooded the cellar.

Afraid of what she might see, yet unable to keep from looking, she slowly turned around. Her eyes widened. It was him. The man who thought he was a vampire.

He looked dead.

She moved slowly, warily toward him.

She could see no sign that he was breathing. He had fresh, ugly burns and painful-looking blisters on the skin of his face, hands, and arms. Summoning her courage, she touched his cheek. His skin was cold, as if he had been dead a very long time. In spite of all he had done to her, she felt a surge of pity for him.

Gingerly she picked up his arm and placed her fingertips over his wrist. There was no detectable pulse.

She laid her hand over his chest. She couldn't feel a heartbeat.

The word *vampire* whispered through her mind again. They slept during the day. They went *Poof!* in the sun. She thought of the paper on the kitchen table. What if he was a vampire? A real vampire? The sunlight streaming through a partly open curtain in the kitchen could have caused those dreadful burns, if the mythology was accurate. There was no evidence of a fire in the house, no smell of smoke.

A last will and testament, and the badly burned body of a man who thought he was a vampire. Had he intended to kill himself? It was the only answer that made any kind of sense, even though it made no sense at all. Why would he want to kill himself? Why would he put her name in his will? He didn't even know her.

She looked around, wondering where he kept his coffin. And suddenly it all seemed too possible, too real.

Shivering, she ran up the stairs as fast as she could and slammed the door behind her. What should she do now? Call the police? She dismissed that idea even as it crossed her mind. How could she explain her presence here? What if they accused her of killing him?

What if he really was a vampire?

People killed vampires, at least in the movies. They dispatched them by driving wooden stakes through their hearts, or cutting off their heads, or both. They burned them, or drenched their bodies with holy water. Driving a stake through a vampire's heart was always depicted as very messy, with the vampire waking up, screaming and hissing, while great fountains of blood gushed everywhere. Not that she was likely to find a stake lying around, especially in a vampire's house.

What should she do?

She went back into the bedroom in search of something to wear. Opening the closet, she found the sweater and jeans she had been wearing the night she decided to kill herself. How long ago that seemed now!

She found her sandals under the bed. She dressed quickly, ran her fingers through her hair, and hurried out of the house. Only to come to a stop once she reached the sidewalk. She had no idea where she was.

She glanced over her shoulder. The house loomed behind her, looking ominous somehow. Maybe it was the windows, tinted dark to block the sun. Maybe it was the gothic architecture. Maybe it was knowing there was a body in the cellar.

She looked up and down the street, wondering which way to go, turned left for no reason except that it put the sun behind her.

Her pace increased until she was running, running like a woman being pursued by demons.

Ramsey woke with the setting of the sun, his body feeling as if it were on fire. With a groan, he rolled onto his side. For a moment, he lay there, hands tightly clenched, trying to breathe through the pain.

He knew the woman had been in the cellar. Her scent was all around him. He knew, just as certainly, that she was no longer in the house.

He rose up on his hands and knees, head hanging, panting like a dog. He stayed that way for several minutes; then, with one hand braced against the wall, he gained his feet.

Every breath, every movement, was a new adventure in pain.

It seemed to take forever to climb the stairs. When he reached the top, he sat down, feeling as though he had just climbed Everest.

Feeling dizzy, he stood up and staggered down the hallway to his bedroom. Feeling as though he were moving through thick mud, he changed into a long-sleeved shirt to cover his burned arms, and a pair of soft, loose-fitting trousers. The touch of cloth against his seared flesh was agonizing. He found a pair of dark glasses to shield his eyes. A hat, pulled low, kept his face in shadow.

Taking a deep breath, he left the house.

He needed help.

He needed blood.

He needed Chiavari.

Chapter 11

Chiavari was waiting for Ramsey on the front porch. "Come in," he said.

"I can't take this anymore," Ramsey said. "I want you to end it, now."

"We've already had this discussion," Chiavari said curtly.

"Look at me!" Ramsey removed his hat and glasses, rolled up the sleeves of his shirt. "Damn it, look!"

"What the hell happened to you?"

"What do you think?"

"Spend a little too much time in the sun, did you?"

Ramsey swore. "I tried to kill myself. I want out of this life. I will not live like this! I have become what I hated, what I hunted. It has to stop. Now!"

"Six months, Ramsey. That's all. To a man with eternity before him, six months should not be too difficult."

"You don't understand! You wanted to be a vampire. I don't! I hate what they are. I hate what I have become." He ran a hand through his hair, wincing as his fingers encountered burnt flesh. "I found a woman. I kept her a prisoner in my house. Do you understand? I tied her up and I fed off of her like a damned leech. What kind of depraved monster does that?"

"Come in and sit down, Ramsey," Chiavari said quietly. "You are in pain. You are not thinking clearly."

"I don't want to . . ."

"Come in the house. We can't talk out here."

With a sigh of resignation, Ramsey followed Chiavari inside.

Chiavari gestured at the sofa. "Sit down."

"I don't need a lecture."

"I know what you need better than you do." Chiavari sat down beside Ramsey and extended his arm. "Old blood is the best blood. Go on, take what you need."

Ramsey met Chiavari's gaze and shook his head. "No."

"Do it."

Ramsey glanced around. "Where's Marisa?"

"She went to the theater with an old friend from work. You need not worry, she won't be home for hours. Drink, Ramsey." His voice was low, soothing, almost hypnotic. "Drink."

He wanted to refuse. There was a great intimacy in the sharing of blood between vampires. He did not want to accept Chiavari's blood again, did not want to be further in the man's debt, but his need was too great, the pain and the hunger beyond bearing, the promise of relief too tempting. With a low growl, he took hold of Chiavari's arm and sank his fangs into his wrist.

And drank.

And drank.

Power flowed into him, sweeping through his body and limbs like a great healing flood, washing the pain away in a scarlet tide. He saw flashes of Chiavari's life . . . his childhood in Italy . . . his wife, Antoinette . . .

his son and his daughter, who had been slain by Alexi Kristov. And, like a rapidly fast-forwarded videotape, glimpses and images of Chiavari's prey down through the centuries. And over all, the scent and the taste of the blood, reminding Ramsey of the night when Chiavari had needed blood to survive. Their roles had been reversed then. It had been Chiavari drinking voraciously.

"Enough!"

Chiavari's voice penetrated the red haze that surrounded him.

"Ramsey, enough."

Sated with the vampire's ancient blood, the roaring hunger within him stilled and slept, the pain receded, a dim shadow of what it had been. Ramsey glanced at Chiavari and looked away. They had ever been enemies, yet this alliance, the blood bond they shared, was a bond as intimate as that of mortal lovers. A bond first formed as an uneasy alliance to hunt Kristov. Kristov, who had wooed Chiavari's wife behind his back; Kristov, who had slain Chiavari's children and changed Antoinette into a mindless creature caught between life and death, with no will of her own.

In a brutal act of kindness, Ramsey had taken Antoinette's head and heart and put her tortured soul to rest, a deed that haunted him still. He looked at Chiavari again. "Do you think she suffered?"

Chiavari did not have to ask who he was talking about. "I don't know. I pray not. I owe you an eternal debt for . . ." His voice broke. "For releasing her. If, in six months, you still wish to be destroyed . . . I will repay that debt."

Touched by the soul-deep pain in the vampire's voice, Ramsey laid a comforting hand on Chiavari's shoulder.

Chiavari's surprise showed in his eyes.

Realizing what he had done, Ramsey jerked his hand away.

Chiavari smiled faintly before he raised his arm to his mouth and ran his tongue over the twin holes in his wrist. "Can you think more clearly now?"

"If you mean, have I changed my mind, the answer is no. But as you said, six months is only a moment in the life of a vampire." Ramsey stood abruptly. "I'll be back in six months to collect on that debt."

"I will be here."

Ramsey nodded curtly. "I would rather you didn't tell Marisa about this."

"Are you still in love with her?"

Ramsey met Chiavari's unblinking gaze. "I will always be in love with her. Good night." He took a deep breath. "And thank you."

Leaving Chiavari's house, Ramsey stalked the dark streets of the city. He fancied he could feel the other vampire's blood flowing through his veins, mingling with his own. He could certainly feel the results. Strength flowed through him; the pain of his scorched flesh lessened with each passing moment. Had he not hated what he had become, he would have rejoiced in his power. The blood of three ancients flowed in his veins. But for that, the sunlight would have killed him instantly. Pity he had not thought of that sooner. He would not try such foolishness again. Somehow, he would endure the next six months, and then he would go back to Chiavari and demand that the vampire destroy him, as promised.

And until then, what?

He stopped and sniffed the air. Kelly had passed this way recently. He would know her scent, her heartbeat, anywhere. Following the Siren call of her blood, he crossed the street, his yearning for her carrying him swiftly across town. He paid no heed to his surroundings; the fact that he was now in a part of town considered dangerous by ordinary men did not register on him at all. Her scent drew him relentlessly until he found himself standing outside a seedy boardinghouse.

He sensed the street punk before he saw him— smelled the metal of the knife in his hand, the drugs that clung to his clothing and clouded his mind.

He turned to face him, his teeth drawn back in a feral snarl.

The boy was no more than fourteen or fifteen. His eyes widened when he saw Ramsey's expression; his face paled when he realized he was no longer the hunter but the prey. He took a step backward, the knife falling from his hand, clattering on the sidewalk.

"No." The word whispered past his lips as the vampire's hand closed around his throat.

Ramsey gazed into the boy's eyes. Sheer horror stared back at him. The stench of the boy's terror filled Ramsey's nostrils, stirred his hunger. A low growl rose in his throat; his fangs lengthened.

"No."

A sob, a barely audible plea for mercy.

With a cry of self-disgust, Ramsey thrust the boy away. The boy stumbled back, turned, and fled.

Ramsey stared after him, appalled by what he had almost done, by the blood lust that had engulfed him. He had just fed. How could he hunger again so soon? Six months. How could he go on like this for six months?

The breeze shifted, carrying the scent of earth and trees, the strong aroma of fried food, the stink of unwashed bodies. The breeze shifted again, teasing his nostrils with the scent of jasmine.

The sound of applause drew his attention.

"Bravo!"

Turning, he saw Khira crossing the street toward him. She was beautiful, he thought, the most beautiful creature he had ever seen. She wore a black cloak over a wine red gown.

"Is this how you pass your time?" she asked with a throaty chuckle. "Frightening little boys?"

"I guess you would have killed him."

She shrugged, a graceful movement of her slim shoulders. "Perhaps. Certainly even you can see he would have been no great loss. When he gets over his fright, he will be on the hunt again. We vampyres can perform a useful service to society, you see, by preying on the predators." As was her habit, she linked her arm with his. "Come, walk with me."

Ramsey glanced over his shoulder. Kelly would have to wait.

"Slumming, are you?" he asked.

"I was going to ask you the same question." She shuddered with mock horror. "What brings you to this dreadful part of town?"

"I was going to visit a . . . a friend."

She looked at him, her blue eyes filled with laughter. "You cannot lie to me, Edward."

"All right, I came to see a woman."

"The woman whose life you saved and nearly took. I see." She stopped walking. "Do you wish to go back?"

He shook his head.

Khira patted his arm and started walking again. "So, *mon ami,* how do you like being immortal?"

"I hate it."

She looked truly surprised. "But why?" She flung out her arms and twirled in a circle, her long gown swirling like flames around her ankles. "It is so lovely to be immortal on a night such as this! Look around you, Edward. The world is yours for the taking."

"You mean the night is mine for the stalking."

"That, too," she replied, as if it were the most wonderful thing in the world. "To be immortal is to be free!"

"Is it? Do you never miss the light of day, the taste of food and drink, the love of a man? A home, children?" He hesitated. "The warmth of the sun on your skin?" He had reveled in its touch for a moment, until pleasure turned to excruciating pain.

She frowned at him. "You wasted no time on those things when you were mortal. Why do you yearn for them now?"

The truth of her words slammed into him. He had never fully appreciated the world around him. He had eaten when he was hungry, slept when he could find the time. He had never noticed the beauty in a sunrise or a sunset. The rising sun meant only that the undead would go to ground; the sunset meant they would be abroad, hunting the night. He had lived out of his car, slept in motels, his only friends other hunters. As for women, he had loved only two. Ironic, he thought now, that the first had been killed by a vampire, and the second had married one. He hadn't had a home since he was sixteen, had never wanted a home or a wife or children, knowing they would only tie him down or become pawns in a dangerous game. His whole life, his whole reason for living, had been to destroy vampires.

His thoughts turned back in time to his first successful hunt. . . .

"Take him." Grandfather Ramsey handed Edward a sharpened stake made of ash, and a mallet made of oak. "One quick blow."

Edward took the stake from the old man's hand and placed it over the vampire's heart, lifted the mallet, and drove the stake into the sleeping vampire's chest. For all their powers and physical strength, vampires were remarkably fragile while resting. The stake pierced the vampire's flesh. Blood had gushed from the wound, spraying Edward's face and hands and arms. . . .

"Edward? Edward, such a gruesome thing to be remembering, and on a night such as this!" Her voice was lightly chiding, but with an edge of malice.

He shook the grotesque image from his mind. "Perhaps, like most people, I had to lose what was truly important before I realized what I had lost."

"Forget all that for now. Come, let us hunt the night."

It was in his mind to refuse. Hunting with Khira was always dangerous, he mused ruefully, and then he grinned. Perhaps, while prowling the night with her, he would find an end to the horror that his life had become.

She looked at him and smiled. "There is always risk, of course, *mi amour*. But that only makes it all the more delicious, does it not? Are you ready?"

He nodded, wishing she would stay out of his mind.

"Let us go, then." Tightening her grasp on his arm, she whisked them across town.

Somewhat stunned by the suddenness of it, Ramsey glanced at his surroundings. They were in a house. A mansion, he amended, with shimmering crystal chandeliers and polished marble floors. The room, as large as a football field, was filled with men and women clad in evening attire. An orchestra was playing Rachmaninoff.

He leaned toward Khira. "What are we doing here?"

"Visiting an old friend," she replied. "Here's our host now."

Ramsey turned to see a tall, slender man striding toward them. He had short brown hair, brilliant blue eyes, and appeared, outwardly, to be in his mid-thirties.

He was a vampire—of that Edward had no doubt.

"Good evening, Khira," the man said. He bent over her hand in a gallant old-world gesture. "How good of you to come."

"It's good to see you, too, Kyle."

Kyle's gaze moved over Ramsey, coldly assessing. "And who is this?"

"This is Edward Ramsey. Edward, this is Kyle LaSalle."

Shock, disbelief, rage. They all flitted through the vampire's eyes. "Ramsey! You brought a vampire hunter into my home!"

"Calm down, Kyle. He is one of us now."

Ramsey knew a moment of surprise when he realized the other vampire had not detected what he was. He felt LaSalle's power push against him. For all his years, Kyle LaSalle was weak, his power easy to brush aside. Ramsey effortlessly resisted the other vampire's attempt to probe his mind. He compared LaSalle's power to Chiavari's as he sidestepped LaSalle's puny efforts to slip past his defenses. Comparing LaSalle to Chiavari was like comparing a snowball to a blizzard. Keeping his face impassive, he unleashed his own power.

LaSalle took a step backward. He stared at Ramsey, his eyes narrowed. "Who are you?"

Khira placed her hand on Edward's arm. "He is mine," she said, and Ramsey heard the fine edge of steel beneath the soft velvet of her voice. "My blood runs in his veins, as does the blood of Grigori."

A hiss whispered through LaSalle's clenched teeth. "Why have you brought him here?"

"If we are not welcome, you have only to say so."

"Of course you are welcome." LaSalle bowed stiffly from the waist. "Please, make my home yours."

"That is my intention," Khira replied.

LaSalle smiled, but it was cold, forced. "As you wish. If you will excuse me, I must see to my other guests."

Khira lifted a graceful hand, dismissing him.

"I guess I must be a little confused," Ramsey remarked. "What just happened here?"

"Kyle will be moving out, and I will be moving in."

"Here?" Ramsey exclaimed. "You're moving in here?"

"Yes. It's a nice place, don't you think?"

"He's leaving, just like that?"

"Of course."

Ramsey shook his head. "I still don't understand."

"It is quite simple, really. I have decided to stay in the city for a while."

"Getting a straight answer out of you is like pulling teeth," Ramsey muttered.

"Such an amusing choice of words." She smiled sweetly. "But my answer is simplicity itself. I am staying. He is leaving."

"What if he had refused to go?"

"He could challenge me, of course, but he would lose, and he knows it. He has never been strong. He is not even strong enough to challenge you, *mi amour.*"

Ramsey grunted softly. "Did you visit Dracul, too?"

Her blue eyes turned to ice. "Yes, I did."

Ramsey remembered the article in the paper, the speculation that the rock star had met with foul play. "Did he just pack up and leave town?"

"In a manner of speaking, yes."

"He's dead, isn't he?"

She plucked two glasses of dark red wine from the tray of a passing waiter. "Here, have a drink. Kyle's wine cellar is quite famous."

Ramsey accepted the delicate crystal goblet she offered him.

She smiled at him, the expression reminding him of a well-fed cat. "Shall we drink to my new home?"

"Why not?" Holding the goblet by the slender stem, he lifted it to the light. It was a lovely shade of crimson. Like fresh blood. He sloshed it around gently, watched the scarlet drops slide slowly down the glass. The translucent liquid clung to the crystal. Again, the resemblance to blood was remarkable.

Ramsey inhaled deeply. The bouquet was like the essence of summer captured, fermented, and freed again. Like lost innocence, when a warm summer evening was meant for romance, not hunting.

He took a sip, the taste and the aroma mingling on the back of his tongue. Heightened by his vampire senses, he savored every drop, relishing the warm mellow glow that spread through him. It was a shame that food was now denied to him, he mused. If wine tasted this good, what would a nice, juicy steak taste like?

"Come," Khira said, "I should like to take a look at my new home."

"Are you going to drive all the vampires out of the city?" he asked as he followed her down a wide corridor lined with plush maroon carpeting. The walls were a stark white, lined with framed book covers and literary awards.

Khira opened a door at the end of the hallway. "This is a lovely room, is it not?" She stepped back so he could look inside.

It was a bedroom. The walls and carpet were white. The drapes and bedspread were black. There was an easy chair upholstered in red, a small black lacquer table. A single abstract painting done in red, black, and white adorned the wall above the bed.

"Lovely," he agreed. He followed her into the room, felt a sense of unease when she shut and locked the door behind him. "What about Chiavari?"

"What about him?" She glided across the floor and sat down on the edge of the bed. The hem of her scarlet gown pooled around her feet, like blood.

"Damn it, answer me!"

"We are hunters, predators." Her voice, though soft, hit him with the force of a slap. "LaSalle and the others may have reached some sort of understanding, some sort of truce, but it means nothing to me. They will leave at my invitation or suffer the consequences."

He started to speak, but she cut him off with a wave of her hand. "I do not answer to you or to anyone. You are a mere infant, Edward. I could crush you with a thought."

He didn't argue. He could feel her power flowing through the room, crawling over his skin, invading his mind. And then it was gone. "All right. You've proved your point."

She smiled complacently. "As for Grigori, he may stay so long as it pleases me."

"And me?"

She raked her nails lightly over his cheek. A caress? Or a warning? And then she patted the bed beside her. "You, too, may stay, so long as you please me."

Chapter 12

The scent of jasmine still clung to him when he woke the following evening. Khira had tried to seduce him in LaSalle's bed. She had been mildly amused, and then angry, when he declined. She had let him feel her power then—let him know his refusal was as useless as a candle in a dark wind—and then she had withdrawn, leaving him breathless and sweating.

"You were so willing the last time," she had murmured. "So strong for one so young—so virile! So like my Grigori of old. I could take you now, willing or not, but it is so much more pleasant when you are willing. And you will be willing. . . ."

He stared at the ceiling, her words purring through his memory, and shivered. Would he? The memory of the night when they had hunted and then slept together was both repugnant and thrilling. Sitting up, he pushed the vivid images aside to consider what she had said about driving the other vampires from the city. It had been a subtle warning, but a warning just the same. She had killed young Dracul, he had no doubt of that. He grunted softly. On one level, he was pleased that there was one less vampire to haunt the world. He knew she would have killed LaSalle without a qualm, couldn't help wondering if she had already warned Madame Rosa and Noah Fox to get out of Dodge, and if they would go without a fight. He had felt her power, up close and personal. Unless the others were very strong, any fight with Khira would have only one conclusion. With Chiavari, the outcome would be less certain. Of them all, Chiavari was the only one who might possess the power necessary to thwart her. Of the two, Chiavari was clearly the lesser of two evils. Chiavari was disciplined. Even within the constraints of his hunger, he was almost merciful. He did not kill indiscriminately, as did Khira. Would Chiavari go at Khira's whim? Leave the city unprotected?

Ramsey swung his legs over the edge of the bed, ran a hand through his hair. What the hell would he do if she told him to leave? He had no ties in the city, no reason to stay, and while he didn't mind leaving if it was his idea, he didn't like the idea of tucking his tail between his legs and skulking away like a whipped cur. Nor could he live with the idea of leaving the unsuspecting community without some measure of protection from Khira. His blood might be mingled now with that of the undead, but in his heart and soul he was still a Ramsey, sworn to protect the innocent from the ravages of the undead.

The memory of her power sliding over his skin cooled his rising anger. He would worry about Khira later. She had not yet called for a showdown, and now, with the Hunger clawing at his belly, she was, for the moment, the least of his worries. Need burned through him, the pain like shards of glass flowing through his veins, overshadowing every other thought, every other desire.

Rising, he showered and dressed, then left the house. He eased his hellish thirst on the first person he found. His mind grasped hers. His arms imprisoned her, and he took what he wanted, what he needed, as though it were his right. He accomplished his task quickly, taking no pleasure in it. Releasing the woman, he vanished from her sight.

Not yet satisfied, he walked on, searching for another victim. Without conscious thought, he found himself standing on the street across from Kelly Anderson's apartment.

Why, he wondered, why was he drawn to this woman? It was more than a hunger for her blood. He could satisfy his demon thirst anywhere.

He stood there for a full five minutes, staring up at the window of her apartment, not questioning how he knew which one was hers. He murmured her name, and a moment later, she opened the window and looked down at him.

Come to me.

The command rose in his mind effortlessly.

A moment later, she was there, walking toward him, her hair falling over her shoulders like waves of black silk. She was beautiful, he thought, and for once it wasn't the desire for blood that filled his mind.

Clasping her hand in his, he took her home. He locked the front door, turned on a lamp. And all the while, she stood in the middle of the room, unmoving.

"Kelly."

She stared at him, her expression blank, like a robot's.

He hesitated a moment, then freed his hold on her mind.

"You!" She glanced at her surroundings, her eyes wild. "How did I get here?"

"I brought you here."

She backed up, one hand going to her throat. "Leave me alone. Please."

"I will not hurt you."

"Yeah, right. Why did you bring me here?"

"I just . . ." He clenched his hands, wishing he had more experience with women. "I just want to talk to you."

"I don't believe you." She stared at him, her eyes wide with fear. "I saw you . . . lying in the basement. I thought you were dead. You were burned, your face, your hands and arms . . . and now . . ." Her gaze moved over him. "It's like nothing ever happened. There's not even a scar! Who are you? *What* are you?"

"You know what I am, Kelly. Say it."

"No." She took another step away from him. "It's not possible."

"The proof stands before you. Refusing to say it will not make it any less true."

"There's no such thing." She shook her head in denial. "It's impossible."

"Say it." His voice was soft, gentle, yet demanded an answer.

"Vampire," she whispered hoarsely.

He nodded slowly.

"You kept me here against my will. You . . . you drank from me."

"Yes." And he wanted to drink from her again.

He could hear the rapid beat of her heart, intensified by the fear building within her. Her gaze darted around the room, lingered on the door, came back to his face. He knew the moment she made her decision, was waiting for her when she reached the front door.

She screamed, a wordless cry of terror.

"Kelly." He took hold of her hands in an effort to calm her.

She kicked him in the shins, drove her knee into his groin with all the strength at her command.

He doubled over in pain, his breath hissing between his clenched teeth. But he did not release his grip on her hands.

When the pain subsided and he could breathe again, he straightened. "Damn it, I'm not going to hurt you."

"Then let me go."

"Will you promise to listen to me if I do?"

"Yes," she replied quickly. Too quickly.

"You can't elude me, Kelly. You can't outrun me. So you might as well sit down and listen to what I have to say."

Apparently realizing the truth of what he said, she went back into the living room and sat down on the edge of the sofa, her hands clenched so tight the knuckles were white.

"I'm listening," she said, her voice sullen, like that of an angry child.

"I'm sorry if I frightened you. If I hurt you. I have only been a vampire a short time and I . . ."

Her eyes widened in surprise.

"And I am not sure yet what I am doing, or how to do it," he finished, determined to say it all.

She stared at him. "So, you're like a fledgling vampire, is that it? And you thought you'd practice on me?"

"No. I want something from you." He held up his hand. "Not your blood."

"What, then?"

"I've seen where you live. I know you haven't any money."

Defiance flashed through her eyes. "So?"

"I want you to kill me." The words seemed to flow of their own volition.

"What?"

"I'll pay you well."

She bounded to her feet. "You're even crazier than I thought."

"Sit down."

She didn't argue but sat down on the sofa once more, her body poised for flight.

"I can't go on like this."

"You don't like being a vampire?" She spoke slowly, quietly, as though trying to humor a lunatic.

He shook his head, then dropped down onto the chair across from her. "I didn't want this life. It was thrust upon me." He closed his eyes as the horror of that night washed across his memory. And then he poured his memories into the girl's mind.

Kristov had pushed him against a wall, held him there while he buried his fangs in Ramsey's throat. It had been Chiavari who had pulled Kristov off him, Chiavari who drove a stake through the other vampire's heart. Ramsey remembered no more after that until he woke in Chiavari's arms, the vampire urging him to drink from the cut in his wrist. Chiavari's voice had been soft yet compelling, as soothing as a mother's lullaby.

Drink, Ramsey, he had urged. *Drink your fill.* And Ramsey had done just that, suffusing his depleted body with the accursed vampire blood until Chiavari jerked his arm away. He remembered the confusion that followed, the horror he had felt when Marisa told him what had happened. It had been Marisa's idea to bring him over, but it was Chiavari he blamed.

He could still hear Marisa's sweet voice asking if he would rather be dead, and his own sharp reply: *Of course I would!* Now, as then, he wondered how he could feel the same and be so different.

Stunned by what had happened that night, he had thanked Chiavari for saving his life, and then left the house. Thanked him! His lips twisted. Thanked him for making him a monster . . .

A low groan brought him back to the present. Suddenly aware of the effect his thoughts were having on the girl, he cut the connection between his mind and hers. She was lying back on the sofa, her eyes closed, her face drained of color.

"Kelly, are you all right?" he asked. "Kelly?"

Her eyelashes fluttered, and then her eyes opened. She sat up slowly, looking at him as if she had never seen him before. "You really are a vampire, aren't you? It's not a game you play."

He nodded. "Will you help me?"

"I can't. Not like that. Not . . . not kill you. I'm sorry."

"Damn it, why not? I'll make it worth your while."

"Because it's murder."

"How can it be murder," he asked bitterly, "when I am already dead? Hell, there won't even be a body if you drag me out into the sun."

Her face grew even more pale.

"I'm sorry," he muttered. He was ashamed of his weakness, ashamed of asking her to do what he himself had failed to do.

"Is it so awful?" she asked. "Being a . . . a vampire?"

"I was born to hunt them. It's what my family has done for generations. It was my sole purpose in life, my reason for living. And now . . ." He laughed bitterly. "Now I am what I have always hated, what I have spent my life hunting. And you ask if it's awful?" He laughed again—a cold bitter sound, like leaves fluttering over a grave. "You wanted to die when I found you. Now I want to die. Perhaps we could meet death together."

She shook her head. "No. I was wrong to even think of it. And so are you. Suicide is a sin. My granny taught me that life was precious, and not to be wasted. I . . . I never thanked you for saving my life."

Rising, she crossed the short distance between them,

hesitated a moment, then bent down and kissed his cheek. "Thank you."

He looked up, his gaze meeting hers. "You're welcome."

She smiled down at him, and in that moment he knew he wanted to live long enough to kiss her, just once.

Ramsey took a deep breath, afraid he was about to make a fool of himself. Again. He cleared his throat, wishing he had been blessed with Chiavari's innate charm.

"Kelly, I want to ask you something. . . ." When she started to speak, he held up his hand to silence her. "Please, hear me out. I know you've had a hard time lately, that you've been unhappy, and that you think you have nothing to live for. . . ."

"How do you know all that?" she demanded. "Did you read my diary?"

"I read your mind."

She blinked at him, then sat down hard. "You did what?"

"I read your mind when I took your blood."

"That's terrible! How could you do such a despicable thing?"

He felt a sudden urge to laugh. "Please, just listen. I am about to make you a proposition."

"I already told you, I'm not into murder. And I'm not into whoring, either."

"Damn it, woman, just listen!"

She made a face at him, then folded her hands in her lap. "Go on."

"I want you to move in here with me. Purely platonic," he added quickly.

"You need a better place to live, and I . . . I could use someone to keep an eye on things during the day. I'll make it worth your while. It will only be for a few months. Six at the most."

She shook her head. "Thanks, but I don't think so." She looked at him warily. "Can I go now?"

"I wish you would stay."

She regarded him steadily for several moments. "You don't want a housekeeper; you want a companion, don't you? Someone to keep you company in this mausoleum."

"Yes."

"How do I know I could trust you to behave?"

"You have my word as a gentleman."

She laughed out loud. "What about your word as a vampire? Do I have your word that you won't . . ." She grimaced with revulsion. "That you won't drink my blood again? And that you'll stay out of my thoughts?"

"Yes."

"I must be out of my mind," she muttered. "Totally, completely bonkers."

He leaned forward. "Then you'll stay?"

"For a week," she said. "We'll try it for a week."

"A month," he countered.

She thought about it for a moment, then nodded. "All right. One month." She tilted her head to one side. "Do you sleep in a coffin?"

"No."

"I thought that was mandatory."

He shrugged. "I think it's something only Hollywood and old-world vampires are into."

"Where do you sleep, then?"

"In a room off the cellar."

She studied him for a long moment, her eyes narrowed. It was tempting to read her thoughts, but he refrained from doing so.

"Okay," she said at last. "I'll move in tomorrow, if that's okay with you. Could you call me a cab?"

"Take my car."

"Are you kidding? It would probably get stolen before the engine cooled off."

He grunted softly. He had never been particularly concerned about material possessions, probably because he'd never owned much more than a beat-up Chevy and the clothes on his back, but he was fond of the Porsche.

He called for a cab, walked her to the door when it arrived, then stood there, watching her drive away, wondering if she would come back.

Chapter 13

APPLE SUNDOWN

Kelly packed the last of her meager belongings in a cardboard box, took one last look at the shabby one-room apartment she had lived in for the past seven months, and left the apartment. If she never saw the place again, it would be too soon!

Tucking the box under her arm, she went downstairs and climbed into the waiting taxi. It had been a long time since she could afford such a luxury. She dropped the box on the floor, gave the driver Edward's address, and settled back on the seat, one foot tapping nervously.

Last night, just before she left, Ramsey had slipped her the key to his house, and a hundred dollars in cash. It was the most money she'd had at one time in years. She, who had once made ten times that for an afternoon's work—although it was hard to remember those days now, clouded as they were by the trying years in between.

She glanced down at the meager belongings in the cardboard box and wondered for perhaps the thousandth time how everything could have gone so wrong so quickly and permanently back then. Of course, the major thing that had gone wrong had been her relationship with Doug. When that began to fall apart, she hadn't been able to concentrate on her career, her personal well-being, or anything else. She had blamed herself at first, and tried harder and harder to make it work, even though her heart was breaking. Her uncertainty in their relationship had shown in her work, until the work began to dry up. She wouldn't have cared then, if she could have won back his love.

Now she grimaced at his memory, and at her own naïveté. She had given her heart to a two-timing gigolo, and he had shattered it. Perhaps beyond repair. The booze, the pills, the self-degradation had followed in a descending spiral of self-destruction that had led her to that pier—and to Ramsey.

Strangely, she felt no need for a narcotic fix today, nor even a good, stiff jolt of cheap whiskey. All of that was behind her now, in a way she didn't quite understand. She was starting a new life. Kelly Anderson, vampire baby-sitter. The thought made her laugh out loud.

She wasn't laughing when the cab driver deposited her and her belongings on the sidewalk in front of Ramsey's house. Even in the light of day, it seemed to gather darkness around it. It didn't really look like a normal house. More like some Hollywood version of Dracula's mansion. She wondered if Ramsey had picked it for that very look. Did vampires have a sense of humor?

Even after all she had seen and heard, such a question seemed preposterous, even unspoken. Actual vampires in twenty-first-century Los Angeles. Who would believe it?

Hugging the cardboard box to her chest, she climbed the stairs, put the key in the lock, and opened the door. She stood on the porch for a moment, wondering if she was making the biggest mistake of her life. But no, she had made that already, with Doug.

Taking a deep breath, she crossed the threshold and closed the door behind her.

She was struck by the stillness of the house. Had it been a living thing, she would have said it was holding its breath.

It was a just a little past noon. Hours until dark. Hours to change her mind.

She dropped the box on a chair in the living room and toured the house. There were two bedrooms downstairs, one of which she remembered all too well. The second bedroom was done in forest green and white. It was obvious the house had been remodeled, she mused, since she didn't think indoor plumbing had been common when the house was originally built. Certainly they didn't have bathrooms like these, with sunken tubs and separate shower stalls big enough for two. She had seen the kitchen before, and she passed it by. There was a formal dining room, empty of furniture. No surprise there, she thought with grim humor. She was reasonably certain Edward didn't host any dinner parties, at least not at a table.

A family room had been added to the back of the house. It was large and oblong, with a marble fireplace, thick forest green carpet, and large windows covered by heavy drapes. The furniture was of dark wood, covered in a dark-green-and-burgundy print. There were no pictures on the walls, no knickknacks of any kind, nothing of a personal nature.

There were three bedrooms upstairs. The first two looked as they must have when the house was built. The paper on the walls was dark, with a patina of age that argued it hadn't been changed since the house was built. The floors were hardwood. The furniture looked antique: four-poster beds and oak rocking chairs and highboys with oval mirrors.

The third bedroom was obviously the master bedroom and had been redecorated recently. The walls were painted a beautiful shade of French blue. The rug, a rich, deep pile, was the same color. The bedspread was a blue-and-white print; the curtains were white. There was a small sitting room between the bedroom and the bathroom.

The third floor was a large empty room with a single round window that overlooked the backyard. There were bars on the window.

With a shiver of unease, she left the room and hurried down the stairs to the first floor.

Grabbing her belongings, she went back upstairs to the blue bedroom, thinking she would feel more comfortable with the ground floor between herself and Edward. Dropping the box on a chair, she flung open the curtains, frowned when she saw that the windows were covered with some kind of film to shut out the sun. Tomorrow she would scrape the windows. He might have to live in the dark, but she wanted light, and lots of it.

She hung her few clothes in the closet, put her cosmetics and her toothbrush in the medicine cabinet in the bathroom, dropped her comb and brush on the counter.

She didn't have much, and it didn't take long to put it all away.

Going back downstairs, she realized she was hungry. The stale bagel that had been breakfast had done little to sustain her. Now that the nervous excitement of moving in was wearing off, she was starving. She went into the kitchen in search of food. And found none. Well, of course not, she thought with a wry grin. Vampires always dined "out."

Not only was there no food in the house, but there were no dishes, no silverware, no glasses, no pots and pans.

Hands on her hips, she stood in the middle of the floor, foot tapping, trying to decide if she wanted to go out for something to eat, or just order a pizza.

It was then she saw the envelope with her name on it. Inside was a sheet of paper.

> *Kelly,*
>   *I have my doubts that you will actually show up today, but in case you do, you will find the key to my car and some money for food in the drawer to the left of the refrigerator.*
>
>   *Edward*

Opening the drawer, she pulled out a key ring with a single key, and four crisp one-hundred-dollar bills.

"Geez, Louise," she muttered, "how much does he think I eat?"

She found the car in the garage. A black Porsche with less than five hundred miles on it.

Feeling as if she had just won the lottery, she opened the door and slid behind the wheel. She closed her eyes for a moment, inhaling the new-car scent while she ran her hand over the soft leather upholstery. It had been years since she'd had a new car, since she'd had a car of any kind.

Smiling, she put the key in the ignition and switched on the engine. The exhaust made a low, throaty sound, and the car seemed to awaken, crouching like some predatory beast ready to spring. She thumbed the garage door remote clipped to the sun visor, studied the gear diagram on the shift lever, and gingerly eased it into reverse.

She stalled it when she tried to find first, and her

next few gear changes were clumsy, but driving a stick, learned on an old Honda, soon came back to her. It felt good to be behind the wheel of such a sleek car.

Her first stop was a steak house. The waiter seemed somewhat dubious when she ordered the largest cut of prime rib they had; later, he seemed a little bemused that she had finished every bite and still had room for chocolate cheesecake. He grinned at her when he brought the check, as if wondering where she had put it all.

Feeling slightly stuffed, replete, she left the waiter a generous tip, pocketed the change from one of Ramsey's hundreds, and headed for the mall. With her hunger taken care of, her next priority was shopping! If this was a dream, she wanted to buy some new clothes before she awoke.

She picked up a couple pairs of jeans, three tank tops, a sweater, a couple of T-shirts, some new underwear, six pairs of socks, a new pair of Nikes, and a watch to replace the Rolex she had hocked. She also bought a saucepan, a frying pan, a coffeepot, a set of silverware, a set of dishes and matching glasses.

She piled her packages in the passenger seat and drove to the grocery store. It was wonderful to be able to shop without worrying about the cost, to pick up a carton of chocolate ice cream and a jar of hot fudge and not have to worry about how she would look in front of the camera. She had no one to impress anymore, no one to answer to except herself. It had been a long, hard battle fighting her way out of the mire of drugs only to find that, when she was clean again, no one wanted her. It had been that realization that had sent her to the pier that fateful night.

She wheeled the cart down the produce aisle, filling the basket with fresh fruits and vegetables. She bought bread and milk and orange juice, coffee and sugar, salt and pepper, butter and eggs, a box of Rice Krispies, a couple of New York steaks, a package of pork chops, a couple cans of tuna. She picked up a bottle of garlic salt and grinned, wondering if having garlic on her breath would repel the vampire in the house. She bought dish soap and cleanser and dish towels, shampoo and conditioner, a new hairbrush and toothbrush, toothpaste, deodorant. A bag of M&Ms, a six pack of 7-Up.

"Junk food junkie," she muttered, and tossed a package of Oreos into the cart.

At the checkout stand, she bought a pack of gum and a *TV Guide*, then frowned, trying to remember if he had a TV.

A cute boy loaded her groceries into the trunk. With his blond crew cut and blue eyes, he reminded her of Edward. She grinned, wondering what the boy would say if she told him she was moving in with a vampire.

A glance at her new watch showed it was almost four when she pulled into the driveway.

It took several trips back and forth to carry everything into the house. Humming softly, she put the groceries away, then carried the other bags up to her room. Next time she went out, she was going to buy a CD player.

She put her new clothes away, then went into the bathroom, bent over the tub, and turned on the tap, mentally adding bubble bath to the list of things she had forgotten.

It would be easy to get accustomed to this, she thought, if it weren't for the monster sleeping in the cellar.

She bathed and shampooed her hair, dressed in a new pair of jeans and a T-shirt. Surprisingly, she was hungry again. Or maybe not so surprising, she thought, unable to remember the last time she'd had more than one meal a day.

She went downstairs, reveling in the feel of the thick carpet beneath her bare feet. In the kitchen, she made a tuna sandwich and a big green salad and poured herself a glass of milk.

She sat at the table in the kitchen to eat, constantly glancing back and forth from the clock to the door that led to the cellar, wondering how soon after sunset he rose. Wondering again if she was making the biggest mistake of her life, although how anything or anyone could be a worse disaster than her affair with Doug was hard to imagine. Even a vampire seemed a better choice.

Needing something to occupy her mind, she bypassed the dishwasher and washed her few dishes by hand. A vampire. What would it be like to be one of the undead? In the movies, they were comic heroes in search of love, or rabid monsters in search of blood. Edward seemed decidedly lacking in humor. . . .

And then there was no more time for thought. She turned to reach for a dish towel, and he was there, standing in the doorway, a curious expression on his face.

She smiled tentatively, her heartbeat accelerating. "Hi."

"Good evening."

He lifted his head, sniffing the air, reminding her of a wary coyote she had seen years ago when she'd gone camping in the mountains with her parents.

She lifted her hand in a vague gesture. "I sort of made myself at home. I hope you don't mind."

"Of course not. My home is yours for as long as you stay." His gaze moved to her throat, to the pulse rapidly beating there. His nostrils flared; his hands curled into tight fists.

A moment ago, she had thought he was smelling the food she had eaten. Now she wondered if he was smelling *her*. She took a quick step backward, grunting softly as her back slammed into the countertop.

He swallowed hard, his breathing suddenly labored.

His gaze, hot and hungry, met hers, and then, before she had time to be truly afraid, he was gone.

Ramsey hunted the dark streets, the back alleys. He had been a fool to ask Kelly to share the house with him. Even now, the scent of her hair, her skin, her blood, filled his nostrils and teased his senses. She was beautiful, more beautiful than any woman he had ever known. More beautiful, more desirable, than Marisa.

Kelly. His heart ached for her; his soul cried out for her; his body yearned for one touch, one night in her arms, freely given.

Bitter laughter rose in his throat, mocking his desire. Except for Katherine, no woman had loved him when he was a mortal man. How could he expect one to love the monster he had become? He lacked Chiavari's old world charm and handsome facade.

A short time later he found his prey, an old man huddled in a doorway, saw himself reflected in the watery gray eyes. A monster out of a nightmare.

With a wild cry, he took hold of the man, his fangs piercing the flesh of his throat. There was no gentleness in him, no mercy, only a cold bitter rage.

This is what you hunted, what you hated. This is what you are! The words reverberated through his mind.

He threw back his head, his laughter ringing out in the night. Fate, it seemed, had a cruel sense of humor.

He drank again, drank until the man's heartbeat grew faint, drank until the man's body grew cold, limp.

Kelly's image rose up in his mind, her deep brown eyes filled with sadness and reproach. He saw himself as she would see him: his eyes burning, fangs dripping blood. Filled with shame and regret, he drew back.

He had seen Chiavari hunt. To his credit, the vampire was never cruel.

Ramsey looked down at the man lying back across his arm. His neck had been cruelly savaged. Blood stained the collar of his faded shirt, dripped down his neck.

With a cry of denial, Ramsey reeled backward, horrified by the savagery of his act. As gently as he could, he settled the man into a corner of the doorway, took off his own coat, and draped it around the man's shoulders. Removing his wallet, he stuffed what cash he had into the man's pockets.

"I'm sorry," he muttered as he backed away. "So sorry."

Kelly was sitting in the living room, trying to concentrate on a late-night movie, when Edward returned to the house.

She looked up when he entered the room, her eyes widening when she saw his face. "What have you done?" she exclaimed softly.

"I almost killed a man."

"I didn't know vampires felt remorse."

Sinking down on the chair across from the sofa, Ramsey cradled his head in his hands. "I can't go on like this. Damn it, I cannot!"

"I thought vampires liked to drink blood," Kelly said.

He thought of Khira, who gloried in it, and of Chiavari, who had accepted it. "Some do."

She shuddered. "How can you drink it?"

He looked up at her, his expression tortured. "I crave it, and the fact that I crave it so desperately—that I enjoy the taste so much—sickens me. Do you understand?"

"Yes. No." She shook her head. "Not really. Is that why you tried to kill yourself?"

He nodded. "I sought out the vampire who made me, and begged him to end my existence. He refused."

"Why?"

"He told me to wait, to give myself time to grow used to my new lifestyle. Damn it, I don't want to grow used to it!" He slammed his fist down on the table beside him. There was a sharp crack, and the table split in two. He grabbed the lamp before it fell to the floor.

The girl looked at him, her eyes wide and scared.

Muttering an oath, Ramsey hurled the lamp against the far wall. The shade crumpled, the porcelain shattered. He saw each individual shard fall.

Kelly jumped to her feet and ran toward the stairs.

"Don't go!"

She paused, one hand gripping the banister, her knuckles white, her whole body trembling.

"Kelly."

She turned slowly to face him.

He stood in the doorway. "Tonight, when I was about to kill that poor man, I thought of you waiting for me here. I saw myself through your eyes. It is the only thing that saved him."

She tilted her head to one side in a gesture that was becoming familiar. "Me?"

"Yes. Help me, Kelly. For the love of heaven, help me."

"How? What can I do?"

"Your blood . . ." He took a step toward her, paused when she backed up against the wall.

Her hand flew to her neck. "No!"

"Please, hear me out."

She glanced up at the top of the stairs, then looked at him again, her heart pounding. "I'm listening."

"A few drops of your blood soothes the hunger within

me. If you would let me . . ." He swore softly. Asking her was harder than he had expected. "If you would let me drink a little from you each night before I go out, I think it would be easier on those I hunt. I know it would make it easier for me."

She shook her head ruefully. "Why did I ever agree to come here?"

"Does that mean you will do it?"

"I don't know." She massaged her throat. "Why does my . . . my blood soothe you? It's no different than anyone else's."

"I don't know. I only know that it does."

She hesitated, her mind racing. Would he take it by force if she refused? It was gruesome to think of him biting her neck, yet perversely flattering to think that her blood soothed him.

"Please." The word whispered past his lips, filled with quiet desperation.

"All right. You'll only take a little?"

"Yes. A few drops."

"Now?"

"No, it's not necessary. But I can't help wondering . . ."

"Why I agreed?" She shrugged. "You saved my life. I'm glad now that you did. And maybe, if you do as your friend suggested and wait a few months, you'll be glad to be alive, too."

"He is not my friend."

"Oh. Well," she said briskly. "I think part of your problem is that you spend too much time brooding about how awful it is to be what you are. I think you need to get out more, see people."

He laughed, a sharp, bitter sound.

"I mean it. You must have some friends. . . ."

He thought briefly of Marisa and Chiavari. "No."

"Well, I don't either, not anymore. So, we'll make new ones."

"Kelly . . ."

"You can't just sleep in your tomb all day and hide out in this house all night. You'll go nuts. I'll go nuts." She descended the stairs and walked briskly toward him, grabbing him by the arm as she passed by. "Come on."

"Where are we going?"

"To the movies."

"Now? It's ten o'clock."

She looked at him and laughed. "So what? We have all night. Let's go."

It was his first date with a woman since Katherine.

The theater seemed to press in on him, his nostrils filling with the mingled scents of soap, perspiration, shampoo, toothpaste, a hint of marijuana, chocolate candy, soft drinks, popcorn and butter, chips and cheese . . . and blood. The scent of it surrounded him, yet it was the scent of Kelly's blood that called to him, beckoning him with the promise of sweet relief.

Why did the need to take blood from others repulse him and leave him hungering for more, yet a few drops of Kelly's blood taste like the sweetest nectar on his tongue, soothing his hunger, calming his tortured soul?

As though she read his thoughts, she turned to face him. His gaze met hers, hot and hungry—not for blood but for the taste of her kisses.

Slowly, so slowly, he closed the distance between them, and when she didn't back away, he claimed her lips with his.

He had expected her to slap him, or push him away, or scream in revulsion because a vampire was kissing her. Instead, her hand slid around his neck to cup his nape.

It was not his first kiss. He was, after all, forty-two years old. But even Katherine's first kiss had not affected

him as profoundly as did this one. He was stunned when
Kelly's tongue met his. It was a kiss that went on forever
and ended too soon.

"Oh, Edward," she murmured.

"Forgive me," he stammered, "I didn't . . . I don't
know what got into me. I . . ."

She laughed softly. "Don't apologize, Edward," she
whispered as she drew his head toward hers. "Just do
it again."

The movie, the theater, the people around him: all
were forgotten as her lips touched his. Soft, warm, yielding, more intoxicating than whiskey had ever been. He
felt like a teenager on his first date: clumsy, uncertain,
his hormones raging. She murmured his name, clinging
to him as though she might never let go.

He never remembered what the movie was about, or
even who was in it. All he remembered from that night
was Kelly sitting beside him in a dark theater, and the
intoxicating taste of her lips on his.

He drew back, somewhat embarrassed, when the
lights came on.

After the movie, they went for a long drive. Not much
was said, but the silence between them was easy, comfortable.

When they returned home, he kissed her good night
in the living room, stood at the bottom of the stairs,
staring after her like a lovesick schoolboy until she was
out of sight.

So many hours until dawn. Taking off his coat, he
tossed it over a chair, frowned as someone knocked on
the door. He knew a moment of trepidation. He had
no friends in this town, no acquaintances to speak of
save Chiavari and Marisa, and he didn't think they would
be calling at this hour of the night.

Chiding himself for jumping at shadows, he opened

the door. "Khira!" She was a vision of shining silver hair and a whisper of black silk.

She smiled her most beguiling smile. "May I come in?"

"I don't think so."

"Surely you are not afraid of me?" she chided.

He shrugged.

Khira glanced past him. "Such a quaint little place," she said, laughing softly. "Will I find Barnabas Collins lurking in the hallways?"

"Very funny." He stepped outside and closed the door behind her. "What brings you here?"

A pretty pout teased her lips. "Aren't you glad to see me?"

"Sure."

"You've been with a woman." Her nostrils flared. "She's here. That little mortal you were playing with."

"So?"

She glided toward him. Reaching up, she dragged one fingernail over his cheek, hard enough to break the skin. "I told you before, I don't like to share. Not territory. Not anything."

He grabbed her wrist, forcing her hand away from his face. "I don't like jealous women."

She ignored his grip on her arm. Rising on tiptoe, she licked the blood from his cheek. "Who is she?"

"No one."

Her gaze burned into him like blue fire. "You've fallen for her, haven't you?"

"Of course not."

"I'm in the mood for a little fun," Khira said. "Come, hunt with me."

He wanted to refuse, but it seemed wiser to do as she wished. And so he smiled back at her and followed her out into the night.

* * *

Khira quickly found a young man to her liking. He was tall and blond, with green eyes and a trim, athletic build. Her hunger was a palpable thing as they followed her prey into a nightclub.

Ramsey sat back and watched her, mildly amused as she flirted with the young man, plying all the tricks of an old-fashioned Southern belle. The man was polite but uninterested, and Ramsey's amusement quickly turned to revulsion as Khira slid into the man's mind, bending his will to hers.

Ramsey followed her outside, trailing behind as she led her prey down a dark street. He watched as she toyed with him, making him kneel at her feet. He kissed her hand and declared she was the most beautiful woman in all the world. Like a queen granting favors, she placed her fingertips on his shoulders and bade him rise, and then she gathered him into her arms— arms that could easily have broken him in two—and buried her fangs in his neck.

The man struggled against her, and Ramsey knew she had released control of his mind, that the man knew her for what she was. His eyes were wide with horror as he looked death in the face, his voice high-pitched with terror as he realized there was no hope of escape.

The rapid beat of the man's heart echoed in Ramsey's ears. The scent of terror, of blood, filled his nostrils, and he had an overpowering urge to join her, to feast upon the man's terror.

His fangs lengthened as the Hunger surged to life within him, and he took a step forward, and then another, the lust for blood thrumming through his veins.

Khira looked up, her bright-blue eyes glowing hotly, her lips and fangs stained crimson.

The man was barely breathing now. His face was ashen, his heartbeat slow and heavy in his chest. He looked at Ramsey, hoping for a savior. "Help . . . me . . ."

Khira's laughter rolled through the darkness like smoke from a funeral pyre.

Ramsey halted, sickened by what he saw, by his eagerness to be a part of it.

"You can be a man with a peculiar lifestyle, or you can be a monster. . . ." He heard Chiavari's voice echo in the back of his mind.

"Please," the man gasped. He held out his hand in a feeble gesture of entreaty. "Help . . . me . . ."

Khira caressed the man's face with one pale hand. "There is no help for you, my handsome one," she said. "No escape." She smiled at Ramsey. "Come, join me."

He shook his head and backed away.

"Come, Edward; it is time to accept what you are. Finish him."

"No." Since becoming a vampire, he had thought of himself as a monster, but there was only one monster here, and it was Khira. She was like Kristov in her thinking, and that sickened him. Once, he had thought all vampires were evil, but he knew now that he had been wrong. Chiavari had told him he could be as good or as bad as he desired. Looking at Khira, he knew she was evil disguised in beauty.

He took a last look at the man imprisoned in the vampire's arms. There was no way to save him, except to bring him across. He was too far gone.

"Edward! Do not defy me. Edward!"

"No."

He spoke softly, but Khira felt his power ripple through the air. He was very powerful for a newly made vampire. Even more powerful than she had first suspected. But then, considering his bloodline, that was

not surprising. She wondered if he had any inkling of
the strength he possessed.

"You fool!" she hissed. "It is time to accept who and
what you are!"

He shook his head. One last look at her, at the blood
dripping from her fangs, and then he was gone, speed-
ing through the night toward the only one who seemed
to care. Kelly.

"You cannot run away from what you are!"

The sound of Khira's voice chased him down the
street.

Chapter 14

Marisa glanced at the clock as the knock came again. "Who on earth can that be?"

Grigori kissed her cheek as he rose from the sofa. "It's Ramsey."

Marisa glanced at the clock. It was almost two A.M. People did not make social calls at such an hour. Of course, for vampires, two in the morning was not considered late.

She felt a shiver of unease. Ever since his last visit, she had been troubled about Edward. She thought she might be picking it up from her husband, who, on more than one occasion, had alluded to the new vampire's unexpected power and constant mental turmoil. During the hunt for Alexi, Edward had often come to see her. It was unsettling to think of him now, roaming the night like those he had once hunted.

She heard muffled voices as Grigori opened the front door, then their footsteps: Grigori's, light, almost soundless; Ramsey's, heavier, more determined.

"Hello, Edward," she said when he entered the room.

"I'm sorry to come calling so late. Or so early."

"Vampire social hours," she said, smiling. "We were just watching an old movie."

He matched her smile, with no hint of loathing or pain. She observed him closely. He looked different somehow, though she couldn't put her finger on it. Perhaps it was just that he was "aging" as a vampire, that he was becoming more comfortable with what he was. Once, she would not have noticed him in a crowd; now, he exuded a sense of power and self-confidence that he had not possessed before.

"Please," she said, "sit down."

Ramsey sat on the love seat, his fingers drumming on the arm. Grigori resumed his place beside her on the sofa. Almost before he was settled, Ramsey stood up and began to pace.

Marisa looked at Grigori, a question in her eyes.

"Ramsey, did you come here to wear a path in our carpet?" Grigori asked, his voice tinged with amusement.

Ramsey paused in midstride to glare at Chiavari. Then, blowing out a sigh of exasperation, he sank down on the love seat again. "Khira," he said heavily. "I've angered her."

Chiavari nodded slowly. "Not a pretty sight when she's angry."

Ramsey grunted softly.

"What happened?" Marisa asked.

As quickly as possible, Ramsey related his activities with Khira: the hunt, the victim, Khira's insistence that Ramsey finish the poor devil off. He glanced at Marisa. She looked pale. How could such things bother her so much when she lived with a vampire? Vampires survived by feeding off the lives of others. Chiavari was no exception; he had fed from her on more than one occasion.

"She wanted me to kill him," Ramsey said, "but I just couldn't do it."

"So, he's still alive? That man?" Marisa asked hopefully.

"No. Khira loves killing too much to be merciful. Besides, he was too far gone. . . ."

"There's something else," Chiavari said. "Something you are not telling us."

"The other night, she wanted me to . . ." Ramsey cleared his throat. "The other night . . ."

"Go on," Chiavari said, "What did she want you to do?"

"Soon after she got here, she took me hunting." Ramsey glanced at Marisa, then looked away. "And then she took me to bed. I don't know what I was thinking! I guess maybe I wasn't thinking. The other night, I refused." Ramsey glanced at Marisa again. "She seems to think that I belong to her now."

Grigori slid a sidelong glance at his wife and sighed heavily. "Khira does not take rejection well," he said. "As I recall, she is not accustomed to having anyone tell her no. About anything."

Ramsey nodded.

Marisa met her husband's sideways look with one eyebrow raised. "You seem to be speaking from experience."

" 'Twas in another country," Grigori said, and smiled wryly. "And besides, the wench is . . . Do you really want me to answer that?"

"That's some kind of quote isn't it?" she asked.

"Yes, from *The Jew of Malta*. Marlowe. Khira was determined I know all the arts, become a polished gentleman. Now, I ask you again, do you really want me to answer your question?"

"Yes," Marisa replied, and then shook her head. "No, I don't want to know."

"Khira has always been impulsive," Grigori remarked. "She is a very sexy, very sensual creature. I suspect she was that way before the Dark Gift. Totally self-absorbed. And with the power she has now . . ." He shrugged. "She has no need to consider anything but her own gratification. She often acts without thinking." He shook his head. "One would think she would have gained a little maturity, a little self-control, over the ages."

"She scares me," Ramsey admitted.

Chiavari chuckled softly. "Smart man. I should stay out of her way until she cools off, if I were you."

"That's my plan," Ramsey muttered. "Damn, I don't have a hope in hell of defending myself against her."

"There is an unwritten law among our kind: Vampyre does not kill Vampyre," Chiavari said.

"You killed Kristov."

"Yes. It happens from time to time. Khira killed the one who made her. And I suspect she has killed others who got in her way."

"She killed Dracul," Ramsey said. "She told him to leave town. Apparently he refused."

Chiavari nodded. "She is a law unto herself. I suspect she has destroyed LaSalle, as well. I no longer sense his presence in the city."

"He's gone. She told him she wanted his house. And he gave it to her, just like that."

"It is a wise man who gives her what she wants."

Marisa laid her hand on Grigori's arm. "Perhaps we should leave town."

"Is that your wish? To leave here?"

"No, but I don't want her coming after you."

"She has always had a, shall we say, a fondness for me," Chiavari said wryly. "I do not believe she will do me any harm."

Ramsey glanced at Marisa, then turned his attention

to Chiavari once again. "She may be fond of you. But what of Marisa?"

"To harm what is mine is to harm me," Chiavari said.

"Do you think you could take her in a fight?"

"I don't know," Chiavari grunted softly. "I hope I never have to find out."

"Me, too," Ramsey said fervently.

"Be careful, Edward," Marisa said. "Promise me."

"*Careful* is my middle name," he said, rising.

Chiavari stood up. "I'll see you out."

"Good night, Edward," Marisa said.

"Good night." Ramsey followed Chiavari out onto the porch. "So?"

"Be careful of Khira. She can be ruthless and utterly cruel."

Ramsey nodded. "I know. I've seen what she's capable of. I'm no match for her."

"Perhaps not yet," Grigori said, "but you are not helpless or weak. Only young in the ways of the Dark Gift. There is powerful blood in your veins, Ramsey. Mine. Alexi's. And Khira's. She will find it difficult to destroy you if you keep your wits about you. If she threatens you, reach deep down inside yourself and call on the power that is there."

"Why didn't you tell me this before?"

"You did not need to know before. You were far too interested in being destroyed then. Now that someone else may want you dead, you seem to have a new interest in staying alive. The longer you survive, the stronger you will become. And you are surprisingly strong already. You did refuse her, after all. Twice. And you are still alive."

Ramsey stared at Chiavari, his mind reeling as he sought to understand what he'd just been told. Almost against his will, he felt a flash of hope. "Am I as powerful as she is? As you are?"

"To my knowledge, no Vampyre who still lives is as powerful as Khira. As for myself . . ." Grigori shrugged.

"Is there any way to keep her from reading my thoughts?"

"You can learn to guard your thoughts. It takes practice and a good deal of self-control, but it's like anything else. The more you do it, the easier it becomes."

"Can I block you, too?"

"Try."

Grigori focused on Ramsey. "You are thinking of a woman. Kelly. She sleeps in your house. You are afraid she may be in danger. From Khira. And from yourself."

"If I can't block you, how can I hope to block Khira?"

"The bond between the two of us is more immediate and therefore stronger. Try again."

Ramsey imagined himself building a wall between his mind and Chiavari's. A thick concrete wall. It took every ounce of concentration.

Chiavari laughed softly. "Well done."

Ramsey grunted.

"As I said, it will grow easier with practice. Do not hesitate to call on me if I can be of help."

"You're telling me the truth? About blocking you?"

"You did surprisingly well, considering it was your first attempt. Practice."

"I will." He hesitated, then added, "Thank you."

"Good night."

Ramsey thought about what Chiavari had told him as he walked home. He could have transported himself there with a thought, but he had always enjoyed walking. The night was cool and crisp, with a hint of fall in the air. With his vampire eyes, he saw the world so clearly— the beauty, the ugliness.

"There is powerful blood in your veins." Chiavari's words echoed in his mind. *Powerful blood.* It eased his fear of

Khira a little to know he wasn't completely helpless, completely at her mercy.

He let his mind expand, reached down inside himself. He could feel the power resting deep within him, waiting to be summoned. It frightened him even as it filled him with a sense of exultation.

Even if he couldn't beat her, he would give her one hell of a fight.

Chapter 15

The next few days passed swiftly. Ramsey soon grew accustomed to having Kelly in the house. She quickly adjusted her schedule to his so that she could share the long hours of the night with him.

Upon rising, he showered and dressed, then met her upstairs. She was understandably nervous the first few times he took her blood. Exerting all the willpower he possessed, he took her gently, always careful to take no more than a few small sips. And though he yearned to do so, he avoided kissing her again. Under the circumstances, it seemed like a further violation somehow.

He left the house immediately after feeding, not wanting to meet her gaze, afraid of what he might see there.

It seemed miraculous to him that a few drops of her blood so quickly eased his insatiable craving, made it possible for him to stay rational while he hunted—to take only what he needed from his prey, to leave them alive and unhurt.

By the time he returned to the house, she had eaten

dinner and was usually in the living room, watching TV
or reading a book. He was aware of her constant furtive
looks, knew she was curious about him. Curious. And
attracted. And repelled.

Her warmth, her very life, drew him like a beacon.
He basked in her nearness, delighted in the hours they
spent together. He bought a chess set and taught her
to play. She bought a game of Scrabble and beat him
every time. During those times, with his hunger
assuaged, the intimacy between them was almost too
much for him. She drew him like a magnet, but still he
resisted. Sometimes he had the feeling his resistance
disappointed her. It would have been so easy to probe
her mind, to see what she was thinking, but he had
promised he would not.

He had told her to make herself at home, and she
took him at his word. Soon, his house, once devoid of
any but the bare essentials, began to look like a home.
There were pictures on the walls, mostly seascapes;
flowering plants in colorful pots on the tables; colorful
figurines of dragons and wizards on a shelf.

Sometimes, sitting in the living room while she fussed
in the kitchen, he could almost pretend he was human
again, a mortal man living with a beautiful woman. He
had never lived with a woman before, never truly realized what enchanting, changeable creatures they were.
She filled his house with light, made him laugh in spite
of himself. She had a lovely, clear voice. He enjoyed
listening to her sing while she washed the dishes or
cleaned the house.

By the end of the second week, it seemed as though
she had always been there. As the third week came to
an end, he was convinced that she was as attracted to
him as he was to her, despite her continued deep-seated
revulsion at what he was.

And now the end of the fourth week was drawing

near. He had fed early this night, wanting to spend more time at home, with her. He sat in the living room staring at the TV, trying to work up the nerve to ask Kelly if she would stay another month, wondering what he would do if she refused. He could hear her in the kitchen, opening cupboard doors.

He looked up as she breezed into the room. A month of having enough to eat and getting plenty of rest had made a marked change in her appearance. Her skin was smooth and clear; the dark shadows were gone from her eyes. Her cheeks were no longer hollow; her figure had filled out, making him all too aware of her sweet feminine form.

"I'm hungry," she said. "Think I'll go out to eat."

"I always eat out," he muttered sourly.

She looked at him a moment, brown eyes wide with surprise, and then she laughed.

"What's so funny?"

"Well, that's the first thing I thought when I looked for something to eat my first day here, that you always 'eat out.' Were you reading my mind already?"

He was stung by her accusation but could not deny it. "I have not read your mind since I promised I would not."

Her expression softened then. "You're really very sweet when you want to be, you know that?"

He didn't know what to say to that, and she laughed again—a merry trill.

"What's so funny now?" He almost glared at her.

"I never imagined a vampire could blush," she said.

And it was true. He could feel his ears burning. But the glow was in her eyes again. She laid a gentle hand on his forearm.

"Come with me," she coaxed. "I don't like to eat alone." And then that devilish merriment took over again. "You should understand that," she said, grinning at him. "You never do. Eat alone, I mean."

This time he laughed in spite of himself. "All right," he agreed. "What are you in the mood for?"

It seemed strange to be talking about food. Though it had been only a few months since he had become a vampire, it seemed as if centuries had passed. His was a warm liquid diet now. He tried not to think of all the things he would never taste again: rare steak, succulent lobster, potato chips, a good cup of coffee, apple pie, ice cream on a hot summer day.

"Italian," Kelly decided. "Let's go to the Olive Garden."

In the past, it had been one of his favorite places. She ordered veal parmigiana, soup, and salad. He ordered a bottle of red wine and sipped a glass while she ate. He couldn't decide which tempted him the most: the meal he couldn't eat, or the girl sitting across from him. Light played in her silky black hair. Her skin was soft and smooth, her cheeks the color of ripe peaches, her lips full and pink and tempting.

Once, she looked up and caught him watching her. Her cheeks flushed hotly, and she looked down at her plate again. "Do you want to try a bite?"

A bite. His gaze moved to her neck, to the pulse beating in the hollow of her throat, as he shook his head.

"Have you tried to eat since you became a . . . you know? How do you know you can't?" She speared a piece of meat and offered it to him. "Try it."

The smell of veal filled his nostrils and turned his stomach. "I can't."

He must have looked as green as he felt, because she withdrew the fork and said, "I believe you. I'm sorry."

"So am I," he replied. "More than you can ever imagine."

They finished the meal in silence.

After dinner, they drove to the beach and walked barefoot along the shore. It was a calm, clear night. The moon painted ever-changing silver shadows on the water.

After a while, they stopped to watch the waves. Ramsey's gaze moved over Kelly. She looked beautiful standing there with the ocean behind her. Moonlight shimmered like molten silver in her hair; her skin looked soft and oh, so touchable. He wished, not for the first time, that he possessed a little of Chiavari's easy charm with women.

"Kelly?" He took a deep breath, the need to kiss her stronger than his need for blood. He knew he should turn away, afraid that one kiss would not be enough. Afraid that a taste of her lips would ignite his hellish thirst. But she was looking up at him, her brown eyes shining in the moonlight, her lips slightly parted, moist, inviting. He cleared his throat. The kisses they had shared at the movies had been much in his mind, but he had lacked the courage to kiss her again, afraid of being rebuffed. "I was thinking about the other night, at the movies. . . ."

"Were you? So was I."

"What were you thinking?" he asked.

"I was thinking maybe we should kiss again—you know, to see if it was as wonderful as I remember."

"Kelly . . ." He swept her into his arms, a part of him still expecting her to push him away or slap his face or laugh out loud, but she did none of those things. Instead, she leaned into him, her head tilting up, her eyelids fluttering down.

And he kissed her, there in the moonlight. Kissed her, and it wasn't enough. He wanted to inhale her, to drink her essence, to absorb her very soul into his own. She was sweet, so sweet. Heat sizzled between them, hotter than the sun he would never see again. Why had he waited so long?

"Oh, Edward . . ."

She looked up at him, breathless. She was soft and warm and willing. He covered her face with kisses, whispered praises to her beauty as he adored her with his hands and his lips. He closed his eyes, and desire rose up within him, hot and swift, and with it the overpowering urge to feed. He fought against it. He had fed well before coming here, yet the Hunger rose up within him, gnawing at his vitals, urging him to take what he wanted.

"This is crazy," she murmured breathlessly. "We hardly know each other."

"Crazy," he agreed. Her scent surrounded him. The rapid beat of her heart called to the beast within him. He deepened the kiss, at war with himself, felt his fangs lengthen in response to his growing hunger.

With a little cry, she drew back. She touched her lower lip, now stained with a drop of scarlet. He watched, hungry and horrified, as she licked the blood from her lip.

"Forgive me," he said hoarsely. "I did not mean to . . ."

"It's all right, Edward, but maybe we'd better . . . hmm . . . slow down a little."

His arms dropped to his sides and he backed away from her. "We should go home."

He was quiet on the drive back to the house. Kelly studied him surreptitiously as he drove. How could she be attracted to this man who wasn't a man at all? Worse yet, she was afraid she was falling in love with him.

Vampire. The word whispered through her mind, conjuring images of wraithlike figures in swirling black capes, pale skin, bloodless lips.

There were times when Edward looked pale, but he

didn't look like a monster. More like a middle-aged beach boy with his athletic build, golden hair, and bright-blue eyes.

Vampire. Even now, after living with him for almost a month, after letting him drink her blood every day, it was hard to believe. Sometimes, sitting on the sofa watching TV, they seemed like any normal couple spending a quiet evening at home.

She licked her lips, remembering the wonder of his kisses, his horror when he saw the blood on her mouth. Was she insane to stay with him, to put her life in his hands? What if some night, instead of taking a few drops of her blood, he took it all?

The thought chilled her, and she wrapped her arms around herself, suddenly cold.

"Are you all right?" Ramsey asked.

"Fine."

His gaze met hers, seeming to probe her very soul. "Second thoughts?"

"Not really."

He pulled into the garage, switched off the ignition. "Do not lie to me, Kelly."

She sighed deeply. "Sometimes it's just so hard to believe."

"Yes, I know what you mean. There are nights when I wake up and for a minute I almost forget, and then . . ."

"Then?"

"I hear your heartbeat, and I feel that damnable hunger stir to life inside me."

"Do you ever see the vampire who made you?"

Ramsey nodded. "He lives not too far from here."

The knowledge surprised her. "Are there a lot of vampires running around in the city?" It was hard enough to accept that there could be one; more than that was inconceivable.

"More than you might think. I know of four besides myself."

"Who are they?"

"Chiavari, he is the one who brought me across. And then there's Khira, who brought him across. Noah Fox . . ."

"The billionaire businessman! I don't believe it."

"It's true. Me, of course. And Madame Rosa."

Kelly laughed. "Madame Rosa? You're kidding! I saw her on the Leno show one night. She was amazing."

"I don't imagine any of them will be around much longer."

"Why not?"

"Khira."

Kelly looked at him askance.

"She's a very old vampire, and very powerful. And she doesn't like to share territory with other vampires. She's already gotten rid of two of them. Shall we go inside?"

"Yes, let's." Kelly slid out of the car and glanced over her shoulder, her gaze probing the shadows.

"It is all right," Ramsey said. "We are alone."

He felt her relax when they were in the house, with the lights on and the doors locked. "You will always be safe here," he said. " A peculiar truth about vampires is that they cannot enter a dwelling without being invited. And Khira has never been invited." He paused. "Kelly?"

"Yes?"

"You must never, under any circumstances, invite a stranger into this house. No one. Not ever!"

She regarded him through eyes wide with trepidation and curiosity. "What does she look like? Khira?"

He shook his head impatiently. "It doesn't matter . . . she has incredible powers . . . but she cannot force her way in here. Never open the door for anyone you don't know. It's the only way you can be safe here when I'm away. Promise me!''

"All right, all right. Geez, stop worrying. I promise.'' She looked at him, a smile hovering over her lips despite the seriousness of their conversation. "I don't want anyone nibbling on my neck but you.'' She squeezed his arm. "I like it that you're so protective of me, Edward. It makes me feel safe.'' And then, with one of those sudden changes of direction he was getting accustomed to, she tilted her head to one side, regarding him with unabashed curiosity. "Do vampires ever get married?''

"Some do.''

"Do they marry other vampires?''

"I don't know about that. I only know of one who is married, and he is married to a mortal.''

"Who's that?''

"Chiavari.''

"Could we visit them? I'd like to meet a woman married to a vampire.'' Her eyes were glowing again. "Maybe she has something to share with me, some advice. You know, how to keep your vampire happy?''

He closed his eyes. Marisa. Once, he had hoped to make her his wife.

"Edward?''

"Sure.'' He opened his eyes and Marisa's image faded from his mind. "I'll call them.''

They agreed to meet at a nearby theater the following night. A double date, Ramsey mused. He had never been on a double date in his whole life.

Kelly came downstairs dressed in a pair of slinky black pants and a pale-pink sweater. Her hair fell over her shoulders like a fall of black silk. She smiled nervously when she saw him waiting for her. "Maybe this isn't such a good idea.''

"We can stay home," Ramsey said, hoping she would change her mind. He wasn't crazy about the idea of spending the evening with Chiavari and Marisa.

She thought about it a minute, then shrugged. "Let's go."

Ramsey spotted Chiavari's black Corvette when they pulled into the theater parking lot. Chiavari and Marisa were waiting outside the theater.

Marisa looked beautiful as always, her face framed in a cloud of dark-brown hair, her green eyes bright with life.

They spent a moment making introductions. Marisa shook Kelly's hand, kissed Edward on the cheek. Chiavari bought their tickets, and they entered the lobby.

"Grigori, would you get me some popcorn?"

"My pleasure, *cara*. Kelly, can I get you anything?"

"A Coke, please."

The three of them stood to one side, waiting for Chiavari. Ramsey felt Chiavari's power crawl over his skin, so strong, so unmistakable, he wondered that the other people in the theater didn't feel it as well.

"I must admit I was surprised when Grigori told me you'd called," Marisa said.

Ramsey smiled at Kelly. "I was a little surprised myself."

"Have you two known each other long?" Marisa asked, glancing from Edward to Kelly and back again.

"A few weeks." Kelly and Edward answered at the same time.

"Let's go," Chiavari said. He handed the popcorn to Marisa, a Coke to Kelly. "The show's about to start."

The lights dimmed as they took their seats. Settling back, Ramsey wondered what the audience would think if they knew there were two vampires in their midst. It seemed suddenly funny—ludicrous, even—that he should be there. He had never thought of vampires as going out on dates. Even though he had known it wasn't true, in his mind he had always pictured the undead forever lurking in the dark-gray shadows of midnight, preying on the young and the helpless.

About halfway through the show, Marisa leaned toward Ramsey. "Does Kelly know?" she whispered.

He nodded, and she smiled at him. She smelled of lavender soap and warm womanly flesh. And Chiavari. The vampire's scent clung to her, a clear mark of possession. Once, the thought of her being with Chiavari would have roused his jealousy, but no more. Impossible as it seemed, Kelly had become his world, his reason for continuing his existence.

They went out for a late dinner after the movie. Marisa and Kelly chatted like two old friends, discussing the movie they had just seen, the latest White House scandal, the outrageous new fall fashions.

Chiavari insisted on picking up the check. While he paid the bill, Marisa took Ramsey aside. "She's charming, Edward. I think she's in love with you."

"What?"

"You heard me."

"Don't be ridiculous. What woman would love me now?"

"Edward, you're a wonderful man. Why shouldn't she love you?"

"It's not right." But his pulse was accelerating nonetheless. Could it be true . . . ?

"Why not?" Marisa asked.

For a moment, he wondered if she was reading his thoughts. "She is alive. I am not. It's as easy as that."

"Oh, for goodness' sakes! You're not dead. The dead don't walk and talk."

"All right, undead. Not dead. Call it whatever you want, it just isn't natural for her to be with someone like me."

"So, you don't think I should be with Grigori?"

"You know I don't."

"Edward, get over it. You're the same man you always were."

He laughed at that—a harsh, ugly laugh filled with bitterness. "No, Marisa, I am not."

"Grigori and I are happy together, Edward. There's no reason why you and Kelly can't have a good life together."

"How can you even think that? Chiavari is no good for you. He never was. Sooner or later, you will regret being his wife."

Marisa shook her head. "No, never."

Kelly had been watching them; now she came over. "Is something wrong?"

Ramsey smiled at her. "No, nothing's wrong." It was a good thing he couldn't eat anything, he mused, because a lie like that would certainly have brought it all back up.

Kelly was unusually quiet as they drove back home. Time and again, he considered probing her mind to learn what was wrong, but he had promised not to invade her thoughts. And even if he hadn't promised, what right did he have to invade her privacy just because he could?

"Is something wrong?" he asked.

"What? Oh, no, nothing. Marisa's very nice, isn't she?"

He nodded.

"They seem very happy together."

He nodded again.

"He's very handsome."

Ramsey swore under his breath.

"He's very powerful, isn't he?"

"Do we have to talk about him?"

"Why, Edward, I believe you're jealous." She looked at him, her expression shrewd. "You are jealous, aren't you? Because I think he's handsome?" She frowned when he didn't answer. "Because of her? That's it, isn't it? You were in love with her. Are you still?"

"It doesn't matter anymore."

Her teeth worried her lower lip for a moment. "Maybe I'd better leave."

"No!"

"I think it's for the best."

"Kelly . . ." He reached for her hand, but she pulled it away.

"I'll leave in the morning."

He didn't say anything. Maybe it was for the best. He was getting much too fond of her, becoming too dependent on her. And in spite of everything, he believed what he had told Marisa. It wasn't natural for the undead to pair up with the living. Sooner or later, it was sure to lead to disaster.

He focused his attention on the road. It stretched ahead of him, long and black and dreary, like his future.

Chapter 16

"What were you and Ramsey talking about?" Grigori asked. "It looked serious."

"It was."

Grigori pulled off the freeway onto a narrow side street. "Are you going to tell me," he asked, putting the gear shift in park, "or make me guess?"

"She's in love with him."

Grigori laughed softly. "A blind man could see that."

"He's worried about it. He thinks it's wrong for them to be together."

"I see." He slid a glance at the woman beside him, attuned, as always, to every gesture, every nuance in her voice and expression. He wondered if she knew that Ramsey was in love, not with Kelly but with her.

"I told him that he was being ridiculous, that you and I were perfectly happy together."

Grigori grunted softly, wondering who she was trying to convince.

"I told him there was no reason he couldn't have a good life with Kelly."

"Go on."

"He said . . ." She turned her head and looked out the window.

"What did he say?"

"He said that sooner or later I would regret our marriage."

Grigori's hand tightened on the steering wheel as he fought to maintain his calm. Damn Ramsey! That sanctimonious jackass! "Do you believe that?"

"No."

"Marisa, look at me."

She turned her head. He could see her face clearly even in the darkness—the soft curve of her cheek, her full pink lips—but it was her eyes that held his gaze. She had beautiful eyes, as green as fine jade. Expressive eyes that could not lie.

"I don't regret anything," she said fervently. "I love you, Grigori. I always will."

He couldn't wait any longer. Switching off the engine, he drew her into his arms and kissed her, heat spiraling through him like summer sunshine as she melted into his embrace. It had ever been like that between them, he mused. A look, a touch, and the fire that had pulsed between them from the first sprang to full flame.

He murmured her name as he kissed her, the sweetness of her kiss flowing over him, soothing him, arousing him. She tilted her head to one side, granting him access to her throat, moaning with pleasure as his teeth grazed her neck.

"Marisa?"

He didn't take from her often, took only a few small sips when he did, and never without asking her first. She found it very endearing somehow, especially since she had never refused him, would never think of refusing him.

There was no pain, only a quick heat followed by a languid sense of pleasure. And then he was kissing her again, his clever mouth arousing her, making her think of dark nights and satin sheets and the ecstasy of his body pressing against hers.

"Let's go home," she said. "Hurry."

He smiled at her, his eyes hot as he opened the door and got out of the car. Rounding the vehicle, he opened her door and swept her into his arms.

"What are you doing?" she gasped.

"Taking you home the fastest way I know how," he said.

There was a faint roaring in her ears, a dizzying sense of incredible acceleration as he moved through the night with preternatural speed toward home.

She was laughing when he set her on her feet in their living room moments later. "You really were in a hurry, weren't you?"

He nuzzled her neck, his tongue a flaming caress against her skin. "Tell me you aren't?"

She wrapped her arms around him, her heart pounding with joy and excitement. Once, she had been afraid of him, but no more. No more.

He was the air she breathed, the center of her world, the reason for her existence.

She closed her eyes, felt his power breathe across her skin. One day soon, she would ask him to make her as he was. But not now. Not tonight. Tonight she was content to be mortal.

She sighed his name as he kissed her again and she was caught up in the magic that was Grigori.

Chapter 17

Noah Fox bade his financial adviser good night, then went to the window and gazed down at the driveway below. As soon as he was certain the man was off the premises, he called downstairs and informed his staff he was retiring for the night and would have no further need of their services.

Going into his bedroom, he took off his designer dress shirt, slacks, and loafers and donned a pair of black sweats and tennis shoes. It was a simple matter to leave the grounds without being seen.

He had not fed for several days, preferring to hunt the night when the hunger was clawing at his vitals, when the driving need for sustenance added zest to the chase, making the reward all the sweeter.

He had always harbored a secret yearning to be an actor, and he indulged the fantasy when he was on the hunt. Some nights he played the English lord: polite, polished. Some nights he played the rogue: brutal, arro-gant. At other times he took on the persona of a swashbuckling pirate; sometimes, like tonight, he pretended he was just an ordinary mortal out for a late-night walk.

At one time or another, he had hunted the plush homes of Beverly Hills and the cardboard shacks of the homeless, plundered the beaches, roamed the desert resorts and mountain cabins.

He prowled the streets of the city, preying on the young and the old, male and female, but young females were his prey of choice. He loved the smell of them, the taste of them, their innocence and vulnerability.

He licked his lips as he walked down the deserted street. Dark-gray clouds hung low in the sky. He was passing an alley when he felt it: a heaviness in the air. It made every hair on his body stand at attention.

He had never been a coward. Even as a mortal, he had feared little, but he was afraid now without knowing why.

A gust of jasmine-scented wind slapped his face and he whirled around, his gaze probing the night. "Who is it? Who's there?"

His only answer was silence, and a feeling of being closed in by an otherworldly power stronger than his own. "Show yourself, damn it!"

Was it his imagination, or did he hear a faint sound of mocking laughter?

It had been decades since he had known fear, but he felt it now, creeping down his spine, coiling around his insides like the cold bony fingers of certain death. Was this what his victims felt as he closed in on them, this horrible sense of doom, of knowing that, no matter how fast they ran, there was no escape?

And he was running now, skimming across the ground with preternatural speed, yet the other stayed close behind him, driving him out of the city toward the small wilderness area that bordered the southeast edge of the town.

Trees and thick shrubs rose up before him, and he ran toward them, as if they could offer him refuge from the terror that stalked him.

With a cry, he fell to his knees and began to dig into the dirt, hoping to find sanctuary deep in the earth. Too late, too late. A strangled cry escaped his lips as a hand closed over his shoulder and lifted him effortlessly to his feet.

It was then he got his first glimpse of his pursuer. He almost laughed with relief—until he looked into her eyes. How could such a beautiful woman have such hellish eyes?

"Hello, Noah."

He licked his lips. "Khira."

"Didn't you get my message?"

He nodded, his movements jerky, like a puppet on a string. "I was going to leave tomorrow night."

"You were supposed to leave last week."

"I . . . I had some . . . some matters of business that I had to take care of."

A smile curved her lips. He wondered if it was meant to be reassuring. It wasn't.

Her fingers dug into his shoulder, the nails piercing the cloth and the skin beneath. The smell of blood filled the air. His blood. Red. Dark.

He stared at her, mesmerized, as her lips drew back to reveal her fangs. "After tonight, you won't have to worry about business anymore."

"Khira . . ." He tried to pull away from her.

She laughed softly. He was a tall man, strong and lean, but he had no strength at all compared to hers. She reveled in her power, her strength. As a mortal woman, she had been nothing but chattel, without rights, without physical strength. Subject to her father's will, she'd had nothing to say about her life, her future. Had her father been so inclined, he could have sold her and no one would have questioned his decision. But now—ah, now—no man on earth was her equal or her master.

"Khira . . . please . . ."

"Vampire blood is the sweetest of all," she murmured, and with a low growl, she buried her fangs deep in his throat, and drank and drank, drinking his strength and his blood, his memories and his knowledge.

He struggled helplessly against her, his heart beating frantically. His hands clawed at her, locking on her arms in an effort to break her hold, but to no avail. His essence filled her, flooded her, warmed her. She held him to her until his heart beat its last, until the spark that had been Noah Fox ceased to exist and all that remained was a dry, empty husk.

She left the body concealed behind a clump of shrubbery. The dawn's light would dispose of the remains quickly and efficiently, leaving nothing behind.

Licking the blood from her lips, she left the park.

Chapter 18

Kelly was gone when Ramsey rose the following night. The house was empty, silent as a tomb. An apt comparison, he mused bleakly.

He showered, dressed, then wandered through the dark, quiet house. He paused in the third-floor turret room, staring down at the grounds below. Where had she gone? Back to that seedy hotel? Or one like it?

Why had she really left? He couldn't believe she was jealous of his feelings for Marisa. The few weeks he had shared with Kelly had been the happiest of his life. He smiled bitterly. Or death. She had banished his loneliness. Her blood had soothed the ravening hunger within him, made it manageable. There had been times when he had felt almost human again. And her kisses . . . He closed his eyes, remembering. Sweet, so sweet. Damn her for making him think they could have some sort of life together, for giving him hope and then running away.

He opened his eyes and stared into the darkness.

He could stand here until dawn, then jump from the window. Perhaps landing on the flagstones below would render him unconscious before the sun incinerated him. And perhaps not.

Kelly.

His heart ached for her; his body cried out for the relief that only her blood seemed able to provide.

Kelly.

His mind screamed her name.

Turning away from the window, he went downstairs. It was then he saw the newspaper lying open on the living room table. The headline read:

NOAH FOX, RECLUSIVE MILLIONAIRE, MISSING FOUL PLAY SUSPECTED

He read the story quickly. According to his household staff, Fox had spent the previous evening in his study with his financial advisor, Bryan Knowlton. Knowlton had left the house at midnight. Again, according to his staff, Fox had spent the remainder of the evening watching movies in his study, and then gone to bed. It was his habit to sleep during the day, and his absence hadn't been noted until a little after six o'clock, when the butler went in to lay out Fox's attire for the evening. The butler reported that there was no sign of violence in the room. Other members of the household staff had been questioned. No one had seen Fox since the night before. No one had heard anything in the night. No one had come to the house after Knowlton left.

Ramsey tossed the paper onto the kitchen table. It was possible that Fox had decided to leave town, but it seemed doubtful. If he had left on his own, wouldn't his staff know? Wouldn't his financial advisor know? Fox had lived in the city for over twenty years. Certainly, he would have taken his clothes and personal effects.

Unless he didn't have time. Unless something had scared him so badly he had run for his life.

Ramsey chuckled mirthlessly. There was nothing scarier than Khira. He could hear her voice in his mind, as clearly as if she stood beside him. *I don't like to share.* One way or another, Noah Fox was gone from the city; that much was certain.

Ramsey grunted softly as he left the house. "Three down, three to go."

That night, he hunted with a single-mindedness that would have made Khira proud. He had no mercy in him that night, his only thought to satisfy his hunger. The beast raged within him, clawing at his vitals, demanding to be fed.

Only when he was bent over his victim, his savage thirst slaked at last, did he give a thought to the woman in his arms. Only then did he realize she was hardly breathing, that her heartbeat was faint and labored.

He looked up as familiar laughter reached his ears. "Khira."

She materialized before him: regal, ethereal, a vision with silver hair and blue eyes that could be as warm as a summer sun or as cold as winter ice.

She floated toward him, her feet not touching the ground. "Finish her, Edward. Accept what you are." Her voice moved over him, soft and seductive, sweetly coaxing. "You will never be at peace until you do."

"Are you at peace?" he asked. "How many lives have you taken to satisfy your monstrous lust for blood? Do none of them haunt you?"

"How dare you speak to me like that?" Power coalesced around her. He felt it sizzling through the air, prickling the hair on his arms, raising the hair on his nape.

She could be the answer he was looking for, he thought, if he just had the guts to push her a little harder. But not tonight. He glanced at the woman in his arms. "How do I revive her?"

"You don't. Take her, Edward!" Her eyes flashed blue fire. "You want to. I know it. And so do you."

"No."

She glared at him in disgust, and with a wave of her hand, she was gone.

Ramsey stared at the woman in his arms. He couldn't let her die, damn it; he couldn't. With a savage cry, he willed himself to the nearest hospital. Blocking their presence from the security guard at the door, he moved down the corridor until he found an empty gurney. He laid the woman on it, covered her with a blanket, then summoned a doctor to her side and vanished from the building.

The night stretched out before him: dark and empty like his past. Like his future. Feeling a sudden need for the company of others, he speeded across town.

The nightclub was crowded, filled with people who, for reasons of their own, were more comfortable hidden in the shadows than basking in the light. The atmosphere was dark, the air heavy with the odor of too many bodies, too much booze.

A single couple swayed on the small dance floor, their bodies so closely entwined it was hard to tell where one ended and the other began.

Ramsey found a place at the end of the bar and ordered a glass of red wine.

"Edward? Edward Ramsey, is that you?"

Ramsey turned at the sound of his name, smiled at the man shouldering his way through the crowd toward him. "Tom!"

Tom Duncan slapped him on the back. "Ramsey, you old son of a vampire hunter, how the hell are you?"

"I'm good. What are you doing in L.A.?"

"On the hunt, as always," Tom replied. He sum-

moned the bartender and ordered a screwdriver. He
punched Ramsey on the arm. "We haven't hunted
together in years. Remember the last one?"

Ramsey nodded.

*He stood beside the vampire's coffin, watching while Tom
placed heavy silver chains across the vampire's neck, chest, and
legs, then placed a large silver cross on her breast, over her
heart. The vampire had awakened the moment the silver touched
her skin. The air had filled with the stink of scorched flesh.
The vampire had cursed them, hissing and screeching when
she discovered she could not move. Her eyes had blazed red
with fury and fear when Ramsey placed the stake over her
heart. He had lifted the heavy wooden mallet without hesitation.
It never failed to surprise him, the amount of blood that foun-
tained from the killing wound.*

The vampire had screamed once.

It had been Tom's lot to take the head. . . .

Ramsey's gaze moved over his old friend. He looked
the same as always: his dark brown hair worn short, his
brown eyes wary and watchful, old beyond his years. A
heavy gold cross on a thick gold chain hung from his
neck.

"I heard there were several vamps here in the city,"
Tom said, "so when I finished up my last hunt, I thought
I'd come here and give you a hand." He slapped Ramsey
on the back. "I've got my gear in the car. You got a
line on any of them?"

"One or two," Ramsey said.

Tom drew back a little. "You okay? You look a little
pale."

"No worries," Ramsey said. He sipped his wine. Tom

was one of the best hunters in the world. If he truly wanted to die, Tom was the answer.

"So, who's the head vamp in the city? Last I heard, it was Chiavari. I sure would like to take him out! What a coup that would be."

Ramsey nodded, his mind racing. Tom could be the answer to everything. All he had to do was tell the hunter where Chiavari lived, where Madame Rosa lived, where Khira lived, and where he himself lived, and leave the rest to Tom. Even though they had been friends for more than fifteen years, Ramsey knew Tom wouldn't hesitate to stake him if he knew Ramsey was a vampire. The man was relentless, tenacious. Merciless. Ramsey had taught him everything he knew.

Tom tossed back his drink and ordered another. "So, what do you say we meet up tomorrow afternoon and start sniffing around?"

"I wish I could," Ramsey said, thinking quickly, "but I'm leaving town."

"Damn, where are you headed?"

"The beach, the mountains—who knows?" The lie rolled easily off his tongue. "I wouldn't admit this to anyone but you, but after that business with Kristov, my nerves are shot. I need a break."

Tom nodded. "That was a rough one, huh?"

"You have no idea."

"How long are you gonna be gone?"

"I'm not sure. A month, maybe more."

Duncan pulled out a scrap of paper and a pen and scribbled down his address and phone number. "Give me a call when you get back. And don't worry, I'll look after things here while you're gone."

With a nod, Ramsey shoved the paper into his pants pocket.

Tom grinned at him. "And try to get a little sun, will ya? You look as pale as one of the undead yourself."

* * *

After leaving the bar, Ramsey walked the streets for hours, his mind in turmoil, his loyalties oddly divided. His first instinct was to tell Tom where the vampires of the city rested and let Tom destroy them. But how could he destroy Chiavari without hurting Marisa? And what of Madame Rosa, whom he had never met? And what of Khira . . . ? Of them all, Khira was perhaps the only one who posed a threat to both vampire and mortal alike. She was an indiscriminate killer—cold, efficient, ruthless. Just like Tom, he mused. Just like he himself had been until Grigori Chiavari turned his life upside down.

It was near three A.M. when he found himself standing outside Chiavari's house. It was the only house on the block with lights still burning. He debated a moment, then walked up the long drive.

The door opened before he could knock. Grigori stood there, shirtless and barefoot. "Ramsey. What the hell are you doing here at this time of the morning?"

"It's nice to see you, too."

Chiavari took a step back. "Well, come on in, as long as you're here."

"I've had more gracious invitations," Ramsey muttered.

"I've had more gracious guests."

Ramsey followed Chiavari into the living room, which was dark. "Where is Marisa?"

"She is upstairs, watching TV." Chiavari sat down on the sofa. "Sit down, and tell me what brings you here."

Ramsey dropped into the chair across from the sofa. "There's a hunter in town."

The words hung in the air between them.

"So," Chiavari said at length. "Anyone you know?"

Ramsey nodded. "Tom Duncan."

"I've heard of him. It is said he is one of the best."

"Yes. He knows you are here."

Chiavari grunted, apparently unconcerned.

"He wanted us to hunt together. I guess I don't have to tell you who he wants to hunt."

"I can guess. Does he know about the others?"

"I don't know." Ramsey laughed softly. "He told me I looked a little pale. I told him I was leaving town. A vacation."

"Might be a good idea. Until you decide whose side you are on."

"I'm not on any side," Ramsey retorted.

"Aren't you?" Chiavari laced his hands behind his neck. "Then why are you here?"

"Because of Marisa."

Chiavari's eyes darkened. "What about her?" he asked, his voice low and dangerous.

"She loves you. I do not want to see her hurt."

"I thought you told her she would be better off without me."

Ramsey grunted softly. "She told you that, did she?"

"Of course. We have no secrets between us. So, you came to warn me to spare Marisa?"

"I would kill you myself if I thought it would make a difference, but she loves you. Getting rid of you will not make her love me." He wasn't even sure he wanted her love now. It wasn't thoughts of Marisa that tormented him, but thoughts of Kelly.

"So, we have two killers in the city." Chiavari stretched his arms across the back of the sofa. "Khira and Duncan. But then, we are all killers, are we not?"

Ramsey took his leave shortly after that. Chiavari's words echoed in his mind as he made his way home. Funny, he had never thought of himself as a killer when he had destroyed vampires. You couldn't kill something that was already dead. He hadn't felt like a killer until he had taken that woman's life, until he had listened to the last faint beat of her heart. The fact that he hadn't meant to kill her didn't lessen his guilt. By accident or design, the woman was still dead, and it was his fault.

Duncan and Khira. Between the two of them, the city would soon be free of vampires. As for himself, he never wanted to kill again. There was blood enough on his hands already. And yet, without Kelly, the urge to kill grew stronger every night. Without her, life, such as it was, was not worth living.

Chapter 19

Kelly tapped her fingertips on the tabletop, her gaze moving restlessly over the crowd. Several couples were dancing to some sad country song. She stared at the drink in her hand, so far untouched. She hadn't craved a drink while living with Edward, but for the past week it had been all she could think about. Just one drink to help her forget, to ease her loneliness—her sense of having betrayed him, failed him. As she had failed at so many things.

She lifted a hand to her neck, wondering what was wrong with her that she should miss his teeth at her throat. It had been strangely erotic, having him drink her blood. She missed his dry humor, the touch of his gaze moving over her, hot not only with hunger but with desire. He had wanted her. She had known that from the first, yet he had ever been a gentleman. She remembered his kisses, the strength of his arms around her. No matter that he was a vampire, she had felt safe in his embrace. Protected.

Loved.

She pushed the drink away. Drugs, pills, booze. They weren't the answer to her problems. They never had been.

Rising, she picked up her handbag and left the bar. It was raining. Grimacing, she crossed her arms over her breasts and hurried down the street, wishing she were closer to home.

At first, she thought it was just her imagination, but then she heard it again, the sound of a heavy footstep. She paused, as if she were tying her shoe, and glanced behind her but saw no one. She wanted to run; instead, she walked briskly, her head up, her shoulders back. *Don't look like a victim.* Moving around the corner to the parking lot, she fished her car keys out of her purse.

She was slipping the key in the lock when a hand fell on her shoulder and spun her around. Before she could scream, he clapped his other hand over her mouth.

He was big. In the dark, that was her first and only impression. He dragged her toward the back of the parking lot, slammed her up against the wall of a building. Her stomach churned at the sour smell of his breath, roiled with fear as he grabbed a handful of her hair and bent his head toward hers.

Edward! Edward, help me!

She repeated the words over and over again as her attacker forced her down to the ground, his hands hot and heavy at her throat . . .

Ramsey whirled around, surprised when he didn't see Kelly standing behind him. Her voice had sounded so real, so near. It took him a moment to realize he was hearing her cry for help in his head.

He let his intended victim fall to the ground untouched. Seconds later, he was moving through the night with preternatural speed, his passing no more than a blur, a cool ripple in the air.

He took in the scene at a glance: Kelly writhing on the ground, her shirt torn, one eye black, the man pinning her down with one hand at her throat while the other tugged at her jeans. Rage consumed him, filled him, enveloped him, until his only thought was to destroy the man who had dared attack his woman.

Silent as death itself, he struck. Lifting the man as though he weighed nothing at all, he hurled him against the wall. There was a sickening crunch of bone as the man struck the wall, then landed in a puddle of rainwater. He didn't move. The scent of blood filled Ramsey's senses, but for once he had no desire to feed— knew he would rather starve to death than touch a drop of the man's blood.

Kelly looked up at him, dazed, a trickle of blood oozing from her lower lip. "Edward," she gasped, her voice raw. "You came."

She groaned when he scooped her up in his arms.

Ramsey brushed a kiss across her brow. "I'm sorry." Holding her gently, he willed them to his house.

He sent his thoughts ahead so that when they arrived, the lights were on, a fire burned in the hearth, a hot bath awaited her.

When he would have put her down, she clung to him, her face buried in the hollow of his shoulder. Great, shuddering sobs racked her body.

"We need to get you out of these wet things," Ramsey said.

"Not now; just hold me, please."

Feeling awkward and uncertain, tormented by her nearness, by the hunger she aroused in him, he dropped down into the easy chair beside the fire and held her close, one hand lightly stroking her hair.

"Did he . . . Kelly, did he . . . ?" He could find no tactful way to ask if she had been raped.

"No. You got there before he . . . before . . ." Tears flooded her eyes, soaked his shirt.

For the first time since Chiavari had given him the Dark Gift, Ramsey was grateful to be a vampire, grateful for the power that came with it. This night, he had truly killed a monster, he thought, and it hadn't been a vampire.

He held her and rocked her until her tears subsided, and then he took her upstairs. Keeping his gaze averted, he helped her out of her damp clothes, lifted her into the tub.

When he turned to go, she caught his hand. "Stay with me."

"Kelly . . ."

"Please. I don't want to be alone."

He glanced over his shoulder, relieved to see that bubbles covered her up to her shoulders. Certain he was making a mistake, he sat on the edge of the tub, his hands clenched at his sides. Did she know what she was doing to him?

"Are you sure you're all right?" he asked.

She nodded. "I am now." She ran her hand over his shirtfront. "You're all wet."

He shrugged. Rain, heat, cold: he was impervious to it all now.

"How have you been, Edward?"

He frowned at her. "How can you worry about me after what happened to you tonight?"

She lifted one hand to her face, winced when her fingertips touched the bruise on her left cheek. "I don't want to think about that. Not now."

He looked at the bruises on her face, thought of what that monster would have done to her, and was glad all over again that he had gotten there in time.

When she began to wash, he stood up and turned his back to her, but he couldn't shut out the sound of the water sloshing around her, couldn't keep his imagination from going wild, couldn't help wishing it were his hand holding the cloth that was moving over her body.

"Edward?" she called softly. "I need a towel."

He jumped as though scalded. Keeping his back to her, he pulled a towel from the shelf and handed it back to her.

She stood up, and he heard the water sluicing down her body. An aching need pulsed through him. He swore softly. Was she deliberately trying to drive him crazy?

He plucked his robe off the back of the door and offered it to her, again without looking at her.

He cursed his preternatural hearing, which allowed him to hear each move she made, no matter how small or how quiet. He could hear the cloth whispering over her skin as she slipped into his robe, hear her tying the sash around her waist. Hear each breath. He cursed the difference in their ages. She was young and fresh, with her whole life shining before her. He had been almost twice her age when Chiavari brought him across, and now he felt ancient, corrupted, a creature of the night whose soul was shrouded in blood and death and darkness.

He went suddenly still at the touch of her hand on his back.

"Thank you for saving me, Edward."

Slowly he turned to face her. "I will always be here when you need me, Kelly."

She looked up at him, her gaze intent upon his face. "Always?"

Unspoken between them was the knowledge that he did not want his life to go on, that he had tried to end his existence and failed.

"Kelly . . ."

"Always, Edward? Can you promise me always?"

"Will you stay with me this time, Kelly, no matter what happens?"

"Yes."

"Then I promise I will be here for you for as long as you wish it. You are the only light left for me," he said, his voice thick. "I don't think I am strong enough to go on without you. Promise me you'll never leave me again."

Her hand cupped his cheek. "I promise." She tilted her head to one side, a faint smile curving her mouth. "Do you think we should seal our vows with a kiss?"

He slid his arms around her waist and slowly drew her toward him. "Kelly . . ."

Rising on her tiptoes, she put her arms around him and murmured, "Kiss me, Edward."

The press of her body against his, the whisper of her breath across his face, filled him with an aching tenderness the likes of which he had never known. He drew her closer, crushing her breasts against his chest. Sweet, so sweet. He kissed her tenderly at first, afraid to hurt her, afraid that he would somehow repulse her, that she would change her mind and pull away.

He was startled when he felt her hips move against his groin, felt her hands slide down to cup his buttocks, felt the tip of her tongue brush his lower lip.

"Kelly . . ." He gasped her name as desire flared within him, hot and bright as Fourth of July firecrackers.

She opened her eyes and smiled up at him, a lazy seductive smile. "Yes, Edward?"

He cleared his throat. "What are you doing?"

"What does it feel like I'm doing, silly? I'm kissing you. Isn't that what you wanted?"

"Yes, but . . ."

"But?"

"Before when we kissed . . . that time on the beach . . . you said . . ." He was almost stammering. "I mean, you said we needed to slow down."

"Well, that was then," she said softly. "And this is now. A girl can change her mind, can't she? And I've changed my mind." She looked up at him, her eyes shining. "Have you?"

"I . . ." He felt his breath catch in his throat. He had hunted dangerous vampires, looked death in the face, but nothing had ever frightened him quite so much as his attraction to the woman gazing up at him through the thick veil of her lashes.

"What is it?" she asked. "What's wrong? You want me. I know you do."

"More than I have ever wanted anything," he admitted. "But I can't. Not now."

"Why?"

"I'm afraid I am not in control." The violence earlier, the smell of blood from his victim, the rush of the kill, the musky scent rising from Kelly: all called to the beast within him. Hunger clawed at his vitals, squeezing tighter, tighter, until the pain was unbearable.

She moved toward him, one hand outstretched.

He drew back. "Don't!"

Her arm fell to her side. "Should I leave?"

He shook his head miserably, afraid she had misunderstood. "I need—that is . . . oh, Kelly."

Damn it, it was humiliating to need her like this, to have to ask her for that which no one should take.

But he didn't have to ask. Seeing the torment in his eyes, she lifted the hair from her neck, turned her head to one side. "Take what you need, Edward."

"Damn it, Kelly . . ."

"Just do it, Edward," she said, her voice thick. "I want you to . . ."

A low growl rose in his throat as he lowered his head,

the beast stretching its claws, coming to life, rejoicing in what he was about to do. He felt his fangs lengthen, heard the increased beat of her heart, smelled her fear and her excitement as his hands curved over her shoulders, holding her firmly in place.

"Do it," she urged gently. She was trembling. "Do it. I want you to, Edward . . . but don't hurt me, please."

He drew back. Took a deep breath. This was Kelly. He needed her. She trusted him. Exerting every ounce of self-control he possessed, he lowered his head again. Ran his tongue over her neck in a loving caress.

Groaned softly as he took what she offered.

Wept, as he felt her hand caress his cheek.

"It's all right, Edward," she said with a sigh. "It's all right."

Closing his eyes, he let her sweetness assuage his unnatural hunger even as her nearness fanned the flames of his desire.

Chapter 20

Marisa was seated at a corner table when Kelly entered the restaurant. She was a pretty woman, Kelly thought—impeccably dressed in a beige suit and white silk blouse.

"Meeting for lunch was a good idea," Marisa said, smiling as Kelly took the seat across from her. "I'm glad you called."

"I'm sorry I'm late." Kelly spread her napkin in her lap. "Did you order already?"

"No. I'm in no rush."

"The days are long sometimes, aren't they?" Kelly said wistfully.

Marisa nodded. "Indeed, they are. And getting longer as the season wears on. I'm not looking forward to summer at all. Shall we order?"

Kelly nodded. Marisa ordered a Chinese chicken salad and iced tea; Kelly ordered a turkey club sandwich and lemonade.

When the waitress left the table, Marisa leaned forward. "I have a feeling there's more to this meeting than just lunch. Is something bothering you?"

"I'm in love with Eddie."

"Eddie!" Marisa laughed. "I've never heard anyone call him that."

Kelly grinned self-consciously. "I don't call him that out loud, but that's how I think of him." She placed her hand over her heart. "In here."

"Does he feel the same about you?"

"I don't know. I hope so."

"But?"

"He scares me sometimes," Kelly said, her voice low and urgent. "He's so unhappy being a vampire. Did you know he tried to kill himself?"

"Grigori told me."

"It was awful." She shuddered with the memory. "I found him in the cellar. I was sure he was dead. His skin was horribly burned, and . . ." She broke off.

"And you're afraid he'll try again?"

"Yes. But what really scares me is the way he seems to need my blood. He says it soothes him. Why should my blood be any different from anyone else's? And what if someday he can't stop? What if he . . . ?" She couldn't say the words out loud.

Marisa covered Kelly's hand with her own. "I don't think Edward would ever hurt you, deliberately or otherwise. He's a strong man. As for why your blood soothes him, I'm sure it's because he loves you. And the need for blood lessens as vampires age, if that's any comfort."

"Are you happy with Grigori? Are you ever sorry you married him?"

"Happy, yes. Sorry, no."

"But what about children?"

"That's difficult. I always wanted a big family. But I love Grigori with all my heart and soul. I can't imagine a life without him. And someday . . ."

"Someday what?"

"I'll become what he is so we can be together forever."

Kelly's eyes widened. "You want to be a vampire?"

"Not really, but it's the only way we can truly be together forever."

"I think it would be wonderful to be a vampire," Kelly confided. "Oh, not the blood part. I'm not sure I could do that. But just think: never to grow old, never to be sick. I could live without the sun. I've always been a night person, anyway. But the blood part . . ." She shook her head. "I just don't think I could do that."

Marisa drew her hand away and leaned back in her chair when the waitress arrived with their order.

Kelly grinned at Marisa when the waitress left the table. "Do you think she heard what we were talking about?"

Marisa laughed softly. "I hope not. You know, I read up on vampires a little after I met Grigori. It's no wonder no one believes in them. I mean, one book said that you could become a vampire if a cat jumped over your corpse, or if you were the seventh son of a seventh son. Who would ever believe such nonsense?"

"Well," Kelly said thoughtfully, "I suppose superstitions were a lot stronger in the past. I think people found ways to explain the unexplainable the best way they could."

"Yes, I suppose so."

They ate in silence for a few moments. Kelly glanced around, wondering what people would think if they knew she was in love with a vampire. Vampires in Los Angeles. Who would believe it? Sitting here, in a cozy restaurant, it seemed impossible.

She lifted a hand to her neck, felt a warmth where Edward had bitten her the night before. She had a sudden mental image of him lying in the cellar, trapped in his deathlike sleep.

"Have you ever asked Grigori what it's like for him during the day?"

"Of course. He told me it's natural for him to sleep during the day. He also told me that only young vampires are helpless when they sleep. He said he could sense the presence of others. I know there were times when he was aware I was in the room. He can stay awake a little after daybreak, and he can rise before the sun sets now. He told me that vampires, like humans, have a strong instinct for survival." Marisa paused a moment before going on. "He's also told me that the blood in Edward's veins is very powerful."

"Oh? Why is that?"

"Edward was brought across by Grigori. Grigori was brought across by Khira. Both of them are very old and very powerful. And he also has the blood of Alexi Kristov. It's a powerful combination. I should imagine he will soon be able to remain awake after sunrise and awaken before sunset. And as I said, the need for blood lessens as they grow older."

Kelly looked thoughtful for a moment. "So," she mused, "if Edward were to make me a vampire, would I be as strong as he is?"

"I would think so."

"How long are you going to wait until you let Grigori—what's the term? Bring you across?"

"I'm not sure. I was going to do it this year, after Christmas, but I think I'll wait a few more years. I want to spend as much time as I can with my family, especially my parents. Summer's coming. My folks have a cabin up at Big Bear, and we always spend a part of the summer up there. We usually go up there for Easter, too, and sometimes for the Fourth, or for Christmas. That's especially nice, with the snow and all."

"Sounds like fun," Kelly said wistfully. "I don't have any family—well, my mother, but she moved to England when she got married again. I haven't seen her in, gosh, must be four or five years."

"I'm sorry. You're welcome to the come up to the cabin with us this summer."

"I don't think so. I'm afraid to leave Eddie alone, you know?"

Marisa nodded. "Another time, maybe, when he's more at ease with what he is."

"Do you have a big family?"

"Not really. Besides my mom and dad, there's just my brother, Mike, and his wife, Barbara, and their four kids. But we're close. And we always have a good time when we get together."

Kelly nodded enviously. Her only family was her mother and her father, unless she counted her mother's three ex-husbands and her dad's two ex-wives. "Is Grigori going with you?"

"If he does, he won't stay with us at the cabin. It's a little difficult to explain why he sleeps all day."

"I guess it would be," Kelly said, grinning. "Of course, you could always tell them the truth. Who would believe it?"

"I don't know," Marisa said, her expression somber. "Maybe no one. But if just one person believes, well, you have to be careful, Kelly. The word *vampire* is like the word *shark*. People panic at the mere mention of either one."

"Well, I guess that's true. But sharks are a real threat. No one believes in vampires these days."

"I do," Marisa said. "You do."

"Good point."

"Did Edward tell you that there's a vampire hunter in town?"

"A vampire hunter? You mean like Van Helsing in Dracula?"

"Yes, and he knows Edward."

"He didn't mention it to me."

"I'm sure he didn't want to worry you. Kelly, don't be afraid to love Edward. He needs it more than anyone I've ever known."

Kelly thought about Marisa's words while she drove home. While she cleaned the house. While she showered and brushed her hair. She dressed in a silky green blouse and black jeans and then went downstairs. She tried to read the paper while she ate dinner, but she saw Marisa's words in the newsprint, heard them while she did the dishes and put them away. *Don't be afraid to love Edward. He needs it more than anyone I've ever known.*

It was raining again. She lit a fire in the hearth, then curled up on the sofa to wait for Edward to rise.

She loved him. If he loved her, perhaps they could have a life together. She had already adjusted to his lifestyle. Perhaps . . .

She felt his presence in the room, turned slowly to face him. His eyes, a deep fathomless blue, gazed back at her. A flame burned in their depths—a hunger that went beyond desire, beyond need.

He glided toward her, soundless, a predator on the scent of blood. Her gaze moved over him. He wasn't darkly handsome like Grigori. Grigori looked like a vampire should look, with his black hair and eyes. But not Edward. Dressed in a white sweater and gray slacks, he looked like the angel she had once thought him to be.

Her heart pounded wildly, thundering in her ears, as he sat down on the sofa beside her. "Edward." His name slid past her lips, hardly more than a whisper.

"Don't be afraid of me," he said.

"I'm not." It was a lie, and they both knew it.

"I will not hurt you; I swear it."

She offered him her throat, closed her eyes as he bent his head toward her. His breath was warm against her neck, his hand cool on her arm. There was no pain this time, only waves of pleasure that were oddly sensual.

"Kelly?"

Her eyelids fluttered open and she stared up at him. "It didn't hurt at all this time."

"Guess I'm getting better at it," he muttered.

"I love you, Eddie."

"Eddie?" He swore softly. "No one has ever called me that."

"I'm sorry, I won't do it again."

"No, no, I like it." He stared at her, blinked, and blinked again. "What did you say?"

"I love you."

"Kelly!" He shook his head. "You can't."

"But I do." Tears burned her eyes. "You're still in love with Marisa, aren't you? She's beautiful. I had lunch with her today."

"You did?"

She had shocked him this time; she could see it in his eyes. "Yes. We had a nice visit."

"What did you talk about?" he asked, his voice wary.

"What do you think?"

"That's what I was afraid of." He shook his head. "And you're still here."

"She told me there's a vampire hunter in town. Why didn't you tell me?"

"I didn't want to worry you."

"That's what she said. Is it someone you know, from before?"

Ramsey nodded. "He is an old friend. We have worked together in the past."

"Does he know? Did you tell him?"

"Hell, no. He probably would have staked me on the spot."

"But you said he's your friend!"

"He was, when I was human. He would be my enemy now, as I would have been his if the situation were reversed."

"I'm sorry, Eddie."

"Kelly." His hand stroked her cheek, slid around to cup the back of her head, slowly drew her closer.

Her eyelids fluttered down as he kissed her. His kiss was warm and tender. She felt his need, his desire. His loneliness. Once again, she heard Marisa's voice in the back of her mind. *Don't be afraid to love Edward. He needs it more than anyone I've ever known.*

Almost as if she could read his mind, she knew it was true, knew he had been lonely most of his life. He had dedicated his heart and soul to destroying those he considered evil, and now, in a cruel twist of fate, he had become what he hunted. He had lost his reason for living, and the loneliness, the emptiness, was slowly eating him alive.

She put her arms around him and drew him closer, her body pressing against his, her hands moving restlessly over his back, under his sweater. His skin felt warm beneath her fingertips. Her blood had done that.

She was breathless when they drew apart. She gazed into his eyes a moment, and then she kissed him, her tongue sliding over his lower lip. He gasped, his arms tightening around her, crushing her close.

"Eddie . . ."

"Kelly, I . . . we shouldn't . . ."

"Don't stop," she whispered. "Please don't stop."

"Have you ever . . . you know?"

She titled her head to the side, a question in her eyes. "Made love, you mean?"

He nodded.

"Of course. Haven't you?"

"Just once," he admitted. And then wondered if Marisa had told her about Khira. Girl talk! He was in uncharted waters in every direction. "Well . . . twice," he amended.

She was smiling at him tenderly. "You still remember how, don't you?"

"It doesn't matter."

"Why not? Oh!" Her cheeks turned scarlet. "You can't, can you? That's why Marisa can't have children. Oh, Eddie, I'm sorry."

He looked at her, his brow furrowed, his mouth agape. And then he laughed. "Is that what you think? That I'm a eunuch?"

"Yes. No. I don't know. I thought . . . Marisa said . . ."

"Vampires are sterile, Kelly. The dead cannot create life." His arms fell to his sides, and he stood up. "This will never work."

She reached for his hand, pressed it to her breast. "It doesn't matter."

"Of course it matters. You are a young woman with your whole life ahead of you. You deserve a man—a whole man, one who can give you children, one who can share your whole life, not just half of it."

"It doesn't matter. None of that matters."

"Damn it, Kelly . . ."

"It's true. I love you, Eddie, for better or worse. You said you loved me before. Did you mean it? If you don't, say so, and I'll leave, but if you do, then at least give us a chance. Please give us a chance."

He dropped to his knees in front of her. "I do love you, may heaven help us both. I love you more than I have ever loved anyone. And I need you, more than you can imagine." His knuckles stroked her cheek. "And not just your blood. But I'm so afraid . . ."

She put her fingertips over his mouth. "Don't be."

He took her hand from his mouth and kissed each finger. "You're the one who should be afraid," he murmured, and then, unable to resist her any longer, he stood in one convulsive movement, lifted her into his arms, and carried her up the stairs.

As soon as they entered her bedroom, doubts plagued him again. "Are you sure about this, Kelly?"

She nodded. "I'm sure, Eddie."

He smiled faintly. *Eddie.* Hearing that name on her lips made him feel more human somehow, younger, carefree. He lowered her to the bed, sat down beside her, and drew her into his arms. He felt like a teenager, nervous and unsure of himself.

Kelly wrapped her arms around him. "Kiss me, Eddie."

Her lips were warm and sweet, like honey kissed by the sun. He held her tighter, afraid to let her go for fear she might vanish. She moaned softly, a purely feminine sound of pleasure that sang through every fiber of his being. She leaned into him, her breasts flattening against his chest as her tongue danced with his. Desire blazed within him, hotter than the fires of the unforgiving hell that surely awaited him.

He groaned, the ache of his need painful in its intensity.

His senses came alive at her touch. His nostrils filled with her scent: shampoo and toothpaste, the soap she had bathed with, the chicken she'd had for dinner, a hint of smoke from the fire in the hearth, and over all, the tantalizing scent of her blood. His tongue stroked her lips, her neck, the taste of her skin more intoxicating than wine. He listened to the sound of her breathing, the beat of her heart, the soft sounds of pleasure rising in her throat. His hands slid under her sweater. Her skin was satin-smooth beneath his fingertips, warm with life.

He swallowed a gasp of surprise when she took his hand and placed it over her breast.

"Kelly." Her name was a groan, a plea.

Her clever hands removed his sweater; he kicked off his shoes. She shrugged out of her blouse; his hands were trembling visibly when he removed her bra.

"You are beautiful," he murmured. "So very beautiful."

He drew her into his arms, felt the warmth of her skin against the coolness of his own. Desire pounded through him. His fangs pricked his tongue.

He pressed her down on the mattress, one of his hands trapping both of hers over her head.

She gazed up at him, fear clouding the passion in her eyes. "Eddie?"

Fighting for control, he took a deep breath. The scent of her blood aroused his hunger. The beast roared to life, demanding to be released.

He opened his eyes, and for a moment he didn't see Kelly; all he saw was a way to end his pain, satisfy his hunger.

"I love you, Eddie," she whispered. "No matter what, I love you."

He closed his eyes, his whole body trembling as he fought against the pain, the hunger. It was a battle he could not lose. Doing so meant losing Kelly, losing his one chance at finding a measure of happiness in the hell that was his life.

"Let me," he whispered.

She turned her head to the side and closed her eyes, but not before he saw the tears trembling on her lashes.

It was the bravest thing he had ever seen anyone do.

He released her hands and slowly bent his head toward her. Murmuring her name, he ran his tongue over her skin, felt his fangs prick the tender flesh of her neck.

Her blood, the sweetest nectar in all the world. It soothed him, conquered the unnatural hunger, freed his natural senses to respond to her own need. She was reaching for him, her hips moving restlessly. "Please, Eddie . . ."

"Kelly. Kelly."

He had taken her blood, and it had forged a link between them that could not be broken. He whispered her name over and over again as he drew her back into his arms, his hands and lips adoring her as he claimed her at last—claimed not only her body but her passion and her love. Joined flesh to flesh, her thoughts became his, so that he knew what she was feeling, what she was thinking. What she wanted. He granted her desires before she could utter them, pleasured her as no other man ever would.

He had heard that people in love considered themselves two halves of the same whole, two souls but one flesh. He knew now what that meant, knew it in ways that mere mortals would never know.

It was an experience like no other. He was in his own body and in hers, experiencing everything she felt. Every sense was heightened, sharpened. She was his now, mind and body and soul, and he would love her and protect her as long as he had the power to do so.

Chapter 21

Madame Rosa took her last bow and left the stage. It had been a good night. The crowd had been with her; the volunteers from the audience had been willing to go along with her. She sensed their skepticism, their unbelief, yet, by the end of the show, she had made believers out of all of them. Of course, with her powers, it was easy to read their minds, to call up incidents from their past, to tell them (in a hushed whisper) the dark secrets they were hiding.

She loved the crowds, the applause. In days gone by, she had been an actress, a singer, a magician. And before that, the confidante of kings, a spy for worried queens.

Ah, she mused, such good times they had been.

She shivered as she stepped out of the theater and felt a brush of preternatural power sweep over her.

Khira!

The area reeked of the older vampire's malevolent presence.

For a moment, Rosa stood rooted to the spot. It had

been years since she felt fear, centuries since she had been in the presence of a vampire whose powers were stronger than her own. What to do, what to do? And then it was too late to do anything.

Khira materialized before her. "Rosa."

Rosa bowed her head slightly. "Khira. I had heard you were in the city, but I didn't believe it. What brings you here?"

"Boredom," Khira replied. She smiled, displaying her fangs. "Such an interesting spectacle you put on this evening." Her eyes glinted like blue ice—cold, impenetrable.

"You were there?" Rosa exclaimed, her eyes widening. "At my performance?"

"Yes. How gullible these mortals are."

Rosa smiled in agreement, her mind racing. Khira was not one to visit or make small talk. Why was she here? The answer came with blinding clarity.

With a shake of her head, Rosa took a step backward. "There's no need for violence between us. I'll leave the city tomorrow night."

Khira smiled. It was a predatory smile—cold, merciless. "There are too many vampires in this part of the world." Her voice was flat, devoid of feeling.

Rosa stared at the other vampire, and then, dissolving into mist, she fled.

The sound of Khira's laughter chased her down the street.

Chapter 22

Breathless and unfulfilled, Marisa stared up at Grigori as he rose up on his knees on the bed. Why had he stopped?

"Hey." She tugged on a lock of his hair. "Hey, why do I have the feeling all of a sudden that I'm alone?"

"What?" He looked down at her, his dark eyes shuttered, his jaw set. His long black hair framed his face.

A shiver ran down her spine as she looked into his eyes. She had known for months what he was, had seen him when the Hunger was upon him, had seen him helpless and in pain. She had seen him at his best and at his worst. Lately, caught up in the excitement of their marriage, she had put the thought of what he was from her mind. The hours they kept no longer seemed strange, and she had come to enjoy the night, to see the beauty in it. They often went walking when the city was asleep. With any other man, she would have been afraid to prowl the dark streets alone. But with Grigori, she had never been afraid. Until now.

"What is it?" she asked tremulously. "What's wrong?"

He looked at her a moment longer, his vampire self evident in every taut line of his body, and then he blew out a deep, shuddering breath. "You might say I just felt a disturbance in the Force."

"What?"

"Nothing." His expression softened as he lowered his head and kissed her.

"Grigori, tell me . . ."

But he was kissing her again, his mouth hot as flame. She moaned softly, everything else forgotten as his clever hands worked their magic upon her all-too-willing flesh.

Later, after Marisa fell asleep, Grigori slipped out of bed. He gazed down at her a moment, the love he felt for her almost a physical ache. In all his years, in all his life, he had never loved another the way he loved her. She looked so beautiful lying there, her hair spread like brown silk upon the pillow. A faint smile curved her lips. She looked, he thought, like a woman who had been well and truly pleasured, and he knew a brief moment of satisfaction before he turned away from the bed.

Naked, he went out into the yard and let the darkness envelop him. Eyes closed, he let his senses expand. The wind sighed over his skin. He heard the distant roar of traffic on the freeway, the sound of a young couple arguing about money, a cat prowling among the trash cans behind a market, the scratching of a rodent digging under one of the shrubs.

Earlier, he had heard Madame Rosa's frightened cry, felt her life force go out, and knew Khira had struck again. Khira. Powerful. Ruthless. Without remorse. Without scruples. What were they going to do about Khira?

He didn't think he had anything to fear from her. For all her bluff and bluster, she had always been fond of him. But what of Marisa? If Khira truly wanted to hurt him, she would do it through Marisa. Was he strong enough, powerful enough, to keep her safe?

He had been an unutterable fool to invite Khira into their home. Should she take it into her devious mind to hurt Marisa, she had only to wait until he was hunting far from home to make a move. He knew Khira's ability. She could be here and gone before he could sense her presence and return. She had been invited in, and now nothing would keep her out. He would have to be on his guard every minute until this matter with Khira was resolved.

He glanced up at their bedroom window. He could hear the soft, even sound of Marisa's breathing, the soft rustle of sheets as she turned over. *Marisa.* She had rescued him from centuries of loneliness, filled his heart with love, given him a reason to rise in the evening.

A thought took him back to her side. He would not go out hunting this night.

Sliding under the sheet, he drew her into his arms and held her close, his mind touching hers ever so gently. She was dreaming, dreaming that he was making love to her on the floor in front of a blazing fire.

Whispering her name, he turned her dream into reality.

Chapter 23

Kelly slept as late as she could, not wanting to let go of the dream, not wanting to leave the night behind. Never in all her life had she experienced such a night, or such a lover as Edward. His kisses had been sheer magic; his touch had aroused her to fever pitch. Most amazing of all, she had known what he was feeling, what he was thinking, as their bodies came together. Ecstasy. Bliss.

Knowing she couldn't put it off any longer, she slid out of bed. She showered, dressed in a T-shirt and a pair of faded blue jeans, and went into the kitchen.

She grimaced when she opened the refrigerator. It was empty save for some butter, a couple of cans of root beer, and a loaf of white bread rapidly turning blue. She tossed the bread in the trash, then checked the cupboards and sighed her annoyance. There was butter and jam but no longer any bread. Cereal but no milk.

"Looks like it's time to go shopping again," she muttered, wondering how one person could go through so much food so fast.

She made a fresh pot of coffee, then found a scrap of paper and began writing a shopping list.

And all the while, her gaze moved to the door that led to the cellar. Edward was sleeping down there. The phrase "sleeping the sleep of the dead" ran unbidden through her mind.

He had thoughtfully left his car keys on the counter. Pouring herself a cup of coffee, she left the house. She picked up her things from the boardinghouse where she had been staying before moving in with Edward again. After collecting her belongings, she went to the market and stocked up on food and wine.

After thanking the box boy for loading her bags in the back seat, she slid behind the wheel of the Porsche and switched on the ignition. Pulling out of the parking lot, she flipped on the radio, grinned when the words to "Eddie, My Love" filled the air. Her heart swelled with happiness as she sang along.

When she stopped at a light, a sports car pulled up beside her. She glanced over at the driver, who gave her a wink and a smile, then revved his engine. She smiled back at him, and when the light turned green, she put the pedal to the metal and left him at the line.

She was grinning when she pulled into the driveway. "Home at last," she murmured. The thought sobered her. She hadn't had a real home since she lived with her parents, and now she was living with Dracula in the house of dark shadows.

After she put the groceries away, she dusted and vacuumed, wondering if he knew she was there. What was it like when he slept? Did he dream? Was he aware of what was going on around him? Would he hear her if she spoke to him? Marisa had said Grigori was aware of what went on around him, but he was far older in the vampire life than Edward.

Leaving the vacuum in the middle of the living room, she went to the door that led to the cellar, and carefully made her way down the stairs. She found the light switch and, turning it on, frowned as she glanced around the room. At first she didn't see anything that looked like a door, and then she saw it. It was about a third the size of a regular door, painted the same color as the walls. There was no handle, no knob.

She knelt in front of it, wondering why it was so small. Anyone trying to get inside would have to crawl through on hands and knees. But perhaps that was the idea, she thought. It would certainly slow down any unwanted intruders, unless they were midgets. Or creatures of the night.

"Edward? Eddie, are you in there? Can you hear me?"

When there was no answer, she went back upstairs, anxious for nightfall.

Her voice penetrated the thick blackness that trapped him. He struggled toward awareness, cursing his inability to move. At first, he had feared she was in danger, that she needed his help, but there was no tension in her voice, no threat of fear, merely curiosity. He had always believed that vampires were totally oblivious to what went on around them when trapped in the Dark Sleep, but now he knew differently. He might be oblivious to others, but not to Kelly.

Pleased by the realization, he let himself fall back into the darkness once more.

She was waiting for him in the living room when he woke. She had dressed with care in a blue-and-white sundress and white sandals. Her hair fell around her shoulders in shimmering ebony waves. She smiled when she saw him. As if it were the most natural thing in the world, he crossed the room, bent down, and kissed her.

Her hands circled his neck. Drawing him closer, she deepened the kiss.

Ramsey drew back, his eyes glinting dangerously. "Careful, Kelly girl."

She smiled up at him as she tilted her head to one side. "Drink, Edward."

He needed no urging. He took what he needed, felt her sweetness move through him, filling him with a sense of peace, soothing the ravening hunger within.

"I'll be back soon," he promised. Kissing her again, he left the house in search of prey.

He felt Khira's presence almost immediately, spreading like a dark stain across the quiet summer night. Moments later, she was at his side, linking her arm through his.

"Edward, *mi amour!* How I have missed you!" She smiled up at him. "So tell me, my fair one, have you finally accepted what you are?"

"I guess so."

"Prove it to me, then. Come, hunt with me."

"I have other plans."

She pouted prettily, but he saw the predator behind the coquette. "Come with me." Her voice was as soft as velvet, but he heard the steel beneath.

He hesitated and then nodded. Kelly could wait. Khira would not.

They hunted in the heart of the city, preying on drunks and derelicts. She was not interested in killing on this night, but in the thrill of the hunt. She fed with wild abandon, toying with her victims, drinking greedily, then moving on. Ramsey watched, repulsed yet fascinated. She felt no guilt, no compassion. Once, she looked up at him, her fangs dripping blood, and he saw the exhilaration in her eyes.

It was near three in the morning when she grew tired of her sport. Giving him a kiss on the cheek, she bade him good night and vanished into the darkness.

With a weary sigh, Ramsey willed himself home.

Kelly was asleep on the sofa, her head pillowed on her arm. Kneeling beside the sofa, he kissed her cheek. "I'm sorry, Kelly," he whispered. "Forgive me."

Her eyelids fluttered opened, and he saw she had been crying.

"Kelly!"

Distressed by her tears, he drew her down into his lap and cradled her against his chest. "I meant to come right back," he said, "but I ran into Khira."

Kelly's eyes widened. "What did she want?"

"The same thing she always wants: a hunting companion. I dared not refuse her."

"You're afraid of her."

"Damn right. She is a killer, totally without mercy. And she is very powerful. Probably the most powerful vampire alive."

Kelly shivered. "You said you went hunting with her. Did she . . . did you . . . kill anyone?"

"Not this time."

Her eyes filled with horror. "You've killed before?"

"Just once," he admitted, "but it was an accident. You must believe that."

"I believe you."

"I will never forgive myself," he said. "I didn't mean for it to happen, but it was all so new to me, and the craving . . . Kelly, you cannot imagine the pain." Agitated, he lifted her onto the sofa, then stood up and began to pace the floor. "I know, that's no excuse for what I did, but . . ." He clenched his fists, slammed one against the wall. "Damn Chiavari! This is all his fault."

Rising, Kelly went to stand behind him, her arms sliding around his waist. "Eddie, don't. Please don't. I hate to see you torturing yourself this way."

"How can you stand to be with me after what I've done? I'm no better than Khira, no better than any of the vampires I have hunted."

"That's not true! You're a good, decent man. If you weren't, you wouldn't feel so guilty. And you're not to blame, not really."

"I'm nothing but a monster."

"Stop that!" She pressed a kiss to his back. "You're nothing like them, do you hear me? If it will make you feel better, you can take my blood, as much as you need, whenever you need it."

He laughed, a hollow sound devoid of humor. "You don't have that much blood in you, Kelly."

"I don't know anything about being a vampire, Eddie. I can't imagine what it's like, what you're going through. I wish I could help."

He turned to face her, his arms sliding around her waist. "You do help, just by being here. I don't know what I would do without you."

His arms tightened around her as she rested her cheek on his chest. Contentment flowed through him. He could do this, he thought; with her help, he could control the beast within him, learn to live with what he was.

Kelly sighed. "I love you, Eddie."

Marisa's voice echoed in the back of his mind: *"Grigori and I are happy together, Edward. There's no reason why you and Kelly can't have a good life together."*

"Kelly." He brushed a kiss across the top of her head. "Heaven help us both, I love you, too."

* * *

On Thursday, Marisa called and invited Edward and Kelly over to play cards the following evening.

"Cards?" Kelly muttered after Edward hung up. "How can she want to play cards at a time like this? Doesn't she know what's going on?"

"I don't know. Maybe Chiavari hasn't told her."

"Just a nice normal night with a couple of friends, is that it?" she asked.

"Normal," Ramsey muttered. "My life's never been normal."

They arrived at Chiavari's home a little after eight on Friday night. It was raining again, unusual for Los Angeles. "But perfect for a meeting of vampires," Kelly remarked, laughing.

Marisa had set up a card table in the living room. A fire blazed in the fireplace. "What shall we play?" she asked when they were all seated at the table. "Canasta? Pinochle? Hearts? Rummy?" She looked at Grigori and wiggled her eyebrows. "Strip poker?"

"Very funny," Grigori muttered.

"I like hearts," Kelly said.

"Hearts, it is," Marisa said. She slid the deck in front of Grigori. "You deal."

At first, they made small talk about the weather, about the movie Marisa and Grigori had seen the previous night, but eventually Kelly's curiosity got the best of her and the talk turned to vampires.

She looked at Grigori. "How long have you been a vampire?"

"Over two hundred years."

Two hundred years, and he looked no more than thirty.

"It's so hard to believe."

"Vampires are as old as mankind," Grigori remarked. "Every culture has recorded their existence, mostly as myths and fables. Some few have been recorded, like

Elizabeth Bathory, who was known as the 'Bloody Countess.' She murdered hundreds of young women. Not only did she drink their blood, she bathed in it, as well."

"Oh, that's disgusting," Kelly exclaimed, wrinkling her nose.

"There were others. John Haigh, who was known as the Vampire of London. Fritz Haarmann, known as the Hanover Vampire, Peter Kurten, the Vampire of Dusseldorf."

"Did you know any of them?" Kelly asked.

"No. In any case, they were not true vampires."

"Well, it's easy to believe there were vampires in the old days, but today . . ." She shook her head. "Who would believe it?"

"Tell her about the ranchers in Ojai," Marisa said. She looked over at Kelly. "It always gives me the shivers."

"What ranchers?" Kelly asked, her eyes bright with interest.

"About twenty years ago, some ranchers in California began finding cattle with their throats cut and drained of blood," Grigori said. "They decided a vampire was to blame. When they searched the area, they found a large stone box at a crossroads. As they neared the box, a large black dog attacked them. One of the men threw holy water on the dog and it ran away. When the men reached the box, they pried off the lid. . . ."

Kelly shuddered. "You're kidding!"

"No. They found a body inside."

Her eyes widened. "Really?"

"Indeed. They staked the creature and left the area, and, if the story is to be believed, no more dead cattle were ever found."

"You made that up."

"Sadly, I did not."

Kelly pondered that for a moment, then asked, "Can you do all the things vampires do in the movies? You know, turn into a bat, change into a mist, influence the weather—that kind of thing.''

Grigori smiled indulgently. "I don't know about other vampires, but I've never turned into a bat. We do, however, have many powers that mortals lack.''

"Like the ability to read minds,'' Marisa said with a wry grin.

Grigori smiled at her. "Yes. For that reason, vampires make good magicians and psychics.''

"Like Madame Rosa,'' Kelly remarked.

Sadness flickered in Grigori's eyes. "Yes.''

"Do you like being what you are?''

"As I said, it's a good life in many ways.''

Kelly leaned forward. "But?''

Grigori looked at Marisa. Not long ago, she had been certain she wanted to be what he was, but he knew she was having doubts, knew she had been having second thoughts ever since Khira had mentioned her regret at not being able to bear a child.

"I had lived a full life as a mortal,'' Grigori went on, his gaze on Marisa's face. "I had been married, had children. They were killed by a vampyre, and I chose this life to avenge their deaths. I was not aware of all the ramifications, of course. It is not easy, to be a vampyre. To watch those you love grow old and die. It is not easy to say good-bye to the sun. Not everyone can survive in a world of darkness.''

"Do you still miss the daylight?'' Kelly asked. "Even after so many years?''

He nodded. "But the loss of the sun was a small price to pay to avenge the deaths of my children.''

"Would you be mortal again, if you could?''

"I don't know.''

"So, you do like being a vampire?''

"I am used to it,'' Grigori replied. "After two hundred years, I doubt if I could go back, even if it were possible.''

"Kelly, let's talk about something else," Ramsey suggested.

"But I want to know all I can, Eddie."

"Leave her alone, Ramsey," Grigori said. "I don't mind answering her questions."

But later that night, after Ramsey and Kelly had gone home, Grigori found himself thinking of his wife and children again. The memory of losing Antoinette a second time stirred his anger, and his hunger.

He went to Marisa and drew her up into his arms. He hugged her tightly for a moment. "I'm going out," he said curtly. "I won't be long."

He prowled the dark streets, becoming a part of the night and the darkness, his thoughts chaotic. He wondered if Marisa was regretting her decision to marry him. She wanted children, and he could not fault her for that. He remembered his son and his daughter, the exquisite joy they had brought into his life, the laughter and the good times. He had loved being a father, wrestling with his son, taking walks with his daughter, telling them stories at night. What right did he have to deny Marisa the chance to have children, to experience the love and happiness he had known? He had loved her and wanted her and swept her into his world, selfishly thinking his love would be enough.

His hunger stirred, growling within him. *When you are out of control, people die.* Those were the words he had spoken to Ramsey. He repeated them now, to himself.

He found a young woman sitting on her front porch. Wrapped in a heavy jacket, she was watching it rain, her expression somewhat wistful. Effortlessly he cocooned her in his power, then bade her come to him. Like a sleepwalker, she rose and walked toward him. Taking her by the hand, he led her into the shadows, the beast within him clawing at his insides as the scent of her blood filled his nostrils.

He took her quickly, at that moment hating what he was doing, because it seemed to emphasize the distance, the difference, between himself and the rest of the world. Between himself and Marisa . . .

Marisa. Pain twisted his heart. He loved her desperately, needed her as he had never needed anyone, even Antoinette.

He closed his eyes, and only then did he become aware of the heavy, irregular beating of the woman's heart. With an oath, he drew back, his gaze frantically searching her face. She was pale. Too pale? He swore again. It had been decades since he had taken a human life, but he was perilously close now. Why? Why, after so many years, did he have this sudden urge to glut himself with blood?

Sweeping the woman into his arms, he carried her into the house and placed her on the sofa. He found a bottle of apple juice in the refrigerator and poured a glass, then carried it to her and commanded her to drink it.

When she was finished, he covered her with the afghan neatly folded at the end of the sofa. He stood there, watching her for several minutes, listening as her heartbeat grew stronger, steadier.

His mind gained a link with hers. *You will remember nothing of this night.* He searched for her name. *Sally Anne. Nothing beyond the time I called you to me. You will remember only that you sat outside and watched the rain, then came inside to get something to drink and fell asleep on the sofa.*

He was about to go out the front door when a battered pickup pulled into the driveway and a man got out, his shoulders hunched against the rain. Father, husband, boyfriend—he didn't know. Nor did he care.

A thought took him home.

Marisa had gone to bed. He stood there, watching her sleep, his heart aching with love. He should let her go. She would object. She would swear she loved him, that children weren't important, that she would never love anyone else, but, in time, she would find love again with a man who could share her whole life.

As though sensing his presence, her eyelids fluttered open. "Grigori?" She sat up, sleepy-eyed and beautiful.

Sitting on the edge of the bed, he gathered her into his arms and held her tight. He inhaled the scent of her, felt her arms slip around his waist, the silk of her hair against his cheek, the warmth of her body chasing away the coldness in his own. Guilt rose up within him. What right did he have to love this woman?

"Is something wrong?" she asked.

"No, *cara*, nothing's wrong." He kissed her cheek, her neck, shuddered with the need to taste her sweetness. Even though he had just fed, he felt empty inside.

She snuggled against him, one hand brushing the hair away from her neck. "Drink, Grigori," she urged softly.

He shook his head, denying himself the pleasure he sought.

"Grigori? What is it? What's wrong?"

"Marisa . . ."

Her hand cupped his cheek, soft and warm and tender. "It's all right, Grigori. Take what you need. I give it to you freely, willingly, as always."

And he closed his eyes and surrendered to the need burning within him.

Chapter 24

"Eddie, do you think you'll ever like being a vampire?"

"I don't know." They were home, in the backyard, sitting on the swing Kelly had bought earlier that day. Ramsey slid his arm around her shoulders and drew her closer.

She looked at him, her gaze searching his. "Do you still hate it?"

He thought of what he had lost: his humanity, the sun, the ability to sire a child to carry on the Ramsey name. He thought of the hunger, the darkness, the aloneness, the sense of being separated from the rest of the world. And then he thought of what he had gained: his increased senses; his immunity to sickness and disease and aging; his ability to read minds, control thoughts, move through the night faster than a thought.

"Not as much as I used to," he admitted slowly. His arm tightened around her shoulders. "If I weren't a vampire, I never would have met you."

"That's true," she said brightly. Leaning forward, she kissed him.

"Why were you asking Chiavari all those questions when we played cards the other night?"

"I was just curious. I've been thinking . . . Marisa's going to let Grigori bring her across. I don't want to be the only one who's not a . . ."

"Forget it, Kelly! Don't even think about it."

"I'm afraid of growing old, Eddie. I'm afraid of losing you."

"You will not lose me."

"You say that now. But how will you feel when I'm old and ugly? When people start thinking I'm your mother, or your grandmother?"

"Kelly . . ."

"I know you think of yourself as a monster, but I don't see you that way. I want to be like you."

"I've never done it." He shook his head. "It's too dangerous, Kelly."

"I'm willing to risk it."

"I'm not!"

"Maybe Grigori could . . ."

"No!" he said firmly, and left her sitting there, alone, in the dark.

She asked him the next night and the next, and every night for the next two weeks. And every night he refused, but the thought was always there in the back of his mind, teasing, tempting. He couldn't help thinking how nice it would be to have someone to share his life with him, someone who would understand, who would always be there. And even as he considered it, he wondered at the change in him. Once, he had killed vampires. Now, he was thinking of creating one.

She was waiting for him when he woke the next night. Sitting on the sofa, the lamp turned low, her hair falling over her shoulders like a river of ebony, her body clad in a nightgown that was no more than a whisper of peach-colored silk, she waited.

He might have thought of himself as dead, but his body came instantly to life, humming with need, with desire. "Kelly . . ."

She held out her arms. "You're hungry," she said, her voice low and sultry.

"Hungry" didn't begin to describe what he was feeling. Lost in the heat of her eyes, he moved across the floor like a sleepwalker, sank down on the sofa beside her, drew her into arms that trembled.

She tilted her head up and back, exposing the slender column of her throat. Her blood called to him, more enticing than any perfume, more intoxicating than the finest brandy.

"Do it, Eddie."

He knew what she wanted, knew she was deliberately tempting him. He should turn away, leave the house before it was too late.

"No." He shook his head even as he felt his fangs lengthen, felt the hunger awake and stretch its claws.

Her nails dug into his arm. "Do it, Eddie. Now."

He was afraid. Afraid for her, for him. "If I take too much . . ."

"You won't."

"This isn't something you want to rush into, Kelly girl. There is no going back once it's done. You need to be sure."

"I am sure." She cupped his face in her palms and kissed him deeply.

Desire and need clashed within him, fighting for control. She was sweet, so sweet. So warm, so alive. All that would change if he did as she asked.

She deepened the kiss, her tongue stroking his, her hands sliding up and down his back. His body responded to her touch, his desire growing. And with desire came the overwhelming need to feed. The hunger clawed its way to the surface as he held her closer, closer.

His lips slid down to her neck.

She moaned softly, her hands clutching at his shoulders, her fingers digging into his flesh.

She shivered as his fangs pierced her flesh, tensed as fear of the unknown overcame her eagerness. She cried his name, her voice hoarse, uncertain.

But he was past hearing. He drank deeply, aware of nothing but the pounding of her heart, the panic that made it beat harder, made the blood flow faster, sweeter. A distant part of his mind told him she wanted him to stop, but there was no going back, not now.

He drank and drank. Drank until her heart was beating in rhythm with his, until it slowed, almost stopped. He drew back abruptly, stared at her in horror. She lay across his lap, her head lolling over his arm, unmoving, barely breathing, as pale as death.

"Kelly! Kelly!"

Fearing he had taken too much, he bit his wrist and held the bleeding wound to her lips.

"Drink, Kelly," he urged. "You must drink. . . ."

Khira lifted her head, the young man in her arms momentarily forgotten as a new heartbeat rode the dark wings of the night.

"Ah, Edward," she murmured. "What have you done?"

Grigori paused on the narrow wooden pier, a sudden chill running down his spine.

"What is it?" Marisa asked. She glanced around the

park, wondering if Grigori had sensed danger lurking in the shadows. They walked here often in the evening. She remembered the first time they had come here, shortly after they met. She hadn't known he was a vampire then, only that he was dark and handsome and strangely compelling. That night, walking hand in hand through the park, had made her feel like a teenager with her first crush. She looked up at Grigori. He was wearing the same black sweater he had worn that night. It was a color that suited him, making it seem as if he were a part of the night itself.

He swore softly. "There is a new vampyre in the city."

"What do you mean?"

"Ramsey brought Kelly across."

"How do you know?"

"I can feel it." Grigori took her hand and started walking again. He turned left at the end of the bridge and made his way toward the shallow stream that cut through the middle of the park. "He would have been wiser to wait a while."

"What do you mean?"

"In a word, Khira."

"Oh."

"Exactly. Khira has already destroyed most of the vampyres in the city. To my knowledge, there were only three of us left; Ramsey, Lisa, and myself.

"Lisa? I've never heard you mention her before."

"She is Rosa's fledgling, and still new to the Dark Gift." Grigori shook his head. "Ramsey should not have brought Kelly across until Khira left town."

"Do you really think she'll leave?"

"She will go back to Italy sooner or later; I have no doubt of that." He stopped walking and drew Marisa into his arms. "I don't want to talk about her now. Do you remember the first night we came here?"

"Of course. You asked me what scared me, and I said vampires."

He nuzzled her neck. "Are you still afraid of vampyres?"

She slid her fingertips through the hair at his nape. "What do you think?"

"I think we should go home."

"Do you?" Standing on tiptoe, she nibbled on his lower lip. "Why?"

He drew her up against him, letting her feel the obvious evidence of his desire. "That's why."

She looked up at him and batted her eyelashes. "Why, sir," she drawled in her best Southern belle imitation, "whatever do you mean?"

Grigori burst out laughing. "Minx!"

"Minx! Minx, am I! Sir, if I had a fan, I should strike you with it."

He ground his hips against hers. "Do your worst, Miss Scarlett."

"My worst, sir? Oh, no, I shall do my best."

"Do not tempt me, *cara*, or I shall take you here, now."

"You're kidding, right?" Marisa asked, suddenly serious.

"No."

"But . . ."

He stilled her protest with a kiss as he swept her into his arms and carried her up the side of the hill until he came to a large weeping willow tree whose branches brushed the ground. Inside the shelter of the branches, he sat down, then slowly fell back, drawing Marisa down on top of him.

He had kissed and caressed her all the way up the hill. Now, locked in his arms, with his mouth warm on hers and his hands sliding seductively over her body, she had no thought except to pleasure him and be pleasured in return.

She moaned his name as his fangs brushed her throat. What would it be like to be able to give him the same kind of ecstasy he gave her?

Chapter 25

"What happened?" Kelly stared up at Edward, wondering why she felt so strange. She glanced around. Even though the room was dark, she could see clearly. "You did it, didn't you?"

He nodded. Had she changed her mind? Would she hate him now?

She sat up, seeing the room through vampire eyes. He felt the excitement thrumming through her.

"I'll never get any older!" She held out her hands and looked at them as if seeing them for the first time, and in a way, she was. She was a vampire now.

Rising, she ran to the back door and darted out into the yard. She gazed up at the moon, and it was beautiful as never before. She looked at a nearby tree, and she knew it was alive, could almost hear it breathing.

"Eddie, this is wonderful! And we'll be together forever!" She twirled around, caught up in the newness, the wonder.

He watched her from the doorway, waiting for the inevitable.

The pain hit her suddenly and without warning. Terrified, she doubled over, her arms wrapped around her waist. "What's happening?"

"You're dying."

"What do you mean?" She lifted her head and stared at him, her eyes wide with panic. "What have you done to me?"

He glided across the yard. "It happens to us all." Taking hold of her arm, he eased her gently down on the ground.

"I'm afraid!" Her hands clawed at his arm, her nails drawing blood. "Eddie, help me!"

"Don't be afraid. It is only mortal death, and soon over."

He had never seen it happen, though of course, he had experienced it. It had happened only moments after he left Chiavari's house the night Chiavari had brought him across. He had studied vampires all his life, so he had known what was happening; but it hadn't made it easier or any less terrifying, and so he held Kelly's hand while her body emptied itself of mortal fluids and his vampire blood infused her system.

When the pain had passed, he took her into the house, bathed her tenderly, then carried her down to his room in the cellar. He tucked her into bed, sat beside her until she fell asleep. When she woke tomorrow night, she would be wholly vampire. He only hoped she would not regret it.

He felt Khira's malevolent presence prowling in the yard, knew a swift moment of relief that he had never invited her into the house. He could feel her power pounding at him, demanding entrance.

"No way," he muttered, and with preternatural speed, he was up the stairs and out of the house.

She was waiting for him on the front lawn. "Looking for me?" he asked coolly.

"Why have you done this?" she demanded.

He shrugged. "She wanted it."

"I will have no more vampires in my territory." Her eyes flamed with the heat of her anger.

"You will not touch her," he said flatly.

Khira glared at him. "Need I remind you that you are fortunate to still be alive yourself, Edward?"

"Perhaps. Your threats grow tiresome, Khira."

"Do you doubt my ability to carry them out?" she demanded. But he detected a flicker of unease beneath her anger.

"You have killed three vampires since you have been here," he said. "But they were not me." Wrapped in the cloak of his own power, he met her gaze impassively. "I am not weak like LaSalle. You said yourself that I am strong. But even you do not know how strong."

"Why . . . Edward. Would you bare your fangs to me?" Her eyes were blue again, almost teasing. "To defend that . . . that . . ." Her voice trailed off, as though words failed her.

"She is mine," he said. "Mine. And none of your concern."

"I told you. I do not like to share my territory."

"L.A. is a pretty big town. I think there's room enough."

"It is not a matter of room, Edward."

"Damn it, leave her alone! Leave me alone!"

Fury blossomed in her eyes. He gasped and reeled backward as pain engulfed him, white-hot pain that exploded through every nerve, every muscle, every cell of his body. Trembling violently, hardly able to breathe, he wrapped his arms around his chest, then dropped to his knees as the agony increased. Head bowed, he closed his eyes, praying for an end to the awful agony that threaded through him. On fire. His blood was on fire, scorching his veins. He rocked back and forth, choking back the cry that rose in his throat. Pain. He had never known such excruciating pain, not even when he went out to meet the dawn.

Then, on the heels of the pain came rage. Rage such as he had never known. He was on his feet again, facing her. Forcing her power back upon itself. Her lips drew thin. He saw her blink, surprised. And then that trace of uncertainty again. He did not attempt to press, for fear of triggering another attack.

They stared at each other, the silence stretching between them.

Khira relaxed ever so slightly. "There is powerful blood in your veins, Ramsey," she admitted grudgingly. "Mine. Alexi's. And Grigori's. And something more . . . that rage of yours. That fury. Generations of Ramseys and their dirty calling . . . all concentrated in you. I could kill you now—oh, don't think I couldn't—but . . ." She paused, and he read the uncertainty in her eyes.

He said nothing, only watched her through unblinking eyes, waiting, wondering if it was all a bluff.

"It would cost me," she said. "Drain me." She regarded him for several moments. "Be careful of your tongue in the future," she warned, but he saw the doubt in her eyes, heard the confusion in her voice. "Keep your little fledgling. She is of no consequence. Surely not worth fighting over." She smiled coolly. "Not at this moment, anyway. Only be careful she does not cross my path."

He nodded, but she was already gone.

After going down to the cellar to make sure Kelly was resting comfortably, he left the house again, his mind reeling. He had met Khira's power and she had backed down! It was a heady feeling, diluted only by his weakened state; he had given a lot of blood to Kelly. Had he been at full strength, would he have been able to deflect Khira's power completely?

He prowled the dark streets hungrily. A sudden awareness, like a cold wind blowing over his skin, warned him he was no longer alone.

"Chiavari."

The vampire materialized out of the shadows. "Ramsey." The accusation was clear in his voice. "Why?"

"She wanted it."

"Do you know what you've done? Khira . . ."

"Has already visited me."

Chiavari lifted one brow. "Indeed?"

"Yes. I . . . thank you."

"For what?"

"You may have saved my life tonight. Khira attempted to exercise her power over me a short time ago. It hurt! Hurt like the very devil, but I remembered what you said about my having powerful blood. It must be true. She backed down. She said she could take me, but it would weaken her."

"Did she indeed?" Chiavari waved his thanks aside. "The test of your strength is good news."

"Good news? She almost . . ."

"Good news indeed," Chiavari said. "It means that, combined, we have the power to face her, if it comes to that. But you should not have brought Kelly across, not now. It complicates things. Weakens you, makes you vulnerable."

"Is that why you haven't brought Marisa across?"

"What I do is none of your business."

"But you want to."

Without conscious thought, they fell into step side by side and walked down the street.

"Yes, and no," Chiavari answered.

"I don't understand."

"We stay the same as we are when we change," Chiavari explained. "And yet we don't. Each individual reacts differently to the Dark Gift. Some embrace it." His gaze moved over Ramsey. "Some reject it and die. Some become drunk with power. Some, like Kristov, revel in the darkness of it."

"Did it change you?"

"For a time."

"And what of Khira?"

"Khira is a law unto herself. She always has been."

"So you said before."

"Do you doubt me?"

"No." Ramsey shuddered, remembering the pain she had inflicted on him with no more than a thought. He had managed to withstand her this time, but what of next time? He had surprised her tonight. If there was another confrontation, she would be ready for him.

Chiavari paused. Lifting his head, he sniffed the air. "There," he said.

Ramsey followed Chiavari's gaze and saw a couple standing in a parking lot, laughing.

"Blood for two," Ramsey muttered with a wry grin. "A girl for me, and a boy for you."

They were crossing the street when a voice called out, "Hey, Ed!"

Ramsey swore under his breath as Tom Duncan came hurrying toward him.

"Who is this?" Chiavari asked.

"He's a hunter," Ramsey replied, pasting a smile on his face. "And an old friend."

Duncan slapped Ramsey on the shoulder. "How was the vacation?"

"What? Oh, it was good."

Duncan nodded, but his attention was on Ramsey's companion. "Have we met?"

Chiavari shook his head. "Enjoy your friend, Ramsey," he said. "I'm going home."

"Hey, now, don't run off," Duncan said. "I didn't catch your name."

"I didn't give it."

Ramsey's gaze darted from Duncan to Chiavari and back again. The tension between the two of them was almost palpable.

"Any reason not to?" Duncan asked.

Ramsey groaned inwardly. Duncan might be built like a pro fullback, but he was no match for a vampire like Chiavari, not after dark.

"So, Tom," Ramsey said, hoping to distract his friend, "are you on the hunt?"

"As always," Duncan replied, his gaze steady on Chiavari.

Ramsey swore softly. His hunger, his need to replenish the blood he had given Kelly, cried out for the warm, sweet relief that Tom's presence denied him. But he had to defuse this situation.

"Let's go get a drink, Tom." Ramsey put his arm around Duncan's shoulder in a friendly gesture. "What do you say?"

"Sure, sure." Tom Duncan fixed Chiavari with a hard look. "I have a feeling we'll meet again."

Chiavari nodded. "Any time."

Ramsey practically dragged Duncan down the street. "Are you crazy?"

"We should have taken him."

"You are crazy! Do you know who he is?"

Duncan nodded. "Grigori Chiavari." He stopped in the middle of the sidewalk. "Why isn't he dead?"

"What do you mean?"

"I know he was involved in the Kristov mess. Why didn't you take Chiavari out at the same time?"

"He saved my life."

Duncan's eyes widened in disbelief. "I don't believe you. Why the hell would a vampire save your life?"

"It's a long story."

"Then you'd better start now." Duncan made an abrupt stop in front of a local bar. "I need a drink. Come on, you can tell me all about it over a glass of whiskey."

Ramsey followed Duncan into the bar. They found a table in a dark corner and sat down. Duncan ordered a whiskey, Ramsey a glass of wine.

Sitting back in the seat, Ramsey related, as briefly as possible, everything that had happened with Chiavari and Kristov, save for the last, damning part of the story.

"Grigori could have killed me, but he didn't." Ramsey took a sip from his wine glass. "That's it."

Duncan leaned back in the booth, his expression thoughtful. "Why do I have the feeling there's something you're not telling me?"

"I don't know. You tell me."

Duncan swirled the liquor in his glass. "Well, for one thing, you look different."

Ramsey tensed. "I do?"

"Yeah. I can't quite put my finger on it. . . ." He swore softly. "It's your clothes! That's it!" Duncan laughed. "You're not wearing brown!"

Ramsey muttered an oath. "You're too funny for me. I'm going home."

"But it's more than that," Duncan said, suddenly serious. He leaned forward, his gaze intent on Ramsey's face. "You look—I don't know—younger. What'd you do on that vacation of yours, anyway, get a face-lift?"

"Yeah," Ramsey said, laughing it off. "I had liposuction on my hips, too." Reaching into his pocket, he withdrew a ten-dollar bill and dropped it on the table. "Have another drink on me. I'm going home."

Duncan tossed down his drink. "Meet me here tomorrow. We'll go hunting."

"Never on Sunday," Ramsey muttered, and left the table.

He felt Duncan's gaze follow him as he made his way to the door. He knew his old friend would not rest until he had uncovered his secret. And when he did, one of them would die.

Chapter 26

Marisa was waiting up for Grigori when he returned home. He paused in the doorway, letting his gaze move over her. She was sitting on the sofa, her legs curled beneath her, a book open on her lap. She looked incredibly young, incredibly desirable.

"What's the matter?" he asked, stepping into the room. "Couldn't you sleep?"

"I was worried."

"Were you?"

"Is everything all right?" She closed the book and put it on the coffee table. Rising, she put her arms around him, stood on tiptoe, and kissed him.

It didn't occur to him to lie to her. "There is a new hunter in town."

Fear flickered in her eyes.

He smiled down at her. "Nothing for you to worry about, *cara.*"

"Worry?" She forced a smile. "Who, me?"

"He is a friend of Ramsey's, which makes it all the more interesting."

Her eyes widened. "You met him?"

Taking her by the hand, he led her to the sofa and sat down. Drawing her down beside him, he put his arm around her shoulders. "Yes. Tonight."

She clutched his arm, her gaze searching his. "You're in danger, aren't you?"

"Cara . . ."

"You are! I can feel it."

"Calm down, *cara mia.*"

"Calm down? Have you forgotten Alexi?" She twisted out of his embrace and began to pace the floor, and then turned to face him. "Let's just move. Now. Tonight."

He would have laughed if she hadn't looked so serious. "Marisa . . ."

"I'm so afraid of losing you."

Rising, he drew her into his arms once more. For a moment, she stood there, and then she drew back a little so she could see his face.

"You said he was a friend of Edward's. Does he know about Edward?"

"No."

"But he knows about you?"

"Oh, yes, he knows."

"How long do you think it'll take before he finds out about Edward? And what do you think he'll do?"

"If the situation were reversed, Ramsey would know already." The hunters had lost their best man when he brought Ramsey across, Grigori thought. Ramsey'd had an instinct that could not be taught, an instinct for detecting vampires that Tom Duncan obviously lacked. "As for what Duncan will do . . ." He shrugged. "Who can say?"

"He'll come after you, won't he?" It wasn't really a question.

"I'm more worried about the threat posed by Khira."

"Khira? Why? I thought she was your friend, that the two of you were . . . you know, more than just friends."

"Khira is not swayed by feelings of friendship or loyalty. She is, first and foremost, a predator. Jealous of her territory."

"Her territory! You were here first."

"That makes little difference. Though there is no royalty among vampires, Khira has always considered herself the queen. And none of us, save perhaps Kristov, had the guts or the power to change her mind."

"She's another reason why we should just move," Marisa muttered. "Why are you being so stubborn?"

"If you really want to move, we will."

"You mean it?"

He nodded. "I mean it. But for now . . ." He swung her into his arms and headed for the stairs, "I mean to move you in another way."

Ramsey undressed in the darkness, slid under the sheets, and drew Kelly into his arms. Would she still be glad for the doings of this night when she rose tomorrow? Or would she hate him?

He thought about all that had happened since Grigori gave him the Dark Gift. As much as he had fought against it, it hadn't been all bad. He enjoyed the power, his heightened senses, the added physical strength.

He regarded Kelly thoughtfully. She was a beautiful young woman, more beautiful than any woman he had ever known. He couldn't help wondering if she would have looked at him twice if he had been plain old Edward Ramsey, vampire hunter, instead of Edward Ramsey, vampire. There was an allure, a glamour, that all vampires possessed, making them seem more beautiful, more handsome, more attractive than mere mortals.

It had worked its magic on him. He could already see the subtle changes his vampire blood had made in Kelly, too. Her skin seemed to glow. Her hair was thicker, more lustrous than before. He had often wondered if it was the vampire allure that had attracted Marisa to Chiavari—a thought that, at one time, had left him feeling both angry and envious. But no more.

He brushed a kiss across Kelly's cheek.

She stirred, her eyelids fluttering open. "Eddie?"

"Yes, love?"

"Did you really do it?"

He went suddenly still. "Yes."

She turned to face him, her arms sliding around his waist to hold him tight. "Now we'll be together forever, won't we?"

"Forever," he whispered.

Unless Duncan discovered his secret.

Unless Khira decided there were too many vampires in the city.

Chapter 27

Kelly stared at the middle-aged woman who stood in front of her, under Edward's thrall. "I can't," she said, grimacing. "I just can't drink her blood."

"Why not?"

"I just can't." She looked up at him, her eyes wide.

"Damn it, Kelly, I thought you were sure about this. Didn't you think it through?"

"I guess I just sort of skipped this part. All I really thought about was how nice it would be for us to be together forever. I never thought about . . . about this part of it."

That wasn't entirely true. She remembered telling Marisa she didn't think she could drink blood. Somehow, that essential part of being a vampire hadn't seemed important last night. Last night, all she had thought of was becoming what Edward was. If she was a vampire, they could be together forever. She would never have to worry about growing old and helpless.

"Well, you'd better start thinking about it. It's part

of what you are now. A vital part, whether you like it or not."

"Isn't it . . . doesn't it taste . . . awful?"

He looked at the woman standing between them. Her blood called to him, sang to him, promising an end to the hunger stirring within him. He had thought to be repulsed by the almost incessant need for blood—knew he should be horrified by the mere idea—when the truth was just the opposite.

"Awful?" He laughed softly. "Try it and see."

"I can't." She shuddered, tears glistening her eyes. "I can't bite her. I just can't!"

She turned away when he bared his fangs.

This is what I am. The words played through his mind as he took what he needed, what he wanted.

When he was done, he released the woman and sent her away, and then he bit his wrist and offered it to Kelly.

She looked at him in horror, but the hunger was there, burning like twin flames in the depths of her eyes.

He caught her gaze with his. "I can make you drink, and then wipe it from your mind, Kelly, if that's what you want."

"I don't know." She looked at the blood welling from his wrist, licked her lips, then looked away. "Maybe just this once."

"Look at me."

She did as he asked; her eyes filled with trust. He spoke to her mind, bending her will to his, his eyes closing as her mouth closed over his wrist. He let her drink as much as he thought she needed, closed the wound in his wrist, wiped the memory from her mind, and then released his hold on her.

She blinked up at him, her expression confused. "What happened?"

"Nothing, love, let us go for a walk."

Arm in arm, they strolled down the street. Ramsey felt like a new father as he watched Kelly take in the sights and sounds around them through her newly acquired vampire senses. It was, he recalled, like experiencing the world for the first time. His hearing had become more acute; his vision was nothing short of amazing. Colors were not only brighter, but they had depth and texture. His sense of touch was remarkably sensitive, his sense of smell keener. His sense of taste, however, had been pared down to one single flavor: the coppery tang of blood. It should have been repulsive, but it was not.

He glanced over at Kelly. Her revulsion to taking blood was an old taboo from her life as a human. Once she got past it, she would be fully vampire. As he was.

Vampire.

It still seemed unreal, like a bad dream, a nightmare that would end the next time he woke. Only it never ended. And even though he had come to enjoy the powers of the Dark Gift, he couldn't shake the constant fear that he would become like Khira—a remorseless killer.

You can be as good or as bad as you wish. Grigori's words echoed in the back of his mind. A good vampire? He had already killed one woman. How would he live with himself if he killed again?

Murder is murder, Ramsey, whether you're killing vampires or killing humans for their blood. It is all the same; only the reasons are different.

He had killed vampires without a qualm; now their deaths weighed heavily on his conscience. He had never questioned whether they were "good" or "bad." He had viewed them all as evil and destroyed them. Could he ever find forgiveness?

He frowned. Perhaps he was not truly guilty of murder. Didn't that sin lie with the vampire who first bestowed the Dark Gift? If so, then he was responsible for killing Kelly. . . .

"Eddie?"

He turned to face her, horrified at the thoughts chasing themselves through his mind. "Did you say something?"

"What's wrong?"

He forced a smile. "Nothing for you to worry about."

"Let's don't have any secrets, Eddie, please?"

"Forgive me, love. I've just been having some dark thoughts, you know?"

"About what?"

"About vampires I have killed. About you."

"What about me?"

"Have I damned your soul? Am I damned for bringing you across?"

Her eyes widened. "You are having deep thoughts, aren't you? How can you be damned for what you did, when I asked you to do it?"

"What about the vampires I have destroyed? Am I guilty of murder?"

"I don't know, Eddie, but I don't think so. You did what you thought was right at the time. Anyway, vampires are already . . ." She looked up at him, her eyes wider than ever. "Already dead. I'm dead, aren't I?"

"You knew that."

"Dead!" She held up her hands, turned them one way and another, touched her face. "What have I done?" Her fingers dug into his arm, her nails breaking the skin. "What have I done?"

"Kelly . . ."

She stared at him as if seeing him for the first time.

"Kelly, I warned you there was no turning back."

"I know." She shivered. "I guess you were right. I didn't really think it through. I was so caught up in the wonder of it, the newness. I've never known a high like that before . . . I can't have children, can I?''

"No."

"I never really wanted any, you know? But it was always an option, till now."

"I never should have brought you over. You are so young."

"Don't blame yourself. I begged you to do it."

"And now you're sorry. After a while, you'll hate me for it."

"I could never hate you, Eddie. Never!" She smiled up at him. "I love you."

"Do you? I wonder."

"What does that mean?"

"Vampires have an allure, an attraction, that mortals don't possess. Maybe you just fell in love with the illusion."

"No, I don't believe that."

"Well," Ramsey said heavily. "We will never know, will we?"

"It really bothers you, doesn't it?"

He couldn't deny it, so he said nothing. For a time, they walked in silence, together yet apart. She was right, he supposed. He had done what seemed best at the time. At any rate, there was no way to change the past, no way to restore the lives he had so callously taken.

Thoughts of vampire killing brought Tom Duncan to mind. How long could he avoid hunting with his old friend before Duncan got suspicious? How long before Duncan realized the truth? And when he did, which of them would survive?

Grigori felt her presence as soon as he left the house. It swamped his senses like sweet poison—alluring but fatal. He continued down the street, ignoring her in hopes she would tire of the game and leave him alone. But it was not to be.

A whisper of air, the scent of jasmine, and she was there, linking her arm through his. His gaze moved over her in frank male appreciation. Whatever else she might be, she was blatantly beautiful. Her dress, of midnight blue velvet, clung to her perfect figure.

"Buona sera, il mio amore."

"Khira."

She looked up at him through the veil of her lashes, a seductive smile caressing her lips. "Will you come hunt the night with me, my handsome one?"

She never gave up. She was like a child who was certain she could have her own way if she just asked often enough.

His first instinct was to refuse, as always, but then it occurred to him that it might be wiser, safer for all concerned, if he acquiesced to her wishes. But he had one stipulation.

"No killing."

She grinned up at him as her hand slid down his arm, her fingers intertwining with his. "No killing," she agreed.

They stalked the night like the shadows of death, creeping up on their prey, silent as moonlight. She had always loved the hunt, loved to let her victims see her for what she was before she took them. She fed on their terror, wanted it, needed it, as much as their blood. She was not troubled by right and wrong. No, not Khira. She reveled in what she was, her excitement palpable. Contagious. They hunted for hours, prowling in dark alleys, cruising high-class nightclubs, slinking around in cheap dives. Her nearness and her laughter were as intoxicating as whiskey.

He had all but forgotten the thrill of the hunt, the excitement of the chase. For too many years, he had fed out of necessity, taking what he needed quickly, efficiently, painlessly. But now ... He looked at the woman in his arms. She stared up at him, her expression blank, her mind linked to his. A single drop of crimson stained the pale skin of her neck. He looked at the pulse throbbing in her throat, and he wanted to drain her dry, wanted to take it all, every heartbeat, every memory, every drop of life.

"Remember," Khira said, her voice gently mocking. "No killing."

He glanced up to find Khira watching him, a knowing look in her eyes.

"Take her," Khira said, her voice filled with triumph. "You want to; you know you do! Why fight it any longer? This is what you are, Grigori, what you were meant to be!"

The truth of her words seared his brain. He had not killed in decades, but the urge to abandon all control, to unleash the ravening beast within him, was all but overpowering. With a wordless cry, he thrust the woman away from him, released her with a thought, then turned and fled.

The sound of Khira's laugher followed him down the street.

Marisa looked up as he burst into room, her expression startled. Usually, he entered the house so quietly she didn't hear him.

"What is it?" she asked, seeing the haunted look on his face. "What's wrong?"

Crossing the floor, he dropped to his knees and buried his face in her lap, his arms wrapping so tightly around her waist, she could scarcely breathe.

"Grigori, what is it? What's wrong?"

"I went hunting with Khira."

"So? You've hunted with her before."

"But tonight . . . tonight she reminded me of what it is like to truly be Vampyre."

"I don't understand."

He shook his head, his whole body trembling. "I don't think I can explain. It's . . . how can I tell you . . . ?" He swore a vile oath. "She made me hungry again as I have not been in over a century. I held a woman in my arms, and I wanted to . . ."

His arms tightened around her even more. He couldn't say it, couldn't tell Marisa how he'd longed to bury his fangs in the woman's throat and take everything she had, everything she was.

He looked up at Marisa. She was beautiful, happy, with a family that loved her. How could he make her what he was? How could he subject her to the hunger that plagued him? What if, once the deed was done, she hated him for it?

"Grigori?" She was watching him through wide, troubled eyes. "Talk to me. Tell me what's wrong. I want to help, but I need to understand."

He shook his head. There was no way to explain, no way to make her understand the icy fear that was spreading through him, the awful suspicion that he had been kidding himself all these years. He looked up at her, his gaze drawn to the pulse throbbing in the hollow of her throat. Marisa's blood. How often had he tasted it and wanted more?

He jerked his arms from around her waist, gained his feet, and began to pace the floor. Damn Khira! One night of hunting with her had reawakened cravings he thought he had conquered over a century ago.

Blood. It was all he could think of. The craving, worse than any addiction that plagued mankind. Blood. Hot. Warm. Sweet. What had Khira done to him, that he should feel this way after so many years?

An oath escaped his lips.

He heard Marisa gasp, knew she was seeing the hunger that writhed within him.

"Go to bed," he said thickly. "Now!"

She didn't question him. Rising, she walked out of the room and up the stairs. She didn't look back. But she didn't run. He could have kissed her for that, but he didn't dare go near her. Not now.

He paced the floor, too agitated to sit still. He could hear Marisa moving about upstairs, could hear the heartbeats of the city, each one calling to him with a Siren song of blood that was his for the taking. And over all, the sound of Khira's taunting laughter, and the echo of her words in his mind:

"This is what you are, Grigori, what you were meant to be!"

Chapter 28

Marisa woke in midafternoon. Accustomed as she was to spending the silent predawn hours awake with Grigori, she had not been able to sleep last night when he sent her up to bed. Only with dawn had her eyelids grown heavy, and when sleep finally came, her dreams had been filled with shadowy images of Grigori chasing her, his eyes glowing red, his fangs dripping blood. Khira had been mixed in there, too, and Edward. Once, she had awakened, or thought she had awakened, to find Grigori staring down at her.

He had not come to bed at the sun's rising, leaving her to wonder where he was now that the sun was up.

Feeling bleary-eyed and not the least bit rested, she showered, then pulled on a pair of old jeans, a sweatshirt, and a pair of tennis shoes and went downstairs. She poured herself a cup of coffee, then stood at the window, wondering where he was. Was he sleeping elsewhere in the house? If not, where would he go?

Carrying her coffee with her, she wandered through

the house looking for him, but he was nowhere to be found.

Returning to the kitchen, she refilled her cup, then sat down at the table. Where had he gone? What had happened last night to affect him in such a way? Khira ... what had the vampire done to him? She had never been afraid of Grigori before, but last night ... She shivered with the memory.

Gulping the last of the coffee, she grabbed a pair of gardening gloves and left the house. She needed to be outside, in the sunshine. She drew on the gloves, determined to pull the weeds that grew alongside the driveway. She'd never gotten around to calling a gardener. Now she was glad. She needed to be busy, needed something to occupy her mind.

It was a beautiful day, clear and sunny. How long since Grigori had seen the daylight? Did he remember what it was like? The touch of the sun? The glory of a sunrise?

She thrust the thought from her mind. Gazing around the yard, she imagined how the grounds would look once they were landscaped. She would have to decide what kinds of flowers and trees she wanted, and where she wanted them. Maybe, instead of hiring someone, she'd just do the job herself. Heaven knew she had plenty of free time.

She paused on the thought. Unless Khira drove them away from here. That dark thought cast a pall on the brightness of the day. She would not think of that now, would not let Khira ruin what was a lovely day. She wandered through the yard, pausing now and then to imagine this plant or that in a particular setting. She could buy some sod to replace the weedy grass, maybe put a wrought-iron bench under the big old oak tree on the east side of the house, plant some flower beds on either side of the porch and under the front windows.

It might be fun to do it herself. Maybe some night-blooming jasmine . . . She hit her forehead with the heel of her hand. What was she thinking? That was Khira's scent. Honeysuckle would do just as well.

She stood in the sun, gazing around the yard. Where was he? Last night was the first night he had not shared their bed. She had missed falling asleep in his arms, missed waking with him beside her. Damn it, where was he?

She checked her watch. Almost four. Hours yet until he would rise from wherever he had gone. Where had he gone? *Khira* . . . the vampire's name slid through her mind like oily, black smoke. Surely he hadn't gone to stay with Khira. Still, they had once been lovers . . .

She shook the thought from her mind, only to have it rise again. Khira had made him what he was. There was a bond between the two of them that could not be broken—a bond she would never be able to break, one she would never be able to share.

Until you become a vampire.

She pushed the thought from her mind. She would not think of that now.

With a sigh, she decided she would start weeding near the street and work her way back up the driveway. When she reached the house, she would reward herself with a root-beer float.

When she reached the front gate, she was surprised to find it open. Grigori always locked it. She was about to close it when a sudden shiver ran down her spine. Turning, she gasped as she came face to face with a man she had never seen before.

"Excuse me!" she exclaimed. "You gave me quite a start."

He stared at her through blank gray eyes. "You will come with me," he said woodenly.

Revenant.

She recognized him for what he was instantly. She took a step backward, chilled by the empty look in his eyes. Whoever the man had been, he was forever lost now, his mind no longer his own. Soulless, mindless, a creature made by a vampire, yet not a vampire. Alexi Kristov had turned Grigori's first wife, Antoinette, into such a creature. When Ramsey and Grigori joined forces to hunt Kristov, the ancient vampire had used Antoinette against Grigori. To rescue her from her thrall to Kristov, Grigori had brought her all the way across, given her the Dark Gift. But Antoinette could not endure being a vampire. She had begged Grigori to release her, but it had been Ramsey who had laid her soul to rest.

The creature took a step forward, his arms outstretched. "Come."

She didn't waste time or energy arguing. Instead, she turned and ran for the house. *Grigori! Grigori! Help me!* She screamed the words in her mind, screamed in terror as the revenant tackled her from behind. She cried out again as her knees slammed against the driveway.

She lashed out at him, kicking and scratching, but it was no use. He was oblivious to her blows. He grabbed her by the hair and pulled her to her feet; then, lifting her into his arms, he carried her down the driveway and out the gate.

She raked her nails down his face, hoping, praying, that someone would come along to save her, but there was no traffic on the street.

She struggled anew as he opened the passenger door to an old pickup truck and thrust her inside. As soon as he closed the door and started for the driver's side, she reached for the door handle. There was none.

Fear rose up in her throat, making it difficult to breathe, to think.

She sat as close to the door as she could get as the revenant slid behind the wheel. He looked at her through soulless eyes as he reached into his pocket and pulled out a hypodermic needle.

"No!" Marisa begged. "Please, don't."

She might as well as been talking to a piece of wood. He held her immobile with one hand, slid the needle home with the other.

A moment later, everything went black.

Grigori! Grigori! Help me!

He swam through thick layers of darkness, drawn out of the abyss of the Dark Sleep by the fear and panic in Marisa's voice.

Grigori!

He fought against the blackness of eternity that ensnared him, his need to protect his woman stronger than the darkness that weighed him down.

Struggling, he sat up. He felt the weight of daylight press in on him, knew the sun was still high in the sky by the lethargy that engulfed him. With an effort, he gathered his power around him, sent it outward. *Marisa!*

She was in danger. The thought slammed into him, his alarm growing when his mind couldn't connect with hers. Panic drove him to his feet, and he left the attic and made his way down the stairs. He ignored the pain that seared his eyes as he left the protective darkness of the attic. Knowing she wasn't in the house, he still searched every room, including the cellar.

Marisa!

He sent his thoughts outward again, shutting out the myriad everyday sounds that assaulted his senses. His mind brushed Ramsey's and Kelly's. They were deeply asleep. He sought Khira, but she blocked his thoughts effortlessly, even in sleep.

He paced the floor in the living room, the need to find Marisa clawing at him. Torn with the need to find her, he opened the door, but the heat of the sun, the glaring light, drove him back inside. He could do nothing until the sun began to set.

Eyes burning, skin crawling from the brush of the sun, he went back upstairs and took shelter in their bedroom. He buried his face in her pillow, his senses filling with her scent.

He whispered her name as the darkness descended on him, drawing him down, down.

Marisa . . . I will find you.

He sent the thought outward, hoping she would hear it.

He would find her. He would find those who had taken her, and they would pay the ultimate price for their folly.

Chapter 29

Khira stirred as she felt Grigori's anger flow over her. Snuggling deeper into the blankets, she smiled into the darkness. *You will not find her,* she thought. *Unless you do as I say, you will never see her again.*

Feeling pleased and a trifle smug, she closed her eyes and fell back into the thick velvety blackness of the Dark Sleep.

Ramsey moaned softly, his rest disturbed by the rush of power that flowed over him, painful in its intensity. Beside him, Kelly slept soundly, her body unmoving, barely breathing. In the brief time before the Dark Sleep laid hold on him once more, he wondered again if he had done the right thing in bringing her across.

Grigori woke the moment the sun began its descent. He dressed quickly in a pair of jeans and a black sweatshirt, jammed his feet into his boots, put on a pair of sunglasses, and left the house. The sun, though not at its zenith, felt like spiders crawling over his skin as he left the shade of the front porch.

Marisa!

Try as he might, he could not sense her presence.

Swearing softly, he willed himself across town to the mansion that had once belonged to Kyle LaSalle. He wondered if LaSalle had put up a fight or simply moved out at Khira's whim.

She was waiting for him at the door, a tall, slender figure clad in a gown of flowing crimson silk. Her silver-blond hair shimmered with red in the light of the setting sun.

"Where is she?"

"Quite safe. For now."

"Damn it, Khira, where is she?"

A lazy smile curved her pale pink lips. Taking a step backward, she beckoned him to enter.

"I don't have time for this," Grigori said curtly.

"On the contrary, you have nothing but time. Come in, *mi amour.*"

Knowing it was useless to argue with her, Grigori entered the house. A long hallway done in black-and-white tile led to a large square drawing room dominated by a floor-to-ceiling fireplace. The walls and carpet were white. A fire burned in the hearth, adding a note of cheerfulness to the room. Dark furniture. Dark drapes at the windows. A dark painting on the wall depicted a stag in full flight from a pack of wolves. On the mantel, a vase held a single bloodred rose.

"I'm here," he said. He removed his sunglasses and slipped them into the pocket of his jeans. "What do you want?"

"What I have always wanted. You."

He almost laughed, and then he realized she wasn't making a joke. "Why? Why now, after all this time?"

She flowed toward him, the red silk of her gown trailing behind her like a river of blood. "I have missed you, my handsome one. Last night was like old times. Do you not remember the fun we had, in the beginning?"

"I remember."

"I want it again." Eyes burning, she ran her finger over his cheek, down his neck, splayed her fingers over his heart. "You owe me your life, Grigori. I wish to share a part of it, for a time."

He shook his head. "Khira, what you want is impossible. I love Marisa. She's my wife." He took a deep breath in an effort to calm his anger, his fear. "Where is she?"

"As I said, she is well—for now."

"This reeks of blackmail. What is it you want of me?"

"I want a year of your life, Grigori. I want you to come back to Italy with me."

"And do what? Be your gigolo?"

"My companion, *mi amour*. Only a year. Such a little bit of time. It seems a fair exchange, does it not, for the life of your woman?"

"And where will Marisa be during this year?"

"Asleep, I think, like the princess in a fairy tale." She laughed softly. "You can awake her with love's first kiss when you return."

"I want to see her. Now."

"Not until we have an agreement." She smiled, then moved across the room and sat down on the sofa. Her skirt had a long slit up one side. It parted now to reveal the smooth length of a shapely leg.

He stared at her, his hands clenching and unclenching at his sides. "I can't believe you mean this, that you think I'd even consider it."

"You can refuse, of course."

He didn't have to ask what the consequences for

Marisa would be. Khira was a killer, quick and efficient and without remorse. He took a step toward her. He could kill, too, if need be.

He took another step forward and her power slammed into him, driving the breath from his body. Twin flames burned in her eyes, flowed across the space between them, poured over him like liquid fire. Though she hadn't moved, he could feel her hand at his throat, slowly choking off his breath.

"All right." He forced the word through clenched teeth. "You made your point."

She held him in her grasp another minute, then let him go.

He felt suddenly limp. Had he been alone, he would have dropped to his hands and knees, but he refused to give her the satisfaction.

"You always were stubborn," she mused. "And strong. Though, in time, I think Ramsey will be stronger, even stronger than he is now." She gazed into the distance, considering what she had said. "Perhaps when our year is over, *mi cara*, I will persuade him to be my companion for a time. . . ."

"Ramsey can fend for himself. Where is Marisa? I want to see her. Now."

Khira shook her head. "You can be quite wearisome at times, did you know that?"

"Damn it!"

Khira laughed softly. "Very well, you may see her." She stood up. "Follow me."

He paid little attention to the rooms they passed through, save to note that all the windows were covered with heavy black cloth.

Khira paused when they reached a narrow door off the kitchen. "She is down there. You will not be able to awake her."

"What have you done?"

"She is unharmed, only deeply asleep."

Brushing past Khira, he opened the door. A long flight of stairs led him into what had once been a wine cellar. Dozens of dusty cobwebs festooned the ceiling and corners of the room. He could hear the sound of mice scurrying away, smell the decay of rotting wood.

He sensed a presence in the room. Not Marisa. Though he detected her scent, he had no sense of her being there. Two heartbeats. One very faint. One heavy and dull.

He made his way through the darkness to another door. Taking a deep breath, afraid of what he might see, he opened the door and stepped into the room.

It was small and square. A man, or what had once been a man, sat in a chair in the corner, his eyes vacant, his expression empty. He stood up as Grigori entered the room, but Grigori paid him no mind. His attention was focused on the narrow cot pushed against the far wall, and the woman lying on the cot. Marisa. Her face was pale, her lips slightly parted. Her breathing was slow and shallow. A thick chain made of pure silver shackled her left ankle to the frame of the cot.

He thought briefly of picking her up, cot and all, and making a run for it. But there was only one way out of the cellar, and Khira stood there, waiting. He could hear her breathing, hear the slow, steady beat of her heart.

He crossed the floor. Sitting on the edge of the thin mattress, he drew Marisa into his arms. She was limp, almost lifeless. No dreams played in her mind.

"Marisa." He whispered her name. "Marisa."

There was no response. He tried to speak to her mind, but it was closed against him. He held her for a long while, rocking her gently as he would a child, his fingers delving into the silk of her hair, sliding over the curve of her cheek. Marisa. He remembered the night he had first seen her at the carnival. She had asked him if he had come to see the vampire, and he had replied yes, and then asked her if she believed in the undead. She hadn't believed, not then. Had he stayed out of her life, she would not be here now. Even as the thought crossed his mind, he knew that, had he not followed her home that night, she would have been dead, or worse, at Kristov's hands months ago. He gazed down at her, a finger tracing the line of her bottom lip. She didn't stir, barely breathed. She was so young, so innocent still—he could not let Khira take her life. Perhaps it was time to give her up. Perhaps a year without him would give her the time she needed to decide whether or not she had made a mistake in marrying him.

Lowering his head, he kissed her gently, then laid her back on the cot. If she left him, he would have no reason to go on.

A last glance, a last touch, and he left the room.

Khira was waiting for him at the top of the stairs. "Well?"

"Release her."

"No."

"You can't keep her trapped like that for a year!"

"I can." She held up her hand, cutting off his protest. "But I will release her, Grigori, if you will give me your word of honor that you will come with me to Italy for one year. That you will not contact her during that time; that you will do whatever I wish."

Interesting, he thought, that she would ask for his word of honor when she had none herself. "I'll give you a year, but not in Italy."

"And if I insist?"

He glanced at Marisa. "Then I will do what you want." He looked up at her and forced a smile. "But I think you will be better . . ." He took a step forward, his fingertips stroking her cheek, sliding down her neck.

". . . satisfied, shall we say, if you give in on this one small point."

She regarded him for several heartbeats and then nodded. "Very well. But you are not to contact her in any way. I will know if you do."

"Agreed."

"I suppose you will want to say good-bye?"

"I want this night with her."

She nodded, a queen granting a boon to a peasant. "Very well. I shall expect you back here tomorrow at dusk." Her eyes grew hard and cold. "Do not keep me waiting," she warned. "You will not like what happens to her if I have to come after you."

With a curt nod, he turned away. He wanted to run down the stairs to Marisa; instead, he forced himself to walk.

She was as he had left her: deeply asleep, pale, barely breathing. He looked at the man. "Release her."

The revenant moved with the jerky movements peculiar to his kind as he reached into his pocket, withdrew a key, and unlocked the shackle from Marisa's ankle.

Lifting her into his arms, Grigori carried her up the stairs and into the drawing room. Khira stood in front of a large marble fireplace. She turned as he entered the room.

"Wake her."

"That sounds very much like a demand on your part. I don't like demands."

He choked back his anger. "Khira, I beg of you, please awaken her."

A rush of power swirled around him. Marisa stirred in his arms, sighed heavily. The color returned to her cheeks.

"She will awake when you reach home."

With a nod, Grigori left the mansion. Moments later,

he was at home. A look roused a fire in the hearth. Pulling a chair up in front of the fireplace, he sat down with Marisa cradled against his chest.

She yawned, stretched, looked up at him through eyes cloudy with sleep, and then, noticing her surroundings, she sat up.

"What are we doing down here? Why didn't you come to bed last night?" She looked at the window, frowning when she saw that it was dark outside. She glanced down at her clothing, recognizing the jeans and sweatshirt she had put on earlier that day. "What happened today? What happened *to* today?"

"It's a long story, *cara.*"

She looked at him, troubled by his tone, by the somber expression on his face. "It's bad, isn't it? I don't think I want to hear it, after all."

"Marisa, why don't you go take a bath, and then get something to eat? I have an errand to run, but I won't be gone long."

She wrapped her arms around his neck. "Where are you going?"

"I need to go out."

Her gaze moved over him. "You've already fed. Where are you going?"

"All in good time, *cara.* I won't be gone long."

Rising, he placed her on her feet. Tipping her head up, he kissed her. She leaned into him, softly yielding, her warmth, her scent, enfolding him. How could he leave her?

She was breathless when he released her. "I love you," she murmured. "Hurry back."

It was Kelly who answered the door. She looked much the same as when he had seen her last, and yet his vampyre eyes saw the changes in her, subtle though they might be. The Dark Gift had worked its magic. Her beauty was subtly enhanced; she moved with the smooth, easy grace so common to his kind.

"I need to see Ramsey," Grigori said. "Now."

"He's in the living room. Is something wrong?"

He nodded curtly.

"Come on in," she said, and stepped back so he could enter the house. "Ramsey!"

"I'm here. You don't have to shout." Ramsey frowned when he saw the rage burning in the other vampire's eyes. "What's wrong?"

"In a word, Khira. I have agreed to go spend a year with her. In return, she has agreed to let Marisa live."

"Are you out of your mind?" Ramsey asked incredulously. "She's already destroyed all the other vampires."

"Not all. Rosa had a fledgling. Lisa. She is weak, still new. Khira will destroy her, too, if I don't do as she says."

Ramsey observed Chiavari through hooded eyes. "She's going too far. She's got to be stopped. And you know it."

"Spoken like a true vampyre hunter," Chiavari said bitterly. "I felt her power again today. I fear she is too strong for me. Too strong for you, no matter what happened the other night. It might interest you to know that she may have plans for you after my year is done."

"Alexi was strong, too," Ramsey said. "Too strong for either of us. But together we destroyed him." He smiled wryly. "And I was not half the man I am today, thanks to you."

"You do not understand! Marisa's life is at risk!"

"And you think Khira will keep her word to you?" Ramsey shook his head. "You're not thinking clearly."

Grigori smiled sadly. "It is you who are not thinking clearly. I have no choice but to do as Khira says."

"Like hell! We could . . ."

"She is probably listening to our conversation, even now," Grigori interjected quickly.

Ramsey shrugged. "Then she would be like the condemned man in his cell, knowing the appointed hour of his doom but unable to do anything about it."

Chiavari looked at Ramsey as if he had never seen him before. "Being Vampyre has given you a certain arrogance. . . ."

"Perhaps I always had it," Ramsey said. "It but needed the Dark Gift to bring it out."

"This is foolish talk," Chiavari insisted. "I came here to ask a favor of you."

Ramsey laughed. "What better favor than to destroy your nemesis?"

"I want you to protect Marisa."

"What do you think I'm trying to do, you fool?" Ramsey swore. "Marisa will never be safe as long as Khira walks. Don't you understand that?"

"You are out of your depth, Ramsey. Just protect Marisa, while I do what I must. I won't be allowed to contact Marisa, so I'm depending on you to be there if she needs help with anything. Understand?"

Ramsey nodded. "I understand you're a damn fool. Don't worry about Marisa. I'll look after her. But think, Chiavari; think very carefully. Think of Lisa, who will certainly die. Think of . . ." He paused. "Think of Kelly. Not to mention all the innocents that Khira will slaughter. Damn it, use your head! You are letting your affection from years past cloud your thinking. None of us will be safe so long as Khira exists."

Chiavari nodded. "For once, you are right. I will go with Khira and keep her occupied until we can think of a way to destroy her, together. I am trusting you to protect Marisa until then."

Ramsey nodded, looking pleased.

"Know this, Ramsey. If anything happens to Marisa while I am playing house with Khira, I will give you the death you once came looking for."

Chapter 30

Grigori stood in front of the house he shared with Marisa, imprinting it on his mind so he could picture her here while he was away. A year wasn't such a long time, he told himself again, but a year without Marisa . . . it would seem like an eternity.

Muttering an oath, he climbed the porch stairs and opened the front door. Her scent enveloped him the moment he entered the house, and he took a deep breath, as if to inhale her very essence.

"Grigori?"

He moved into the living room. "Why are you sitting in the dark?" He crossed the room and sat down beside her on the sofa.

"I don't know. It just seemed . . ." She shrugged. "I don't know."

He slid his arm around her shoulders and drew her closer.

"I love you," she whispered, snuggling against him.

"Ah, *cara* . . ."

"I've been sitting here, trying to guess what bad news you'd bring home." Her fingertips drifted over his cheek. "It is bad, isn't it?"

"That depends," he replied, "on how you feel about separate vacations."

"What?"

There was no easy way to say it, no way to make it sound better than it was. "I'm going to move in with Khira."

Marisa stared at him. She would have thought he was joking save for the expression on his face. She felt suddenly sick to her stomach. "Move in? With her?"

He nodded. "For a year."

Marisa shook her head. "Why?" She wanted to say, "What about me?" but she was afraid of the answer.

He told her the rest of it as gently as he could—how Khira had threatened to kill her if he refused.

"So you're going to live with her, because of me?"

"Cara, what else can I do?"

"I don't know." She wanted to cry, to scream, to pound her fists against his chest and demand that he think of something. "When?"

"Tomorrow night."

"So soon?" Rising, she went to stand in front of the window, her back to him so he couldn't see her tears.

He sat there a moment, listening to the tears roll down her cheeks, and then he went to stand behind her, close but not touching. Waiting.

She turned and buried her face against his shoulder. "Why is she doing this?"

Grigori shrugged. "Who can say why she does what she does? She is easily bored. Perhaps she will grow tired of me before the year is out."

Marisa shook her head. No woman, mortal or vampire, would ever grow tired of such a man.

"I'm afraid, Grigori." She wrapped her arms around his waist. "I'm afraid I'll never see you again."

"Hush, *cara*. It will be all right. A year is not so long."

"Maybe not to you. Please don't go. Let's leave town. Now, tonight."

"Marisa, there is no way you can hide from her."

"But you can, can't you?"

He nodded. "I could go to ground, but you and I would still be apart. And I cannot—I will not—take a chance on her taking her anger at me out on you."

She looked up at him, making a valiant effort not to cry. "What will I do without you for a whole year?"

"Spend it doing whatever you wish. Finish decorating the house. Go see your family. Take a vacation."

She nodded, unable to speak past the lump in her throat.

"This might be a good time for you to rethink our relationship."

"What do you mean?"

Taking her hand, he led her to the sofa and drew her down beside him. "Marisa, take a good look at me. You know what I am, how I live. Think about it while I'm gone. We have talked about bringing you over. This will give you a chance to decide if it is what you really want."

"You're tired of me, aren't you? That's what this is all about."

A vile oath escaped his lips. "You don't mean that."

"Then why aren't you more upset by it all? You tell me to do whatever I want, take a vacation. I want to be with you."

His knuckles brushed her cheek. "Marisa . . ."

"Go on," she said, bolting to her feet. "Go play with Khira for a year. Two years! I don't care."

"You don't mean that."

"Don't I?" She had truly hurt him now. She could

see it in his eyes. But it was nothing compared to the hurt she was feeling. She held herself stiff and cold, a cold that radiated from her frozen heart. "I thought you loved me . . ."

"Cara, cara . . ." He reached for her, and for the first time in their relationship, she pulled away. He dropped his hands by his side and stood, stricken.

"I asked Ramsey to look after you while I'm away," he said woodenly. "To protect you."

"Isn't Ramsey afraid of Khira, too?" she asked bitterly. "If she is such a fearsome creature, how can he be expected to protect me, if you can't?"

"Marisa . . . damn it, Marisa, I've got to go with her. There are things you don't know, things I can't tell you! Not when your life hangs in the balance."

"I know enough. Khira calls, and you come running. She is quite beautiful, after all . . ." She forced a smile. "Don't worry about me; I'll be fine."

Grigori reacted as if she had slapped him. "Marisa . . ."

She had never heard his voice so full of pain and longing. But she steeled herself against it.

Grigori felt her resistance. His reaction came naturally, his power reaching out.

Marisa's lips twisted as she felt his power gather in the room. "Will you use your vampire power against me now? Force me to do your will? One last quickie with me before you go to her?"

Her words stopped him cold. "I had better go," he said stiffly. "Good-bye, *cara.* I have always loved you. . . ." He turned away.

And her rebel heart melted, all in a rush. "Grigori . . ."

He stopped, still not looking at her. "Yes?"

She laid a hand on his shoulder. "I'm sorry. Look at me."

He turned slowly. Marisa tilted her head back so she

could look into Grigori's eyes. "I love you so much. I'll always love you. Nothing, no one, can ever change that."

She took his hands in hers. "Can we . . . do we have time to say a proper good-bye?"

He groaned low in his throat. "Oh, my sweet, sweet love," he murmured brokenly, "we'll make the time."

She was crying openly as he lifted her into his arms. He carried her swiftly up the stairs. With a thought, he kindled a fire in the hearth. As the flames flickered, he stood her gently on her feet and lifted her T-shirt over her head. Then he slid her jeans slowly down her legs. He removed her bra and panties with slow deliberation, his eyes burning brighter and hotter than the flames in the fireplace.

She felt their minds join in the sweet familiar way. Excitement rippled through her as his hands glided over her body, awaking her, arousing her. She purred with feminine satisfaction that was leavened with grief and sadness.

"Cara, mi amante . . . mi vita . . ."

She loved the sound of his voice, the way it moved over her like rich black velvet, warm and soft and sensual. She looked at him, and love swelled her heart until it ached. How could she endure a year without him?

She slid her hands under his sweatshirt, ran her fingertips over his belly, his back, reveling in the hard-muscled strength of him. Removing the sweatshirt, she tossed it on a chair, then began to unzip his jeans.

"Careful there," he muttered.

She laughed softly as she eased his jeans down over his hips. He wasn't wearing anything underneath.

"My, my," she murmured.

"I dressed in a hurry."

"Your boots," she said with a grin.

He sat down on the edge of the bed and pulled off his boots and socks. With a sultry grin, Marisa pulled off his jeans, then straddled his hips. "I'm going to miss you so much."

"I know." He fell back on the bed, drawing her with him. "I know."

"Will you call me while you're away?"

He shook his head, his hands moving lightly over her back, his thumbs skimming her breasts. "I have promised her I will not, but I will know if you need me." He nuzzled her neck, his tongue hot against her skin. "Marisa?"

She brushed her hair away from her neck and closed her eyes, yielding to the need in his eyes. Once, the thought of anyone drinking her blood had been repulsive, but no more. It was strangely erotic to know that her blood sustained him, bound them together. There was no pain. With a sigh, she wrapped her arms around him and held him closer, tighter, urging him to take as much as he needed. There was no need for words between them. She knew what he was thinking, what he was feeling. His tongue laved her neck, sealing the wounds.

As he rolled over, tucking her body gently beneath his, she put everything from her mind and gave herself over to the magic, the love, that was Grigori. There would be time for tears tomorrow, but tonight there was only Grigori, filling her, completing her.

Loving her, until dawn stole the darkness from the sky, and they fell asleep in each other's arms.

It was dusk when she woke. She squeezed her eyes shut, not wanting to wake up. She didn't want to face the coming evening, or tell Grigori good-bye. A year. Not long ago, she had complained that time went by too fast, but she knew that would not be true now. The days would drag, and the nights would be unbearable.

She snuggled closer to Grigori, frowned as she felt the tension flowing through him. "Grigori, what's the . . . ?"

She opened her eyes, drew the sheet up to her chin, when she saw Khira standing in the doorway. Dressed in ice blue silk that matched the color of her eyes, her long silver-blond hair falling over her shoulders like a mantle, the vampire looked as cool and beautiful as always. There was a faintly amused look in her eyes.

"It's time," Khira said.

"Khira, get the hell out of here," Grigori said brusquely.

She glanced at Marisa, then fastened her gaze on Grigori. "Don't make me wait too long," she warned, and left the room.

Grigori looked at Marisa. "My ride is here."

She nodded, unable to speak, knowing that if she tried, she would burst into tears.

His gaze caressed her face as he brushed her cheek with the back of his hand. "I can wipe my memory from your mind if it will make it easier."

"No!"

"I know this will not be easy for you, but try and make the best of it. Spend time with your family. Call your friend Linda Hauf. You have neglected her since we got married. And try not to worry. Everything will be all right."

She nodded and forced a smile. He didn't want to leave her. She wouldn't make it more difficult by crying or making a scene.

He kissed her, then slid out of bed and began to dress.

Such a beautiful man, she thought as she watched him. Lithe, supple, perfectly formed. He moved with a fluid grace no mortal could ever hope to achieve. And he was handsome, so very handsome. No wonder Khira wanted him . . .

The thought of Grigori with Khira was like a knife

piercing her heart. She had often wondered how anyone could commit murder, but she understood now. Jealousy and impotent rage flooded her heart, and she wished suddenly that Khira were just a woman, one she could fight on equal terms.

"Marisa, don't."

She met his gaze, knew her thoughts had betrayed her.

"I can't help it."

He pulled on his boots, then sat on the edge of the bed and drew her into his arms. "I love you. Only you. Remember that."

"I know."

"I shall miss you, *cara mia*. I will think of you every night, dream of you every day." His hands slid over her shoulders and down her arms. His gaze burned into hers, his mind brushing hers, and she felt his love wash over her like a warm, sweet tide, seeping into the very deepest part of her, touching every nerve, every cell, every particle of her being. It filled her heart with peace, eased the ache in her soul, overflowed in a cascade of silent tears.

His arms tightened around her. "Ah, *cara*, please don't cry. I cannot abide your tears."

She buried her face in the hollow of his shoulder. "I'm not," she said, sniffing.

He rained kisses on her hair, her cheeks, her neck, the tip of her nose, the hollow of her throat. "I have to go," he murmured, his voice filled with regret. "She is calling me." He cupped Marisa's face in his hands. "I love you. Never forget that."

"I won't."

He kissed her again, slow and long and deep, and then he was gone.

Chapter 31

Kelly rolled onto her stomach and braced her chin on her hand. "It's not right, you know?"

Ramsey frowned at her. "What are you talking about? What's not right?"

"What Khira's doing to Grigori and Marisa. What gives her the right to do such a thing?"

"She thinks she has the power to do it."

"Well, we ought to stop her. You heard Grigori. What if she decides she wants you next? I mean, Grigori and Marisa are married . . ."

"We are going to stop her. Don't worry about that." He frowned at her. "Your concern—is it really for Chiavari and Marisa? Or about you and me?"

She scooted toward him, her teeth grazing his shoulder. "Both."

He put his arm around her and drew her up close to his side. Her sweet, feminine curves fit against the lines of his body as though she had been designed for him. "Are you trying to tell me something?"

She made a low growling sound and punched him on the arm. "I'm trying to get you to ask me something."

Ramsey lifted one brow. "Is that right?"

"You said we'd be together forever."

He nodded.

"Well, I know times have changed, and people live together all the time without getting married, but I . . ."

"Hush, Kelly."

She stilled and looked away, but not before he saw the hurt in her eyes.

Ramsey took her chin in his hand and gently forced her to look at him. "Will you marry me, Kelly?"

"No."

"No! Why not?"

"Because you don't really want to."

"Kelly girl, when I ask a woman to spend forever with me, I mean it."

"You do?"

"I said it, didn't I? I cannot imagine what I ever did without you in my life. I love you, Kelly girl."

"Oh, and I love you!" she said, and launched herself on top of him, smothering him with kisses, caressing and nibbling until he was on fire for her.

Fire. Desire and hunger burned within him. He felt her teeth at his throat, felt a sensual rush as her fangs pricked his flesh. His hands moved over her, lightly stroking, until his need was too great. Rolling over, he tucked her beneath him. She shivered with pleasure as his tongue laved her neck, moaned softly as she yielded to the vampire kiss, bucked beneath him as his body melded with hers. He saw her through a pulsing red haze, his every sense attuned to the woman in his arms, the touch of her, the taste of her, the scent of her— ah, the warm sweet scent of her blood; the musky scent of her heated flesh; the pleasurable pain of her nails raking his back, her teeth nipping his shoulder . . .

"Forever," he said, and carried them both over the edge.

Kelly let out a slow, deep sigh. She had never known love like this in her whole life. Never. Rolling onto her side, she caressed Edward's cheek. "Eddie? We have to do something to help Marisa."

"Like what?"

"I don't know. Think of something. You used to be a vampire hunter. How would you have hunted Khira back then?"

"In the daytime, when she was weak." He grunted softly. "Hell, we don't even know if she is weak in the daytime. No one knows exactly how powerful she is."

"But there's three of us," Kelly argued. "Four, if you count Lisa. And only one of Khira. You told Grigori . . ."

Yes, that combined we might do it. In the back of his mind, he heard Grigori's voice: *"There is powerful blood in your veins, Ramsey. Mine. Alexi's. And Khira's. She will find it difficult to destroy you if you keep your wits about you."*

There had been no mistaking the surprise and, yes, unease Khira had felt when he resisted her.

Together, he and Grigori had destroyed Kristov.

Khira had killed Noah Fox and Prince Dracul and Madame Rosa, and who knew how many other vampires, let alone innocent humans. She was like a plague, a one-woman virus, spreading through the city, preying on the weak.

"One way or another," Ramsey said, "we will find a way."

"So, do you have any ideas?" she asked, her eyes glowing with excitement.

"Not a one," he admitted, nuzzling her neck. "But we will think of something. But first, what do you say we get married?"

The wedding was surprisingly easy to plan. They didn't need a church. Ramsey had no family, and Kelly's mother was in England. Ramsey found a minister who would perform the ceremony outside, in a local park, the following Saturday night.

Kelly wrote out an invitation to Marisa, and then one for Grigori. "It's not right that Grigori can't come with Marisa," she said.

"Chiavari is holding up his part of the bargain by keeping Khira occupied," Ramsey said. "First things first."

"Is there anyone you want to invite?"

Ramsey thought briefly of Duncan, then shook his head. Inviting a vampire hunter to a vampire wedding was just asking for trouble.

"You know, it's a good thing the all-night market on the corner sells stamps," she said with a grin, "or I'd have to ask Marisa to go to the post office for me."

Ramsey shook his head. "It seems silly to send out two invitations when a couple of phone calls would do just as well. Besides, Khira probably won't let Grigori come anyway."

"Well, she'd better!" Rising, she put the invitations in her handbag, stepped into her sandals. "Come on, let's go get some stamps. Oh! What about a license? The offices close before dark."

"I'll take care of it."

"How?"

He winked at her. "Don't worry about it."

"All right." She slipped her arm through his. "Let's go."

They wandered through the market, reminiscing about the taste of food. Kelly stopped in the candy aisle.

"Look at all that chocolate," she said with a sigh. "It's the only thing I really miss. Well, that and ice cream. And hot fudge."

Ramsey laughed. "A real chocoholic, weren't you?"

She stuck her tongue out at him. "Me and a million other women. Besides, don't you know? Dark chocolate is good for you."

"Sure, it is."

"It is! I heard a doctor say it was good for the enamel on your teeth, and good for your heart, too."

He laughed out loud this time. "Your teeth are fine, honey, trust me."

She laughed, too, causing an elderly couple to stop and stare at them.

Grinning, Kelly took Edward's hand. "Come on, let's go get those stamps."

They were heading for the check-out stand when Ramsey came to an abrupt halt.

"What is it?"

"Duncan."

"Where?"

"There." He nodded at a tall man who was reaching for a bag of potato chips.

"Maybe he won't see us."

Ramsey tugged on Kelly's hand, urging her backward, but it was too late.

"Hey, Ramsey!" Duncan called.

"Hi, Tom."

Duncan pushed his cart toward them. He gestured at the groceries inside. "Heck of a way for a single man to spend a Saturday night, ain't it?"

Ramsey laughed. "You need to get yourself a wife."

Duncan nodded, his gaze moving over Kelly.

"You two haven't met, have you?" Ramsey said. "Tom, this is my fiancée, Kelly Anderson. Kelly, this is Tom Duncan."

Duncan held out his hand. "Nice to meet you, Kelly."

"Nice to meet you, too," she said, smiling. "I've heard a lot about you."

"Good things, I hope. I'm about done here," Duncan said. "Maybe I could meet the two of you for a cup of coffee somewhere when you get done with your shopping."

"We just came in for some stamps," Ramsey said. "We thought maybe we'd catch a late movie."

Duncan grunted softly. "Which one?"

"Whatever is playing when we get there."

"Mind if I join you?"

Ramsey glanced at Kelly. "No, we don't mind, do we?"

"No." She forced a smile.

"Good. You going to the theater just down the street?"

Ramsey nodded.

"Just let me pay for this stuff," Duncan said.

They followed him to the check stand, bought a book of stamps, waited while Duncan put his groceries in the trunk of his car. Ramsey didn't miss the fact that Duncan had all the tools of the trade in place: a long, sharp knife, a strong silver chain, a hammer and a mallet, a shovel, a small case that he knew held a silver cross and several vials of holy water.

"Good thing I didn't buy any perishables," Duncan said, closing the trunk. "Shall we go?"

As luck would have it, they got there just as a new movie started. Duncan bought three tickets, insisted it was his treat for horning in, and they entered the theater.

"Eddie, what are we going to do?" Kelly whispered.

"Watch the movie," he said, squeezing her hand. "And stop worrying."

It was good advice, he mused, wishing he could take it himself. He was all too conscious of the man sitting next to him, of the great gulf between them. For the next two hours, he debated the wisdom of telling Duncan the truth and enlisting his help in defeating Khira.

He grinned into the darkness. Unbelievable, that he would be looking for a way to rescue Chiavari when a few months ago he had been determined to kill him. Times changed, he mused ruefully, and so did people. Boy, how they changed!

Duncan nudged him with his elbow. "I'm going out for popcorn. You want some?"

"No, thanks."

"What about Kelly? She want anything?"

"No. We had a big dinner before we left."

With a nod, Duncan headed for the snack bar.

"Do you think he suspects?" Kelly whispered.

"I don't know."

"Would he really kill you if he knew? I mean, he'd be the perfect one to dispose of Khira, don't you think?"

"It crossed my mind, but he would be just as likely to take out every vampire in the city."

Kelly shivered. "I wouldn't like that."

They fell silent as Duncan returned carrying a bag of popcorn and a large soft drink.

"Sure you don't want any?" he asked, taking his seat.

"No, thanks."

Lost in thought, Ramsey paid little attention to the rest of the movie.

Later, walking out of the theater, Duncan asked Ramsey what he was doing the following Saturday night.

Ramsey looked at Kelly and smiled. "I have a heavy date, why?"

"Still hoping we can get together." Duncan looked at Kelly. "And go hunting."

"I told you, I will not hunt Chiavari."

"There are other vamps in the city. One old, one young."

"Khira," Ramsey said, his voice almost a whisper.

Duncan nodded. "I know you said you needed some time off, but I don't think I want to try and take her alone. And who knows how long she'll stick around? We need to take her out now, you know?"

"I can't argue with that."

"Well, I've got my equipment in the car. When do we start?"

Ramsey swore under his breath. How long could he keep sidestepping Duncan's invitation?

Kelly slipped her arm around Ramsey's waist. "You'll have to wait a little while," she said, smiling sweetly. "We're getting married on Saturday."

Duncan's eyes widened. "Married!"

Ramsey nodded.

"Well, I'll be damned! I don't know what to say . . . congratulations, I guess. Married! Hunters never get married."

"Yeah, well, I'm thinking of looking for a new line of work," Ramsey said. "Kelly worries about me."

She gave him a squeeze. "It's time he put away the old wooden stake and found something a little less dangerous to do."

Duncan glanced from Ramsey to Kelly and back again, then let out a deep breath. "Well, I'm happy for you both," he said, "but I hate to lose Ramsey. He's the best hunter we've ever had."

"Thanks, Tom."

"So, do I get an invite to the wedding?"

Ramsey knew a moment of panic. He was scrambling for an excuse when Kelly said, "We're eloping, just the two of us. It's always been a dream of mine, and Eddie was kind enough to let me have my way."

Duncan winked at Ramsey. "Always good to let the little woman have her way before the wedding."

Ramsey smiled. "That's what I thought."

"Well, let me know when you get back in town, and we'll go out and celebrate."

"I'll do that."

With a last, speculative look at the two of them, Duncan turned and walked down the street toward his car.

Ramsey kissed Kelly on the cheek. "That was quick thinking."

"He suspects something, doesn't he?"

"Yeah, I'm afraid so."

Chapter 32

Grigori paused in the doorway, watching Khira as she glided across the floor and took a seat on the edge of the bed. It made a pretty image: the shimmering silver hair, the long ice white gown, the velvet black bedspread against the white carpet.

"I think you will be comfortable here." Her hand slid back and forth over the bedspread, graceful, sensual. Suggestive.

He shook his head. "I want a room of my own." He lifted his left hand and wiggled his ring finger. "I'm a married man, remember?"

She laughed softly. "Only mortals are bothered by such foolishness."

"I promised Marisa to be faithful when I took her as my wife. I will hunt with you. I will stay here in this house with you. But that is all."

Khira glared at him, her blue eyes frosty with anger.

Careful to keep his expression blank, Grigori waited, saying nothing. Would she threaten Marisa's life again?

If she did, if he thought it was more than a bluff, he would do what she asked. Anything she asked. Until the time was right ... He carefully buried the tag end of his thoughts.

But Khira's flash of anger was gone. She smiled fondly, and he knew she was enjoying her sense of power, knew she was certain that no male, vampire or mortal, could resist her for long.

"One of the things I have always loved about you was your old-fashioned sense of morality. I would have thought you would have outgrown it after all these years." She pouted prettily. "But I won't take advantage of you ... yet."

She rose in a graceful swish of white silk. "Come," she said, holding out her hand. "The night awaits."

Marisa moved through the house. What was Grigori doing now? What was Khira doing now? She was angry, angrier than she had ever been—angry at Khira for her outrageous demand, angry at Grigori for acquiescing, angry at herself for being angry at him. He loved her; she knew that without a doubt. Knew that was the only reason he had gone with Khira, and yet ...

"And yet, nothing," she muttered. She had no doubt that she would be dead—or worse—by now if Grigori had refused the vampire. But she couldn't shut out the image of Grigori in Khira's arms, couldn't forget how well they looked together, silver moonlight and black shadow.

How could she endure a whole year without him? What would she do? He had suggested she go visit her family for a while, and perhaps she would. And she needed to call Linda. They had been such good friends when Marisa was working at Salazar and Salazar, but since the wedding, she had cut herself off from everyone she knew. It would be good to see her mom and dad again, to have lunch with Linda and get caught up on her life, but not now. Now she wanted to scream, to break things . . . like Khira's graceful neck.

"Damn!" She sniffed back her tears. She would not cry. She wouldn't! But the tears welled in her eyes, rolled down her cheeks. If she missed him this much after only one night, how would she get through all the ones to come?

Tom Duncan strolled down the town's main street, his mind on his conversation with Ramsey the night before. Ramsey was getting married! It was unbelievable, unthinkable. Vampire hunters never married. It was an unwritten law. He had known Ed Ramsey for almost fifteen years. They had faced death together more times than he cared to recall. He had saved Ramsey's life; Ramsey had saved his. They couldn't have been any closer if they were blood kin, and that was why he knew something was bothering Ramsey, but what?

Duncan paused at the curb. It was more than just Ramsey having a rough time with his last kill. They had weathered bad patches before and come through them smiling. No, something else was eating at Ramsey, something big. Something bad, so bad Ramsey wouldn't talk about it.

Duncan crossed the street, his hands shoved in his pockets. Whatever was bothering his old friend, he would discover what it was, sooner or later.

He swore under his breath. What the hell kind of friend was he? Something was bothering Ramsey, and he meant to find out what it was. Like any good vampire hunter, Tom had connections in high places. It shouldn't be too hard to find out where Ramsey lived, now that he had taken up a permanent residence. Then, too, there would be a marriage license on file. . . .

The following evening, Tom pulled a piece of paper out of his shirt pocket and double-checked the address. Unbelievable. What had Ramsey been thinking when he bought a place like this? It looked like a Hollywood set for one of Christopher Lee's old vampire movies.

With a shake of his head, Tom stuffed the paper back into his pocket and switched off his car's engine. If this was old Ed's idea of home sweet home, then Ramsey had been in the vampire business way the hell too long.

He walked up the drive, climbed the stairs, rang the bell, and listened to it echo inside the house. Damn, the place gave him the creeps.

He smiled as the door opened and he saw Kelly standing there. "Hi. Is Ed home?"

Kelly blinked at him. "Is he expecting you?"

"No, just thought I'd drop by and say hello. Is he home?"

She glanced over her shoulder, then stepped backward. "Come on in."

He followed her down a dark entryway into the living room.

Ramsey did not seem surprised to see him, which kind of surprised Duncan.

"What the hell are you doing here?" Ramsey asked flatly.

Tom grunted. "I'm happy to see you, too."

Ramsey smiled faintly. "Come in. I didn't mean to bite your head off. We weren't expecting anyone; that's all. Sit down."

"But you weren't the least bit surprised it was me." Tom sat on the sofa. Something wasn't right. He glanced from Ramsey to Kelly, wondering if he'd interrupted a fight. They both looked tense. Especially Kelly. She sat on the arm of a chair, one foot tapping the floor while she gnawed on a thumbnail.

"Why should I be surprised?" Ramsey asked. "Finding an address in L.A. should be child's play to an old hunter like yourself. What brings you here?"

Tom lifted one shoulder and let it drop. "I was just bored and thought I'd look you up. There's vampires to be hunted, Ed. You've vacationed long enough."

Ramsey and Kelly exchanged nervous looks.

Tom stood up and shoved his hands in his pockets. "I think I came at a bad time."

Ramsey also stood up. "As a matter of fact, we were just about to go out to dinner."

"Mind if I join you?"

"We would love to have you join us," Ramsey said quickly, "but we're going to a friend's house. Kind of a private party for the bride and groom. You understand?"

Tom nodded. "Sure. Another time, then. Just one thing: do you know where Khira holes up?"

Ramsey shook his head. "Sorry, I can't help you."

"Best guess?"

"I really don't know."

"All right. Sorry to have bothered you."

"Tom, wait. If you find her, be careful. Chiavari is with her."

Duncan raised one brow. "Chiavari and Khira? What brought that about?"

"You might say she is throwing her weight around a little."

"I don't follow you."

"You don't have to. I just wanted you to know that you might be walking into more than you bargained for if you go after her."

"I see. Well, thanks for the tip. It was nice to see you again, Kelly."

Her smile looked forced. "You, too, Tom. Good night."

Kelly watched the two men leave the room. As soon as they were gone, she began to pace the floor. She whirled around when Edward came back into the room. "Do you think he knows?"

Ramsey blew out a sigh that seemed to come from the deepest part of his soul. "I'm afraid so."

Duncan was waiting for Ramsey when he left the house the following night.

"Evening," Ramsey said.

Duncan didn't waste any time. "She's a vampire, isn't she?"

Ramsey nodded warily.

"And you're going to marry her?"

Ramsey nodded again.

"Why?"

"Because I love her."

Duncan shook his head. "Something's not right."

"We've been friends a long time, Tom, but my private life is just that. Private."

Ramsey shoved his hands into his pant pockets, his face impassive under Duncan's probing gaze, though he was anything but calm on the inside. Tom was his best friend. What happened in the next few minutes could change that forever.

"What is it?" Duncan asked. "What aren't you telling me?"

"You're better off not knowing."

"Damn it, I have a right to know! We've been through too much together for you to be hiding something from me now. I already know you're marrying a damned bloodsucker. What could be worse than . . . ?'' He broke off and stared at his friend. "No, it can't be."

Ramsey clenched his hands, his body tense, ready to fight or flee.

His posture was not lost on Duncan. "You're not!" Duncan swore colorfully. "Damn it, Ed, tell me it's not true. You didn't . . ."

"No, I didn't go looking for it. You know me better than that."

"Then why? How?" Duncan swore again. "When?"

"What difference does it make? It's done."

"Damn it!"

"It happened the night Kristov was destroyed. I was dying. Chiavari saved my life."

"Took it, you mean!" Duncan ran a hand through his hair. He stared at his old friend, the differences obvious now that he knew. Why hadn't he recognized them before? "What's it like, being a vampire?"

"Better than I expected. And worse. So, now that you know, what are you going to do about it?"

"Damned if I know. If it was anybody but you . . ." Duncan shrugged. "I've never hesitated to do what I had to do before."

Ramsey nodded. Neither of them had ever shown mercy or pity to the vampires they hunted and destroyed, or suffered any pangs of remorse when the deed was done. He wondered if Duncan felt the sudden tension between them as keenly as he did. He had told Kelly that Duncan would not hesitate to destroy him. Not long ago, he would have welcomed an end to his existence. But not now. He silently thanked Chiavari for insisting he give his new lifestyle some time, even as he wondered if he would be able to kill his best friend if it should come to that.

"So . . ." Duncan said, clearly as ill at ease as was Ramsey. "What do we do now?"

"I guess that's up to you," Ramsey replied. "But we agree on one thing. There are vampires to be hunted in this city. One particularly, and that's Khira. She's more powerful than even Kristov. More evil. She's destroyed other vampires, and who knows how many mortals. Her lust for blood seems insatiable."

"Vampires don't destroy vampires," Duncan remarked. "You know that. It's one of their rules."

"One Khira's already broken," Ramsey said.

Duncan observed his old friend closely. "You'd hunt her with me?"

Ramsey nodded.

"Good vampires versus the evil ones—what a concept!" Duncan shook his head. "The last disrespected minority?" A smile twitched at the corners of his mouth. "You're still Ed Ramsey, though, aren't you? Mr. Morality, through and through."

"Thanks, I think," Ramsey retorted dryly.

Duncan banged his fist repeatedly, distractedly, against the fence post. "Damn, I've got a hundred questions running around in my head."

"They will have to wait." He could feel the force of Kelly's hunger, feel his own rising in response. "I've got to go."

Duncan's eyes narrowed thoughtfully.

Ramsey looked away, unable to meet the speculative look in Duncan's eyes. "Don't ask."

"You need to feed." It wasn't a question.

"So, are you willing to cooperate with a . . . with me?" Ramsey asked. "In this Khira business?"

"The greater good for the greater number," Duncan said sadly. "Without you, I don't have a snowball's chance in hell of bagging Khira, and we both know it. And you need to feed to be strong. I know that, too. Hell, I can't believe I'm going to say this, but . . . good hunting. We'll talk tomorrow. . . ."

Ramsey could wait no longer. He vanished from Duncan's sight. In the house, he grabbed Kelly by the hand and then sped into the night.

He didn't stop until they were far from home.

"What is it?" Kelly asked. "What's wrong?"

"Duncan was waiting for me outside."

"Does he know?"

"Yes."

She stared at him, wide-eyed. "Did he try to . . . ?"

"No, we just talked."

"What about Grigori? And Lisa? Will they be safe from him?"

Ramsey grunted softly. "I wouldn't worry about Chiavari. If Khira can't protect him, no one can. As for Lisa . . ." He shrugged. "I don't know where she is. But you are my biggest worry right now."

"Me? Why?"

"You must learn to feed on your own." He held up his hand to stay the protest he read in her eyes. "If anything happens to me, you will need to know how."

"Nothing's going to happen to you!"

"I hope you are right, but you still need to know how. And tonight is as good as any to learn."

They moved silently through the night until Ramsey found a teenage couple in a park, smoking pot. He mesmerized them both, which was remarkably easy, given that their minds were already fuzzy.

He took the girl in his arms, wondering absently what it was that caused such a pretty kid to dye her hair purple. He looked at Kelly. "Take the boy."

She enfolded the boy in her arms, holding him as if he were made of glass.

"I'll tell you what Chiavari told me. You can make this pleasant for those you take, or not. It is up to you. You needn't worry about the boy's blood. If it was unclean, you would know it. And you must be gentle.

Human flesh . . ." He looked at the girl in his arms. "Human flesh is very fragile."

Kelly nodded.

"Let his blood call to you. Listen to the beat of his heart."

He saw the hunger rise within her, nodded to himself as she lowered her head. The scent of blood wafted through the air.

Watching Kelly feed fueled his own hunger. He spoke to the girl's mind, telling her not to be afraid, and then he unleashed the beast within him, wondering what Duncan would think if he could see his old friend now.

Chapter 33

Marisa poured herself a cup of coffee and carried it to the table. She had kept Grigori's hours for so long, it seemed odd to be up when the sun was still high in the sky. She smiled faintly as she glanced at the wedding invitation lying on the table. Edward and Kelly were getting married day after tomorrow. She hoped they would be happy together.

Though she wasn't in the mood to shop, she supposed she would have to go out and buy them a gift. She wondered if they had invited Grigori, and if Khira would allow him to attend.

She stared into her cup. It was hard to get excited about anything these days. No matter where she was, or what she was doing, all she could think of was Grigori . . . Grigori living in Khira's house, hunting with her. Grigori had told him that Khira was a sensual creature, one who didn't like being told no. They had once been lovers, Grigori and Khira. The thought of the two of them together was like a dagger in her heart.

She slammed her hand on the table. She couldn't think of it any more or she'd go crazy! Grabbing her handbag, she left the house. A day of shopping was just what she needed. It had been a long time since she had spent a day at the mall.

But forgetting Grigori was impossible. The car she drove had been a gift from him. She smiled with the memory. In the nights before the wedding, he had brought her a gift every day: white roses by the dozen, yellow ones, pink ones, a single, perfect, bloodred rose, chocolates and perfume, a diamond necklace that was so beautiful it took her breath away. Her car was the most extravagant gift of all. She well remembered the night he had given it to her.

He had given her a small square box that night, handed it to her with a wink.

When she had asked him what it was, he had told her to open it and see. Stomach fluttering with excitement, she had lifted the lid. A key rested on a bed of blue velvet. She had looked up at him and asked if it was the key to his heart. He had laughed softly and told her it was the key to her new car. She had thought he was kidding until he told her it was parked out front. When she had gone to the window to look, she had seen two Corvettes parked at the curb, a sleek black one and a red convertible. When she had asked him which one, he told her to take her pick. She had scolded him for being so extravagant, saying it must have cost a fortune to buy two such expensive cars. *"I have a fortune, cara mia,"* he had replied. *"Let me spend it on you."*

She lifted her hand to the gold filigree heart at her throat. It, too, had been a gift from Grigori. He had given her so much, but his love was the best gift of all.

She wandered through the mall. It felt good to be out and about, to be in the company of ordinary people doing ordinary things. She passed young women in business attire who were obviously on a lunch break from work, mothers with small children, and elderly women sitting on benches, watching the world go by. She felt a pang of regret as she smiled at a little girl with long blond pigtails. If she accepted the Dark Gift from Grigori, she would never have a child of her own. She thrust the thought from her mind. She had come here to keep from thinking of Grigori and what he might be doing with his ancient lover. She turned back to the task at hand. What kind of wedding gift did one buy for a vampire couple, anyway? They didn't need dishes, glassware, or silverware, had no need for crock pots or toasters or popcorn poppers. New bedding was a possibility, but she didn't know if they rested in beds or—she shuddered—in coffins. Finally, she settled on a crystal vase and a pair of matching candelabra.

Pleased with her purchases, she stopped at Mrs. Field's and bought a dozen dark-chocolate-chip cookies. Another simple human pleasure that would be denied her if she accepted the Dark Gift.

She was leaving the mall when she had the sudden, unshakable feeling that she was being watched. She glanced over her shoulder, remembering the monster who had kidnapped her, but she saw nothing out of the ordinary. Could Khira be trusted to keep her word and leave her alone while Grigori was with her?

She had just convinced herself she was imagining things when a man seemed to materialize out of the crush of people walking through the parking lot. He positioned himself squarely in her path. She stopped abruptly, heart pounding.

He raised a placating hand. "I didn't mean to frighten you. You have nothing to fear from me."

"Who are you? What do you want?"

"I'm Tom Duncan."

Tom Duncan. The vampire hunter. Her heart seemed to drop to her feet. "Why are you following me?"

He fell into step beside her. "A friend of yours asked me to keep an eye on you."

"Oh?"

"Ed Ramsey."

"I see." *Bless you, Edward,* she thought. "Well, thank you."

Duncan blew out a breath. "Hell of a mess," he muttered.

Marisa nodded. "This is my car," she said. "Oh, I guess you know that."

He grinned at her. "I'll follow you home, make sure you get there all right."

"Thank you."

"You won't have to worry much longer."

"What do you mean?"

"We're working on a plan to dispose of Khira permanently."

Marisa's eyes widened. "Are you crazy?"

"It's gotta be done. There's no telling how many she's killed," Duncan said flatly. "We rarely find a body when a master vampire makes a kill. But there's been a sharp increase in missing persons in the last few weeks. I'm not talking runaways. I'm talking men with good, steady jobs. Women with kids at home. People who have no reason to suddenly disappear."

Marisa felt suddenly faint. It was Khira. She knew it was. She braced her hand against the car door. What if Grigori was also responsible? She knew he was capable of violence. She had seen it firsthand. She knew he had killed when he'd first been made vampire, but he had assured her he hadn't killed anyone in over a hundred years, and she had believed him. Had it all been a lie?

She felt suddenly faint. "What about Edward? And Grigori? You aren't . . ."

"No. Just Khira."

"Everything all right here?"

Marisa glanced past Duncan to see a security guard in a green cart. "Yes, fine," she said. "Thank you." Unlocking her car, she opened the door and put her package on the seat.

Duncan waited until the guard had driven away before saying, "She's ruthless. A female Kristov."

"I know. Edward and Grigori are both afraid of her."

"Yeah, well, I can understand that."

"Grigori wasn't sure that they . . ." Her words trailed off as a young mother with two children approached. The woman looked at Marisa and Duncan curiously a moment before unlocking her car and settling her children inside. She glanced at them again before sliding into the driver's seat and pulling out of the parking lot.

"Go on," Duncan said.

"I was saying that Grigori wasn't sure they could destroy her, even with their combined powers."

"Well, we need to find a way, and soon." He pulled a card out of his pocket, wrote a number on the back, and handed it to her. "Call me if you need me."

"Thank you." She thought about everything Duncan had said to her on her way home. Could he be trusted? He had said he was only after Khira, but what if, once Khira was destroyed—assuming she could be destroyed—Duncan decided to destroy Edward and Kelly and Lisa, too? And Grigori?

She blew out a sigh as she pulled into the driveway, wondering if this nightmare would ever end. She had been so certain all their troubles were behind them when Kristov had been destroyed.

She saw Duncan's car slow down as it went past the driveway. He waved and smiled.

Edward trusted him. She only hoped she wasn't making a mistake in doing the same.

Chapter 34

It was her wedding night. It was the first thought to cross Kelly's mind when she woke. She glanced over at Eddie.

He winked at her. "Tonight's the night," he said, grinning.

"You haven't changed your mind, have you?"

"Not a chance, love. Have you?"

"No way." She moved closer to him, one leg draping over his, her arm resting on his chest.

He slid his hand around the back of her head and kissed her. "How much time do you need to get ready?"

"How much time do I have?"

"We are supposed to be there in an hour."

"An hour!" She jumped out of bed. "You expect me to be ready in an hour?"

Ramsey laughed softly. "Take as long as you need, Kelly, my love. They will not start without us."

* * *

The park was dark and quiet. A winding stream glistened like a ribbon of black silk in the light of a full yellow moon. The air was fragrant with the scent of trees and grass and flowering shrubs.

Kelly looked up at Edward when they reached the place they had chosen. "Maybe you were right. Maybe Khira won't let Grigori come. But Marisa said she'd be here."

"Stop worrying," he said. "You're here, and that's all that matters." His gaze moved over her. "Did I tell you how beautiful you are?"

"Yes, but tell me again."

"More beautiful than any woman in the world," he said. "More beautiful than anything or anyone I've ever seen."

And it was true. She had decided against traditional white; instead, she wore a sleeveless gown of soft, shimmering black.

"Like Vampira, Mistress of the Dark," she had said, grinning.

"Mistress of my heart," he replied. "Look, here comes Marisa now."

Kelly glanced over her shoulder to see Marisa walking toward them, a package tied with a white bow in her hands. Even from a distance, Kelly could see the sadness that shadowed the other woman's eyes.

There was a ripple in the air, a change that sent a shiver down Kelly's spine.

And then, in a scene reminiscent of a horror movie, Khira appeared, materializing out of the deep shadows of the night in a shimmer of iridescent silver. She looked ethereal in a golden gown that clung to her body like a second skin. Her hair shimmered in the moonlight.

"What's she doing here?" Kelly exclaimed softly.

A moment later, Grigori appeared at Khira's side. Tall and elegant, clad all in black, he was the handsomest man Kelly had ever seen. She did not miss the look that passed between Marisa and Grigori. The love that flowed between them made her heart ache. Marisa started toward him, then stopped when he shook his head.

"I guess we should have known she wouldn't let him come alone," Ramsey muttered. He swore under his breath as another young woman materialized, looking lost and alone. "Lisa," he said. "Damn, this just keeps getting worse."

Holding back her tears, Marisa hurried forward to hug Kelly. "You look lovely."

"So do you. I'm glad you came."

Marisa nodded. Nothing would have kept her away, not when there'd been a chance that Grigori would be here.

The minister arrived a few minutes later.

The service was brief. The atmosphere tense. Kelly could feel Marisa's longing, Khira's jealousy, Grigori's barely restrained anger, Lisa's fear. And over all, Khira's power roiled like a storm waiting to strike.

Kelly smiled at Edward when the minister asked if he would have her as his wife "for as long as you both shall live."

"Forever." Edward squeezed her hand as he whispered the word.

"Forever," Kelly repeated.

She gazed into Edward's eyes as the minister pronounced them man and wife, felt his love surround her as he lowered his head and claimed his first kiss as her husband. A kiss that went on and on. She leaned into him, all else forgotten as his love surrounded her.

She was breathless when he released her.

The minister offered his congratulations, accepted his fee, and left the park.

Marisa and Lisa came forward to hug her and wish her well.

Khira glided forward with queenly grace. "I do hope you don't mind my coming uninvited," she said coolly. "I was certain my lack of an invitation was merely an oversight." Her gaze moved over Kelly, glittering like shards of ice blue glass. "I do wish you well, my dear."

Turning toward Edward, she kissed him, and when she drew back, there was blood on his lower lip. Looking smug, she moved away to speak to Lisa.

Grigori hugged Kelly and then shook Edward's hand. "Be good to each other."

"Is there anything you want me to tell Marisa?" Kelly asked quietly.

Grigori looked past her to where Marisa stood. "Only that I love her more than my life."

Khira's voice cut across the night. "Grigori, let us go." She reached for his hand and then stopped. Lifting her head, she sniffed the air.

Blood. The scent of it filled Kelly's nostrils.

Tom Duncan crawled forward, then swore softly as something sharp sliced into his left hand. Rocking back on his heels, he stared at the shard of glass protruding from his palm. *Damn. Damn, damn, damn!* Even in the darkness, he could see the blood pooling in his hand.

He peered through the bushes, froze as Khira turned his way. Head lifted, she sniffed the air.

"I knew this was a dumb idea," he muttered.

Grabbing his handkerchief, he wrapped it tightly around his palm, then reached into his pocket and withdrew a large vial of holy water. He touched the wooden stake tucked into his waistband to make sure it was still there.

All the vampires were looking in his direction now. He could feel their senses reaching out, testing the air for danger.

And then Khira was there, fire blazing in the depths of her ice blue eyes. "Looking for me?" she asked.

He tried to draw his gaze from hers, grunted as she grabbed a handful of his hair and jerked him to his feet.

"Edward," she purred, glancing over her shoulder. "How thoughtful of you to provide refreshments for your guests."

"Let him go," Ramsey said.

"Before we've dined? I think not."

"He's a friend of mine," Ramsey said. "Let him go."

Khira shook her head. Baring her fangs, she bent over Duncan's neck. He went limp until he felt her fangs graze his throat; then, with a cry, he jerked his hand up, splashing the contents of the vial into her face.

Khira shrieked with pain, but she didn't release him. Lifting him off his feet as though he weighed no more than a child, she slammed him to the ground with enough force to drive the breath from his body. The holy water made sizzling sounds as it burned her skin. Duncan stared up at her, his stomach churning. He tried to rise, but he was helpless, held immobile by the strength of her will alone.

She was going to kill him.

"No!" With a feral cry, Ramsey launched himself at Khira.

She struck him with the full force of her power and he went flying backward, his back slamming into a tree, hitting it so hard that the trunk split in half.

Momentarily freed from her hold on him, Duncan tried to crawl away, but her power caught him again. He screamed as pain engulfed him, writhed in agony as her hellish power spread through every nerve, every cell. And then, blessedly, miraculously, he was free.

He curled in on himself, hardly able to breathe.

Through a red haze, he watched Ramsey and the two female vampires attack Khira. It was a silent, deadly dance. Preternatural power sang through the air, crackling like lightning. It was like nothing he had ever seen before.

Khira sent Kelly and Ramsey reeling backward and then, with a savage howl, she grabbed the young female vampire and buried her fangs in her throat.

Ramsey and Kelly rushed toward Khira once again, but her power, strengthened by the blood of the young vampire, hurled them backward. The girl whimpered softly as Khira continued to drink, draining her of blood, of life, and when she was done, Khira lifted one clawed hand and ripped the young vampire's heart from her chest. She flung the corpse aside and turned on Kelly. A wave of her hand sent Kelly to her knees. Kelly screamed in agony. Bloodred tears welled in her eyes.

With a savage cry, Ramsey launched himself at Khira.

It was then that Chiavari moved in. Grabbing Khira by the arm, he tried to pull her away from Ramsey. She turned on him in a fury, power radiating from her like sparks from a brush fire.

A voice whispered urgently in Duncan's ear. "Get up! We've got to get out of here!"

Duncan stared up into Marisa's eyes.

"Hurry!" she said.

He nodded and tried to stand, but his legs wouldn't support him.

"Come on!" Grabbing him by the arm, she pulled him to his feet and dragged him to the street where her car was parked. Opening the door, she shoved him inside, ran around to the driver's side, opened the door, and slid behind the wheel. She could hear Grigori's voice in her mind, telling her to get the hell out of there before it was too late.

Duncan glanced out the rear window. "Step on it!"

"Where are you staying?"

He gave her the directions to his motel, then sank back against the seat and closed his eyes. He hurt all over.

"Are you crazy?" Marisa asked. "What the hell were you doing there?" She shook her head. "You weren't going to try and destroy her tonight, were you?"

"No. We weren't ready."

"Then why . . . ?"

"There was no way to know what Khira would do tonight. Ramsey wanted me to be there as backup. Some backup," he added bitterly.

"How much further?"

"A couple blocks. It's on the right side."

"Will she follow us?"

"I don't think so," he said wearily. "She's fed off another vampire. That should hold even Khira for at least a while."

She drove the rest of the way in silence. When she reached the motel, she pulled into the lot and switched off the engine. "Will you be all right?"

"Oh, yeah," he muttered. "No worries."

He opened the door, took a deep breath, and stood up.

"Are you sure you'll be all right?"

"Yeah. I'm not so sure about you, though."

"Me?"

"I don't think you ought to go home tonight."

"Why not?" she asked, and then nodded. "You're probably right."

"Come on," he said, "help me inside."

She grabbed her bag, slid out of the car and locked the door, then walked around the car. She slipped her arm around his waist and they walked slowly toward his room.

Marisa glanced over her shoulder while he fumbled for his key. "What if she finds us?"

"Well, vampires aren't supposed to be able to enter a dwelling uninvited." He opened the door and staggered inside. "I sure as hell hope she knows that."

Marisa followed him inside, shut the door, and locked it.

It did little to make Duncan feel safer. Having felt the force of Khira's power, he doubted if he would ever feel safe again.

Duncan fell onto the bed nearest the door. The room looked pretty much like every other motel room he'd ever seen. There was an ugly brown carpet on the floor, a pair of queen-size beds with flowered spreads, drapes heavily lined to shut out the sun, a cheap painting of a landscape on one wall, a mirror on another, a chest of drawers with a television set on top, a sagging overstuffed chair by the single window.

Muttering an oath, he closed his eyes. He had never felt so miserable in his whole life. Not when he'd had the flu. Not when, at the age of sixteen, he'd caught a bad case of chicken pox. Not last year, when he had come down with food poisoning.

He opened one eye to find Marisa staring down at him. She was a pretty woman, he thought absently, and wondered how the hell she had gotten mixed up with a vampire.

"Can I get you anything?" she asked.

"Coffee. Hot. Black."

"Only if they deliver," she replied, shivering. "I'm not going outside until the sun's up."

"In the bathroom. Courtesy coffee."

She grimaced, then left the room.

Duncan tried to relax, but it was no use. He kept seeing the look in Khira's eyes as she slammed him to the ground, couldn't shake off the sheer terror that had turned his blood to ice when she turned the full force of her gaze on him. He had tangled with a lot of powerful vampires in his day, but never, never anything quite like Khira. He wondered if she was able to move about during the day, if she was immune to sunlight.

She wasn't immune to holy water, though. That was something, at least.

He took some grim satisfaction in that remembered shriek of horror and the sight of her face, the skin steaming and seeming to melt away. She had hurt him, yes, but he had gotten in his licks . . . The thought made him feel better. She was dangerous, but so was he.

"Here." Marisa's voice.

He opened his eyes as the scent of coffee tickled his nostrils.

"Can you sit up?"

"I think so." It took all his strength to pull himself into a sitting position. When he had his back braced against the headboard, she handed him the cup. "Thanks." He took a sip, sighed, and took another drink. The hot, bitter brew slid down his throat.

"What did she do to you?" Marisa asked.

"Beats the hell out of me." He drank the last of the coffee and put the cup on the table beside the bed. "Ramsey told me your husband is shacked up with Khira."

"He is not shacked up! He's . . ." She turned away, but not before he saw the anguish in her eyes.

"Hey, I'm sorry. But he is living with her, right?"

She nodded. "She told Grigori she'd kill me unless he agreed to spend a year with her."

"And when the year is up, what then?"

"I think . . . I think she's hoping that he'll want to stay with her."

"Will he?"

"I don't know."

It was a question that haunted her long after Duncan had fallen asleep. Sitting in the chair by the window, her legs curled beneath her, Marisa thought about Grigori. She had been drawn to him from the moment she first saw him, mesmerized by his voice. She recalled thinking it was richer than dark chocolate, more intoxicating than wine. She remembered the night, soon after she had met Grigori, when she had felt Alexi's presence outside her apartment. Grigori had gone out to meet him, and they had struggled. Grigori had returned, his cheek bleeding from where the other vampire had stuck him. The wounds had been deep, down to the bone. The sight had made her sick to her stomach, yet the wound had healed before her eyes. *Vampire.* She had not wanted to believe it, had fallen in love in spite of what he was.

She thought of the horrible night that Alexi had been destroyed, the night Grigori had, at her urging, bestowed the Dark Gift upon Edward. So much had happened since then.

She recalled all too clearly the night Grigori had come home after hunting with Khira. He had never spoken to her of that night, but she had known what he was feeling, had sensed his struggle to suppress the darkness within him. One night of hunting with Khira had destroyed the peace he had fought so hard to achieve, awakened cravings he had thought long subdued.

She had seen the demon within him that night, seen the raw, aching hunger for blood. What would he be like after spending a year with Khira? Would the Grigori she loved return to her or be lost forever? Where was he now?

She closed her eyes, her soul searching for him, her heart aching, her arms yearning to hold him.

"Grigori." She wrapped his name in her love and sent it out into the night, hoping he would hear.

Chapter 35

Khira paced the floor of her bedroom, her eyes blazing, her hands curled into tight fists. Curses spewed from her mouth like venom, filling the air with the poison of her hatred.

Grigori stood in the doorway, every muscle taut, his face impassive as he waited to see where her fury would lead. Earlier, it had taken all the strength he possessed to drag her off Ramsey and out of the park. He only hoped Ramsey had sense enough to take Kelly and leave town, or at least go to ground until Khira's rage ran its course, until they could formulate a plan to destroy her. And Marisa . . . He dared not send his power into the night searching for her lest his thoughts betray her whereabouts to Khira. Surely the vampyre hunter, Duncan, would have sense enough to lie low and take Marisa with him.

Absently he rubbed his fingertips over his wrist. As soon as they had reached home, Khira had grabbed his arm and fed. She had not asked. There had been no gentleness in her as her fangs had ripped into his flesh. He had steeled himself for a fight to the finish then, certain that, caught up in her rage, she would kill him without a thought. But she had stopped well short of draining him, and he knew it had been her way of reasserting her dominion over him, proving to him— and perhaps to herself—that she was still in control.

She had not needed to feed so soon, not after she had drained Lisa of blood in what had been an act of cruelty, not of necessity. Khira hadn't been in need of anything but a reaffirmation of her power. Duncan's use of the holy water had shaken her badly. She was nothing if not vain of her appearance.

His gaze moved over Khira's face. Already the effects of the holy water were fading. By tomorrow or the day after, her skin would be as unblemished and flawless as before.

Looking at her now, her features contorted with hate, he wondered how he had ever thought her beautiful.

"We are not all monsters." Her words from long ago echoed through the corridors of his mind. *"Look at me. Do I appear a monster to you?"* She had not looked like a monster then. With her regal bearing and costly attire, she had looked like a queen.

She did not look like a queen now.

She whirled around, pinning him with her venomous gaze. "Say something!"

"What would you have me say?"

"I want you to tell me why you took their side." Her voice rose. "I want you to tell me why you did not come to my aid when they attacked me!"

It was the question he had been waiting for. And dreading.

"Why?" Teeth bared, she flew at him.

He ducked out of her way, whirled around to face her. "Stop it."

She drew herself up to her full height. "You dare to tell me what to do?" she demanded imperiously.

"Enough is enough. You are acting like a spoiled child."

"You betrayed me."

"I did nothing of the kind."

Renewed anger flared in the depths of her eyes. "I expected you to fight at my side."

"And do what?" he retorted. "Help you destroy Ramsey? I did not save his life to have you take it from him."

Her eyes narrowed. "Why did you save him?"

"Because, in spite of everything he was, everything he believed, I respected him."

"You are a fool!"

"But not a tyrant."

She glared at him. "A tyrant? Because I demand loyalty?"

"What have you ever done to earn it?"

She placed her hand over his heart. "Have you forgotten that I made you what you are, Grigori?" she asked, her voice deceptively sweet.

"How could I?"

Her fingers dug into his flesh. "I gave you this life, my handsome one. I can take it from you just as easily."

"You think so?" he asked, his own considerable anger rising to meet hers. "Then try! Go on, do it! I grow weary of your threats."

He had pushed her too far this time. As soon as the words were uttered, he knew with a dreadful certainty that he had made what might be a fateful mistake. She bared her fangs in a feral snarl, her eyes glittering like blue hellfire.

She was going to kill him.

Her power lashed out at him with sudden force. His knees buckled beneath the weight of it, but did not give. He bit back the groan that rose in his throat. There was no pain in the world quite like it. Even the hot kiss of the sun was not as excruciating as the cold fire that flowed through him now, burning him from the inside out.

Gathering his strength, he met force with force, his legs spread, his head high.

They faced each other, unmoving, as their wills clashed. Slowly, inexorably, he felt her strength begin to erode his own. In that moment, when her power flowed over him and through him, he knew he had no hope of defeating her. Not now, not alone. She had taken only a little of his blood, but it had been enough to weaken him and strengthen her. What a stubborn, arrogant fool he had been to challenge her in her present mood. Had she known he would defy her? Had she purposely set out to rouse his ire in hopes of bringing him to his knees?

He swore under his breath. He would not submit to her. Nor was he strong enough to defeat her in a head-to-head confrontation. But he was still strong, and smart enough to end the battle before she anticipated his intent.

Drawing from the deep wellspring of Marisa's love, he reached down inside himself, gathered his power around him, and in a last desperate maneuver, flung it outward, momentarily blocking Khira's attack. Using the last of his strength, he willed himself out of the room and out of the house.

Her outraged cry followed him into the night.

"I will destroy you! I will destroy all of you! And your woman, too!"

Marisa bolted upright. "Something's wrong!"

Duncan switched on the light next to his bed. "What's the matter?" he asked sleepily. "Bad dream?"

"No. It's . . ." She glanced around the room. "It's Grigori. He's in terrible pain."

She had gone to bed fully clothed, shy in the presence of a man who was little more than a stranger. Throwing back the covers, she slipped out of bed and went to the window, where she pulled the heavy drapes aside. The sky was just turning light.

Chilled, she folded her arms across her chest. "Grigori has quarreled with her. He's run away. Grigori," she whispered. "Grigori, my life, my love, where are you?"

He fled the mansion, fled the city, with the sun rising behind him, and with Khira's last angry words ringing in his mind: *"I will destroy all of you! And your woman, too!"*

"Like hell," he muttered. With the help of Ramsey and Marisa, he had destroyed Alexi Kristov, once the most powerful vampire that had ever lived. They had done it once. They could do it again.

He fled through the weak light of early dawn, feeling the lethargy of the Dark Sleep pulling at his weakened limbs, until he found what he was looking for: a barren stretch of ground. Using the last of his strength, he burrowed into the earth, clawing at the dirt with his fingers, digging deep, deeper, in a frantic effort to escape the rising sun.

Panting, he gathered the dirt around and over him, blotting out the first deadly rays of the rising sun. His last thought was of Marisa, and then he was beyond thought as the Dark Sleep enveloped him, pulling him down, down, into nothingness.

* * *

Kelly snuggled against Edward. "Will we be safe here?"

"We should be." Edward glanced around the room. It was a first-class hotel in an expensive part of the city. The desk clerk had been reluctant to admit them without any luggage, but Edward had used his Dark Power to cloud the man's mind, and now he and Kelly were reclining on a big round bed in the bridal suite. The carpet was plush, the furniture elegant, the bathroom, with its sunken tub and double shower, bigger than most of the houses he had lived in.

"She killed that poor girl," Kelly said, shuddering at the memory. "Killed her for no reason."

Edward nodded. Stroking Kelly's hair, he stared into the darkness. He was appalled by the events of the night, by his own shortsightedness and stupidity. He should have known that Khira would not allow Grigori out of her sight. Guilt for Lisa's death lay heavy on his conscience. And yet it was Khira who was to blame. Khira who must be destroyed.

He squeezed Kelly's shoulder. "Try not to think about it."

"What are we going to do?"

"We're going to find Duncan and Marisa tomorrow night," he replied. "It's time to end this."

Duncan woke late the following afternoon. Except for being hungry enough to eat a very large horse, tail and all, he felt surprisingly fit considering all that had happened the night before.

He glanced at Marisa. Exhausted by her worry for her vampire lover, she was asleep, her cheek resting on her hand. It looked as if she had cried herself to sleep. He could hardly blame her. Being married to a vampire couldn't be easy at the best of times, and now . . . he shook his head. Now it must be hell.

When his stomach growled again, he got out of bed. Going into the bathroom, he made a cup of coffee, then turned on the shower. When the water was hot, he undressed and stepped into the stall, carrying the cup with him.

Standing under the soothing spray, he reckoned it was sometimes the small things in life that were the best. If he had been alone, he would have stayed in the shower until the water got cold, but he was pretty sure Marisa wouldn't appreciate that. The least he could do was leave her some hot water.

He turned off the faucet, toweled himself dry, dressed, and brushed his teeth. When he reentered the room, Marisa was awake. "Hope I didn't wake you."

"No."

He jerked a thumb over his shoulder. "I left you some hot water."

She nodded wordlessly.

Crossing the floor, he sat down on the bed beside her. "It'll be all right. You'll see."

She shook her head. "You don't know how awful it was the last time . . . fighting Alexi . . . I don't think I can go through all that again."

"I guess it was pretty rough, huh?"

"You have no idea."

"That's the night Edward was changed?"

She nodded.

"How'd it happen?"

"Edward was under Alexi's control. He had drugged Grigori, then drained some of his blood to weaken him. Alexi told Edward to take the bowl filled with Grigori's blood and dispose of it. I begged Edward not to leave me, but he was helpless to resist Alexi's power.

"But Grigori had taken Edward's blood and he was

able to speak to his mind. I didn't know that at the time, of course. I fought Alexi, but he only laughed at me."

She heard Alexi's voice in her mind again, as real as it had been that horrible night.

"Fight me all you wish, woman; you cannot escape me. I will take you here, now, and there is nothing you can do about it. Nothing Chiavari can do to save you." Wicked laughter bubbled up from his throat. *"I know the power of those chains. He does not have the strength to remove them. Even now, the silver burns his flesh and weakens his powers. Only a vampire who has lived as long as I could withstand them. And he is but a babe compared to me."*

He gazed down at her, his eyes glowing with hatred. *"He took Antoinette from me, and now I shall take you from him. I will defile you, here, in his presence, and then I shall destroy him. And when that is done, you will be mine for a hundred years. And he will know it. In whatever hell he finds himself, he will know it."*

She shook her head, trying to throw off the horrible memory. "I was so afraid. I looked at Grigori, but he couldn't help me, and I knew Alexi was going to kill me. And suddenly . . ." She took a deep breath. "Suddenly, Edward burst into the room. His mouth was smeared with blood. I knew it was Grigori's, that he had . . . had drank the blood from the bowl. His eyes were wild. He had a stake in his hand, and he hurled himself at Alexi."

"Good old Edward," Duncan said. "Got him like that, huh?"

"Not quite. Alexi was unbelievably strong. I dragged the heavy chain off Grigori and let him drink from my wrist."

She remembered the prick of his fangs, the oddly sensual flow of blood from her vein. He seemed to drink forever, yet it was only a handful of seconds, and then he put her from him and rose to his feet.

"Go on," Duncan urged quietly.

"Edward and Alexi were still struggling. Edward had plunged the stake into Alexi's chest, but he had missed Alexi's heart. The vampire pulled the stake from his body and tossed it aside. And then he flung Edward against the wall and held him there. And he . . . he drank and drank. And suddenly, Grigori was there. He grabbed the stake and plunged it into Alexi's heart."

Her voice was flat, expressionless, as she relived the horror of it all. "Alexi screamed. It was an awful sound. Grigori twisted the stake, driving it deeper and deeper. Alexi sank to his knees. His face turned a hideous shade of gray. Grigori told me to get the chain and put it over Alexi." She laughed hollowly. "I don't know why. I mean, he was dead. Again. I thought Edward was, too. He was . . . he was lying on the floor. His throat was . . . was gone. I asked Grigori if he was dead, and he said no, not yet."

She looked at Duncan, hoping for his understanding. "I couldn't let Edward die, not when he'd saved us. I asked Grigori to save him. He didn't want to. He told me Edward wouldn't like it, that he would rather be dead. But I couldn't let him die. There had been so much death already . . ." She smiled faintly. "Grigori told me I'd have to take the blame. He made me sit down and covered me with a blanket, then told me to close my eyes. But I didn't. I couldn't."

Duncan leaned forward. He had killed vampires, and he had a pretty good idea of how the Dark Gift worked, but he had never seen anyone brought across.

"Grigori knelt on the floor and drew Edward into his lap. He turned Edward's head to the side. I saw Grigori take a deep breath, and then he bent over Edward. I couldn't see much. I don't know how much time went by, probably not more than a few minutes. And then Grigori bit his own wrist and placed the bleeding wound to Edward's lips and told Edward to drink.''

"And he did," Duncan said.

"Yes, he did. It was . . ." She shook her head, at a loss for words to describe adequately what she had seen.

Grigori had looked at her then, his eyes dark, fathomless, penetrating. *This is what I am, what I have always been.*

"It was like a miracle," she went on. "The horrible wound in Edward's throat healed in just a few minutes. His color returned. He didn't know what had happened at first."

Edward had glanced from Chiavari to Marisa. "What the hell happened?"

"How do you feel, Edward?" she had asked.

"I feel fine," he retorted. "I want to know what the . . ." His words trailed off when he caught sight of Alexi's body. "Is he dead?"

She shrugged. "I hope so."

"He's dead," Grigori remarked. He regarded Ramsey through narrowed eyes. "How do you feel?"

"Why do you two keep asking me that? I feel . . ." Edward frowned. "I feel funny." He looked at Alexi again. "I stabbed him, and then he . . ."

Edward lifted one hand to his throat. "He bit me. Ripped my jugular. I remember . . . what happened?"

"You were dying," she told him.

Edward stared at Grigori, a look of horror spreading over his face. "You didn't? For the love of all that's holy, tell me you didn't!"

"It was my idea," she said. "He didn't want to."

"You told him to turn me into one of them? How could you?"

She remembered standing up, the bedspread clutched to her chest. "Would you rather be dead, Edward?"

He had scrambled to his feet and backed away from them both. "Of course I would . . ." he began, and then, shoulders slumping, he buried his face in his hands.

"Well, he seems to have adjusted readily enough now," Duncan remarked drily.

"Perhaps," she said. "He went through—so much pain. He tried to walk out into the sun, to destroy himself. He even asked Grigori to destroy him. He was very troubled. And then Kelly came into his life. . . ."

"Ah, true love," Duncan said with a twist of bitterness. "What happened to Kristov's body?"

"Grigori dragged it out onto the balcony. He said the sun would take care of it."

"Hell of a story."

She nodded.

"You're worried about him, aren't you? Chiavari?"

"Of course. I love him." She clutched his arm. "You're not going to try and kill him, are you? Or Edward? Or Kelly?"

"Sounds like you're trying to put me out of business. Killing vampires is what I do. It's all I know."

She let go of his arm, her gaze probing his. "I thought Edward was your friend."

"He was. He is." Duncan shook his head. "Damn, I don't know what to do anymore." He ran a hand through his hair. "I've spent close to fifteen years hunting vampires. I've always believed they were evil, that they had to be destroyed." He stood and began to pace the floor. "Look at Kristov! The man was a monster. And Khira? She's even worse. She's killing people every night. Who knows how many of the people on the city's missing-persons reports are dead and gone, killed by her hand?''

"Grigori wouldn't . . .''

"He's killed, too. And, damn it, so has Edward.''

"So have you.''

"Vampires are already dead. You can't kill something that's dead.'' Agitated, he slammed his fist into the wall. Life had been so simple before. He had been one of the good guys. The undead were the bad guys. Black and white. No shades of gray. And now . . . he swore under his breath. Right or wrong, he couldn't kill Edward.

"Tom?'' She looked up at him, a silent appeal in her eyes. "I love Grigori.''

"All right, all right. I won't hunt him. Or Edward.''

"Or Kelly?''

He swore again. "Or Kelly.''

"Thank you.''

"Yeah, sure,'' Tom muttered ruefully. "Who knows? Maybe I can go into the movie business as a consultant on horror movies. Or write the next bestseller. *Vampires Are Us.*''

Chapter 36

Shifting shadows, a subtle change in the pulse and rhythm of the city, of the earth itself, as night spread her voluminous cloak across the face of the land.

Edward Ramsey came awake at the setting of the sun, all his senses alert. He sent his power outward, testing the air, but he detected no hint of danger.

He brushed a kiss across Kelly's cheek. Her skin was cool. She lay unmoving beside him, still caught in the deathlike sleep of their kind.

Their kind. *I am a vampire.* Even now, it was still hard to believe.

He smoothed a lock of hair from her brow. Even though he knew she would awaken soon, even though he knew her utter stillness was normal for a vampire, he found it disconcerting to see her like that, vulnerable and helpless—and more so to know that, when caught in the Dark Sleep, he was just as vulnerable, just as helpless.

She stirred a short time later, her eyelids fluttering,

opening. She smiled when she saw him gazing down at her. "Hello, husband."

"Hello, wife."

She rolled over, draping her body across his, her fingertips trailing up and down his thigh. "We didn't get much of a honeymoon night, did we?"

Ramsey shook his head. "Maybe we can make up for it tonight."

She smiled a slow, sexy smile. "Are you reading my mind?"

"I hope so."

Ramsey folded her into his arms, his mouth finding hers, his hands moving over the smooth skin of her back. Their lovemaking was sometimes tender and sweet and sometimes, as now, filled with a dark fire edged with a fierce hunger. His power rose within him, emphasizing every sensation. He breathed in the scent of her skin, closed his eyes as he tasted her lips. It crossed his mind that, if not for Marisa and Chiavari, he would never have met Kelly. He would have been dead these past months, killed by Kristov's hand, never knowing the joy he had found in Kelly's arms.

She clung to him, her body moving against his like a living flame, her hands and lips igniting his desire. She whispered erotic suggestions in his ear, some that were wickedly funny, some inventive but quite impossible, even for a vampire.

He took pleasure in her release, in the way her body shuddered beneath his, in the touch of her fangs at his throat. His own release came soon after, an explosion that rocked him to the core of his being, heightened by the rich, coppery taste of her blood on his tongue. . . .

Awash in contentment, he held her close in his arms, the scent of her blood arousing another hunger.

Kelly drew back so she could see his face. "Do you think it's safe to go out?"

"I hope so." He offered her a wry grin. "We could hunt in the hotel, I guess."

"Yeah, right."

"We need to go out, anyway," Ramsey said. "We have to find Marisa and Duncan."

"Do you really think Khira can be destroyed? That we can destroy her?"

"I don't know, but we have to try. She has to be stopped. She is as bad as Kristov ever was. Hell, she's worse."

"You're not a hunter anymore."

"But Duncan is. If I had any doubts about killing her before, they're gone now." He swore under his breath. "She has to be stopped before she kills us all."

Grigori rested deep in the heart of the earth, letting its warmth surround him, letting its energy flow into him, rejuvenating him. He summoned his power, flung it out into the vast reaches of the night. He felt Ramsey's determination to destroy Khira, Kelly's trepidation. He closed his eyes as his senses brushed the essence that was Marisa. Marisa, so warm and vital and alive, her love for him strong and unwavering. And over all, the evil canker of Khira's anger, spreading across the city like a dark stain, polluting everything it touched.

He stirred as the sun went down, drawn to the surface by the heartbeat of the city, a low quiet thrumming that sang like sweet music in his ears, urging him to rise, to feed.

It was a call he could not refuse. Not now, when the need for blood was pounding through him, merciless, relentless.

He burst forth from the earth filled with renewed strength and a powerful thirst. A thought took him down to his favorite hunting grounds at the beach. He prowled the darkened streets until he found a young couple necking in a late-model convertible. His mind closed on theirs, held them immobile while he quickly took what he wanted. What he needed. What he craved.

When he had drunk his fill, he wiped his memory from their minds, released them from his hold, and vanished into the ever-changing shadows of the night.

Marisa smoothed her skirt, wishing she had a change of clothes. A hundred dollars for a new dress, and it was ruined, stained with dirt and with Duncan's blood. "How's your hand?"

"Okay, I guess. Hurts a little."

"You probably need some stitches."

He shrugged. "Too late now."

She jumped, startled, when someone knocked on the door.

"Relax," Duncan said. "It's probably just the pizza."

She nodded. They had considered going out for something to eat but, in the end, had decided to play it safe and stay in. While she showered and washed her hair, Tom had called out and ordered a couple of pizzas.

Duncan went to the door. "Who is it?"

"Ramsey."

Startled, Duncan glanced over his shoulder at Marisa.

"Maybe we shouldn't let him in." She didn't think they were in any danger from Edward, but after what she had seen at the park, she wasn't feeling any too safe.

"I trust Ramsey," Duncan said. "If he wanted to kill me, he could have done it already."

Marisa nodded. "All right."

Tom unlocked the door, his confidence waning some when he saw the two vampires standing there.

"So, are you going to invite us in?" Ramsey asked, one brow raised in amusement.

"Sure, come on in, " Duncan said, and stood back to admit Edward and Kelly.

Marisa glanced from one vampire to the other. Edward was clad in a bulky light-blue sweater and a pair of black jeans; Kelly wore a bloodred sweater and a pair of white pants. From the vibrant glow in their cheeks, it was obvious both had fed recently.

For a moment, the tension in the room was thick enough to cut.

It was Duncan who broke the silence. "What brings you here, Ed?"

"What the hell do you think?" Ramsey retorted. "We need to talk."

With a nod, Duncan shut the door and slid the bolt home, then sat down on the edge of his bed. "You two might as well sit down and be comfortable."

Edward and Kelly sat on the other bed, holding hands.

Marisa sat in the room's only chair, one leg curled beneath her. "Have you seen Grigori?"

Ramsey shook his head. "I tried to locate him, but I couldn't. He's put up a mind block."

Marisa leaned forward. "You don't think he's . . ." She couldn't say the word.

"No."

"Why would he shut his mind against me?"

Kelly reached out and squeezed Marisa's hand. "I'm sure it's to protect you from Khira."

"Yes, Khira," Duncan said. His gaze settled on Ramsey. "Are you ready to tell me where she is?"

"She's staying at the LaSalle mansion. She . . ." Ramsey paused, his gaze darting toward the door. "Someone's here." He lifted his head and sniffed the air. "Did you order a pizza?"

Duncan nodded. A moment later, there was a knock

on the door. Duncan opened the door a crack and looked out, then opened the door. He paid for the pizzas, handed the boxes to Marisa, then closed and locked the door.

Marisa set the boxes on top of the dresser. The first was ham and pineapple, the second sausage and pepperoni. Swimming in tomato sauce. It reminded her of blood.

"I don't think I'm as hungry as I thought," she murmured, turning away.

"I used to love pizza," Kelly remarked.

Duncan took a slice of sausage and pepperoni. Leaning one hip against the edge of the dresser, he wolfed it down. Looking at Ramsey, he smacked his lips appreciatively as he grabbed another slice and then sat down on the bed again.

"So," he said between mouthfuls, "what's Khira doing at the LaSalle place?"

"She saw it. She decided she wanted it." Ramsey shrugged. "She took it."

Duncan wiped his hand across his mouth. "What about LaSalle?"

Ramsey snorted disdainfully. "He left without a whimper."

"So." Duncan grabbed his third slice of pizza and munched it thoughtfully. "I guess I'll go pay her a little visit tomorrow morning." He looked at Ramsey. "I sure wish you were going with me."

Ramsey nodded. "I wish I could."

"You would be wiser," remarked a deep voice, "to visit her in the afternoon."

"Grigori!" Jumping to her feet, Marisa hurled herself into his arms when he suddenly appeared in the middle of the room. "Where have you been? How are you?" She ran her hands up his arms and over his shoulders, her gaze searching his face. "Are you all right?"

"*Cara*, you worry too much." Lowering his head, he kissed her tenderly.

She leaned into him, all else forgotten. He was here; he was well. For now, that was all that mattered. Khira, the danger they were in, everything else faded into the distance, swept away by the heat spiraling through her, by the sweet ecstasy of his lips on hers, his arms surrounding her.

Ramsey's voice penetrated the haze of passion. "You two coming up for air any time soon?"

"Maybe they'd better get their own room," Duncan remarked dryly.

Marisa felt her cheeks grow warm at the banter of the two men. Grigori smiled down at her. Lifting her into his arms, he sat down in the chair she had vacated, and settled her on his lap.

"You left her?" Ramsey asked, one brow raised in disbelief. "You left Khira? What about Marisa?"

"I'm not afraid," Marisa said. She looked up at Grigori. "Not as long as you're here."

Chiavari's arm tightened around her. "Marisa is in no more danger than the rest of us now. Khira intends to kill us. All of us."

Duncan swore softly. "Like hell."

"Exactly," Ramsey said. He looked at Duncan and smiled broadly. "Looks like we'll be working together again, after all."

The room fell silent a moment. Ramsey squeezed Kelly's hand. He could feel her fear. She wasn't the only one who was afraid, he thought. They all were.

"We need a plan," Ramsey said. "Khira's powerful, and she's smart. She won't go down without a fight."

Duncan nodded. "It'll have to be during the day."

"Maybe," Chiavari said. "And maybe not."

"What do you mean?" Marisa asked, her gaze searching Grigori's face. "You don't intend to fight her at night, when she's at her strongest?"

"Maybe you would rather not be involved," Ramsey said, addressing Chiavari. "You and Khira share a lot of history."

"She cannot be allowed to go on as she is," Grigori said quietly. "She is a danger, not only to us, but to everyone in the city."

"So, we're agreed," Ramsey said. "She must be destroyed."

Grigori nodded, his arm tightening around Marisa. He would do whatever he had to do to keep her safe.

"So," Ramsey said, "we need a plan."

"I've got a plan," Duncan said. "I'll go in tomorrow afternoon, stake her, and take her head. What could be simpler?"

"Almost anything," Grigori said dryly. "You don't know what you're dealing with here."

"She's a vampire, isn't she?" Duncan retorted. "I don't care how powerful she is. A stake through the heart will stop her clock, just like anybody else's."

Darkness moved through Grigori's eyes. "I am surprised you have survived this long, vampyre hunter." There was no mistaking the disdain in the last two words. "How have you hunted us for so long and learned so little?"

Duncan stood up. "I've made ten kills," he said. "Ten kills in almost fifteen years. She'll make eleven."

"Go, then," Grigori said, his voice as hard and cold as ice. "Try and take her. We will bury what is left of you, if there is anything left to find."

"What's that supposed to mean?" Duncan asked, bristling.

"It means you are a fool if you think you will be able to walk into her lair, find her, and stake her. She has not survived a thousand years by being careless or foolish."

"We know where she lives. It shouldn't be that hard to break in."

"You do not know if she rests there," Grigori said, his voice filled with contempt. "You know nothing of her habits. Or if anyone guards her lair while she sleeps."

Duncan glanced at Ramsey, his expression uncertain.

"He's right," Ramsey said. "You're letting your eagerness overcome your good sense." He held up his hand, silencing the protest he saw in Duncan's eyes. "I know you better than anyone, Tom. You're a good man, a capable hunter. And ten kills is an impressive record. But you've never gone up against a vampire as powerful as Khira, believe me. I've felt her power. I know what she can do."

"He's right," Grigori added. "As for being vulnerable during the daylight hours, she told me that the daylight has little power over her anymore. If you go charging into her house expecting to find a . . ." He glanced at Marisa. "A sleeping corpse, you may find yourself facing an enraged vampire who is very much awake. And far stronger than any mortal."

Duncan sat down, his face pale. "All right, you convinced me. Now what?"

Ramsey grinned ruefully. "I guess we still need a plan."

Khira stormed through the city like a dark angel of death, hunting and killing with relentless fury. With each life she snuffed from existence, with each steaming draught of life's blood, her strength increased—and with it, her rage.

Grigori had left her. Forsaken her. How dare he! Did he really think himself strong enough to resist her fury? The thought gave her pause. Perhaps he did, but he would soon realize his folly. He had underestimated her anger, her strength, her passion for vengeance. When she found him this time, she would drain him and destroy him without effort. Without regret. She had given him the Dark Gift of life, and she would take it from him.

Even as she ensnared another victim, she was aware of Grigori. He had not even bothered to leave the city but had simply gone home to that—that—wife of his. He was there now, waiting. Waiting for her. He did not seem particularly afraid, when he should be cowering from the wrath to come. From where had he found this sudden courage, this need to defy her?

Disposing of the last body, she drew in a deep breath and blew it out in a long shuddering sigh. She was ready now, impatient for the confrontation to come. Her eyes narrowed as she focused all her energy on Grigori.

He was not alone with Marisa.

The vampyre hunter was there, the one who had dared attack her. She lifted a hand to her face, assuring herself that no scars remained from the holy water he had splashed over her. She had already marked him for destruction, had believed she might have a difficult time finding him after he had felt her power. She smiled. They had joined forces, the vampyre hunter and the vampire, making it that much easier to find them both. Khira discounted Marisa's presence. The puny mortal was no threat. And it would be such a pleasure, poetic almost, to feed on Grigori's woman after the battle.

But where was Ramsey? She searched but could not find him or his woman. Had they left town? Or had Ramsey grown strong enough to conceal himself—and his little slut? She knew a momentary pang of regret. She had been drawn to Ramsey from the first, attracted to his cool facade and growing power. If she had concentrated more on him, perhaps he would be at her side now, aiding her against Grigori and the hunter, Duncan.

She dismissed the thought even as it formed. She had never been foolish enough to trust those of her own kind. She was a law unto herself.

Still, her inability to locate Ramsey troubled her.

No matter. She was full of power. She could feel it seething within her, her anger growing, feeding on itself. It was time. She would destroy them all: the vampire hunter, Edward and his fledgling, Marisa, Grigori . . . She closed her eyes, imagining a world without Grigori in it.

Why, Grigori? Why have you done this?

"I asked only for a year," she whispered. "A year out of our immortality to spend together again. And you promised!" Anger overcame sentiment. "You lied to me! Humiliated me!"

But it was more than that. He had wounded her pride by leaving her to go to another woman. A mortal woman. Her voice rose as her outrage flamed high once more. "You will pay for your folly," she vowed. "Before the night is out, you will have paid the ultimate price."

She felt a familiar sense of pleasure as she gathered her power around her. She embraced it, reveled in it, and then, with a wave of her hand, she went to make her final preparation for the battle to come.

"What if she doesn't come?" Marisa asked.

"She'll come," Grigori said. He sat back in the easy chair, looking calm. "Her pride will bring her."

Duncan was playing solitaire. He turned over a card, the ace of clubs. "Got all four aces up now," he said with satisfaction. "My only concern is, what if she goes after Ramsey first?"

"She can't find Ramsey. I can't. And I know where to look. Ramsey is our hole card. So to speak." Grigori smiled. "Your five of hearts can go up now."

"I've got a good feeling about this," Duncan remarked as he played the five. "Yessir, I think I'm going to win this hand."

"Let's just hope we win the battle."

They both seemed so calm, Marisa thought. Was she the only one who was afraid? She hated waiting, wondering, not knowing. Too nervous to sit still, she stood and began to pace the floor in front of the hearth, trying not to look at the sharpened wooden stakes lying in obscene innocence on one of the end tables. A finely engraved solid silver dagger with a triangular blade ending in a needle point lay next to them. Tools of the trade, Duncan had called them. He had two vials of water at his elbow. He didn't have to tell her what they were. She knew it was holy water. She shuddered at the memory of the damage it had done Khira's features, the way it had eaten into the vampire's flesh.

She fingered the thick silver chain around her neck. She had not worn silver since she met Grigori, but tonight he had insisted. She wore wide silver bracelets on her wrists, as well. She didn't want to be here, didn't want to face Khira. Coward that she was, she wanted only to leave town. But Grigori had refused. No matter where they went, Khira would hunt them down sooner or later. Better to end it now, he had said. And Ramsey and Duncan agreed with him. Khira had to be destroyed, and there was no one else to do it. When they had first discussed their plans, Grigori had told her there was no need for her to stay, but then he had changed his mind. Alone and unprotected, Marisa would draw Khira like a beacon on a dark night. Give her a hostage to use against him. Defeat him before he had a chance to fight.

"How long do we have to wait for her to act?" Marisa asked. "I hate waiting, not knowing . . ."

"It shouldn't be much longer," Grigori said. "I've felt her in my mind. She knows we are here, and that

Duncan is with us. She suspects we are plotting against her. One of her revenants is watching the house even now.''

Revenants. Marisa shuddered.

"She will be here," Grigori said, and went suddenly still.

"What is it?" Marisa touched the chain around her neck again. "Grigori . . ."

"Damn it, I should have expected this," Grigori said tensely. "Duncan! The front door . . ."

The rest of his words were drowned in a splintering crash as the front door exploded inward.

There was the sound of heavy footsteps, and two huge men burst into the room. Another followed. And another . . . and another.

They were all built like football linemen—tall and massive and muscular. They fanned out toward the room's occupants without a word. They moved fast enough, but in a disjointed shamble, mouths slack.

Their eyes were dead.

Marisa's stomach churned with fear. She ran across the room toward Grigori without thinking about the silver she wore—until she saw him flinch away. She ducked around behind him—far enough away so the silver would not weaken him.

By then, two of the revenants were on him, while two more closed in on Duncan. She couldn't see the vampire hunter past their bulky bodies.

They seized Grigori's arms. Marisa felt him gather his power, felt it crawl along her skin, lift the hairs at her nape.

With a savage cry of rage, Grigori broke free. He shoved one of the revenants away, and at the same time, he snatched the other to him, his hands folding over the creature's bulky shoulders in an obscene parody of a lover's embrace. Jerking the revenant's head down and to the side, he exposed its muscular, corded neck. The creature he had thrown off was shambling back to the fray, grunting furiously.

Grigori buried his fangs in his prey's neck and drank deep as the other one laid his hands on him and tried to pry him away from his kill.

Across the room, one of the creatures blocking her view of Duncan sagged suddenly and collapsed. Eyes glazed with the heat of battle, Duncan coolly planted his foot on its chest and withdrew a bloody stake. But before he could set himself to strike again, the second creature drove him to his knees with a clumsy round-house blow.

Marisa shrieked as a huge hairy arm circled her waist and lifted her off her feet. The grip tightened relentlessly, cutting off her breath.

"Grigori!" She gasped his name.

He flung his prey aside, spun out of the grasp of the second, and was at her side in the blink of an eye. She couldn't see what he was doing behind her, but the revenant's arm fell away and he dropped heavily to the floor.

Duncan was up again, struggling with one of the attackers. She scrambled toward the wall and turned, her mind reeling, her nostrils filling with the scent of blood.

A stake was raised in the air, the end dripping blood.

It took her what seemed like forever to realize it was not wielded by Duncan, but by one of the revenants. And that it was aimed at Grigori's back as he battled the creature who had seized her.

Shadows blurred across her vision, moving fast.

And suddenly Ramsey was there, his grip locked on the wrist of the revenant who held the stake. Kelly was there, too, struggling with the creature who had almost bested Duncan.

Marisa watched with horrified fascination as Ramsey looped his free arm around the revenant's neck and snapped it with one powerful stroke.

Kelly screamed as the monster she had attacked broke her left arm and hurled her to the floor. Ramsey immediately launched himself at the creature. Duncan grabbed a stake from the table and tossed it to Ramsey, who drove it through the revenant's heart.

The room stank of blood and fear and violent death.

The surviving revenants pressed their attack, utterly oblivious to the fate of their fellows.

And then, Khira was there.

Her triumphant laughter filled the room. "Sorry I'm late, children. I had to wait until Ramsey and his little trollop came out of hiding."

Like a whirlwind, she spun through them. A single blow sent Duncan flying across the room. He slammed into a wall and slid to the floor, boneless as a rag doll. A revenant turned and plodded toward him.

Khira backhanded Ramsey out of her path and grabbed Kelly. Snatching her upright, she curled her fingers into hooked claws and raked them down the girl's body, opening a great, gaping wound from shoulder to thigh. With a scream, Kelly collapsed to the floor.

Ramsey almost reached Khira, but she spun away, flying at Grigori. A revenant was bending over Kelly, a stake in his hamlike fist. Ramsey spared only a glance for Grigori before lifting the revenant high and breaking its back over his knee.

Khira stalked toward Grigori, her eyes blazing with the anger and jealousy of two hundred years. She waved her hand toward the table, and the remaining stakes went up in flame.

Whimpering softly, Kelly curled in on herself, her body lying in a pool of her own blood. Marisa wondered if Kelly, being a new vampire, possessed the resilience to overcome her wounds on her own. Ramsey fell to his knees beside Kelly, his face stricken. Over in the corner, Duncan and the last revenant wearily hammered at each like two tired prizefighters.

Marisa stood transfixed, unable to move. They were going to die, all of them.

Khira's gaze burned into Grigori. "Have you nothing to say to me?" she asked with a sneer. "No last words?"

Marisa wrapped her arms around herself. She was trembling all over from what she had seen, from what she knew was coming. She could feel Khira's power growing stronger by the moment, could feel it pushing against Grigori, could feel Grigori's power pushing back. He had fed well, but so had Khira. How many people had died this night to strengthen her? How many more would die when there was no one left to thwart her?

It was a silent, deadly battle. Khira reeled backward as Grigori's power pierced her own, but only for a moment. Slowly she lifted her arms, drew them together over her head, her eyes burning, burning, as she gathered all her power and focused it on Grigori.

He groaned low in his throat as pain engulfed him. "Ramsey . . ."

Khira whirled and waved her hand at Ramsey, who had started toward Grigori. Her power wrapped around him and flung him back against the wall. He lay there, trapped in the web of her power, unable to move.

And then she turned to Grigori once more. "It did not have to end like this," she said. Her power slashed at him like a whip, driving him to his knees. "And now, because of you, they will all die, your woman last of all."

"No." The word was torn from his throat.

"Yes. I will drain her of every drop. Think of that while you writhe in hell."

"Marisa . . ." He gasped her name as white-hot pain splintered through every fiber of his being.

Marisa stared at him, tears coursing down her cheeks. They had underestimated Khira's strength. All this time, she had been toying with them, playing with them, letting them think they had a chance against her, but it no longer mattered, Marisa thought dully. If she was to die, so be it. Without Grigori, she had nothing to live for.

She glanced at Ramsey, helpless in the clutch of Khira's power, at Duncan, who seemed to be holding his own against the last revenant, at Kelly, lying in a pool of blood, at the dead creatures who had once been men, their lives destroyed because of Khira's jealousy. She looked at Grigori, writhing in agony because he was too fine and decent to run away and leave the city at Khira's mercy. And she was suddenly ashamed of her cowardice. People had died, were dying. Grigori was in agony. If she was to die, she would die fighting!

Before she realized what she was doing, before she had time to talk herself out of it, she grabbed the dagger from the table and plunged it to the hilt into Khira's back.

The vampire screamed, a high-pitched wail of pain and rage and disbelief that echoed off the walls and reechoed in Marisa's mind.

Slowly, so slowly, Khira turned, her face a mask of agony, her eyes ablaze with hatred. She stood there for stretched seconds, her power shrinking around her.

"You!" The word hissed from her lips.

Marisa took a step backward, but there was no need. The life went out of Khira like an extinguished flame and she fell slowly, gracefully to the floor.

There was a moment of complete and utter silence. And then, as if they had all been released from some sorcerer's spell, they all moved at once. Ramsey scooped

Kelly into his arms and carried her to the sofa, murmuring that everything would be all right.

With a final uppercut, Duncan slammed his last antagonist back against the wall. The revenant went down, hard. Lips drawn back in a grimace, Duncan jerked a stake from the body of another revenant and plunged it into the heart of the creature lying at his feet.

Marisa knelt beside Grigori. "Are you all right?"

He started to slip his arm around her waist, then jerked his hand away. Marisa frowned at him and then, realizing the problem, she removed the silver she was wearing and tossed it aside. With a wry grin, Grigori slipped one arm around her waist and hugged her tight. She could feel him trembling as the last of Khira's power floated away like smoke in the wind.

"How's your hand?"

He lifted it and showed it to her. There was an ugly red welt where his skin had touched her bracelet. She pressed a kiss to his palm. "I'm sorry."

"Well," Duncan said, his voice filled with exuberance as he took in the destruction all around them. "We did it!"

Grigori stood up, drawing Marisa with him. "We didn't do a damn thing," he said, his gaze resting on Khira's body. "Three vampyres and a first-class hunter, and it was a mortal woman who brought Khira down."

Grigori looked at Marisa, his eyes shining with love. "My woman."

With Khira's death, all the furious energy and pounding fear bled out of the corpse-strewn room.

Marisa stared at the hilt of the dagger, protruding like a silver crucifix from Khira's back. She had thought she might faint when she felt the dagger pierce the vampire's flesh. Then she thought she might be violently ill. Her pulse raced; there was a pressure in her temples.

"Is she really dead?"

"Oh, yeah," Duncan said, grinning. "She's definitely dead."

Marisa shook her head, unable to believe she had done such a thing. A wave of relief, sickening in its intensity, swept over her, followed by disbelief. She had never, ever imagined herself capable of killing.

Grigori's arms enfolded her gently. A distant part of her mind noted that his usually powerful muscles were trembling weakly. His battle with Khira and the revenants had cost him dearly. She leaned into him, shaking all over.

"It had to be done, *cara*," he murmured, reading her thoughts. "You saved my life. You saved us all."

On the couch, Ramsey huddled protectively over Kelly as she fed from his wrist. Remarkably, her broken arm had already mended; the horrible wounds on her slender body had stopped bleeding and were starting to close. But she was pale and weak. Ramsey's eyes were closed and his jaw set. Marisa realized that Kelly, in her need, could drain him.

She looked over at Duncan, who met her gaze and grinned.

"You did it," he said. "By damn, you did it!"

"We all did it," Marisa murmured. "And now I need you to do something."

"Sure, kid. I'll dispose of all this carrion; trust me." His gesture included the twisted bodies.

"Not that," Marisa said.

"Just tell me what you want," Duncan said. "And consider it done."

"Ramsey needs to feed."

Duncan stared at her. "What?"

"He needs blood to replace what he's giving Kelly. He's not strong enough to hunt."

"You want me to . . ." Duncan looked at Ramsey,

then back at Marisa. "This is carrying friendship a little too far, don't you think?"

"No," Marisa said.

"Why can't you do it?" Duncan glanced at Grigori. "You're used to it."

She felt Grigori stir, and put a restraining arm on his trembling shoulder. "Yes," she agreed calmly, "I am. But Grigori needs to feed, too. You have no idea what it cost him to hold Khira at bay until I could . . . could . . ."

"Okay, okay, you convinced me," Duncan grumbled. But he picked up a vial of holy water as he moved toward the couch.

Ramsey opened his eyes to watch him come. His eyes darkened with alarm. Grigori tensed.

"Relax," the vampire hunter said. "A little insurance, that's all. Friend or no friend, you aren't turning me into a damned bloodsucker." He sat down on the sofa, his expression wary. "But you owe me big-time for this, Ed, and don't you forget it."

Marisa tugged on Grigori's arm. "Let's go upstairs."

He followed her up the stairs and into their bedroom without argument and closed and locked the door behind them.

Marisa looked at him, one brow raised.

"Duncan's still a vampyre hunter," he explained quietly. "Ramsey may be willing to put his life in Duncan's hands, but I'm not."

"You don't think Duncan would try to . . ."

"I don't know, but I'm not willing to risk it." He caressed her cheek, his dark eyes smoldering. "I need you, *cara,*" he murmured.

"I know, love." She sat down on the bed, her head tilted to the side to give him access to her neck. "Take what you need."

He knelt in front of her and took her hands in his. "Not just your blood now, *cara mia,* but all of you. Your heart, your soul. Your indomitable spirit." His gaze burned into hers. "Your love."

"You already have them, Grigori. You know that."

"And will you join your life with mine?" he asked, his voice thick with need and longing. "Forever?"

She knew what he was asking. She thought briefly of all she would be giving up, then looked deep into his eyes and thought of all she would be gaining. They had faced life, and violent death, together. From this night forward—no, from the night she had first met him— she had known that her life was forever, irrevocably destined to be entwined with his.

"Yes, Grigori, it's time."

"You are sure, *cara?*"

"I'm sure," she replied, and meant it with every fiber of her being. "I love you."

"As I love you." His hands clutched her shoulders and he rose over her, his dark eyes glowing. "Do not be afraid. I will not hurt you."

She closed her eyes, her heart pounding, not with fear but anticipation, as he drew her into his embrace. She felt a brief, sharp prick, followed by a rush of pleasure as she gave her heart and soul into his keeping.

Chapter 37

Ramsey woke with the setting sun. Kelly slept beside him, a welcome warmth against his back. Turning over, he drew her into his arms, feeling totally at peace for the first time since the night he had awakened to find himself a newly made vampire.

A week had passed since the slaughter at Chiavari's house. Kelly had quickly recovered from the horrible wounds Khira had inflicted on her. True to his word, Duncan had disposed of the bodies, then declared he was taking a much-needed vacation.

Ramsey blew out a sigh. It was still hard to believe that Khira was no longer a threat—that a being so vital, so powerful, one who had lived for hundreds of years, had been brought down by a mere mortal. And a woman, at that.

But Marisa was mortal no longer. He had known the moment Chiavari brought her across, though he couldn't say exactly how he knew. The words "a disturbance in the Force" had him grinning into the darkness, but that was what it had been like. He had felt the change in her, the shift of preternatural power.

The night after Khira's death, Chiavari and Marisa had left the city. "On an extended holiday," Chiavari had said. Ramsey couldn't help wondering if he would ever see them again, bemused by the thought that he would miss them. Both of them.

Kelly stirred in his arms. "You're very quiet," she remarked, dropping a kiss on his forearm. "What are you thinking about?"

"Something that's been in the back of my mind for a couple of weeks."

"Oh?" She turned over onto her side to face him. "What?"

"We need to be prepared in case some other vampire decides to go on a rampage. For all her wicked ways, Khira never left any trace of her kills. Another vampire might not be so neat. If the word gets out that vampires really exist . . ."

She nodded. There would be panic in the streets, hysteria. In days gone by, the very word "vampire" had been enough to start a panic. And while she didn't think that would happen in this day and age, her mother had always told her, "Better safe than sorry."

"So," he went on, "I thought maybe I'd set up a school to train vampire hunters. There aren't many of us left, you know."

"Us?" Kelly asked, looking amused.

Ramsey grinned. "Once a hunter, always a hunter."

"Well, it sounds dangerous to me," Kelly said. "What if they decide to hunt *us?*"

He gave her a wounded look. "They won't know about us. We'll put Duncan in charge."

"What makes you think he'd be interested?"

Ramsey brushed a kiss across her cheek. "We won't know until we ask."

"What makes you think you can trust him?"

"I've taken his blood," Ramsey said, his expression sober. "It will be impossible for him to betray me without my knowledge." He kissed the tip of her nose, his hand sliding up and down her rib cage. "What would you think about buying the LaSalle mansion?"

"Why?"

"Knowing Khira, I'm pretty sure it's as impregnable as a vampire could make it."

She smiled up at him. "Suits me. I always wanted a mansion of my own."

He kissed her again, slowly, seductively, amazed anew that she loved him, that she needed him. Wanted him. Her eyes glowed with the heat of her desire, and he swept her into his arms, silently thanking Grigori for the Dark Gift that had given him forever in the arms of the woman he loved.

Epilogue

Italy
Three years later

Marisa stood on the balcony of their villa, reveling in the quiet beauty of the warm summer night that surrounded her. The scent of earth and trees and a profusion of flowers filled her nostrils.

Grigori had promised her the world, and he had kept that promise. And it was an incredibly beautiful place when seen through her vampyre eyes. Sights and sounds, colors and textures: all were clearer, brighter, more intense—as intense, it often seemed, as her love for Grigori.

She closed her eyes. Grigori. He was everything to her, life and breath, heart and soul. He had brought her across so tenderly, hovered over her as the change took place, his deep voice soothing her, assuring her that there was nothing to fear, holding her safe in his arms as her old life slipped away and she had been reborn a new vampyre in his arms. He had been so afraid that she would regret her decision once it was done, that she would hate her new life and hate him for giving her the Dark Gift.

He had assured her that she would not have to hunt, that he would hunt for them both and nourish her with his own blood, and for the first six months of her new life, that was what they had done. Though she'd had no doubts that she wanted to join Grigori in his life, the thought of what she must do to survive had filled her with trepidation. But it had not repelled her. She was not overcome with a lust for blood, perhaps because Grigori's nourished her so completely, perhaps because she had accepted the change willingly. Whatever the reason, it was but a small part of the whole.

Soon after their move to Italy, she had called her parents and apologized for not going to see them before she left the country, explaining that Grigori had been offered a job in Italy that was too good to pass up, and that it had been imperative that they leave immediately.

She and Grigori had kept in touch with Kelly and Edward and Duncan, their lives forever bound together by that one terrible night when they had destroyed Khira. She had been taken aback when she learned of their plans to open a school to train vampire hunters, but Grigori had laughed. "It sounds just like something Ramsey would do," he had declared. Duncan was in charge of the school, which was funded by Edward and Kelly. They took on only two candidates a year, putting them through rigorous tests of courage, warning them that they were to hunt only those vampires who took human life indiscriminately, warning them that, should they break faith with the school, they themselves would be hunted.

She stirred restlessly, her thoughts turning toward her husband. And a moment later, she felt his presence in the house, felt her heart beat faster as he moved through the house toward her. And then he was there, his arms sliding around her waist to draw her back against him.

"*Cara.*"

"*Il mio amore.*" She sighed. "It's a beautiful night, isn't it?"

"Not so beautiful as you, *il mia migliore cara.*"

She leaned her head against his shoulder, content to be held in his arms. They had left the States shortly after Khira had been destroyed. Marisa had been reluctant to leave at first. Her family was there, after all. But Grigori said it was for the best, that it wasn't wise to remain where they were. She knew it made him uneasy, having Duncan know where they lived, just as she knew that, in spite of all they had been through, Grigori didn't trust Ramsey completely. She had bowed to her husband's wishes without question. His instincts for survival were, after all, much stronger than her own.

But none of that mattered now, not when Grigori was turning her in his arms, gazing down at her through fathomless black eyes, eyes filled with love and desire; not when he was kissing her, wiping everything from her mind but her ever-growing love and need for this man who filled her every waking moment after sundown.

Please turn the page for a special preview of
A WHISPER OF ETERNITY by Amanda Ashley,
coming in early 2004 from Zebra Books.

Nightingale House perched on the edge of a rocky cliff overlooking the Pacific Ocean. The first time Tracy Patterson saw the house she thought it was the most beautiful place she had ever seen. Sunlight glinted on the tall leaded windows. Birds sang in the trees. A covered veranda wrapped around three sides of the house and she had imagined herself sitting there on balmy nights admiring the view of the ocean. The inside of the house had been freshly painted, the oak floors and banisters gleamed with wax.

As much as she'd loved the big airy feel of the house, she'd had every intention of asking the realtor to show her something a little less pricey, so she wasn't sure who was more surprised, herself or the realtor, when she said she'd take it. Once the decision was made, she was sure it was the right thing to do even though it would mean wiping out most of her savings, including the money her grandfather had left her.

Still, a house by the ocean was bound to be a good investment, and she had been pleased with her decision and eager for escrow to be closed.

Now, looking at the place sixty days later, she found herself having second thoughts. The house that had looked so bright and cheerful in the morning looked somehow ominous with night approaching. Windows that had sparkled in the morning sun now reminded her of dark soulless eyes staring out at her.

With the sun setting behind the house, it looked like some huge prehistoric bird about to take flight or perhaps some cobweb-infested castle that the infamous Count Dracula might have lived in. She grimaced as it occurred to her that the only thing missing was the requisite dark and stormy night. She wouldn't have been at all surprised to see a giant black bat hovering overhead or to hear the melancholy wail of a wolf in the distance.

For the first time, it occurred to her to question why there were two chimneys but only one fireplace.

Now, climbing the creaky porch steps, she wondered whatever had possessed her to buy the place. Had she seen it at this time of night instead of early morning, she would certainly have looked elsewhere! Tall trees grew close to both sides of the house, their leaves rattling like dry bones in the evening breeze. Tracy shook her head. Her imagination was really working overtime!

Taking a deep breath, she slid the big brass key into the lock. The door opened with a screech like that of a woman in pain.

How could she have forgotten that awful sound?

"First on the list," she muttered, closing the door behind her. "A little WD-40."

Stepping into the entryway, she was overcome by a sense of unease.

The realtor who had sold her the place had warned her that the two previous occupants had moved out because they believed the house was haunted. Tracy had dismissed the notion out of hand. She didn't believe in ghosts but if they existed, this was certainly the kind of house they would be comfortable in.

Searching for the light switch located just inside the

door, she flicked it on, but the room remained dark. No light penetrated the thick draperies that covered the windows in the living room.

Tracy sighed in exasperation. The electric company had promised the power would be on before she arrived.

The thought of walking into that dark empty house filled her with apprehension. Though she was reluctant to admit it, she had been afraid of the dark ever since she was a little girl.

She grinned to herself. Being a former Girl Scout, she had come prepared. Spying an oil lamp on a long, low table, she searched her pockets for a match. The realtor had warned her that the power was prone to go out during storms and that it might be a good idea to keep a few of the old lamps close at hand, as well as a supply of matches.

Checking to see if the lamp had fuel, she lifted the chimney, struck a match, and touched the flame to the wick.

The welcome flare of light put her fears to flight.

After adjusting the wick, she replaced the chimney and blew out the match; then, lamp in hand, she moved out of the entryway and into the parlor, her tennis shoes making hardly any noise at all on the hardwood floor.

The parlor had high ceilings. An enormous stone fireplace with a black marble mantel took up one whole wall. It was the biggest fireplace she had ever seen, easily large enough to hold a horse. And its rider.

Her footsteps echoed off the walls as she walked across the floor to the windows and drew back the heavy draperies, exposing tall leaded windows. Her mood brightened considerably as the late afternoon light filtered into the room. The trim around the windows and doors were made of oak. The walls, freshly painted, were off-white.

Feeling suddenly lighthearted, she blew out the lamp

and put it on the mantel, then went out to the car to get the groceries she had purchased in the quaint little village situated at the foot of the hill.

The kitchen was large, with windows on three sides. There was a round oak table, cupboards galore, a relic of a gas stove, and a small refrigerator.

After she put the groceries away, she explored the rest of the first floor, opening the curtains and drapes as she went. Wandering from room to room, she mentally remodeled each one as she looked around. In addition to the parlor and the kitchen, there was a large library paneled in dark oak and a small room she guessed had been a sewing room at one time.

A winding staircase led to the second floor. She fell in love with the first room at the top of the stairs all over again. It was the master bedroom. Large and square and papered in an old-fashioned dark blue stripe, it featured a fireplace and a walk-in closet. One of the windows overlooked the backyard, the other overlooked the ocean. A small sitting room papered in the same dark blue stripe adjoined the bedroom. The bathroom had been recently remodeled. It was powder blue with white trim and contained a new sink and an oval tub.

There were two smaller bedrooms farther down the hall, a linen closet, a good-sized bathroom with a pedestal sink and a claw-foot bathtub, and, at the far end of the corridor, a large rectangular room with large windows set in three of the walls. One window had an eastern exposure. She nodded as she glanced outside, pleased that this room also offered a view of the ocean. This would be her studio.

Going back downstairs, she began to unload the boxes from her car.

By nightfall, she had managed to carry the rest of the boxes into the house. Her clothes hung in the closet, her toiletries were in the bathroom, and she was ready for a hot bath. Holding her breath, she turned on the light switch in that room, then murmured, "Hallelujah!" as the light came on over the sink. Silently blessing the electric company for coming through, she turned on the faucet, and added some lavender-scented bubble bath to the water.

While the tub filled, she lit a pair of vanilla-scented candles, pulled a bath towel from one of the boxes, grabbed a paperback from her handbag, and returned to the bathroom. The air was warm now, fragrant with the scent of vanilla and lavender.

Undressing, she turned off the tap, then settled into the tub, book in hand. Scented candles, a froth of warm bubbles, a good book. What could be better?

There was someone in the upper house. Dominic St. John felt the presence of another immediately upon waking. Rising, he took a deep breath, his senses reaching out, testing the night air much the way a nocturnal animal might sniff the wind for danger.

He smiled faintly. He was in no danger from the woman upstairs. He could hear the water draining from the bathtub, smell the fresh clean scent of her as she moved into her bedroom and slipped something silky over her head. A nightgown, perhaps?

A wave of his hand and half a dozen candles sprang to life, casting flickering yellow shadows on the gray stone walls. No one living knew that there was another house beneath the one above, a rather cozy place if one didn't mind stone floors and walls without windows.

Rising, he laid out a change of clothes, all the while following the woman's movements.

He wondered who she was and what had prompted her to buy a house that had been empty for more than five years. Many people had come to look at the house in the last decade. A few had attempted to live there, but he had not wanted their company and it had been an easy thing to drive them away. Dark thoughts planted in their minds, objects that moved or disappeared completely, the whisper of a cold wind down the back of a neck when the air was warm and the night was calm. He grinned faintly. It was all so easy.

Donning a clean black silk shirt, a pair of black trousers and a pair of soft black leather boots, he followed the narrow passageway that led to the back of the fireplace in the parlor. There were many such walkways in the old house. A wave of his hand and the hidden passageway opened.

Dissolving into a fine gray mist, he drifted through the parlor and down the hallway to the kitchen. The smell of roasting meat made his stomach clench even as the scent of animal blood stirred a hunger deep within him.

The woman stood at the stove with her back toward him. She stirred something with a wooden spoon, then lifted it for a taste.

"Not too bad, if I do say so myself," she murmured. Laying the spoon aside, she sprinkled salt and pepper into the pot.

The woman glanced over her shoulder as he floated into the kitchen. Had she sensed his presence? Such a thing seemed unlikely. Few humans had the ability to detect his nearness when he was in an incorporeal form.

She was not classically beautiful, but she was a remarkably pretty woman, with delicate features and fine unblemished skin. Her honey-colored hair fell in a thick braid past her waist. Her eyes were brown with tiny gold flecks, fringed by long dark lashes. Her slender figure was clad in something long and silky. Not a nightgown, as he had thought, but some sort of lounge-around-the-house dress.

Dominic grinned as he drifted out of the room. He had not wanted anyone to occupy the house in the past, but this one could stay. There was something about her . . . something he would pursue at a later date, when his hellish hunger lay quiet. Perhaps one day he would even introduce himself to her, but not now. Now he needed to feed and as handy as it might have been to use the woman, he didn't want to scare her away just yet. It might be amusing, even entertaining, to have company for a while.

Taking on his own shape once again, he made his way to the city located some thirty miles past the quaint village where most of the local people did their business. He never hunted in the village. Not only was it located too close to his lair, but the inhabitants all knew each other. If one of them went missing, everyone would know it in a matter of hours. He had ever been discreet in his choice of hunting grounds.

Walking down one of the crowded cobblestone streets, surrounded by warm mortal flesh and beating hearts, he felt his hunger rise up within him. It was a need that could not be denied, a thirst that could be quelled but never quenched. The beast that dwelled within him had an insatiable appetite, one that could not for long be ignored.

His footsteps quickened as his hunger mounted, and then he saw his prey. She was a few yards ahead, a young woman with short brown hair. He watched the subtle sway of her hips, lifted his head and sniffed the air, sorting her distinct scent from all the others around him.

She looked up at him in alarm as he glided up beside her. Her eyes were gray and clear. He gazed into them, his mind speaking to hers, assuring her that he meant her no harm, and when he was certain she would offer no resistance, he slipped his arm around her waist and led her away from the crowds into a dark alley.

Lost in the shadows, he took her into his arms. For a moment, he simply held her, absorbing her warmth, listening to the whisper of the red tide running through her veins. His fangs lengthened in response to the sound of it, the warm sweet coppery scent of it.

With a low growl, he bent her back over his arm and lowered his head.

He could hear the new owner of Nightingale House moving about in the rooms above when he returned to his lair. Her presence unsettled him, and he paced the cold stone floor, all his senses focused on the woman. He had fed and fed well. Why, then, did this woman's blood call to him? He had a sudden urge to meet her, to hear the sound of his name on her lips, to taste the nectar of life that thrummed through her veins in a warm rich river of crimson.

How best to accomplish a meeting? He did not want to appear out of nowhere and frighten her. A chance meeting, then. Perhaps she would take a walk along the beach some evening after sundown, when the air was cool. Yes, that would be the perfect opportunity.

Smiling at the prospect, he picked up a book of Shakespeare's plays and settled down to pass a quiet evening at home.

The perfect opportunity arrived two evenings later, shortly after sundown. Dominic was returning from the city, walking along the shore, when he saw the woman jogging toward him.

He spent a moment admiring her long shapely legs, the smooth golden tan of her skin, the way her ponytail swished back and forth. Her cheeks were flushed, her blood warm from the run, the smell of it stronger than the faint scent of the woman's perspiration, the ocean, or the salty air.

When she was only a few yards away, she slowed to a walk. He sensed her trepidation at finding herself alone on a deserted stretch of beach at night with a strange man. As far as she knew, he didn't belong here. This part of the beach was private, reserved for the few homes spread out on the cliff above.

As he drew nearer, she stopped walking. He could hear the fierce pounding of her heart as she tried to decide whether or not she was in danger.

"Good evening." He offered her a benign smile. "Lovely night for a stroll."

"Yes." She slipped her hand into the pocket of her shorts. He saw her hand clench, and he wondered what sort of defense she carried in there. A can of pepper spray, perhaps. He watched her summon her courage.

"I'm afraid you're trespassing," she said. "This is a private beach."

"Yes, I know. I have a house nearby."

"Oh, I'm sorry, I didn't know that. I'm new here myself."

He extended his hand. "Dominic St. John."

After a moment's hesitation, she placed her hand in his. "Tracy Patterson."

His fingers curled around hers and he felt it, a sharp jolt of recognition as his essence brushed hers. Excitement swept through him. It was she, his soul mate, the woman he had found and lost countless times through the centuries. He had known her in many guises, by many names.

She was staring up at him. It took him a moment to realize he had fallen silent, that he was still holding her hand.

He smiled. "Pleased to make your acquaintance."

"Thank you." She withdrew her hand from his and glanced back the way she had come. "I should go."

"May I walk with you?"

He could easily read her thoughts by the expressions that flitted over her face. He was a stranger. It was late. For all she knew, he could be the next Cliffside Strangler.

"Perhaps another time," he suggested, fully aware of her apprehension.

"I'd be glad for the company, actually."

"Afraid of the dark, are you?" He asked the question lightly even though he already knew the answer. She had feared the dark in every life.

"Just a little," she admitted.

She turned and started walking back the way she had come. He fell into step beside her, aware of the warmth radiating from her body, the scent of her hair and skin, the beat of her heart.

"Have you lived here long?" she asked.

"Yes, for years." More years than she had been alive in this body.

"It's lovely here. I couldn't believe my luck in finding a house near the beach, even though it was a little more than I planned to spend."

"Nightingale House has been for sale for quite some time."

Startled, she looked up at him. "How do you know that's where I live?"

He smiled to put her at ease. "It's the only house that was for sale on the beach."

"Oh." She laughed self-consciously. "Of course."

"What do you do for a living?" he asked.

"I paint. Landscapes, mostly. What about you?"

"I'm retired."

"Retired?" She looked up at him. "You don't look old enough to be retired."

You'd be surprised, he thought. Aloud, he said, "I made some good investments when I was very young. Now I live off the interest."

"Must be nice."

"Very."

They had reached the long flight of wooden steps that led up to Nightingale House.

"Thank you for walking me home," she said.

"Shall I see you to your door?"

"No, that won't be necessary."

"Good night, then."

"Good night." She started up the steps, paused, and turned to face him again. "Would you like to come to dinner tomorrow night at, say, five o'clock?"

"That's a bit early for me," he replied. "How about a movie later instead?"

"All right. What time?"

"I'll pick you up around seven-thirty."

"I'll be ready." She smiled. "See you then."

He watched her climb the stairs, admiring the sway of her hips, the graceful way she moved. When she was out of sight, he dissolved into mist and followed her home.

Materializing in his basement lair, he dropped into his favorite chair. A wave of his hand started a fire in the hearth. Sitting back, he grinned in mild amusement as he stared at the dancing flames.

He had a date for tomorrow night.

Tracy hummed softly as she plugged in the blow-dryer. She couldn't help noticing that her hand was shaking or deny the butterflies in her stomach. She told herself it was just a case of nerves. After all, she hadn't had a date in the last five months, not since she'd broken up with that creep Richard. But even as she tried to convince herself it was perfectly normal to be excited at the prospect of going out on a date with someone new, and a wickedly handsome someone at that, she knew she was just kidding herself.

There was something intriguing about Dominic St. John, something she couldn't quite put her finger on, something that made her skin tingle with both anticipation and trepidation when he was near. She still didn't understand what it was that had possessed her to ask a complete stranger to come for dinner. She had never done anything like that before and had had no intention of doing so last night.

Thinking of him now, she realized that he had looked vaguely familiar but try as she might, she couldn't recall ever meeting him before. And a man like that would not have been easily forgotten.

When her hair was dry, she brushed it out, carefully applied her makeup.

Was she making a mistake in going out with him? He seemed nice enough, but then, wasn't that what friends and neighbors always said about the boy next door who turned out to be a serial killer? "He was such a nice boy. Never caused any trouble."

She shook her head. She was really letting her imagination run wild this time! She hated this part of dating, hating the "getting to know you" stage. Some of her girlfriends thought that was the fun part, but not Tracy. She'd only had three serious relationships since she graduated from college and each one had lasted just over a year.

Leaving the bathroom, she glanced at the antique clock on the small antique oak table beside her bed. Whoever he was, he was going to be here in less than thirty minutes. Slipping on a pair of sandals, she went downstairs into the living room. She turned on the stereo, flicked on the lights.

She loved this room, she thought, glancing around. Her furniture had arrived yesterday morning and she had spent the day arranging it. The white wicker sofa and chair brightened up the room considerably. The pillows were covered in a variegated blue print. An antique oak bookcase held a number of books and videos. Several dragons, some she had bought for herself, some that had been gifts, decorated the mantel. Her entertainment center took up most of one corner. The next time she went into the village, she would look for an area rug to put in front of the fireplace and another one for her bedroom.

A knock at the door sent her stomach plummeting down to her toes. He was here.

Discover the Thrill of Romance With
Kat Martin